Petrified Hearts:
The Shaking

Book1

By Jaclyn Zant

PRESS

Blessings to yo[u]

Jaclyn 3a[...]

(Num. 6:24

Finding Truth

in Fiction

For Abba. . .
. . .I am pouring-out, just as you said to.

2 Corinthians 4:17

    "For our light and momentary troubles are achieving for us an eternal **glory** that far outweighs them all."

Psalm 62:2

"He only is my rock and my salvation, My stronghold;

I shall not be shaken."

Acknowledgements

To the following individuals I am so very grateful. . .

First, to my husband who has been so supportive of me as I have ventured out and tried my hand at this new endeavor. To Phyllis, who has been my dear friend and main cheerleader throughout the writing of these books. She knew this project would become a series a year before I did!

To my Draft Readers, Karen and Janice—who gave me all kinds of wonderful feedback and encouragement throughout the writing of these books, and my 'Pray-ers,' Donna, Connie, Suzy, Joanna and Faye for investing into me, and into this project, your on-going prayers and encouragements, your friendship, and much more. I absolutely could not have done this without all of you!

To my (Messianic) Rabbi—for being willing to lend his personality and bits of his background to the character of 'Rabbi Sid'. To D. Johnston (*with a 'T'*), my go-to 'Answer-Man,' for his help with the Hebrew language and miscellaneous scripture questions. To my teacher, Mary S., Thank you for coming alongside and helping me in a pinch!

To my co-worker, Mike—former EMT and Emergency Room Nurse, who allowed me to pick his brain and glean from his years of experience in order to bring an added degree of realism to these pages. To Ken Pike, Owner-operator of Perry Air (www.perryairflight.com), who took me on my *Discovery Flight* where I was allowed a brief, first-hand experience of flying a single-engine aircraft, and was also my unsuspecting Technical Consultant for every imaginable question I could come up with relating to aircraft and flying.

And finally, a special acknowledgement to George A. Potter (1949-2014), former Chief of Police of Perry, Georgia—and the namesake for the city of 'Potterville,' In tribute to his coming alongside so many others during their most difficult times, and easing their fears with his encouragements. When this tribute was made known to Chief Potter, his response was this, "I was called upon to help people and succeed as a cop. I have enjoyed my life and helping others."

Also, my thanks to my editor Penny for all her help, and to N. J. Persson for her photograph on the front cover.

Chapter 1

"Gerrard and Son Aviation. . ." Patty spoke into the handset as she brought it to her ear. "No, sir, Mr. Gerrard is not available, may I take a message?. . .Another family member? Well, Rae and Ben are the only ones here right now. . .Okay, I'll put Rae on. Hold please." Patty pressed hold and puzzled for a moment, staring at the phone, and then pressed the button for the overhead page. "Rae, pick up on line two."

Patty's voice overhead summoned Rae from under the instrument panel of Jesse's Cessna. She waved at Ben, drawing his attention to her, then tapped her chest and held her fist to the side of her face, thumb and pinky extended, making the 'phone' sign. She pointed upward, and signed for him to finish up the re-installation of Jesse's annunciator panel. Ben nodded and Rae backed out of the cockpit.

Heading for the phone on the wall outside the break room, Rae pressed the button for line two as she picked up the handset. "This is Rae."

"Yes, this is John Stevenson of the Florida State Patrol. Are you a relative of Lynn Gerrard?"

"The state patrol?" Rae felt her heart skip a beat. "Yeah, she's my mom, why?" A minute later, she burst through the door from the hangar into the front office, eyes wide; frantic. "Where's Dad?" She stared anxiously across the desk extension to Patty.

"He and Riley are at the meeting at Barkley Field. What's wrong?"

"Can you call him?"

"I'm sure he has his phone off, hon."

Hands on her head, Rae pivoted all around her, grimacing; thoughts swirling. "Where's Sam?"

"He's in the air with a student."

"What about Jesse and Luke?"

"Everyone's in the air, Rae—you and Ben are the only ones here." She had never seen Rae in such a state.

Rae wilted, "That was the state patrol—something happened to Mom! We've got to get a hold of Dad!"

Eyes wide, Patty reached for her handset, her hands trembling. "Maybe I can get Riley on *his* phone. What did the state patrol say?"

"He said she was in an accident; they're sending a car for us." Rae's voice trembled, "They're going to be here pretty soon." She glanced around, trying to think. "I need to tell Ben. Patty, can you try to call everyone?"

"I'll try, Rae. What do you want me to tell them?"

"I don't know. The state trooper sounded like it was bad; he said they were taking her to the trauma center. Just tell them to get there as soon as they can." Rae's voice broke on the last word, and she was trembling visibly now. "I need to get Ben."

She turned on her heels and dashed back out the door she had come through, unzipping her coveralls as she hurried across the hangar. Already shrugging them off of her shoulders when she arrived back at the Cessna, she shook an elbow out of a sleeve as she pounded on the cowling to alert Ben of her presence—grabbing his attention away from the annunciator panel.

Inside the cockpit, Ben's head came up, looking for the source of the pounding vibrations. Finding Rae waving at him from under the wing, his forehead furrowed with concern at her distraught expression. Hurriedly, she signed to him the news, beckoning him to come with her as she pushed the coveralls off of her hips and stepped out of them. Stricken, Ben immediately backed out of the cockpit on the other side of the aircraft and unzipped his coveralls as well. Leaving hers on the floor of the hangar, Rae ran to her office and grabbed her wallet, as Patty's voice echoed through the hangar again.

"Rae, the state patrol is here."

When Rae and Ben emerged from the hangar, they found a state trooper holding open the back door of his cruiser, and the pair scrambled in. Anxious thoughts racing through her mind, Rae gnawed on a knuckle as the trooper weaved through the mid-afternoon traffic at a dizzying clip, his siren blaring. Ben reached for his sister's hand and squeezed it; when Rae turned toward him, he signed his desire quickly. She nodded and focused intently on her brother as he began signing a prayer for their mother—and after another glance at the scenery blurring by their windows, for their own safe arrival to the hospital, as well. When the cruiser arrived at the emergency room, the state trooper ushered the two through a side door and down past a row of treatment rooms.

Stopping at the nurse's station, he announced them to the secretary. "These are the family members of Lynn Gerrard."

The unit secretary glanced up and pointed toward a room behind the trio, and down a couple of doors. The trooper steered Rae with a hand to her back, as she reached for Ben's elbow. At the door to the room, their eyes fell on a flurry of activity as several scrub-clad personnel surrounded a still figure on a gurney at the center of the far wall. A monitor above the gurney, near the ceiling, displayed several colorful tracings, each of a different shape and size. A woman in scrubs noticed them come in.

"These are two of her kids," the trooper informed her.

Rae's eyes darted around the room. There was blood on the floor, on the blankets, on the gurney, and on the gloved hands of some of those around it. Rae grimaced, *No. Oh, Lord... No, please!*

The nurse waved in the wide-eyed Rae and Ben, her eyes on the trooper. "Is her husband here?"

"They're still trying to locate him," the trooper reported, and then backed out of the room leaving the siblings there.

A nurse inside the room turned, then spoke to a man in a white scrub coat, pulling his attention away from the gurney. "Dr. Jerrod, her family is here."

The white-coated man turned and glanced quickly at the fearful pair, his shoulders sagging as he and the nurse exchanged furtive glances. The doctor stared at the floor for a moment, then raised his eyes to the two and stepped toward them.

"I'm Dr. Jerrod. Your mother is critical; she has sustained some serious injuries. We are doing everything we can for her, but you need to prepare yourselves."

Ben was trying to follow the doctor's words, but the man in the white coat kept turning his face away, glancing back at the gurney as he spoke. Disconcerted, Ben turned to Rae for interpretation, finding her wide-eyed, stone-faced, and pale. When someone called the doctor back to the huddle around the gurney, Ben jostled Rae's shoulder, gesturing to learn what the doctor had said.

Her face alarmed, her breathing rapid, Rae turned to her brother and signed to him, "Mom is hurt really bad—he said we need to prepare ourselves."

Ben squinted at his sister, signing his response, "Prepare ourselves for what?"

Before Rae could answer, an alarm sounded from the monitor on the wall, grabbing her attention. Her eyes now riveted on the screen, she watched as the spikes of the top tracing grew wider, and progressively further apart. Her knuckle in her teeth again, she gasped.

"Code Blue!" The shout came from the huddle of scrubs around the gurney and a nearby nurse poked her head out the door toward the nurse's station, repeating the cryptic expression—which Rae was certain was not good tidings. Moments later Rae heard it again, this time echoing from the overhead P.A., along with the words, 'Emergency Room.' It was repeated three times successively, and with each repetition Rae' stomach clenched more. Dr. Jerrod stepped onto a small step-stool next to the gurney and began chest compressions on its occupant. Her heart pounding in her throat, Rae saw blood on his nitrile gloves as well.

"Mom!" She lunged toward the gurney, but was caught up short by someone in scrubs who gently, but firmly, pressed her into the periphery.

"You need to stay back, Miss."

Rae stared up at the man as she felt Ben's arms intercept her and draw her close to him. More scrub-clad personnel flowed into the room, pressing Rae and Ben to an inside wall. Rae's mind was awhirl as a cacophony of bells, chimes, and shouts assailed her ears; her eyes darted all around as she tried to make sense of it. Insulated in his silent world from the assault to Rae's ears, Ben was not so distracted. Craning his neck toward the crowd at the gurney, he peered through a triangular gap formed by a man's arm reaching from his torso, and saw the face of his mom on the gurney. A tube protruded from her mouth, a manual ventilation bag attached to it. At intervals, a gloved hand squeezed the large green plastic bulb of the bag, delivering oxygen through the tube. He watched her eyes, open and unblinking, as they stared dully at the ceiling. Ben swallowed hard, tears streamed down his cheeks. He grabbed Rae by the elbow and pulled her toward the door.

"NO!" she protested, but Ben stared sternly into her eyes, beckoning her wordlessly, insistently, to come with him. Alarmed, Rae turned her face back toward the frenzy of activity around her mother, then back to Ben; she signed as she spoke. "No, I don't want to leave her!"

Ben stopped and signed quickly, "Rae, you don't need to see this!" He took hold of her elbow again and pulled her forcibly toward the door. Rae stared behind her as her brother dragged her from the room, *One more day, Lord. . .Please. . .just give me one more day with her!* Someone ushered the two into a quiet room with a comfortable sofa and chair, and they sat clinging to each other until Dr. Jerrod came in and told them their mother was gone, and then left the room. Still clinging to each other, the two now cried openly and uncontrollably.

In another part of the ER, an intoxicated man teetered on an examination table. Beside him on one side, a lab technician drew his blood into several lab tubes. On the other side stood a police officer holding a breath analyzer to the man's lips. Once the man had exhaled into the device, the officer took note of the reading. Then, as the teetering man fingered a broken front tooth, the officer began reciting to him his rights. A moment later a doctor came into the room and, after having the man lie down on the table, began stitching up the small gash on his forehead. All the while, as the man lay on the table, he gazed at the ceiling, dazed, trying to take in and make sense of what had happened.

A half hour later, Sam was escorted to a secluded room and found his two youngest siblings holding each other, exhausted from crying. His own face wet with tears, he joined them on the sofa and they all cried anew. Soon after, Joe Gerrard appeared in the doorway, brokenhearted and distraught. He sank into the sofa and embraced his three adult children. Immediately, Rae reached for him and clung to his neck, tears dampening his shirt collar, and Joe drew his only daughter close, and his sons embraced them all.

When they were cried-out, Joe cleared his throat and blew his nose. "Well, kids. I think it's time we head home. I need to try to get hold of Luke and Jesse. . ." It was all he could choke out. Then he and his children let themselves out of the room and made their way back to the parking lot.

Chapter 2

Two days later, Joe stepped into the kitchen and headed for the coffeepot. Luke and Ben watched him retrieve a clean mug, then he picked up the pot and begin pouring.

"Has Rae been down?"

Both boys shook their heads, but Luke answered, "I knocked on her door; she said she wasn't hungry again. I don't think she ate anything at all yesterday."

Joe sighed. Leaning against the counter, he took a sip of his coffee. "Last night she begged me to let her stay home from the funeral today. I hope I convinced her that if she doesn't go, she might look back one day and wish she had." He joined his sons at the breakfast table. "She needs to say good-bye—we all do; I think she just can't stand the thought of it." He shook his head, "This has been hard on us all, but it's just killing Rae. She's been so upset and angry. I wish I could make it easier on her somehow."

Luke leaned on his elbow, his cheek in his hand. "She said people keep telling her it is God's will that Mom died. I think it's really getting to her."

Dismayed, Joe looked up in surprise, "People have been telling her that? Who?"

"Yeah." Luke shrugged, "I don't know who—mostly phone calls, and a couple of people from the church who came by yesterday. I think she's going to go ballistic if she hears it one more time. She quit answering the phone."

Joe shook his head again, "I suppose they're just trying to be comforting. I don't think they realize what it can sound like to someone who just lost someone they love." Joe stared out the window past Ben. "Well, I see it's raining again. The only thing more cheerless than a funeral is a funeral in the rain."

A few minutes later Joe tapped on his daughter's bedroom door. "Rae?" A moment later, it opened a few inches and a somber face with vacant eyes appeared in the gap. "How are you doing, sweetheart?" Rae only shrugged. "Did you decide to come with us?" he asked. Looking away, Rae nodded, then so did Joe. "Well, I'm glad. It may take a few days, but I think you'll be thankful you did." Rae didn't respond, so he moved on to a different topic. "Sweetheart, could I trouble you to help me with my tie? I can't seem to get it right." Rae pressed her lips together and squeezed her eyes closed, hanging her head for a moment, then nodded without looking up. Her heart suddenly tender, she welcomed a break from the relentless anger. With a heavy sigh, she stepped aside, opening her door to her dad.

Joe sat his tall frame down on the edge of her bed so that Rae could reach his tie easily. Without a word, she stood before him and gathered up the two ends of the necktie in her hands and began. Joe gazed into her sad countenance as she worked. Not far into the task, tears welled up and silently streamed down her cheeks, but she stayed with it; methodically winding and tucking until she slid the knot up to her dad's throat and smoothed down his collar.

She stepped back without looking up. "There you go."

"Thank you, sweetheart." Joe stood and drew her close, hugging her. He raised her chin with a finger and brushed back her hair from her face. *She looks so much like her mom.* He smoothed her hair with both hands, letting his hands come to rest on her shoulders, searched her face a moment longer, and then leaned down and kissed her on the forehead. Stepping out her bedroom door, and into the adjacent bathroom, Joe eyed himself in the mirror examining her handiwork. He pinched the knot, smoothing down the tie, as Rae also stepped to the doorway. Joe nodded to her, "It looks great, sweetheart—your mother would be proud." Rae tried to smile, but could only swallow hard.

When the two came downstairs, they found Rae's four brothers and two sisters-in-law in the living room, lining the sofa, loveseat, and chair—her brothers' neckties in varying stages of disarray. Those who were not currently struggling to tie theirs, sported crooked ties or ones tied with the narrow end in back longer that the wider end in front. When they saw their father's perfectly tied necktie, their eyes shifted pleadingly to Rae.

Silently, Rae stepped to Luke, who was nearest, and reached for his necktie. Luke shifted to the edge of the sofa and leaned forward to make her task easier. Undoing what had been attempted, she began again as her dad leaned against the hallway door jamb to watch. All eyes were riveted on Rae and no one spoke.

Just as his father had, Luke watched her face as she worked, finally he spoke softly. "I guess this is *your* job now."

"I guess so." A whisper being all she could manage, Rae blinked back her tears as she robotically wound and tucked. Then, once again, she pinched the completed knot, sliding it up to his throat and smoothed down his collar and stepped back from him.

Next to Luke, Jesse arched a hopeful eyebrow, having arrived with his tie draped around his shoulders, hoping for help. Rae side stepped over to him and began again. Jesse watched, his chin quivering, "I'm sorry, Rae. I know this must be so hard for you."

Rae swallowed without looking up, her voice still barely a whisper. "It's hard for you guys, too." Jesse only nodded.

Finished, she smoothed down his collar and nodded to his wife, Julie, next to him. Then turned to Sam, who sat with his wife, Janine, on the loveseat adjacent to the sofa. Sam moved to the edge of his seat cushion, as well, and Rae stepped close and began again. His chin tucked, Sam watched her work, and noticed her hands were trembling. After a moment, Rae hesitated and Sam raised his eyes to hers; seeing her struggling emotionally, his heart ached for her. "It's okay, Rae. You can do it," he encouraged, stroking the back of one of her arms. Rae gazed at him forlornly, unconvinced. Swallowing, she drew a deep breath and pressed ahead with her task. At last, she pinched the knot and drew it up to his throat, and once again, smoothed the collar. Before she could step away, Sam stood and hugged her. "Thanks, Rae—you're amazing." Her throat tight and unable to find her voice, she could only hug him in return.

Releasing her hold on Sam, she turned searching for Ben and found him across the room in the chair by himself. Breathing deeply, he hurriedly smudged away the tears that unendingly streamed down his cheeks, using boths hands alternately and inadvertently using the tie in one hand to blot them. Stepping up to her younger brother, Rae signed something the others couldn't see, and Ben signed in return. She nodded, her tears flowing yet again, and retrieved the damp tie from his hand. Draping it around his neck, she began again for the final time. As she slid the knot to Ben's throat and smoothed down his collar, Joe checked his watch.

"The car from the funeral home should be here pretty soon." A moment later the doorbell rang.

After the funeral service, those in attendance gathered in the foyer of their church. From a secluded corner across the way, Rae slid her locket back and forth along its chain as she watched her father and brothers receive condolences from those gathered.

Her dad Graciously nodded and smiled to the succession of mourners as they shook his hand and hugged him; she could tell it was killing him and wondered why he bothered. Her brothers stood nearby, stone-faced—except for Ben, who cried openly despite being seventeen; being deaf, he didn't hide his feelings the way hearing people do. Her three older brothers took turns trying to comfort him. The mourners hugged and shook hands with the other three as well, but not Ben; they didn't know how to talk to him, so instead they ignored him. Glaring, Rae shook her head, disgusted. *Do they think he can't feel just because he can't hear?* She grimaced and teared- up. Unable to bear it, she turned away.

Standing there in the most remote corner of the foyer that she could find and still be in the room, Rae let go of her locket and began absently twirling a ring around her finger. Noticing it, she stopped and gazed at the dainty rose and leaf motif of Black Hills Gold. *Mom's ring. She gave it to me when I was fourteen.* The memory warmed her heart briefly, and then the ache returned. She sighed wearily, struggling to keep the tears at bay. The rain pattered steadily on the window next to her and Rae stared out for a minute, watching the cars swish by on the wet street. It was just another rainy March day in Florida to the people in those cars, but to Rae, it was the second worst day of her life—the worst day being two days ago when her mother died. *If it wasn't for the rain, I'd just get out of here and go for a walk or something.* She sighed, *I still might.* Then, as her thoughts and gaze returned to her dad and brothers, she decided against it. . .*For now.*

She turned her attention back to the people in the foyer. Someone's voice near her caught her attention. ". . .It's God's will that she died."

Rae winced and groaned inside. *I'll bet I've heard that at least twenty times over the past two days!* Eyes narrow, she pressed her lips together, shaking her head slowly as she drew a deep breath; incredulous. *Stupid people. Why do they think that's a good thing to say?* She clenched her jaw until it ached.

Those gathered stood together in small clusters, chit-chatting as though they were at a church social. *I guess a funeral is just another get-together for them.* She glanced around at the other mourners. *Ha! 'Mourners'?—That's a joke!* The widows and divorcees from church had already started closing in on her dad. Rae watched him for a few moments. At sixty-two, Joe Gerrard was still handsome, Rae shrugged—*For an old guy. What is it about women and pilots? They're like moths at a light bulb.* Rae watched the middle-aged single women flit around him. *Wow, some of them are even flirting with Dad right here at the funeral chapel!* She scowled. *Vultures! They're not even waiting until Mom is in the ground!*

She saw her dad glance in her direction, and then say something to Sam. Rae pressed herself further into the corner, hoping he hadn't seen her. He had. Sam looked up at her as her dad spoke something into his ear, then her brother started toward her. *Oh, great.* She glanced around for an escape route, but thanks to her careful selection of this secluded spot, she had none. Her eldest brother crossed the room and stepped up beside her. "Dad wants to know if you're okay."

Rae stared down at the floor, tight-lipped and shoulders sagging; her anger and grief fighting for an exit, feeling like her head might explode. "No, I'm not *'okay'!*" She swallowed hard, and reached up to stop an escaping tear. "How can I be *'okay'?*—I'll never be *'okay'* again."

Sam reached for her and drew her close, hugging her tightly. As he did, he pressed his lips together and blinked back his own tears, staring at the ceiling above him until he could control himself, then he leaned down and kissed the top of Rae's head. He exhaled shakily, "I know."

After a moment, Rae reached up and hugged him back, her face buried in his shirt; her voice pinched and muffled. "When can we get out of here?"

As he held her, Sam gently swayed her from side to side in miniscule movements. "Not soon enough for me."

The upside of the rain was the crowd at the graveside was small. Joe wanted it to be brief and asked that no chairs be set out to discourage lingering, so everyone stood around the casket, either under the tent or their umbrellas, and at the periphery of the twenty or so gathered, stood Rae. Numbed in body, mind, and soul, she let the rain fall on her, making no effort to stay dry. In front of her to her right, she heard someone speaking softly to the person next to them.

"I haven't seen Rae. Is she here?"

The other person shrugged. "I don't know. I heard she isn't taking it well."

Rae scoffed under her breath. *My mom was killed by a drunk driver! Just how does someone take that 'well'?* Irritated anew, she moved away from them several feet. Staring blankly at the backs of the people around the casket, she let her thoughts drift as the minister spoke his platitudes over the deceased.

"...Amen."

The word jarred Rae from her thoughts. *Good, that means he's done and we can finally get out of here.* She turned and started for the car, but stopped short, coming face to face with big hair and heavy make-up.

"Rae! There you are. Oh, my!—you're all wet." The fifty-something woman with dyed red hair smiled far too cheerfully. *So are you,* Rae sneered in her thoughts. She had seen this woman flitting around her dad and brothers at the church and had dubbed her the 'chief moth.' Until this moment, Rae had successfully avoided her, and she now made another attempt. Side stepping, she searched for a quick way around her, but—surprisingly agile for her age—the woman managed to stay in front of her. "Are you okay, Rae?"

"No, I'm not. Excuse me." Rae muttered bluntly, her eyes to the ground. She tried again to step around the woman, but again, the woman stayed in front of her. Rae squinted at her, puzzled and annoyed.

"Rae, you need to forgive the drunk driver who hit her."

Indignant, Rae exhaled forcefully. "I'll leave that to God." She tried again to step around, but the woman laid her hand on Rae's arm.

"You know, Rae, it's God's will that your mom died."

Rae glanced down at the hand on her arm, then up at the woman's face, her eyes blazing. *Why, so you could snatch him up?* Contemplating physical violence—she decided against it for her dad's sake. Instead, she just swallowed hard. "Well, He got His way, didn't He? I hope He's *happy.*" The moth's mouth fell open. She stood stunned just long enough for Rae to step around her and trudge to the car, ready to be away from these people.

But to Rae's dismay, the small crowd who had gathered at the graveside soon gathered at her house. *Don't these people have anything else to do?* Exasperated, she retreated to her room upstairs, closing the door. She kicked off her shoes and hung up her wet coat. After toweling off her hair, she curled up on the bed facing the wall and squeezed her eyes closed, rubbing her feet together, never having felt so alone.

It was after midnight when Rae awoke, still in the clothes she had worn to the funeral and someone had put a quilt over her. Eyes puffy, and still feeling numb, Rae pushed the quilt back and eased out of her bed, switching on the lamp next to it.

Robotically, she slipped out of her black dress and tossed it into the corner, then peeled off her stockings and put on her pajamas. Sitting on the edge of her bed for a moment, she stared at the floor. *All I asked for was just one more day with her, Lord. You couldn't give me one more day?* Rae sighed heavily then eased herself to the floor, her back against the bed and sat there, cross-legged, knees bent, staring at the wall across from her. Out the corner of her eye, resting on the floor next to the night table, her Bible caught her attention. More out of habit than anything else, she reached for it and began leafing through the pages in search of comfort. Her mom always seemed to know just where to steer Rae in the Word to find an answer to whatever problems or questions she was facing; but now her mom was not there to help. Closing the book, she stared at the gold lettering on the cover. "What chapter do you go to when the bottom falls out of your world?" she asked of the book in her hands, "What's the answer to that, huh?—And don't tell me it was God's will!" She snarled at the leather cover before her. Flipping it open again, she stared blankly at the pages before her. After a moment, she began to read from where it opened.

Blessed are the poor in spirit, for theirs is the kingdom of heaven. (Mt.5:3)

She read the words again and tried to let them soothe her, but instead she just felt dead inside.

Blessed are those who mourn, for they will be comforted. (Mt.5:4)

"Okay, here's your big chance. I'm mourning—so, comfort me, already," she demanded of the red ink.

Blessed are the meek, for they will inherit the earth. (Mt.5:5)

"Yeah. That's what she inherited—dirt. We just buried her in it." Her eyes narrowed as she read on.

Blessed are those who hunger and thirst for righteousness, for they will be filled. (Mt.5:6)

She softened for a moment. "That was Mom, for sure—hungering and thirsting after righteousness." A thousand thoughts crowded her mind; thoughts of her mom—one of the few people she knew who actually walked out in her own life what the Scriptures detailed. Suddenly, her face clouded and Rae grimaced, forcing back tears. "But what do they get filled with?" She answered her own question, "Embalming fluid, that's what!"

Shocked at her own words, Rae knew better, but didn't seem able to curb her simmering anger.

Blessed are the merciful, for they will be shown mercy. (Mt.5:7)

"Ha! What kind of mercy was she shown? She's dead!—the drunk guy who killed her got all the mercy!" Jaw clenched, Rae snatched the page out, wrinkled it up, and threw it across the room, trembling. ". . .and he's still out there walking around! *He* gets another day!" She snatched up another few pages and ripped them out. "*His family* still has him with them!" She grabbed up a bigger hunk of pages and ripped them out as well, flinging them into the air. "Where was your mercy for my mom? Do you only show it to drunks?" She shrieked at the pages as they flew into the air. "And what about mercy for me? *One more day!*—that's all I asked you for. *One more day—that's all!* Just to wake her up for one more day! You couldn't do that? You couldn't give me one more, lousy day with her?" Her anger boiling over, Rae snatched out hunk after hunk of pages throwing them around her, screaming at them and God.

Suddenly her door burst open, and a hand flipped on the light switch. Luke stood there at the doorway, wide-eyed—at first with concern, then, as he saw what his sister was doing—with horror. He lunged into the room diving for the floor, and scrambled across it to Rae. "Rae! Rae, stop—don't do this!—Rae!" He tried to restrain her, wrestling the remains of the Bible from her hands. Rae shrieked and snatched it back from him, throwing another cluster of pages into the air. "Dad...!" Luke yelled, trying to contain his sister's flailing arms. *"DAD...!"*

Startled awake downstairs, Joe Gerrard threw back his blanket and flew off the couch. Unable to bear returning to his own bed, the past few nights found him sleeping on the sofa. Spurred on by the shrieks, he took the stairs three at a time and, a moment later, burst through the doorway of Rae's room. Recognizing the pages that floated past him, he gaped, wide-eyed at the sight before him. At once, he was on the floor next to Luke, taking hold of his daughter's wrists. "Rae! Don't do this, baby!—I know you're hurting...!"

Rae wailed and shrieked at him, sobbing and out of control. She struggled against his hold, while Luke stared in shock. Joe tried again to get through to her, *"Rae!* He let go of her wrists and gathered her into his strong arms, pulling her close to him as Rae thrashed and writhed against him. "Rae, sweetheart—it's Dad...The Lord knows your heart is broken, honey; he cares— he really does, baby." He soothed gently while restraining her forcibly. A moment later, his tender words broke through her frenzy. Little by little, Rae settled into his hold, her strength and anger spent. "There you go, baby. . . .that's better. . .that's better..." he soothed.

Rae sobbed pathetically, "I only asked him for one more day, Dad. Why wouldn't he give us one more day?" Her shoulders jerked in spasms as her dad held and rocked her. Stricken, Luke searched his father's face. Leaning close, he stroked Rae's shoulder as his dad murmured soothing words into his sister's ear. Joe met his son's gaze and nodded reassuringly, and Luke nodded in return, his tension easing. Rae clung to her dad, her face buried in his neck, breathing shakily as her dad stroked her hair.

"You're gonna be okay, hon." Joe murmured, "We all are. We're gonna make it through this."

Luke sniffed and smudged away a tear, then glanced around him. Needing something to do while his dad calmed his sister, he began gathering up the torn pages strewn around the room, raking them into a mound with his fingers. That done, he left in search of a trash bag. While he was gone, Joe continued to rock his daughter and stroke her hair until he felt her relax in his arms.

"Are you okay, baby?" Rae shook her head under his chin, and Joe tried a more intermediate step. "Are you okay, *for now?*" This time Rae nodded, her face still buried in his pajama shirt. "You feel like getting into bed?"

Rae hesitated before she nodded again and sniffed, her voice frail and shaky. "I'm sorry, Dad."

"I know, sweetheart. I know." Joe stood and hoisted Rae up after him, just as Luke returned with a trash bag and began gathering the pages into it. Rae climbed into her bed and curled up on her side facing the wall again. Joe pulled her covers over her, then sat down on the edge of the bed and stroked her arm. "You need anything, hon? Can I get you some water or something?" Rae only shook her head against her pillow. "Okay, sweetheart..." He made the decision as he spoke, "Well, I'll be right across the hall, if you need anything."

Luke gathered together the edges of the trash bag and switched off the lamp, then left the room ahead of his dad. Joe followed his son out, but paused at the doorway and gazed at the curled up form under the quilt. He pressed his lips together shaking his head slowly. After another moment, he flipped the light switch down and stepped out, closing the door behind him. In the hallway, Joe reached for the bag in Luke's hands. "I'll get that, son."

Luke stared at him, still alarmed. "Dad, I've never seen Rae do anything like that before."

Joe sighed, "No—me neither. Not even when she was a little girl." Upbeat and cheerful, as her mother had been, they both knew this outburst was in stark contrast to Rae's nature. He sighed wearily, gripping his son's shoulder. "She and your mom were very close." Luke nodded, wanting to understand. After another moment, he returned to his room next to Rae's and closed his door. Joe stood in the hallway holding the partially full trash bag and stared after him, then turned his attention to Ben's door that was still closed; he half-expected to see Ben in the doorway. *I guess sometimes deafness can be a blessing.* Joe headed down the stairs and out to the garage and deposited the bag of torn pages into the trash can, shaking his head sadly as he replaced the lid. On his way back through the house, he gathered up his bedding from the couch and carried it upstairs to the room across from Rae's. He hesitated at the doorway summoning his courage, then stepped in. After arranging the pillow and blankets on the mattress, Joe haltingly crawled between the sheets and lay on his side staring at the empty space next to him. After a moment he reached out his hand and stroked the sheet and pillow. Grimacing, he withdrew his hand and tucked it close to his chest, then turned and cried softly into his pillow.

The next morning, Luke shuffled into the kitchen half-awake, looking for something to eat. He was surprised to see Rae already at the table leaning over her bowl. She had one elbow on the table, her cheek resting in her hand, and several open food items around her. He stared at her for a moment before speaking. "Are you alright?" Rae glanced up at him and shrugged without saying anything. Luke squinted at the array of food choices around her. "What are you eating?"

Rae recited her inventory, "Marshmallow Oaties, cold pizza, pudding cups; dill pickles, and chocolate milk."

Luke wrinkled his nose sleepily for a moment, then arched an eyebrow and shrugged. "You got any more?"

Rae half-grinned and pushed everything nearer to her brother's place at the table as he shuffled over to the cupboard for a bowl, a spoon, and a plastic drinking tumbler, then returned and sat down across from her. Reaching for the Marshmallow Oaties, he poured himself a bowlful, covered them with the chocolate milk, and then filled his glass. When he set down the jug, he reached for a pickle spear and took a bite. "You sure did a number on your Bible last night." Rae looked away and shrugged again. "So what's going on? Are you like, mad at God, or the people at church, or the whole world?"

"I don't know. I'm just mad." Rae opened another pudding cup. "Aren't you?"

"No."

"Don't you care?"

Luke shook his pickle spear at her, glaring, "Listen here, Rae—just 'cause I didn't tear up my Bible doesn't mean I don't care! You got that?"

Rae deflated in her seat and swallowed hard, staring into her cereal bowl. "Sorry,"

Luke hung his head and leaned back in his chair. "Maybe I'm a little mad. . .I don't know. I don't really feel anything right now; I'm just kind of. . .*numb.*" Rae raised her eyes to her brother as he spoke. "It's like it's not real, you know? I mean, I half-expected to see Mom in here making breakfast when I came down this morning." Luke grimaced and shook his head slowly, then sat forward and scooped up a spoonful of cereal and shoved it into his mouth, avoiding his sister's gaze. Rae's shoulders sagged as she watched her brother eat, feeling his sadness.

Having survived his first night alone in his bed, Joe Gerrard emerged from his bedroom. He opened each bedroom door as he came to it, checking on his kids. Rae and Luke were gone, but Ben was still there. Seeing he was awake, Joe entered and sat down on the edge of his bed, and signed to his son silently. "How are you feeling today?" Ben shrugged. Joe tried again, "I thought you'd be downstairs eating breakfast by now." Ben looked away briefly. When he looked back, his father was still signing. "You're not hungry?"

"I don't want to go in there and not see Mom." Ben signed in return, his eyes moist.

Joe swallowed hard and nodded, glancing away for a moment. He sighed and tried again, still signing. "I'm not the best cook, but if you give me a shot, maybe I can scramble us some eggs."

Ben smiled weakly and pushed himself up onto one elbow. As Joe stood, Ben swung his legs over the side of his bed and nodded to his dad. They hugged each other tightly then headed for the door.

In the kitchen, Luke eyed his sister. "So, are you going to church tomorrow?"

"No. There's something I need to do."

"Like what?"

"I don't know, I haven't thought of it yet."

Luke dipped his pickle into a pudding cup and took a bite. "So, you're just going to avoid church for the rest of your life, or something?"

"Maybe."

Just then, their dad and Ben came in, so Luke reserved their discussion for another time. The four nodded to each other, and Ben took a seat.

Rae noticed her dad's briefcase. "You're going to work?"

Joe nodded, "Yes, I thought I would."

Anguished, Rae's eyebrows knitted. "How can you do that? We just had the funeral yesterday!"

Joe tried to keep his tone even. "Well, hon, I haven't been there since we got the news and things are getting really behind." Rae's face clouded up. Seeing her wounded expression, Joe hesitated. "What's wrong?"

Eyes blazing, her tone accused him. "How can you do that, Dad? How do you just go to work and act like nothing happened?"

Luke was indignant. "Rae. . .!"

Joe waved him off, "No, it's okay, son." He sighed and sat down next to Rae. "I'm sorry, Rae, if that seems insensitive to you, sweetheart; I'm not trying to be. There's just been so much upheaval over the past few days—and, well, going to work seems normal. I guess I just want to start feeling normal again."

Calming a bit, Rae could only stare at him. She shook her head slowly, "How can things ever be normal again?"

"I don't know. I guess maybe we just need to work on finding a *new* normal."

Rae pouted, "I don't *want* a new normal."

"Well, hon, the old normal is gone and it isn't coming back, so we best start looking for a new one. It's either that, or be *ab*normal for the rest of our lives." He watched quietly as Rae processed this. After a few moments, her chin dipped and her tense expression eased. Finally, her shoulders sagged, signaling her acquiescence. Joe nodded as he rubbed his daughter's back and studied her for another moment. He glanced around at the food on the table. "So, what are you kids eating?" Luke recited the list and his dad grimaced, shaking his head. "That—*is disgusting.*"

Chapter 3

March in Middle Georgia ushered in not only allergy and lawn mowing seasons, but also, for Heath, the beginning of the long awaited—and long-dreaded—house-selling season. In preparation for putting his on the market, he spent most of his weekend mowing the lawn, edging, and trimming up the bushes and trees in the front yard. After a late lunch, all that was left to do this Sunday afternoon was cut the branches down to size and bundle them for the yard waste detail of the trash collection service. Heath set about sawing and lopping and was well into the job when a voice behind him summoned him from his thoughts.

"How ya doing?"

Heath stiffened. *Oh great—caught outside by a salesman.* Kicking himself for not keeping watch, he sighed heavily. *Which one this time—cable TV or home security?* He turned to the source of the voice, finding a tall, slim, forty-something man with wavy brown hair; fit and tan—like the gym bum his wife had run off with. *No, more like the gym bum's father.* He noted the man's dark slacks and button-down shirt and took a guess. *Cable TV.* Heath smiled politely at the man, more because of his own upbringing than because he was glad to meet him.

The man smiled back, and then looked around. "You look busy."

"I am. Want to help?" *That ought to scare him off.* Nothing will cut short a sales pitch like trying to get a salesman's help in something physical—but, to Heath's surprise—and disappointment—the salesman took him up on it.

"Sure." He stepped toward the pile of branches and Heath sighed. *Great. Now, he'll expect me to buy something in return and be even harder to get rid of!*

As the salesman reached for the loppers, Heath figured his bluff had been called. "Never mind. You don't need to do that." He tried to wave the man off.

"It's okay, I don't mind." The salesman proceeded, however awkwardly, to maneuver the loppers into position around a limb that was much too big for them.

Heath tried again, "No, really—I can do it."

"I don't mind at all." The salesman continued struggling. Heath watched him for a moment, pretty sure the man had never used loppers before.

Seeing the man was determined to help, Heath sighed. "You don't need to, but if you insist. . ." He tucked his saw under his elbow and slipped off his gardening gloves, tossing them over to the salesman. "That limb will need the saw." Heath offered the tool, waiting to see if the salesman would accept it or jump on this opportunity to bow out. Surprised again, Heath watched as the salesman picked up the gloves and put them on, then spread his fingers and examined his hands, front and back, as if that were the first time he'd ever donned such a thing. His examination complete, he accepted the saw from Heath and handled it as awkwardly as he had the loppers. Heath stood back and watched him. *Is he trying to make some kind of point, or something? I hope he don't hurt himself making it. . . I don't want to get caught up in some kind of homeowner's insurance claim when I'm trying to sell the house.* Heath watched the salesman a moment longer, then shrugged and went about gathering and bundling the last of the smaller limbs he had already cut.

Out the corner of his eye, Sid caught Heath watching him, and noted his puzzled expression. Though not accustomed to doing yard work, it seemed to him that if a man would ask a total stranger for help, then he must truly need it, so Sid wanted to do what he could. He had hoped to chat with Heath as they worked, but when Heath stepped away and started gathering limbs around the yard, it made that difficult. Instead, Sid just pressed on, waiting for Heath to come back to his vicinity.

Sid had seen men using a saw before, and now had a new appreciation for how easy they'd made it look. The blade kept getting stuck in the groove he was trying to make; he could only get it going in one direction without it buckling, never back and forth smoothly. Finally, he got through it and decided that, for such a small branch, it seemed like it was a disproportionate amount of trouble, and went back to the loppers. Just then, Heath stepped up next to him, "If you're done with the saw, I'll take it."

Sid turned and glanced up, then up some more, noting Heath's height and large frame at this proximity. He nodded, and Heath picked up the saw and stepped over to a large limb lying on the ground several yards away. Sid watched as Heath made quick work of separating a four-inch branch from it in less time than it took Sid to saw off the two-inch limb he'd just finished struggling with. A moment later, Heath moved to the next branch on the large limb and did the same. The younger man was broad shouldered and muscular, but not overly so. Sid wondered if that was from Heath's job or if he worked out. He thought back on Ruth—no more than five-feet six. *I'm five-eleven and I'm looking up at this guy. How did Ruth produce such a tall, strapping son?*

He must take after his dad. He looked at his loppers and down at the limb at his feet. After another glance in Heath's direction, Sid decided he would focus on the smaller branches and leave the larger ones to him.

After about fifteen minutes, Heath checked to see if the salesman had given up and slipped away quietly, but to his annoyance, the man was still at it and had actually managed to lop off several limbs from his large branch without injuring himself. *Okay, calling my bluff was one thing, but this is getting ridiculous. Now, I'm really going to feel bad for turning down his sales pitch—if he ever gets around to pitching it.* Heath sighed, surveying the yard, deciding that the job was almost done. He was getting uncomfortable that the salesman was still there, so he put down his saw and trudged back over to him. "Well, that's enough for today. Uh, thanks for your help."

The salesman stopped and straightened up. He didn't seem as anxious to leave as Heath had expected—or hoped. Nor did he pounce on the moment to launch into his sales pitch. Actually, completely uncharacteristic of any salesman Heath had ever encountered, this guy hadn't said anything the entire time he'd been working. Once he'd picked up the loppers, he had only smiled a couple of times when he and Heath happened to look up at the same moment. It was awkward, but as far as Heath was concerned, when he got right down to it, everything felt awkward these days. His world had been turned upside down over the past year, and just trying to keep his balance and keep going every day took all of his energy and concentration. Add in caring for his sixteen-month-old son, plus the relentless emotional pain, Heath stayed exhausted. At age thirty, he felt more like forty or fifty. He would not even be working outside now, if he hadn't needed to in order to get the house sold. Selling the house was the final blow after this unwanted and unwelcome divorce. Heath sighed wearily.

"Glad I could help, even if it is just a little bit." The salesman's voice jolted him back from his thoughts.

"Yeah, uh, that was real nice of you. You're the first salesman who hasn't taken off when I offered to let him help."

The salesman grinned broadly and chuckled, "Oh, so that's your way of getting rid of them?" Sid shook his head and chuckled again.

Heath noticed a distinct New York accent, now that the man had spoken more than just a couple of words together. "Yeah, but it usually works. So, I guess I have to disappoint you by saying I don't want cable TV. I'm going to be moving soon, anyway." Heath's tone was apologetic, "but thanks for your help."

The salesman was still grinning. "Well, I hate to disappoint *you*, but I'm not a cable TV salesman." When Heath's eyebrows shot up, Sid removed his right glove and extended his hand. "I'm Sidney Edelberg, or just 'Sid.'" Heath's grimy hand shook Sid's clean, smooth hand. "I'm guessing you're Heath—at least I hope so, if I'm not at the wrong house." Heath stared at him, puzzled, so Sid answered the question he saw in the younger man's eyes. "I'm the Rabbi over at Beth Chesed V' Emet."

Feeling his face flush warm, Heath froze. *Oh, no! I just made my mom's Rabbi do my yard work!—she's going to kill me!* The entire scene replayed in his mind in fast forward, as Heath groped for words. "I'm...I'm so sorry, Rabbi."

Not at all offended, Sid was actually quite amused by the whole thing and grinned broadly again. "It's okay, really. Actually, I came over here to see how I could help, so I'm glad I could do a little something." Heath just nodded, then hesitated, squinting at the Rabbi. *Help? Why does he think I need help?* Seeing Heath's puzzled expression, Sid offered further explanation. "I talked to your mom yesterday—she's concerned about you." Heath arched an eyebrow, then Sid added, "She said you are selling your house."

Heath winced, his head and shoulders sagging. "Um, yeah." He winced again. "Is that all she said?"

". . .And that your wife left."

Heath only sighed wearily. *Great. Now my mom's Rabbi knows I'm a loser.* It had been over a year since she'd left and still the mention of it was like a sword through his chest. He only pressed his lips together and stared at the ground, saying nothing.

Ruth, had spoken to Sid after services the day before, about her son who had gone M.I.A. from services—and serving—at his own church after being devastated by his wife leaving. Since those at his church had moved on from his devastation much more quickly than Heath, and seemed to have largely forgotten about him, she hoped her Rabbi might reach out and try to help. Unsure of how to proceed, Sid had spent much time in prayer and felt the Lord tell him to pay the M.I.A. a visit today.

Sid tried again, "I know sometimes being divorced in the body of believers can make you feel like an outcast, Heath, but you're not an outcast with God. Even though he hates divorce, he doesn't hate divorced people. He's just as grieved as you that your marriage ended, probably even more so." Heath raised wounded eyes to Sid's briefly, then returned his gaze to the ground. The Rabbi had planned on simply making Heath's acquaintance and inviting him to Shabbat services at his Messianic Congregation. But now, seeing the young man so deflated and subdued, Sid could tell he still was grieving a great loss—the young man's whole countenance seemed to confirm that. Seeing the pain in Heath's face, now complicated by this embarrassment, Sid decided to take a step back and change tactics. "I don't know if you noticed, but I'm not from around here," he began.

Grateful for the reprieve from talking about his failed marriage, Heath nodded. "Yeah, I could tell." His leisurely drawl was in stark contrast to Sid's obvious New York accent and rapid-fire speech.

"Oh, you noticed?" Sid feigned surprise. "Well, I don't know if you could tell this, too, but I'm also not very good with gardening tools."

Heath kept nodding, playing along. "Yeah, I noticed that, too."

"What? Was I that obvious?" Sid deliberately exaggerated his embarrassment.

"Yeah, I was getting worried you might lose a finger or something."

"Hmm. . .me too, for a minute there." Glancing in all directions for effect, Sid now spoke furtively. "You know, I've heard that you Georgians are very big on gardening, so help me out here, will ya? If it gets out how I fumbled with those tools, I'll never hear the end of it. I mean, how am I going to keep the respect of my congregation if they find out I don't even know how to use clippers?"

"Loppers."

"Excuse me?"

"Those were loppers."

"Loppers? Really? *Loppers?* I've never heard of that." Sid was genuine for the moment and Heath smiled, in spite of himself. "Okay, loppers, then." Sid grinned, "Well, if they find out I don't even know how to use *loppers,* I'm a dead man. I may as well just pack up and go back to the Bronx." It was so ridiculous, Heath couldn't help grinning as Sid continued weaving the tale designed for Heath's benefit. "Tell you what—let's just keep this whole thing between the two of us. Waddaya say?" When Heath didn't immediately respond, Sid took out his wallet and opened it, and pulled out a couple one dollar bills. "How much is it worth to you? One? Two? I'll even go as high as three dollars."

Heath couldn't help but chuckle; it was the closest thing to a laugh he'd had since his wife had left. He waved Sid off. "Y'all don't need to worry, your secret's safe." He smiled appreciatively at Sid, who smiled back. Heath eyed the older man for a moment. "You want a beer?" He waited, curious what the Rabbi would think about that, and at the same time, not really caring.

Sid smiled. *Ah—the Southern olive branch.* "Thanks, I'd love one."

** *** **

The next morning, Heath pulled up outside his mom's house, unhooked Nate from his car seat, carried him in and set him down inside. Nate ran to Ruth and hugged her knees as she turned to them.

"Good morning, Nate!" She knelt down to hug her grandson, and helped him out of his coat before he ran off out of the kitchen. Straightening up, she greeted her son. "Good morning, Heath."

"Morning, Mom." Heath thought for a moment before speaking. "Uh, Mom?" His voice was almost a whine.

"What, Heath? What's wrong?"

"The next time you send your preacher over to my house, could you warn me that he's coming?"

"Why? So you can find someplace else to be?"

"No. So I don't confuse him with a cable TV salesman and embarrass the snot out of myself."

"Oh, my."

"Yeah."

"Things didn't go well?"

"Oh, things went fine, I guess. He was a good sport about it."

"Well, that's good."

"Yeah. Well, I gotta get to work. Love you." He called out, "Nate, Daddy's leaving!" A few seconds later, his son scurried back into the kitchen, stopping at his daddy's feet, reaching up expectantly. Heath scooped him up. "Bye-bye, Nate-ster, I love you. I'll see you tonight." He kissed his son on the cheek, and then set him down. As soon as Nate's feet touched the floor, he took off again. "Bye, Mom." Heath leaned down and kissed her on the forehead, turning toward the door.

"So, Heath, what did you think of the Rabbi?"

"He's a nice guy, I guess. He's interesting."

"Do you think you'll get together again?"

"No, I don't think so. I mean, unless you send him over again unannounced, I doubt I'll ever run into him."

Heath opened the door to leave, and his mom waved goodbye. *Well, Heath,* she thought, *with Sid, you just never know.*

** *** **

That afternoon in his shop, Heath sat on his stool before the large signboard he had mounted on the wall. Pencil in hand, he busied himself blocking out the first draft of a new sign. The bell on the front door jangled, then his mom's voice came through the shop. "Don't get up Heath. It's just me and Nate."

"Hi, Mom. I'm back here in the work room. What are you and Nate up to?"

Ruth leaned against the front counter. "Oh, just my Monday errands. I thought we'd stop and see if you wanted to get some lunch."

"Sure. Can you give me about ten minutes, or so?"

"No problem, take your time. I need to change Nate and work on my list, anyway."

Heath quickly immersed himself back into the task at hand, trying to get the basic design from his mind to the signboard before it evaporated from his memory. Ruth rounded up Nate and laid him on the couch in the small reception area as she rummaged around in the diaper bag. Once Nate was changed, she pulled out her errand list and poured over it.

The door jangled again, and in walked Sid, drawing Ruth's eyes from her list. "Well, hey Rabbi!—this is a surprise!"

"Hi, Ruth. Yeah, Heath said he had a sign shop around here. I was in Redlands, so I thought I'd stop in and say hi."

"Isn't that nice! I'm sure he'll be pleased to see you again." Ruth stood and leaned over the counter toward the doorway to the back and called out. "Heath, Sid's here!"

Immersed in his project, Heath reached for the upper left section of the signboard. He called back to her without turning around, asking absently, "Sid? Sid, who?"

Ruth blushed immediately, her hand coming to her lips. Amused, Sid couldn't resist. He came around the counter and jumped into the conversation before Ruth had a chance to answer. Standing in the doorway, he shouted across the big work room, grousing in mock-indignation in his best Bronx accent. "'Sid? Sid, who?' What is that?—A knock-knock joke? Sid Edelberg!—you bag of bones!"

The volume and the nearness of the voice startled Heath. Still reaching upward, he cringed immediately and let his forearms fall across his head, his drafting pencil still in hand, embarrassed anew.

"Oh, *that* Sid," he mumbled to himself. He took a deep breath and pivoted on his stool until he faced Sid, grinning sheepishly. "Hey, Rabbi."

Chapter 4

Sid read the same paragraph for the fourth time, and still it wouldn't sink in. *I'm too distracted. Joel's been on my mind all evening; I should just stop what I'm doing right now and give him a call.* No sooner had he finished the thought than the phone rang in another part of the house. *Great. Another distraction.* He waited for Connie to answer it and run interference for him, listening to see if he would be interrupted—though, at this point, it would not make any difference. A moment went by before Connie was at his door.

"Sid? I hate to interrupt you, but Joel is on the phone. Do you want to talk to him or call him back later?"

"Joel?" Surprised, Sid straightened up. *This can't be a coincidence.* "No, that's okay, I'll talk to him." Sid pushed himself away from his desk and left his study. Stretching out on the sofa, he picked up the extension in the den.

"Joel! How ya doing? You been on my mind, man! I was just thinking about calling you. How are things in Florida?"

"I'm fine, Sid. . ." Joel's voice hesitated over the line. "Um, things are going well; real well. The kids are fine, the business is great. I have no complaints."

"But. . .?"

"But what?"

"You tell me! C'mon Joel, it's Sid!—even over the phone I can tell something is up."

Joel chuckled. "Everything is fine, Sid, really—which is why I don't understand why I feel so unsettled. You know, distracted, restless—and every time I pray about it, you come to mind."

"Oh, so when you think 'restless and distracted', you think of me? Thanks a lot, you bag of bones!" Sid teased. "So, what do you think is going on?"

"I don't know, Sid. I've been trying for weeks to figure it out." Sid could hear the strain in his friend's voice.

"So, this has been going on for weeks and you're just calling me now?" He chided his friend, but was struck by this revelation. Unlike Sid's busy intensity, Joel was much more relaxed in nature. It was not like Joel to fret or be anxious about anything for very long; something was definitely bothering him. "So, you feeling like you want to shoot some hoops?"

Joel chuckled again, "How did you know?"

"Because I'm feeling the same way. Is there a court somewhere on the state line where we could meet?"

The two friends laughed, amused at the thought of driving that distance just to play a game of one-on-one—their long-time tradition when something was on either one's mind. When Sid had something to mull over, he liked to do something physical; it allowed him to clear his mind and think, and the same was true for Joel. It was actually how they first met, back in college in Queens nearly over two and a half decades before. They'd struck up a conversation while taking turns at the hoop, and had been close friends ever since. Many an afternoon had been spent at the hoop, solving the problems of the world, or at least their own corner of it.

Joel grinned at his friend's question. "I thought I might come up for a visit, if that's okay."

"What? Are you, crazy? Of course it's okay! I'd love for you to come up!" The more they talked, the more their speech lapsed back to their roots in the boroughs. "How soon can you come?"

"Is now a good time?"

"Of course it is! Any time, really. You wanna come up now? –Then come up now!"

"I thought maybe I'd come Thursday and stay the weekend. How does that sound?"

"That sounds perfect!"

"I don't want to be a bother."

"Oh stop it, you sound like my mother. Just come on, will ya?"

"I'll see you Thursday. Find us a court, okay?"

** *** **

By Thursday afternoon, Sid's two older children were piling on top of 'Uncle Joel' trying to wrestle him to the floor in Sid's den. "Okay, I give, I give!" He declared in mock-defeat. The children relented and let Uncle Joel get up. He climbed to his feet and stood next to Sid, hands on hips, shaking his head at the children who were now wrestling each other in front of him. "Wow, your kids have grown, Sid. It's only been a year since I've seen you, and I can't believe how much they've changed!"

"Mine have changed?!" Sid shot back, "I still can't believe Maddy is married and has a baby!—I used to play hide n' seek with her! Either of the boys serious about anyone?"

"Jake seems pretty serious about his girlfriend, but if you ask him, he denies it; they've been dating for over a year now but he refuses to even think about getting serious until he's done with college—which will be next year. Micah isn't serious about anyone in particular; he's still young. I have this feeling he's not going to think about it until I get married again; it's like he's 'looking after me' or something."

Sid thought back on Joel's family, "They're good kids."

"The best," Joel agreed.

Sid turned for the patio and waved Joel along. Settling into the lounge chairs, a glass of sweet tea in their hands, Sid eyed his friend. "So, what's got you so stirred up?"

Joel sighed, "Well, you're going to think I'm crazy, but it's this dream I've been having."

"A dream? Seriously?"

"Yeah, I know, right? The first time was almost a year ago now, and I've had it a few times since then. Every time I dream it, I get really distracted for a while. Then, just when I've settled down, I have the dream again. This time, it has really been on my mind. I can't seem to shake it."

"So, what's the dream about? Is it something you can talk about?"

"I think that's why you came to mind. I feel like I'm supposed to tell you."

"Go for it. I'm all ears."

"I dreamed I went to synagogue on Shabbat, as I usually do. In my dream, I knew the synagogue was my synagogue, but it didn't look like the one I go to now—but still, I knew it was mine; it was weird. Then there was this woman there. I've never seen her before, but when I saw her, I knew I loved her. I felt like Adonai was, like, presenting her to me, and he said, 'This is my *segula*—treasure her.'"

"Wow!" It was all Sid could think to say.

Joel continued, "Yeah. It was the first time it had occurred to me to think about another woman since Deb died. Sid, the dream was so vivid—even after all this time! It seems as though Adonai is telling me it's time to move on."

"Could be. . ." Sid agreed cautiously. "How long has it been since Deborah died?"

"Four years next month. This whole last year my kids have been trying to get me to start going out again, but I haven't wanted to."

This amused Sid. "So, your kids want you to move on, too?"

"Yeah, you know how they are. They just want me to be happy."

"You're not happy?"

"Well, I'm not *un*happy. You know how it was when Deb died. We were all devastated. I'm doing much better now, but I just haven't felt like I wanted to start looking again."

"What's holding you back?"

"I don't know. I feel okay; I'm not depressed or anything. There just hasn't been anyone who has caught my eye. But this dream has really knocked me for a loop. Ever since I dreamed about that woman, I've been looking for her—every Shabbat. It's so strange. I feel like I already know her and love her. It was just *SO* real. Like it was a vivid memory, instead of a dream. That just sounds crazy, doesn't it?"

"Maybe not. Adonai knows your heart. Maybe He's got someone in mind for you. Do your kids know about your dream?"

"I told Jake a few months ago, and I'm pretty sure he told the others. It was like pouring gasoline on a fire. Maddy really wants to see me married again. You know—she's happily married, so she wants everyone to be happily married." Joel grinned, "She keeps saying it isn't right for me to stay single. She and the boys—especially Micah, keep trying to set me up with their friends' moms!—It's embarrassing!" The two men chuckled. "Anyway, you've been on my heart and mind a lot lately, so I thought I'd come. I don't know why; I just felt like I needed to get away for a few days."

Sid nodded, "I'm glad you came."

Joel thought for a moment. "You know, that's another strange thing, Sid. Everything is going really well, but instead of just being excited about that, I just feel restless—sort of detached from it."

"That's what you said on the phone; it sounds to me like Adonai is getting ready to shake up your life."

Joel grinned, shaking his head, "Ha! I was afraid you'd say that!" He nodded slowly, "Actually, that's my feeling, too. I feel like I need to get going, but I don't know which direction to go or what I'm supposed to do."

"Well, let's pray about it over the next few days, that Adonai will make that clear to you."

"That would be great, Sid." Joel nodded as he spoke, "I would sure appreciate the prayers." A thought occurred to him and he changed the subject. "Speaking of synagogues—when do I get to see your new building?"

Sid shrugged, "How about right now?"

Joel tilted his head. "Okay, great!"

The two stood to leave and began making their way through the house to the front door. Sid called to Connie along the way, "We're going over to the synagogue for a few."

"Okay," she called back. "Dinner will be ready in an hour."

"Eh, we'll be back before then, we're just going to have a look around. Joel hasn't seen it since we broke ground."

Not five minutes later, they pulled into the synagogue parking lot. Joel panned the building and the landscape. "Wow, Sid. This is beautiful! It looks just like Israel." As soon as they entered the sanctuary, Joel's mouth fell open. Pivoting all around, he made his way down an aisle, wide-eyed and excited. "O my word!—this is incredible, Sid! I don't believe this!"

Sid squinted. "What's wrong?"

Joel, still open-mouthed, again turned himself around in the room. Almost speechless, his breath came is short gasps. "This is it, Sid! This is it!"

Squinting, Sid puzzled. "This is *what?*"

"This is the synagogue in my dream! This is it!" Joel stared all around him in excited wonder.

Sid squinted again. "We just finished this building and moved in a few months ago, and you said you dreamed about it over a year ago?" Sid stared in amazement.

His hand on the nape of his neck, Joel craned his head in every direction. "I know it sounds crazy, but this is the synagogue I saw. The inside, those windows...the Bimah...that Ner Tamid! In my dream it was my synagogue!" His thoughts raced. "You know, with how I've been feeling so antsy, like I need to go somewhere, maybe the dream wasn't really about that woman. Maybe it was about moving up here or something. Do you think that dream could be about me coming here to live?"

Sid thought for a moment. "I don't know, Joel. That's certainly possible. Let's pray about it right now." And that's what they did.

** *** **

Two days later, after several sessions of prayer and rounds of one-on-one, it was Shabbat morning and Joel arrived at the synagogue with Sid and his family. Sid's children emptied out of their van and Connie corralled them toward the building. As Sid gathered his Bible and tallit from the van, Joel panned all around again, taking in the building, the landscape, and the people as they gathered together for the service. Sid began to head toward the building, with Joel following behind him, still glancing excitedly around.

"So, do I call you 'Rabbi' while I'm here, or what?" Joel grinned at his friend.

"'Sid' is good." He rolled his eyes. "You bag of bones."

The two chatted as they walked, and Sid greeted those around them along the way. Someone in the next row of the parking lot called out a greeting to the Rabbi, which Sid returned as Joel followed the direction of the shout. Suddenly he froze. Snatching Sid by a shoulder, he pulled him in front, as though trying to hide behind him. Regaining his balance, Sid puzzled at his friend. "What was that for?"

Joel's voice was almost a whisper. "Oh, my word, Sid!— there she is!"

"There *who* is? Where?" Sid craned his head this way and that.

"The woman in my dream!" Joel gestured subtly with an index finger. "There!" Sid traced the trajectory of Joel's gaze and the discreetly pointed finger. "That's her, Sid! She's here!"

Recognizing the woman who was the focus of Joel's excitement, Sid squinted uncertainly. *Andrea Cullen. . .?* Shoulders sagging, he verified, "Her. . .? Right there in the black pants?" Joel nodded hurriedly and Sid winced to himself in disappointment. "Are you sure?"

Not noticing Sid's hesitation, Joel could hardly contain himself. "I'm positive! Who is she? What's her name?"

Sid sighed, unenthusiastic. "That's Andrea Cullen."

Joel pressed, "What can you tell me about her?"

"Well, for starters, you see that man coming up behind her?" Joel nodded expectantly and Sid gestured toward him with his head. "*That's* her husband."

Immediately, Joel deflated. "Her husband. . .?" Confused, he continued to stare over Sid's shoulder at the woman.

Sid turned to him. "You sure that's her, Joel? Maybe she just *looks* like the woman in your dream."

Joel frowned. "No, it's her—I'm positive." Puzzled and dismayed, he shook his head slowly. "I don't understand. This doesn't any make sense."

Full of consternation, Joel followed Sid inside and took a seat near the back. Sid continued up the aisle to the front row, nodding to the two Shammashim, who then sounded the silver trumpets and then a few minutes later, the shofar sounded and the service began. Becoming involved in the worship, Joel pushed his confusion and the woman to the back of his mind. Once the service was over, noticeably subdued, Joel returned to the van, and Sid's house. The next morning, a disheartened Joel waved good-bye to Sid and his family and set out for the long drive back to Jacksonville.

After having spent much time in prayer with Sid during his visit to Georgia, despite his bafflement over the woman in his dream, Joel was convinced in his heart of Adonai's leading to relocate to Heartland. Once he arrived home, he began making preparations to move. Planning to open up an office up there, and shuttle back and forth between it and his main business in Jacksonville, he got right to work on the details.

Though the woman in his dream was definitely off-limits, the lingering questions about her were never far from his thoughts. Puzzled and dismayed, though he tried hard not to think about it, the questions nagged at him. *How could I have been so off-base? How did someone I've never met or even seen before, end up in my dream?! Let alone, someone who is married. . .!* Even more disturbing than the how, Joel puzzled all the more over *why* she ended up in it. There seemed to be no answer to that.

Chapter 5

L ate March and early April in the Cullen household was always an eventful time. With two birthday celebrations and their wedding anniversary within three weeks—and this being a milestone year for two of those events, Andrea had been scrambling for weeks to make those two occasions extra special for all.

Having to work on Shabbat was bad enough, and even though it was only required of her every third week, Andrea was still disheartened whenever her weekend came up and she had to miss synagogue services. But working this particular Saturday was even more discouraging than usual; not only would she miss out on the worship and message at Beth Chesed V' Emet, but this work weekend fell on Matt's twenty-first birthday. She had wanted to celebrate it by giving him a nice party and this Shabbat was the only day that worked out for everyone—except her, and try as she did, she could find no one who could switch with her. She had spent the past two weeks scurrying around making certain everything was in place—not just for Matt's party, but for their twenty-fifth anniversary trip in two weeks. Now, there was only one errand left to do for the party and that was picking up the cake—a task she had reluctantly delegated to Evan because of having to work. With everything else done, all that remained was, finish up and clock-out on time, and hurry home to change, then to somehow, in some way make it to the restaurant by six.

After rushing to finish her charting and give report at the Out Patient Clinic, Andrea hurried to the badge reader and swiped her badge through it, going through her mental check list as she hurried for her locker in the nurse's break room. *Let's see, Donna took care of the decorations, the photographer should already be there. . .I'll get Matt's gift when I get home. . . Evan's picking up the cake. . .I think that's it.* Hurriedly, she grabbed her things, then made a dash out to her car. Pulling out of the parking lot, she glanced again at her watch. *Okay, all I have to do is get home and change clothes and get to the restaurant in the forty-five minutes.* Of course, twenty minutes to her house and back, in heavy traffic, plus changing clothes made that a feat in itself.

Not fifteen minutes into her return trip, her cell phone sounded with Matt's ring tone. "Hi, Matty! I'm running home to change, but I'll be there as soon as I can. Did Donna get the decorations up? Do they look okay?"

"Yeah, they look really good. Um. . .where's Dad?"

"He's not there?"

Matt sighed and Andrea was certain he was also rolling his eyes. "No. I called, but only got his voicemail."

"So, the cake isn't there?"

"No."

"What about the photographer?"

"He's not here either."

"What?" Andrea groaned to herself. Thinking quickly, she made a right turn onto a side street, followed by a U-turn until she was back at the boulevard, then waited at the signal to turn left toward the bakery. *So much for changing clothes; I'll just have to go in my scrubs.* "Okay Matty, I'm heading back to the bakery to pick up your cake. Give them a call for me to make sure they don't close before I get there. Tell them I'm on my way. Meanwhile, when everyone is there, go ahead and let them get seated. I'm sorry, Matty. I'll be there as soon as I can. I'll see if I can call and find out what's keeping your dad." After ending the call with Matt, she tried her home phone and then Evan's cell, getting voicemail both times. *We've been planning this for weeks!—where could Evan be?*

A minute later, Matt's ring tone sounded again. "Mom, the bakery said they were just closing up, but they'll wait 'til you get there."

Andrea sighed, relieved. "Great! Did the photographer show yet?"

"No."

"Okay, I'll give him a call."

"Did you get a hold of Dad?"

"No, I just got his voice mail. Don't worry, Matty, he wouldn't miss this; he'll be there." After a few more reassurances, she ended the call but her forehead furrowed. *Oh Evan, not again! Please be there!*

After picking up the cake, and profusely thanking the bakery staff for waiting for her, Andrea was back on the road. Trying Evan's cell number again, and then their house phone, she got no answer. *Where could he be?* She found the photographer's number in her phone. When the call connected, as nicely as she could, she asked him why he wasn't at the restaurant.

"Your husband called and cancelled last week, Mrs. Cullen. He said he wanted to take his own pictures."

"What?" Andrea's mouth fell open. In her stunned moment, she almost ran through a red-light. Slamming on her brakes, she reached to stop the cake from ending up on the floorboard, losing her cell phone in the process. Retrieving her phone from between her feet, she resumed the call. "Sorry about that. I dropped my phone. When was that?"

"Last week."

"Last week. . .? I didn't realize that. I'm so sorry to bother you."

"It's no problem, Mrs. Cullen. I'm sorry for the mix-up."

"It's not your fault." She rushed to make excuse, "He probably told me and I forgot." They ended the call amicably and Andrea groused as she puzzled over it. "Why didn't he tell me he was doing that. . .?—Is he trying to save money, or something?" Then a new concern struck her. ". . .*Evan* is planning to take the pictures? With what?" Sighing wearily, she shook her head. "I can't believe he did that—and now I don't even know where he is!" She sighed again, speaking to no one but herself, "Sorry Matty, it looks like we're just going to have cell phone pictures of your big party." She worked to quell her frustrations before arriving at the restaurant.

The cake arrived safely, though a little flatter on one edge from the sudden stop, and Matt's party finally started, albeit a half hour late; there was only one catch—the absence of his father. Several times, Matt inquired after him, and each time all Andrea could say was, "I'm sure he'll be here."

Matt only rolled his eyes.

When dinner was finished and the cake was cut, guests around the long table joked and teased as Matt opened his gifts. As the gathering wound down, Matt's twenty-first had been celebrated by all—except his dad, who still had not shown. Growing antsy, and ready for the *real* party to begin, Matt's friends whisked him away to continue their celebration elsewhere—away from the over-sight of his mother. Disheartened over that, Andrea could only pray wisdom over her son, as well as for his safety. As the remaining guests also left, Andrea was all that remained, sitting there alone, staring at Evan's empty seat and the tab for the meal.

Her mind no longer occupied with the details and distractions of entertaining a hoard of jubilant twenty-one years olds, Andrea's thoughts dissolved into worry. *Something terrible must have happened for him to miss this!* She tried his phone again, and again got his voicemail. When she pulled into the driveway at her home, she was surprised and relieved to see Evan's car was there. Hurrying into the house, she found him on the sofa. He had a beer in one hand, and was munching chips and dip with the other as he watched a basketball game on television. He glanced up when she entered.

"Evan! Where have you been? I've been trying to call you for two hours!"

Evan just shrugged, his eyes glued to the TV screen. "Traveling?! That ref is an idiot!" He returned his attention to Andrea, but only partially. "I got some yard work done. Did you notice I trimmed up the bushes? And I took Sally for a walk. I just got back about ten minutes ago."

"You were doing yard work and walking the dog?" Surely she had not heard right.

Curious over her stark expression, Evan glanced over, "Yeah. Where have *you* been?"

Andrea stared at him incredulously. "Where have *I* been? I was at Matty's party, worried sick about you!"

Evan squinted at her. "Was that tonight?" He shrugged, still focused on the TV. "Oh that's right—I forgot."

Andrea could only stare at him. "You forgot?—Evan, we've been planning this for weeks!"

Just then a commercial came on the screen, so Evan gave her his full attention. "You should have called and reminded me it was today, Andrea."

"I did, Evan!—lots of times. Check your voicemail—I've been calling you for the last two hours!"

Evan grasped at another straw. "Why didn't you just call my cell?"

"I did that too—a couple of times."

"You should have left a note, or something before you went to work. This is your fault!"

Incredulous, Andrea's shoulders sagged. "Evan, how is this my fault? Despite all my talk about it and all of my reminders about what I needed you to do, you still didn't remember!—or at least, you only remembered long enough to cancel the photographer!"

Deciding to ignore that last part, Evan pressed, "If you had called to remind me earlier, I wouldn't have missed it! *That's* how it's your fault!" The game and Evan's attention returned to the screen, signaling the end of the matter.

Andrea stood in the doorway of the living room, her heart heavy, and her husband returned to fully focusing on the game, his wife forgotten. Shoulders sagging, she watched Evan as he watched the game—oblivious to her. Wounded, she shifted her gaze to the TV screen. *He forgot because of a basketball game?* She could only sigh again.

** *** **

Already frazzled by the time Thursday arrived, Andrea rushed around the clinic trying to do three things at once, accomplishing none of them. After being summoned to the phone for the third time in the past ten minutes, she sighed, resigned, *Okay, this week is officially rotten.* Stepping over to one of the phones in the work room, she pressed the button for line two.

"This is Andrea. . ."

"Hi Andrea—guess what!" Evan's voice was unusually animated.

Andrea's eyebrows arched. "Evan!—you sound excited!"

Though she could not see him, Evan grinned from ear to ear. "I am!—Jerry has an extra ticket to the semi-finals *and* the championship!—*and box seats!*"

Knowing how much her husband loved college basketball, Andrea smiled, delighted for him. "Really?—That's great, Evan! When is it?"

"When *is* it?" Evan was incredulous, "It's *the semi-finals and the championship,* Andrea! Where have you been?" He didn't wait for her response. "It's next weekend in Atlanta, and then the championship is on Monday! I'm so glad I already requested those days off at work!"

Andrea's countenance fell. "Next weekend? But what about our long weekend to to Destin?"

Evan brushed it aside dismissively. "Andrea, we can go to Destin any time—this only happens once a year!"

". . .And our twenty-fifth anniversary only happens once in a life time!" She shook her head in disbelief. "Evan, I was really looking forward to this—I took time off of work for it!"

"Oh, Andrea, don't be like that! We can reschedule the trip." To him, it was simple, "Just go ahead and work that Monday and Friday and we can just go to Destin some other time." When Andrea didn't immediately respond, Evan insisted. "Andrea, this is *box seats at the semi-finals AND the championship!*"

"Evan, You know I can't just put myself on and off the schedule when I feel like it! Nobody wants to work Mondays and Fridays—I had to do summersaults to get someone to trade those days with me!—I can't just change it back because you changed your mind!"

Evan's tone was decidedly sharper. "I *cancelled* the trip, Andrea—I'm *going* to Atlanta."

Crestfallen, Andrea's mouth fell open. "You already cancelled it?" Her voice suddenly frail, ". . .Before even talking to me?" Crushed, she blinked back her tears. Seeing further discussion would avail nothing, she tried to steady her voice, working to be gracious and understanding—yet feeling neither. "Okay, well. . .I guess we'll go some other time then. I'll see you at home." Lips pressed together, Andrea hung up the phone, unaware that Arlene had overheard everything, gleaning much from Andrea's side of the conversation.

Shaking her head, Arlene sneered. "So, I take it Evan just bailed on your anniversary weekend?" Andrea's sigh spoke volumes to her co-worker. "What was it he cancelled you for?"

"Basketball. The semi-finals and the championship game in Atlanta—a guy at work with box seats has an extra ticket."

"A few basketball games with a guy he works with, instead of your twenty-fifth anniversary?" Not one to mince words, Arlene shook her head in disgust. "Andrea, when are you going to dump that dirt-bag?"

"Arlene, please don't start on me. . ."

"He treats you like you don't exist! When are you going to wake up?"

"Arlene, he's not a drunk, he doesn't chase women, he doesn't slap me around, and he doesn't use drugs or gamble away our money. Just being self-absorbed and inconsiderate is not grounds for divorce."

Arlene only rolled her eyes as she walked away. "It should be. . ."

Sulking over his wife's lack of understanding, Evan subjected Andrea to several days of the silent treatment until Shabbat morning when Andrea, always the peacemaker, finally apologized for her selfishness. Triumphant, Evan packed his bag the following Thursday and headed to Atlanta with Jerry for the weekend.

** *** **

Bone weary, Andrea drove home from work the following Tuesday evening after a very draining day. *I'm so glad I'm off tomorrow. It's my birthday, and I'm not going to rush around and wear myself out like I usually do. I just want to relax.* Evan hadn't made any mention of it, or nosed around for any gift ideas, so she didn't have any expectations that he had remembered. *It's Health Check Day, so at least, I'll get to spend a couple of hours with Ruth—that'll be my present.*

Pulling into the driveway, her eyes narrowed, surprised to see Evan's car was there. *He's home already?* Puzzling over it, she pulled up next to it and headed inside. Setting her tote bag and pocketbook on the table next to the door, she glanced around, looking forward to getting off her feet. Not seeing her husband, she called out, "Evan? You're home early."

"Hi Andrea! Yeah, I took off early." His voice called from beyond the living room. "Come into the kitchen, Andrea. I have a surprise for you."

Andrea stepped into the kitchen and glanced around, wondering if there might actually be a gift awaiting her—but there was only Evan standing by the sink, grinning proudly. Andrea squinted, puzzled. "What's the surprise?" Evan beamed as he turned on the faucet, and then flipped a switch on the wall. A grinding sound arose from the sink, and Evan grinned all the more, then shut off the switch and the water. Delighted, Andrea smiled, "You put in a new garbage disposal? Wow, that's great Evan!"

"Yeah," Evan squared his shoulders, "since you *broke* it a few months ago." He beamed again, "Happy Birthday!"

Andrea winced. "Evan, I didn't break it. I turned on the switch and it wouldn't work. It was over twenty years old—" Stopping suddenly, Andrea arched an eyebrow. "Happy Birthday. . .?" She glanced around the kitchen again, finding nothing that resembled a gift. *Did I miss something?* She eyed Evan and the sink suspiciously. "The garbage disposal. . .?"

Evan nodded proudly, "Yeah, since your birthday is tomorrow, I decided I'd give you a new one for your present and kill two birds with one stone."

"That's my birthday present. . .? Andrea just stared, her countenance sagging along with her shoulders. . .*A garbage disposal?* She sighed, trying to find a positive, *Well, at least he remembered this time.* Swallowing her disappointment, Andrea mustered a smile. "Thank you, Evan. It'll sure be nice being able to use it again." Staring sadly at her 'gift,' that discarded feeling surfaced again. *A garbage disposal. . .how fitting.*

The next morning Andrea let herself sleep an extra half hour before the aroma of pancakes roused her from her sleep and lured her out of bed. Salivating, she shuffled into the kitchen anticipating a birthday treat, but when she arrived, the room was empty, with fresh dishes in the sink. Just then, Evan came around the corner, adjusting his necktie.

"Good morning, Andrea."

"Good morning, Evan." She waited for a moment, but when nothing further was offered, Andrea arched a puzzled eyebrow. "Um, are we going to have breakfast together?"

Evan shook his head. "No, thanks—I already ate. There are some left-over pancakes in the fridge, if you want them." Crestfallen, Andrea declined. Evan only shrugged. "Okay. Hey, I'm out of cash. Can I have a couple twenties?"

"I only have about ten dollars in my purse, but you can have that, though."

Instantly annoyed, Evan eyed her suspiciously. "I saw online that you got a hundred dollars out of the ATM yesterday. You spent it already?"

"No, not spent—gave. They were taking up a collection at work for someone who had a kitchen fire. That's what I got it out for."

Evan bristled immediately. "You gave someone at work a hundred dollars of *MY* money?!"

Taken aback, Andrea squinted at him. "Last I checked, Evan, it's *our* money; I earned part of it, too."

Side-stepping that, Evan stared at her angrily. "Why go giving it away like t*hat? —a hundred dollars...?!*"

"She was in a bind."

"So, what? It isn't my fault her kitchen caught on fire!"

"If it was your fault, it wouldn't be 'helping'—it would be 'owing'." She eyed him uncertainly, "You think you should only have to help someone if their problem was your fault? Where exactly in the Bible did you read that?" A sneer being Evan's only response, Andrea was becoming increasingly appalled. Her eyes narrowed again. "How does a Believer even think something like that, Evan?—Let alone say it!"

"Oh, now are you implying I'm not a Believer?"

"I'm not *implying* anything." Andrea's eyes widened, surprised at herself.

Evan scoffed, "Oh, so you're *saying* I'm not a Believer?—Is that it?"

Her entire history with him rushed to mind, and Andrea swallowed hard. "I don't know, Evan. A tree is known by its fruit—I think that's a question you should seriously look into."

He took a step toward her, challenging, "What fruit. . .?"

Instinctively, she stepped back, but didn't back down. "*Your fruit!*—that attitude for starters, and how you treat Matty and me. I don't know how you do it, Evan. I don't know how you can read your Bible as much as you do and attend services every week and listen to all those messages—and still have those attitudes of the heart and treat us like you do."

Glowering down at her, he sneered, "Oh, so now I'm not treating you right?"

Again, she held her ground. "You be the judge, Evan. Compare what you do, and how you talk to us, with all those books out there on marriage and family. You don't even need to look in the *Christian* marriage section—even *secular* books say you shouldn't treat your family the way you do!"

Indignant, Evan groped to defend, "I provide for you!"

"Yes, you do—and you're a good provider; but there's more to it than providing. What about sharing?"

"Sharing what? I share my income with you!"

Now it was Andrea who stepped forward. "No, Evan. I share *my* income with *you!* You *hoard* yours!" Resisting the rabbit trail, she back-pedaled, "And I'm not talking about money, anyways. I'm talking about sharing your time, your thoughts, your feelings, your life, your... your... SELF! You hoard those, too!" Trembling all over, it seem as though she were standing off to one side, watching herself confront her husband.

Eyes blazing, Evan made several attempts to refute her, but could come up with nothing—which made him even angrier. Reaching for the cliché, he stormed at her. "I can't believe you're saying that *after all I've done for you!*" Again he groped for words, then resorted to his old stand-by. "I don't have to listen to this. I'm late—I have to get to work." He pushed past her, headed for the front door, and slammed it behind him.

Tears streaming down her face, Andrea turned away from him. Now facing the kitchen counter, she wiped her eyes and nose with both hands, then focused on the sink to her left. Stepping closer, she lifted the lever of the tap, and flipped the switch on the wall. Immediately a grinding sound filled the room. She let it run for several seconds then flipped the switch down and turned off the water. In the following silence, she stared dismally into the black hole of her sink—of her life—and sighed long and heavy. "Happy Birthday to me."

Just after lunch, Ruth pushed open the louver door into the kitchen, listening. *Was that a knock...?* Hesitating in the doorway, she listened again. Another few knocks sounded softly and she nodded, *Okay, that was definitely a knock.* She stepped over to the porch door and peeked through the curtains and the glass panes of the upper half.

Her eyebrows arched, "Andrea!" Quickly pulling open the porch door, Ruth waved in her friend. "Andrea, you're early! I sure hope you haven't been out there long. I barely heard your knock!" Her delighted smile faded with one look at Andrea's vacant eyes. "You doing all right, hon?" Andrea just shrugged weakly. "Come on in—let me put on some tea, and we can talk." Andrea set down her tote bag under the small breakfast table, and then plopped down into the closest chair. Filling the kettle from the tap, Ruth eyed her friend, concerned. After setting the kettle on the stove, she joined Andrea at the table, taking the seat across from her. Ruth arched an eyebrow as she ventured, "You look like you're trying real hard to not look like you've been crying."

Leaning on her elbows, Andrea couldn't help smiling slightly, despite her sadness. "I guess I'm not trying hard enough to *not* look like it." She smiled sadly again, averting her eyes as she rested her chin in a hand.

"Tough day?" Ruth ventured.

"Tough month." Still she could not make eye contact.

Ruth took a guess that wasn't much of a reach. "Evan?"

Andrea nodded, her eyes shifting to the table in front of her. "Twenty-five *years* of Evan. This last month has been all those years in a nutshell."

Ruth tilted her head slightly to one side. "It must have been a doozy this time, hon; I haven't seen you look like this in a while." Andrea's shoulders just sagged all the more. Ruth tried again, "I was hoping we'd be able to sit out on the porch when you came today. It's too bad it's raining out."

Andrea rolled her eyes. "Well, I'm sure if you ask Evan, that's probably my fault, too." Her face clouded as she struggled to maintain her composure. "All these years, Ruth, all these years I've been praying. Praying for Evan, praying for our marriage. Praying that God would change me, or him, or both of us—or *something.*" She shook her head dismally. "Why is it taking so long for him to answer, Ruth?"

"I know it's hard, hon, especially with it being so long—but God hasn't forgotten you. He's heard every prayer and caught every tear; and he has seen you standing when everyone else has been telling you to bail and run."

"Except you, Ruth; you're the only one who is standing with me. Everyone else thinks I'm crazy for staying with him."

"No one ever said standing firm for God was a popular thing. In fact, the Bible says it's *not* popular—that's why it's called 'the narrow path.'" Ruth thought for a moment. "You know what, Andrea? This reminds me of dominos—when they set up those displays. You can't see God working, but he's in the background setting up all those dominos, and when he's all finished, and everything is in place, he's going to touch that end domino and all of the dominoes will fall!—and you are going to be dazzled by what he's done." Andrea tried to smile and believe, which was becoming more difficult by the day. Ruth sighed, sad for her friend. "The Gang isn't expecting you for another hour or so. You want to talk about it now, or leave it be for later?" The answer to that question would serve as Ruth's barometer to Andrea's degree of heartbreak.

Andrea sighed long and heavy. "Let's leave it for later. Just talk to me, Ruth—about anything. Just please *talk* to me."

Ruth's heart sank. *This is not good at all.* She nodded, "Okay, hon—we'll just have us some chit-chat 'til you feel up to talking about it." The tea kettle's squeal summoned Ruth back to the stove and she rose from her place. "I got some more of that fruity red tea you like. Can I fix you a cup?"

"Sure, Ruth, that will be fine." Andrea's voice was as expressionless as her face.

Ruth's forehead furrowed. *Her favorite tea didn't even get a smile out of her? She must really be hurting this time.* Saddened for her friend, Ruth just shook her head slowly. *Oh, Lord, please come alongside Andrea and comfort her heart.* Ruth brought over two steaming mugs of tea, then returned with a plate of freshly baked muffins and set it on the table in front of Andrea; in the middle of one of them, stood a lighted candle. Both delighted and anguished at the same moment, Andrea gazed at it.

Ruth smiled encouragingly, "Happy Birthday, hon."

Tears welling up, Andrea's small voice squeaked out the words, "Thank you, Ruth!"

As usual, by the time she left Ruth's, Andrea had received a generous dose of encouragement and felt ready to face the world again. The peacemaker by nature, Andrea sought to make amends and brought up Evan's work number on her cell phone screen on her way home from Ruth's. When the call connected, it wasn't Evan who answered.

"Oh, hi, Jerry. Evan's not at his desk?"

"Hi, Andrea. No, sorry—Evan didn't come in today."

She could hear the puzzlement in Jerry's voice and hurried to cover for her husband. "Oh, that's right—silly me," she chuckled for added effect. "Thanks." Andrea frowned as they ended the call. Forehead furrowed, she stared out her windshield, puzzled. *I watched him leave. . .He didn't go into work today?* She tried his cell number but got his voicemail. Considering their morning, she was not so surprised, and just sighed, *I'm sure I'm the last person he wants to talk to right now.*

By bedtime that night, Evan still had not come home. Anguished in her thoughts, Andrea climbed into bed alone and prayed until she drifted off to sleep. Close to midnight, her eyes popped open to the metallic clacking and grating of the deadbolt sliding, then the sound of the front door opening. She listened as footfalls neared their bedroom. *"Evan. . .?"*

His voice sounded from the dark at their bedroom door. "Yeah, Andrea. It's me."

Dizzy with relief, Andrea reached for her bedside lamp. "Evan, I'm so glad you're home!" When her eyes adjusted to the lamplight, she focused on him, "You look spent. . ."

Evan sat down wearily on the side of their bed. "Yeah, I am." Elbows on his knees, he rubbed his face with his palms.

"I called your work today."

His shoulders sagged. "You did? Why did you do that?"

Andrea shrugged, "I wanted to apologize, but Jerry said you didn't go in today."

"No, I didn't." One hand moved to the back of his neck where he continued rubbing, his other elbow on his knee, that hand dangled loosely. "Andrea, I'm sorry—not just about the money thing this morning, but about everything." Surprised by his contrition, Andrea had expected a rebuke. Wincing, Evan shook his head, the distress in his voice was obvious. "You're right—everything you said. I've wronged you and Matty more than I can say." Genuinely grieved, he hung his head. "Andrea, please forgive me for being such a. . .a *jerk* to you and Matt."

Andrea stared, wide-eyed. She'd heard those words before, but never in such earnestness. "Of course, Evan. Of course—I already did." She stared at him a moment longer, sensing there was more to this. "Did something happen today?"

"Just something that I wish would've happened years ago." He glanced over his shoulder at her, then resumed his hunched position over his knees. "I was so mad when I left; I wanted so bad to say you were wrong—but you weren't. Everything you said was completely true. It's weird, Andrea, it's like God just showed it all to me while I was driving to work. I just all-of-a-sudden got this huge impression that life is too short and I've already wasted too much of it being a selfish, self-absorbed jerk—and I just started bawling right there in my car." Evan began crying anew and Andrea crawled out from under her covers and over to him. He opened his arms and they held each other tightly as he cried, his voice breaking. "Please pray for me, Andrea, I want to be a good husband to you." They clung to each other for a long moment until Evan regained his composure and continued, "I just drove all day. I drove all the way to Columbus and just walked along the river—up and back, over and over, just praying and asking God to forgive me." He sniffed and wiped his nose. "I called Matt on the way home and asked him to forgive me, too. I woke him up!"

Andrea's eyebrows arched. "You did? What did he say?"

"He said the same thing you did." He shook his head slowly, amazed. "He's a good kid." Evan half chuckled, "He takes after his mom."

Andrea hugged him. "I'm glad you're home."

Evan nodded, "'Home' in more ways than one. . ." Suddenly a thought occurred to him for the first time that day. "Oh, Andrea—happy birthday!"

Andrea smiled, nodding. "Yes, it is. . ."

The next morning, too few hours later and short on sleep, both slept past their alarms. They both hurried to get ready for work and Evan called out a quick good bye and dashed out the door—only to return thirty seconds later.

"I'm not getting off to the right start!" He grinned at his wife, "I want to give you a fitting goodbye." He smiled at her earnestly as they parted, both wishing they could just be an hour or two late.

Though her day at the Outpatient Infusion Clinic was as hectic as ever, Andrea sailed through her morning, her heart light.

"What's gotten into you?" Arlene teased.

"It's not what's gotten into me—It's what's gotten into my husband!"

"And what's that?"

"The Holy Spirit, I think."

Arlene rolled her eyes, "Yeah, sure." But it didn't diminish Andrea's enthusiasm one whit.

** *** **

After lunch, the telephone handset to her ear, Arlene beckoned Andrea to the desk as she spoke to the caller, "Yes, here she is right here." She held the handset out to Andrea. "A call for you."

Curious Andrea reached for the phone. "Who is it?"

Arlene shrugged. "He didn't say, but he sounds upset."

Andrea arched an eyebrow. *He?* "Is it Evan?"

Arlene shook her head. "No, it didn't sound like Evan."

Andrea brought the handset to her ear. "This is Andrea. . ."

Arlene watched as Andrea's expression went from puzzlement

to alarm, furrowing her forehead. "What? What happened? ...Oh no! Okay, thank you Jerry." She hung up the phone, her eyes still wide, and raised her face to Arlene.

"What's wrong Andrea?"

"I need to go. . ."

"What is it?"

"That was a co-worker of Evans—he said they found Evan. . . They had to call an ambulance and he's on the way to the ER right now!" Andrea glanced all around her, flustered. "I. . .I still have a patient here. . .!"

"Just go—I'll take care of her. Where's her chart?"

Andrea forced herself to focus. "Um. . .it's in my slot. She's almost finished with her infusion, but. . ."

"I got it, Andrea—just go!"

** *** **

Two weeks after his visit to Heartland, Joel's cell phone rang. Reaching for it, he glanced at the display and smiled, raising it to his ear,

"Sid, how ya doing?"

"Joel. . ." Sid began, and then hesitated.

Suddenly concerned, Joel's forehead furrowed at his friend's voice. "What is it, Sid? Are you okay? Did something happen to Connie? The kids?" He braced himself for what was sure to be bad news.

"No, they're good." Joel sagged in relief as Sid drew a breath. "Joel, I don't know how to tell you this—I don't even know if I *should* tell you this. . ." He hesitated again, searching for the words. "You know that woman you pointed out to me that you said was in your dream?"

Suddenly attentive, Joel leaned forward in his chair, his elbows landing on his desk. Dreading what might come next, his tone was cautious. "Yeah, what about her?" When Sid again hesitated, Joel pressed, "Sid, what—?"

"Joel, her husband died today." Sid awaited his friend's response, but on the other end of the line there was only stunned silence.

Chapter 6

A sleeved CD-ROM in her lips, Rae pulled off her nitrile gloves and pushed open the door between the hangar and the front office just enough to peer in, *Good, Patty's still at lunch.* She stepped back from the door and tossed the gloves into the nearby trashcan. She quickly slipped out of her smudged coveralls, hung them up, then checked herself for any stray smudges as she reached for the door to the office and stepped in. The business may belong to Joe Gerrard, but the front office was Patty's domain—and grease was forbidden.

For as long as Rae could remember, Patty had been their office manager. With her dad and her four brothers—along with the other pilots, and most of their customers all being men, Patty was Rae's oasis in this sea of testosterone. When Rae took her place in the family business their camaraderie grew—much to the dismay of the men, and despite Patty's grandmotherly appearance, the two of them were a formidable coalition in any debate with the men. In addition, since many of those male customers did not initially believe Rae belonged in a cockpit, let alone under the cowling of an airplane, on occasion Patty had intervened as both referee and cheerleader. But all that would change, Rae was certain, if Patty returned from lunch and found even a smudge of grease on her desk or keyboard.

Rae lowered herself into the chair and pivoted to the dino-saur-of-a-desktop computer that faced the door she had just come through, and popped the CD-ROM into its tray. Part of her job as head mechanic was to fill out monthly reports and order parts and supplies. With her time always crowded with more pressing responsibilities, those chores often ended up being put off until the last minute—sometimes longer. Her month-end report was still waiting, and this parts order should have been faxed two days ago.

Down the hall to her right, the doorknob rattled and a door swung open as Joe Gerrard filled the doorway. Seeing Rae at the desk rather than Patty, he stopped short and smiled at his daughter, "Oh, hi, sweetheart. Your printer out of ink again?"

Rae grinned without taking her eyes off the screen. "Yup."

"Where's Patty?"

"Lunch."

Joe considered his options. "Are you going to be here long?"

"For a little bit. I have to finish this parts order, then I need to be at Miller's by two. Whatcha need?"

"I'm expecting an important phone call from Mr. Barkley and I have someone coming in soon about a job, but I need to catch Riley on the apron before he leaves. Will you stay here and grab the phone if it rings?"

"Sure, no problem." Rae smiled, but continued squinting at the computer screen. Her dad smiled and nodded as he headed out through the door to the hangar as she continued her hunt-and-peck mode at the keyboard.

Kirk Sloan squealed his sports car into the parking spot so that it came to a stop crooked and straddling two spaces. Craning his head out the side window, he verified his destination by the old, wood board sign over the doorway before him, that spelled out 'Gerrard and Son Aviation' in peeling red paint. He shook his head in disgust at the unimpressive sign.

Quickly drawing his conclusion, he shook his head slowly. "Pitiful!" He groused in his thoughts. *So this is what I've been reduced to? Groveling for work in a two-bit dump like this just to stay in the air and get my hours in.* He sneered and shaking his head again, as he stared for a long moment at the forlorn shack of a building attached to a partially rusted, corrugated aluminum hangar, trying to decide if it was really worth it to even go in. Kirk loved flying; there was nothing else he desired to do more—or could do; but private piloting jobs were scarce in Florida these days, and it was already May. He needed to secure a job soon—he had bills to pay; mainly the payments on his aircraft and the impressive set of wheels in which he now sat. Groaning, he regarded the old wood sign once more. . .*But seriously—this place? The ad in the newspaper sounded desperate. Well, at least I'll be a shoe-in.* With a sigh of resignation, he pushed open his car door and got out.

Midway through her task, the phone on the desk beside Rae rang sharply, startling her. At the same time, the bell on the front door jangled and the young man, who had finally made his decision to come inside, swaggered through. Glancing up at the door, Rae reached for the ringing phone at the same time, knocking it off its cradle. She scrambled for it for a few seconds before she got hold of the handset. Seeing the girl at the desk fumbling with her telephone, the new arrival arched his eyebrows with a smirk as she brought the receiver to her ear. Rae spoke into the mouthpiece, "Gerrard Aviation. . .Yes sir, Mr. Barkley, just a moment, please."

Seeing that it would be a minute before the girl would be free, Kirk glanced to his right and took a seat in one of the metal and plastic chairs that lined the space in front of the big, front window. He noted the name plate on the desk in front of him—*Patty Clark*, then glanced up, nodding approvingly at the girl with the long, blonde ponytail that sat behind it.

Rae cupped her free hand over the receiver as she stared down at the row of buttons below the touch pad on Patty's telephone, trying to remember which button would connect her to the intercom. Rae worked on aircraft; antique office equipment was not her forte—and this phone of Patty's probably came over on the Mayflower. Along with being old, the labels on all five buttons had long since worn off, so Rae didn't know for sure which one would connect her to the hangar intercom. The hold button was red, so that was a no-brainer; she pushed it and its light immediately rewarded her by oscillating. Triumphant, she bobbed a fist in the air—*Yes!* The grin of amusement from the young man across from her went unnoticed by Rae. *Now, to find the intercom button.*

Patty had worked this telephone for a hundred years and could put her finger on the correct button in her sleep, but since she had gone to lunch—and there was no one else in the office to ask, Rae decided she would have to experiment to find it. She studied the row of buttons for a moment, being certain of only one thing—that if she pushed the wrong button and cut off an important man like Karl Barkley, she was toast!—and simply going to the door and yelling for her dad was out of the question, since her voice would never carry all the way to the apron. So, gingerly she began pressing one button at a time, speaking into the handset with each button, listening for her voice to echo in the hangar next door. Finally, with only one button left, she began to wonder if there was more to connecting to the intercom than just pushing the button. If this last button didn't give her the results she needed, she knew she would have to make a dash out to her dad, after all.

Rae took a deep breath and punched the last button, then spoke again into the handset. To her relief, her voice echoed back in the vast room on the other side of the wall. Pleased, she made her announcement, "Barkley Field on line one." Her words reverberated next door and from the speaker that faced the apron, and then faded away. *Yes!*—she pumped her fist a second time.

A chuckle from near the window interrupted her reverie; the entire process had been very entertaining to the young man in the uncomfortable chair. "Congratulations!"

Rae raised her eyes to the voice and found the person it belonged to leaning back in his seat with one elbow draped over the back of the chair next to him, and one ankle crossed over to the other knee, smirking at her. She eyed the man across from her: tall, blond, lean, and good-looking—and he knew it. The young man smiled at her charmingly and nodded, waiting for her to blush and smile coyly in return. Squinting at him, she scoffed, indicting him in her thoughts. *Pilot.* Growing up in the hangar with her dad and brothers, all of whom flew—including her, she had seen more cocky, self-absorbed young pilots than she could ever count. As far as she could tell, this one was no different. She didn't blush, get coy, or return the smile. Unamused, she instead gave him a frosty stare. "Funny." Then rolled her eyes and returned to her screen.

Accustomed to a more adoring reception from girls, this one's deadpan tone surprised Kirk. Deciding she was just sore about being a klutz in front of him, he cut her some slack; he would smooth it over in no time. "Kirk Sloan," he declared, nodding with a smug smile and a tilt of his head. "I'm a pilot." Confident that bit of information would change the little lady's tune, he waited for her to gush over him—or at least make his presence known to her boss. Rae did neither.

Suspicions confirmed, she only rolled her eyes at his presumption—as though meeting a pilot was a novelty to someone working for an aviation business. "No kidding." Her sarcasm spoke volumes as she returned her eyes to her screen.

Again surprised, Kirk guessed she was just playing hard-to-get and gave her another chance. "The Man in?"

Indignant, Rae turned again to the new arrival, "The Man...?" In that instant, his lack of respect for her father, 'Kirk the Pilot' dropped down a few more notches to 'Kirk the Jerk,' and only earned him another frosty stare before Rae sneered a second time and returned to the task before her.

"...Mr. *Gerrard.*" The pilot exaggerated the name with a hint of sarcasm to clarify his question to this ignorant, but sufficiently pretty desk ornament.

"No." Rae muttered, typing disinterestedly without looking up.

Kirk watched the girl as she laboriously pecked at her keyboard. Amused still more, he chided her, "...And she types, too!"

Rae stiffened, contemplating how she might seriously hurt Kirk the jerk. Just then, Joe Gerrard bounded through the side door from the hangar and made a quick left turn to dash down the short hall to his office. The pilot waited for the girl to make his presence known to her boss but, sliding her locket along its chain, she just squinted at the screen in front of her, trying to think if she'd left out anything from her order.

"Wasn't that him?" Kirk interrupted, with a hint of accusation.

Still fiddling with her locket, Rae's eyes remained on the screen. "Yup, that's him."

"You said he wasn't in." His snide tone implied more.

Rae lifted her eyes to him briefly. "He's in now." Then she turned back to her screen.

Not accustomed to such indifference, now it was Kirk who was annoyed. *What is her problem?* Feeling slighted, and seeing she wasn't making any moves to announce his arrival to her boss, he sighed heavily. Deciding he needed to do her job for her, he took matters into his own hands. Pushing himself to his feet, he casually stepped around from the front of the desk to the side where Rae pecked away at the keyboard.

"I wouldn't go in there. . ." Rae offered without passion, her eyes never leaving her screen.

"He's expecting me," Kirk justified.

"Suit yourself." Rae shrugged, still not looking up, though unable to resist grinning in anticipation as Kirk passed by her.

Showing himself to the boss' door at the end of the hall, Kirk knocked, then let himself in without awaiting a response, closing the door behind him. After a moment, the door reopened and out came a subdued, chagrined, and much less cocky Kirk. Rae glanced up as he passed by without a word and stiffly seated himself in his former seat. She tried hard—but not overly hard—to stifle another grin. Kirk saw it and sneered at her, wanting to get up right then and walk out, but hesitated. *No, I need this job.* Sighing, he just turned and stared out the narrow window at the end of his row of chairs.

As the silent minutes passed, he squirmed uneasily; angry with the girl at the desk because he was angry with himself, and she was handy to blame. He kicked himself in his thoughts, both for walking in on the man he hoped would be his future employer, and for making a fool of himself in front of this girl. *Why is she so indifferent anyway? What's wrong with her?*

Oblivious to his churnings, Rae continued to hunt and peck until at last, she put the final number in the final box. Satisfied, she moused her way to the 'save' and 'print' buttons, and closed the program. Then, to Kirk's relief, she retrieved her papers from the printer tray, and her CD-ROM from its tray, and stood to leave. She stepped out from behind the desk extension just as the door to the boss' office opened and Joe came out. As Rae crossed in front of him on her way to the side door, she grinned matter-of-factly.

"I told him not to go in there."

Joe Gerrard returned the grin, glancing at the dejected pilot across the room. He cocked his head and said loud enough for him to hear, "Did you, now? And he told me you sent him in." They both peered at the pilot as Kirk noticeably slumped even further into his seat. Rae scoffed and then disappeared through the door into the hangar. "Now son," Joe Gerrard beckoned to the pilot, smiling warmly, "c'mon back and we'll have us a little talk."

Twenty minutes later, they emerged from Joe's office and slowly walked up the short hallway to the front, stopping at Patty's desk, which still sat empty. They stopped in front of the computer Rae had used, as Joe concluded his interview with Kirk. "You've got your own aircraft, haven't you?" Joe asked, and Kirk nodded. "Okay then, it looks like you got yourself a job. You'll be an independent contractor, so you'll need to take care of your own tax issues and insurance. Just bring your aircraft over here tomorrow afternoon to get it checked out by my mechanic, and we'll have your paperwork ready and go over it with you—then you'll be set."

"I have my own guy." Kirk answered, lying because he wanted to save the time and money. Contractors were often fine with that, because they did too.

Joe shook his head. "Not around here—too much liability." He spoke pleasantly, but he meant business. "My pilots use my mechanics; I want a mechanic I can trust—too many of them out there these days who'll just take the money and sign it off without ever looking, and too many pilots who prefer it that way." Himself being one of them, Kirk nodded in resentful resignation. *Oh great, he's honest.*

As they ambled out to Kirk's car, Joe continued, "My mechanics will give your aircraft a tune-up if it needs it, and we'll fix whatever is necessary—and you'll pay for all that." Before Kirk could protest, Joe pressed on, "No sense in me paying for something that went wrong before you came here, right?" He didn't wait for an answer, "That way, you and your aircraft will start out fresh with me. You can pay for that outright, or you can work it off your first paycheck or two, if you need to—depending on the cost." The two men arrived at Kirk's car as Joe finished. "Any routine maintenance after that, we'll take care of—and I do mean *routine* maintenance; anything you mess up from not treating your aircraft right is on you. Does that sound fair?" Whether it did or not didn't seem to matter; as far as Kirk could tell, that was just how it was going to be, so he nodded again. "Good." Joe confirmed with a nod of his own. "Rae is the head mechanic, and the maintenance office is in the back of the hangar—you can't miss it. Once it's checked out, you can start flying for me."

Kirk thanked the man who was now his new employer, and shook his hand. The two men nodded their good-byes and Joe headed back to the office. Taking one more look at the dilapidated sign and the run-down hangar, Kirk shook his head miserably, then climbed into his sports car and drove off.

Chapter 7

T he next day, Kirk Sloan returned to Gerrard and Son Aviation as requested, arriving via the runway of the municipal airport, and taxiing over to the forlorn metal building at the end of the apron. He pulled up to the large, double doors at the back of the hangar, identifying his destination by a similar, but larger wooden sign in the same condition as the one he'd seen out front the previous day—with the same peeling red paint. Coming to a stop, he shut down his engine and got out.

Once inside, Kirk veered to his left and angled across the hangar floor toward the the front office. As he approached, he anticipated another encounter with Joe Gerrard's secretary. *This time it will be different. This time I'll turn on the charm and win her over.* Stepping through the door into the office sporting his most disarming smile, Kirk's face fell when he saw the desk sat empty. Disappointed, he shoved his hands into his front pockets and glanced down the short hall to the boss' office. Recalling yesterday's faux pas, he shook his head. *There is no way I'm going to walk back there to his office this time.* He stepped around to the front of Patty's desk and seated himself where he'd sat the previous day, and waited. Eventually, Joe Gerrard emerged from the hangar, and would have walked right on by, if Kirk hadn't said something. "Hi, Mr. Gerrard." Joe stopped suddenly and turned.

Seeing his blank expression, Kirk reminded, "I'm back with my aircraft."

Distracted, Joe hesitated, "Oh, yes. . .uh, um. . ."

"Kirk—Kirk Sloan."

"Yes. Kirk. I'm sorry you had to wait—my office manager took a late lunch." He checked his watch. "She should be back soon to get you going on your paperwork. Let me find someone to show you around in the meantime." Joe stepped around the desk to Patty's phone, and pressed the intercom button. Kirk smirked under his breath. *Well, at least the boss knows how to work the phone!* Joe raised the handset to his ear and spoke into it, "Sam? If you have a minute, would you come to the office?"

After a few moments, the door from the hangar opened and a very tall, thirtyish man with wavy blond hair poked his head in. "Yeah, Boss?"

"Yeah, Sam," Joe gestured to the new pilot, "this is. . .uh. . ."

"Kirk." the young man repeated, trying to hide his irritation—but not trying hard enough.

"Yes. I'm sorry. I'm a little distracted today, Kirk." He addressed Sam again, "This is Kirk—he's our new pilot. Listen Sam, Patty is still at lunch—would you tell him how we run things around here until she gets back, and introduce him to whoever is here? Oh, and let me know when Rae gets back; he needs to have his aircraft looked at."

"Sure, Boss."

"Patty should be back any time," Joe added then headed for his office.

The two young men eyed each other briefly before Sam spoke. "So you're the new pilot?"

"That's right.".

"You been flying long?"

"A couple of years." Kirk's eyes narrowed and the sizing-up began. "You fly?"

Sam nodded, amused at the question. "Yeah, just about everyone here does."

"How long?" Kirk pressed.

Sam's eyebrow arched. "Me? Almost sixteen years now."

Since Sam didn't look that old, Kirk was sure he was exaggerating. "Are you serious? That long?"

Sam nodded. "Yeah, I started when I was twelve. It's pretty much routine when you grow up around it."

Disappointed that the sizing-up left him short, Kirk sighed. "Oh yeah, I guess so."

"Okay, well, I'm Sam. Just about everyone is at lunch or in the air, so there's no one to introduce you to. I guess I'll just show you what we do." Beginning there in the office, Sam gave Kirk the run-down of the types of flights they did and the schedules they kept, answering questions as they came up. When he could think of nothing else to add, they stepped out to the hangar. After a short tour of the different doors and what they led to, Kirk began to feel more comfortable, mostly because he had confirmed in his mind that he was better than this place. Becoming bored with Sam's tour, Kirk's thoughts drifted to the cute girl he saw at the desk in the office the previous day. In his mind, her aloofness just made her more appealing; he enjoyed a challenge. The two came to the shop phone on the wall next to the break room and Sam took this opportunity to show Kirk the particulars of the multi-line phone and the intercom to the office. "If you need to talk to the office, just pick up the receiver and push this button, and Patty will pick it up."

Kirk perked up at the mention of the name. "So, if I want to talk to Patty, I just push this button here?"

Sam nodded, "That's right."

"So, speaking of Patty," he tried to sound casual. "is she. . . um. . . is she seeing anyone?"

Caught off-guard, Sam squinted. "Seeing anyone. . .?"

Kirk nodded, pressing, "Yeah, you know, does she have a boyfriend, or anything?"

Sam shrugged. "Um, I don't think so. Why?"

"I just want to make sure I don't step on anyone's toes."

"Toes?" Now Sam was completely at a loss.

Kirk nodded again. "Yeah, you know, I want to make sure she's free."

"Free of what?"

"I was thinking of asking her out." Kirk spelled it out for Sam, wondering why this was such a hard concept for him to grasp.

"Um, you're talking about our office manager, right?" Sam just wanted to clarify.

"Yeah, that's right, Patty. Do you think she would go out with me?"

Sam eyed Kirk as though he had two heads. "I have no idea. You'll have to ask her."

Kirk ventured again, "Does she go out with people she works with?"

"I. . .I. . . don't know." His words halting, Sam wondered if Kirk was just messing with him. "I'm pretty sure no one here has ever asked her."

"No one here has ever asked her out? Really?" Kirk gaped, amazed. *What's wrong with these guys?*

Sam shook his head. "Not to my knowledge." He was still baffled, but he decided this was getting amusing, *Maybe he just likes older women. . .*

"I think I'll give her a call." Kirk nodded, then studied Sam's face for a moment. Noting his obvious doubt, Kirk challenged him, "You don't think she will, do you?"

Sam raised a palm toward Kirk, and shook his head again. "I didn't say that. I'm just... well...surprised, that's all."

"Shall we make it a bet? How about, say, ten dollars?" Even though he and the little lady at the front desk got off to a rough start, Kirk was certain he could win her over; he knew how to talk to girls and get what he wanted.

"Ten dollars. . .?" Sam stepped back in surprise. "You want to bet ten dollars that Patty—*our office manager*—will go out with you?" Sam was incredulous; he just couldn't figure out this one.

"You think she'll turn me down?" Kirk challenged.

Sam hesitated. "I don't know; I don't want to take your money."

Kirk scoffed, "Yeah, that's what people always say when they know they will lose!" Kirk challenged again, "You can't see her going out with me?"

Mystified, Sam shook his head. "Actually, I can't even picture you asking her." It was all Sam could think of to say.

"Ten dollars says she'll say yes," Kirk goaded, "Put up your money and I'll make a believer out of you."

Sam worked to understand why this was so important to him, wondering if this was the new guy's way of proving himself, or something. *There has to be an easier way, kid!* "If you don't actually ask her, is the bet off?" Sam hoped so; he wanted to offer the poor sap a way out. *It's tough being the new guy.*

"Oh, I'll ask her, you don't have to worry about that!" Kirk emphasized his confidence with a nod of his head. "I'll tell you what, I'll go easy on you. If I don't ask her, you win. If I ask her and she says no, you win. If I ask her and she says yes, I win. How 'bout it?"

Sam could see Kirk was dead-set on making this an issue, yet was completely baffled as to why. *Maybe I missed something.* "This is Patty we're talking about, right?"

"Right." Kirk nodded with certainty.

Sam wanted to be absolutely sure. "Patty?—In the front office. . .?"

"Right again." Kirk was growing impatient. "Odds are in your favor, man—but, I have to warn you, not many women can resist the *Sloan charm*."

Ordinarily, taking bets—especially for something like this—was offensive to Sam, but Kirk's cockiness so irked him that he was willing to make an exception. Deciding he could use an extra ten dollars, Sam shrugged, "You're on." Both reached for their wallets. Just then, Luke came through the door from the front office and Sam diverted to him. "Luke, is Patty back from lunch?" When Luke nodded, Sam handed his brother his ten dollar bill. "Here, hold this." He gestured for Kirk to do the same.

Luke stared at the money in his palm, "What's this about? It looks like a bet." He eyed Sam expectantly.

"Luke, this is Kirk Sloan, our new pilot," Sam explained, keeping his eyes fixed on Kirk while trying to maintain a straight face. "Kirk is betting me that Patty will go out with him."

Luke's mouth fell open. "*Patty?*" He turned to Kirk, not sure he heard right. "*Our office manager?*"

"That's right," Kirk sneered, setting his cash into Luke's hand, "and this guy doesn't think it will happen." Waiting for the punch line, Luke glanced back at Sam, his eyebrows arched. Sam only shrugged and Kirk reached for the phone, "It's this button, right?" Sam nodded, waiting for Kirk to declare it all a joke and call the whole thing off, but then Kirk was actually talking to Patty. "Hi, is this Patty? . . .Yeah, this is Kirk Sloan, the new pilot." Luke stepped closer to his eldest brother, his eyes inquiring. Sam just grinned in anticipation—whatever the outcome, he decided seeing this was worth losing ten dollars. Kirk continued, "Yeah, that's right—Kirk. Do you have a minute that I can come and talk to you? Would you do that for me?" His voice dripped with honey, "I don't think we got off on the right foot yesterday and I want to make it up to you—it would sure make me feel better. . .Right now? Sure! I'll be right there!" Kirk hung up the phone and turned, seeing the two with mouths agape. Kirk grinned smugly at the two dumbfounded men. "She wants me to come *right now.*" Then he turned on his heel and swaggered toward the office door. Sam and Luke glanced at each other, slack-jawed and speechless, staring after Kirk's retreating back.

Patty was no fool—she knew something was up, hence her summoning Kirk to the office. As soon as he swaggered through the door, Kirk stopped short as Patty raised her eyes to him sweetly. His eyes widened in surprised when he saw the heavy-set, middle-aged woman behind the desk.

Hurriedly, he glanced around, puzzled and panic-stricken. "Where's Patty?"

"I'm Patty." Her voice was matter-of-fact.

Kirk shook his head, "No, I mean, the *other* Patty. . ." He stammered, beginning to feel foolish. ". . .the one I just talked to on the phone."

"That was me, I'm the only Patty here." She smiled innocently as Kirk rechecked the name plate on her desk.

"You are the office manager. . .?" He was beginning to feel ill.

"That's right. You said you wanted to make something up to me?"

Kirk's mouth went dry. "Um. . .no, that was all. . ." He back-pedaled feverishly, "I. . . uh. . . just wanted to find out. . . um. . . if you were the office manager. . . .that's all." He felt his face flush. "Well. . . uh. . . that's all I wanted to know, so. . .um. . . I need to get back to work."

Grinning, Patty called sweetly after Kirk's retreating back, "It was nice to meet you, Kirk!" But she didn't get a response.

Kirk burst from the office, stormy-faced, striding stiffly and briskly through the hangar toward the two waiting men who couldn't wait to hear the report.

"So, what did she say?" Sam asked in earnest. "Did you ask her?"

Kirk was not amused. "No, I didn't *ask* her!" His voice was strained. Luke shrugged and handed the twenty dollars to his brother and Kirk's shoulders sagged in defeat. He exhaled forcefully and asked, almost whining, "Who is that lady in there?"

The two brothers looked at each other, baffled. "That's Patty." They shrugged, still puzzled.

"That's not the lady who was the office manager before!" Kirk protested.

"She's the only one we have." Sam countered, amused, not knowing what else to say.

"Since when. . .?"

"Since forever—as long as we can remember," Luke volunteered.

Kirk wouldn't give up that easily. "Where's that other girl who was in there yesterday?"

"What girl?" The brothers asked in unison, honestly not knowing who Kirk was talking about, but finding it hard to keep from smiling, nonetheless.

"The girl with the blonde ponytail," Kirk insisted, "—the *young* girl!" Instantly the brothers knew Kirk was referring to Rae. Luke burst out laughing as he turned and walked away.

"That's a good one, Kirk!" Sam chuckled, shaking his head as he also turned away.

"What's so funny?" Kirk demanded, face flushing again.

"Kirk," Sam called over his shoulder to the poorer, but still non-the-wiser newcomer, "you'd have better luck with Patty!"

Kirk glared after him for a moment, now more determined than ever. "Yeah, we'll just see about that. . ."

** *** **

Back from lunch, Rae and Ben finished up the avionics check on the Piper, then secured the cover plate. Backing out of the cockpit, Rae straightened up and leaned on the wing across from her younger brother. Ben signed as he spoke, "Did Dad hire that guy who came in yesterday?" His speech had a hollow, nasal quality, with some consonants missing due to little use of his tongue, characteristic of many of the Deaf.

"Unfortunately, yes!" Rae rolled her eyes, signing back to him.

"Looks like he made an impression on you, already!" Ben observed, working his hands and smirking.

"What can I say? He's a typical pilot—you know how they are." Rae began to chuckle.

"What's so funny?"

"I was just thinking about yesterday—that guy was being such a jerk!"

"So, you took him down a few pegs, right?" Ben nodded and grinned expectantly.

Rae couldn't help smiling. "Oh, he came down a few pegs, but he did it to himself."

"What did he do?" He couldn't wait for her to tell it. Wide-eyed with amusement, he watched his sister intently as she signed, then laughed out loud. "I can't believe he just walked in on Dad like that!"

Rae nodded mischievously. "He's supposed to bring in his aircraft today to get checked out—" Before she could finish, Rae was summoned to the phone by the overhead P.A., so she gestured to Ben with the phone sign, and then jogged to her office.

Ben nodded and Rae turned and jogged in that direction as he began gathering his tools.

In the front office, Kirk was finishing up his paperwork. Next on his agenda was the head mechanic. As Ben was about finished, movement out the corner of his eye caught his attention. He looked up to see an unfamiliar man approaching him from across the hangar. "Where can I find the maintenance office?" Kirk called from several yards away in a voice that echoed off the walls of the hangar. Unable to clearly read the young man's lips at that distance, Ben waited for him to get a little closer. In her office, Rae was ending her call.

"What do you need?" Ben asked in his hollow, nasal tones.

After losing the bet with Sam, Kirk was running out of what little patience he possessed. "Oh great! They got a *re*-tard fixing their aircraft! Now I've seen everything!" With the man now close enough to see his lips clearly, Ben's eyebrows shot up in stunned surprise over the words. In her office, Rae also heard, and her face flushed with anger.

"MAIn-TEn-ANCe OFFice!" Kirk pressed, exaggerating each syllable, "I'm-looking-for-the-MAIn-TEn-ANCe OFFice. *Comprende?*"

"He's deaf—not stupid." The angry voice came from behind and Kirk whirled around to see the pony-tailed girl standing there, arms folded in front of her, glaring hard at him.

Kirk brightened, "Well, hello, sweet thing!" Intentionally sarcasatic, he cosidered the girl any thing but. "Were you able to figure out your phone yet?"

Bristling at his tone, Rae's eyes flashed in warning. "Watch your mouth."

Kirk just chuckled then nodded toward Ben, who was behind him. "So you've got a deaf guy for a mechanic? That's rich—almost as good as having a *re*-tard."

Deeply offended, Rae shook her head slowly, pressing her lips together, glaring. "What is your problem?"

"*My problem* is that I'm looking for the Maintenance Office. I need to have the head mechanic check out my aircraft so I can get to work," he sneered, "and all I got to help me out is a deaf mechanic and a secretary—or whatever you do—who can't type or answer a phone."

Appalled, Rae checked her reaction and shrugged her shoulders, still glaring. "So ask the deaf guy, he can read your lips. His name is Ben—and remember, you just called him a '*re*-tard' to his face."

Kirk rolled his eyes and turned to face Ben, who had only been able to follow Rae's side of the exchange. Ben waited for Kirk to speak; when Kirk hesitated, Ben prompted him by raising his eyebrows and nodding his head. Resigned, Kirk sighed, rolling his eyes. Then, shrugged with his palms toward Ben, 'Okay, I'm sorry about the 're-tard' crack. . ." Ben nodded and shrugged to Kirk, accepting his apology then prompted him to continue,"Okay, so, you're not hacked or anything, that's good." Speaking exaggeratedly, he figured since the guy was deaf, he didn't need to conceal his sarcasm. "Would you direct me to the office of the head mechanic?"

Ben glanced at Rae, who signed something quickly to him behind Kirk's back. Ben watched Rae for a moment then fixed his eyes back on Kirk. Having noticed Ben's eyes divert, he glanced over his shoulder, finding only the pony-tailed girl still standing there quietly, her arms still folded, so he turned his attention back to the deaf boy. In response to both, Ben pointed out the Maintenance Office to his inquisitor. Kirk followed the trajectory of Ben's point, turning until he saw a small sign next to a window, identifying the building it belonged to as the Maintenance Office.

"Great, thanks." Kirk started off toward the office, passing Rae on his way, offering her a smug smile. "Catch you later, sweet thing."

As Kirk headed toward Rae's office, Ben looked to Rae for further directions, puzzled. Rae quickly signed her response and Ben guffawed silently, nodding as Rae turned and left the hangar. Still chuckling, Ben gathered the rest of his tools and moved to his next task. Kirk stepped through the doorway of the small office finding no one there. Assuming the head mechanic would be back soon, he took a seat across from the desk and glanced around as he waited, finding it surprisingly tidy for a mechanic's office. Kirk shook his head. *Wow, this Ray guy must be a real neat-freak!*

At the end of his patience after nearly an hour of waiting, Kirk threw up his hands. Hoisting himself up from the two-seater couch, he stomped back out into the hangar, calling out for the deaf kid—then remembering he was deaf, he growled aloud, and set out to look for him and found Ben up to his elbows in the engine compartment of the Piper. Stomping up behind him, Kirk poked him roughly on the shoulder several times. Ben glanced up from his work, not surprised to see Kirk—nor that he was angry.

"So when is that head mechanic coming back? What's his name?—Ray? When will Ray be back? I've been waiting in there for an hour!" Ben feigned lack of understanding by squinting with a hand cupped to his ear. Teeth clenched, Kirk growled loudly in exasperation.

Intervening for his youngest brother, Jesse stepped up behind Kirk. "Something I can help you with?"

Kirk wheeled around to face the voice. Temper flaring, he eyed Jesse fiercely. "Can you talk to this guy?" He hiked his thumb animatedly over his shoulder at Ben. Jesse glanced at Ben, then back to the agitated stranger and nodded. Relieved, Kirk rolled his eyes and reigned in his temper. "Can you ask him when Ray will be back?"

"Who are you?" Jesse wanted to know.

"The name's Sloan—*Kirk* Sloan. Who are *you?*" Kirk shot back.

Jesse found himself amused. "The name's *Gerrard*—Jesse *Gerrard*." He emphasized his last name, suggesting to the inflamed young man in front of him that he was addressing the boss' son.

Recalling the sign out front, Kirk backed off instantly, taking the hint. *Oh, so this is 'the son.'* . . Kirk immediately changed his tone, "I'm the new pilot. I'm here to get my aircraft checked out and I've been waiting in the head mechanic's office for an hour."

Jesse nodded then shifted his gaze past Kirk to address Ben, mouthing the words as he signed the question. Ben signed his response, working to stifle a grin. Taking note of the effort, Jesse returned his attention to Kirk, "She's gone for the day."

Kirk squinted, not sure he'd heard right. "*She. . .?*"

"Yeah, 'she'," Jesse reasserted, wondering why this man seemed to be so disagreeable. "Is there a problem?"

"Ray is a girl?" Kirk confirmed, feeling foolish yet again.

"That's right—short for Desirae," Jesse offered, still puzzled.

Kirk sagged, his temper simmering again. "She wouldn't happen to be about, oh, seventeen, this tall," Kirk held out his hand at his chin's height, palm downward, "with a long, blond ponytail, would she?"

Jesse nodded, "Twenty, but yeah—that's her. I guess you just missed her."

Following the conversation over Kirk's shoulder, and able to surmise his end by Kirk's gestures and Jesse's responses, Ben could scarcely contain himself, working to keep his face straight. Upon hearing Jesse's explanation, Kirk turned and shot Ben a glare, then turning back to Jesse, he thanked him and stalked off in a huff. Jesse watched the retreating figure until he disappeared through the door. Suspicious, he turned his attention back to Ben, who quickly retreated to bury his face, and his laughter, under the cowling of the Piper. Not fooled, Jesse approached him and tapped him on the shoulder. Ben forced the grin from his face then turned to face his brother.

"Okay little brother, you wouldn't have anything to do with this, would you?" He asked as he signed. In exaggerated innocence, Ben pointed to his own chest with a slight shrug of his shoulders, struggling to keep his grin at bay. Jesse wasn't fooled, "Rae put you up to this, didn't she?" Ben grinned broadly, and related the incident to his brother. Jesse watched intently, returning the grin. "You two are wicked!" he teased. Ben nodded proudly in agreement. Jesse chuckled to himself as he retreated to the front office door, and disappeared through it.

Chapter 8

Kirk eyed Rae across the hangar from the doorway to the break room, sipping his soda; mystified. He'd been on the job two weeks and still had not made any progress with her. Not accustomed to being dismissed by a girl, it ate at him. *What's with her? She is friendly with every other guy here, but she won't give me the time of day. What's up with that?* He squinted at her, thinking hard. *They all hug on her and tease with her—if I tried to do that, she'd eat me for lunch.* He glanced over this shoulder at the guys in the break room. *They sure seem like they all know each other, like they're all in the same club or something. Maybe they've just worked together for a long time.* He hated being the outsider.

Jesse stepped up and filled a paper cup from the water cooler next to the door. "What's up, Kirk?"

"Oh, nothing, just finishing lunch."

Jesse sipped his water. "You look like you're deep in thought there."

"I was just thinking." He tried to sound detached, "Have you ever had dinner with Rae?"

"Sure. Why?" Jesse only paid half-attention as he scanned the schedule on the bulletin board next to the cooler.

"Oh, no reason. From what I hear, it just seems like she's had a meal with just about everyone."

"Yeah, lots of them—why wouldn't she?" He traced his name on the schedule across the the page, noting the entries.

"I'll bet she has even had dinner with the boss."

Jesse shrugged, turning to face Kirk. "Sure she has." He took another sip of water.

Kirk's eyebrows arched. "Really?" *Wow, she's dated the boss—and his son?* Surprised by Jesse's nonchalance, he had to ask, "That doesn't bother you?"

Not on the same wave-length as Kirk, Jesse squinted at him. "Bother me? No, why would it?"

Again surprised, Kirk eyed Jesse quizzically. "No reason. Is she seeing anyone right now?"

Jesse shrugged, taking another sip. "Not that I know of."

"Would it bother you if I asked her out?"

Now Kirk had his attention; a grin formed in the corner of his mouth. "Knock yourself out."

"So, you and the other guys don't have a problem with me dating her?"

"Why would we have a problem? Rae's a big girl—and don't get ahead of yourself, you're not exactly 'dating' yet." Jesse grinned again, knowing his sister well.

Kirk eyed him smugly, "Well, that's only a matter of time."

Shaking his head, Jesse chuckled. "You're not exactly the first pilot to hit on her, Kirk. I know her; she's onto you guys and the whole 'conquest' thing."

Feeling exposed, Kirk tried to pretend otherwise, "Well maybe there's more to me than that."

Jesse just shrugged. "Maybe, but I doubt it. More to the point, Rae doubts it."

A tad less confident, Kirk pressed, "So, what do you think my chances are?"

"What do *I* think your chances are?" Jesse had heard about the bet over asking Patty out and wondered if Kirk had another one in mind. Eyeing Kirk, who seemed to acutally be waiting for an answer, Jesse smiled and stepped closer. Reaching for Kirk's hand, he turned it palm up, then poured water into it from his cup. "This was a snowball that asked her out once." Chuckling again, Jesse turned and walked away.

Kirk glared at Jesse's retreating back and shook the water from his hand. *Okay, fine, we'll see about that!* He ambled over to the Piper Rae was working on, finding her head and shoulders buried under the instrument panel. "Hi Rae, what's going on?"

Rae glanced over her shoulder. "Work is going on. What do you want, Sloan?"

Determined not to be put off, Kirk pressed ahead. "I was just wondering—you want to go get a burger after work?"

Rae didn't look up. "You're asking me out?—I heard you prefer older women."

Instantly, Kirk's face colored, but he held his temper. "C'mon, give me a break Rae—you were sitting at Patty's desk with her name plate; I thought you were her. So, you interested?"

She scoffed from behind the avionics stack, "Don't even think about it, Sloan."

He resorted to his favorite fall-back line. "C'mon, Rae, we got off on a bad foot; I just want to make it up to you." He grinned to himself, *That usually works—especially with the young ones...*

But not with Rae. "Forget it, Kirk."

Kirk frowned. "Why not? I see you coming and going with just about every other guy around here."

Suddenly, Rae sat up, squinting at him. "Meaning what?— That it's your turn?" She scoffed again, sneering, "The company may be Equal Opportunity, Kirk—but I'm not."

"So, why them and not me?"

"I like them—not you."

"What have they got that I don't?"

"Oh, I don't know, manners...class...*my respect,*" Shaking her head, she turned back to her work.

Stifling his anger, Kirk pasted a strained smile onto his face. "Well okay, maybe not tonight then—but I'm going to keep trying, 'til you say yes!"

"Don't hold your breath, Sloan." Rae spoke it over her shoulder, not caring whether or not he heard—he did.

He kept his voice cheery for the moment, "Well, I'll catch you later." Then glaring, he backed away. *You just wait! I'll win you over girl—just so I can dump you like last week's leftovers!*

Two days later, Kirk arrived for work at his usual time in the morning, and glanced around the hangar furtively, seeing no one in the immediate area, he proceeded quickly into the break room. Hurrying over to the refrigerator, he pulled it open and rummaged through the lunch bags until he found Jesse's. Smiling impishly, he reached in and pulled out a package of cupcakes. Glancing around again, he pulled a chair over to the cupboard above the sink and tossed them in, then closed the door and returned the chair before anyone saw him. Grinning to himself, he hurried out to the apron to do his walk-around and get ready for his charter.

That afternoon around 2pm, Kirk touched down again and taxied back along the apron, stopping outside the hangar. Shutting down his aircraft, he climbed out and glanced casually around him. Certain he had not attracted anyone's attention, he turned again to his cockpit and, gathering up the cable to his headset, he yanked hard, snatching the plug out of its jack. The sudden movement caught Ben's attention as he came around the aircraft at the mooring next to Kirk's. Curious, he ambled closer and watched Kirk for a moment, the sound and movement of his approach masked by the noise and activity on the apron around them. Ben's eyes narrowed. *What's he doing with that?* Suspicious, he squinted, shaking his head. *He's up to something.* Thinking quickly, Ben pulled out his cell phone and activated the video function, then zoomed in on Kirk.

Examining the cable, Kirk was not content with the results of the yank. Producing a shop rag and a pair of pliers from the pocket in the door, he wrapped the rag around the headset cable, then gripped the pliers over it. Taking hold of the plug in the other hand, he twisted and pulled with the pliers until the connection between the cable and the plug was sufficiently loosened. Checking to make certain the pliers had left no marks, Kirk nodded, satisfied with his handiwork—having no idea that the whole of his mischief had been captured on video. Also smiling to himself, Ben pocketed his phone and ducked back around the adjacent aircraft. After stuffing the pliers and shop rag into his duffle bag, Kirk plugged the headset back into its jack, then went looking for Rae. Stepping through the big hangar from the apron, he glanced around, finding Rae up to her elbows under the cowling of a Beechcraft he didn't recognize, and stepped up behind her. "Rae, can you take a look at my aircraft?"

Rae stepped back from the Beechcraft, her arm falling to her side, still gripping her wrench. "What? Again. . .? What have you done to it this time?"

He ignored her question. "My headset is breaking up. I don't know if it's the radio or what. Can you take a look at it real quick?"

Rae rolled her eyes, exasperated in record-time, "Do I look like I'm sitting here knitting?—No, I can't look at it 'real quick'; I'm busy." She shook her head, incredulous.

"Well, I have another charter in the morning; I thought you could look at it tonight."

"Well, you thought wrong—I've got my hands full. Go see if Ben is doing anything if you want it looked at right now."

Not the plan Kirk had in mind, he made a cursory pan of the hangar, hoping he wouldn't see Ben, and to his relief, he didn't. "I don't see him. I'll just wait."

"Well, wait in the break room or something—not here." She turned again to her engine.

Missing her point completely, Kirk pressed ahead with his agenda. "Oh, I don't mind waiting here." Rae rolled her eyes and got back to work. Kirk shrugged, "Besides, I'd rather you looked at it anyway—you always find the problem real fast." Kirk smiled to himself behind Rae's back, smirking at his flattery. He hovered near Rae, as she worked on the Beechcraft, chattering on and on.

After a good five minutes Rae's annoyance was evident. "Don't you have something you need to do, Sloan?"

"No, I'm good."

"What about your flight plan?"

"I closed it."

"Great. How about your mouth? Would you close that, too?"

Not taking her seriously, Kirk chuckled, amused. "That's a good one, Rae." He grinned at her. "I know you like me; your eyes keep telling me so."

Amazed by his conceit, Rae glanced up, grimacing. "Well, if that's what my eyes are saying, I'm pretty sure they're not talking *to you.*"

Kirk just laughed out loud, thoroughly entertained. *I love it when they play hard-to-get; it makes the reward that much sweeter!* And he started up again, chattering aimlessly and getting on Rae's last nerve. Finally, she could take it no more. Closing her eyes tightly, her jaw clenched, she wheeled around, a fist on her hip,

"Sloan, do you *ever* stop talking? I'm trying to work here and it's *annoying*—so just put a sock in it, okay?"

Momentarily taken aback, Kirk's eyebrows arched. Having believed he had been 'engaging' and 'conversational,' he puzzled at her. *Annoying. . .? She must have just misunderstood because she's busy.* Recovering quickly, the smile returned to his face and he played it cool. "Sure, when I run out of things to say." He smiled charmingly, certain she was delighted that he would take the time to talk to her.

Rae eyed him for a moment, shaking her head. "No. . . No, I don't think so, Sloan. You've been going on for, like, ten or fifteen minutes straight and haven't had anything to say *yet.*"

Kirk squinted at her uncertainly, *She's kidding, right?* He decided she was, and after chuckling at her quip, he resumed his discourse. Deciding she'd finally had enough, Rae turned waving her wrench uncomfortably close to his face. "Sloan—go find something else to do!"

Kirk squinted at Rae, then at the wrench, and decided he'd said enough. "Okay, sure, I'll catch you a little later, then."

"Make that *a lot* later." Rae muttered under her breath as Kirk turned and headed for the break room.

Seeing no one in there, he slipped inside quickly. Pulling a chair over to the sink, he stepped up onto it and retrieved a package of cupcakes he'd hidden on the upper shelf of the cupboard a couple of days before. Jumping down, he opened the refrigerator and slipped it into Jesse's lunch bag, smiling to himself, then again pushed the chair back to its place.

Now back in the hangar, Ben glanced around for Kirk. Not seeing him, he approached Rae and signed without speaking, "You been having trouble with Kirk's aircraft lately?"

Rae nodded, quietly signing back to him. "Yeah, and I think something is up. He comes to me every other day with something new wrong with it. It's always something little and stupid, and then he talks the whole time I'm looking at it. I can't get any work done."

Ben grinned knowingly, holding out his cell phone to Rae, the video he'd just made cued-up on its screen. Puzzled, Rae backed away from the Beechcraft, and accepted it from him. "What's this?" Rae signed as she squinted at the screen, "Is that Kirk?" Ben nodded and reached over, touching the play button on the screen. Rae glanced at the time stamp, and signed again, "Did you just do this?" When Ben nodded again, she touched her thumb and index finger to the screen and spread them apart a couple of times to zoom in, trying to figure out what Kirk was up to. Suddenly her eyes widened. Incredulous, she signed to Ben, "Do you believe that?" Shaking her head, she replayed it just to make sure. "Why would he do that?"

Ben signed back with a smirk on his face, "I think he likes you."

Rae's face froze into a glare. "Ben, that is so NOT funny!" Shaking her head again, she fumed at the video.

Emerging from the break room, Kirk stepped out and glanced around. Seeing Rae and Ben near the Beechcraft, he made his way over. Rae finished closing up the cowling just as Kirk stepped up to her. Delighted, he smiled at her. "Oh, great! You done? Can you look at mine, now?"

Rae growled at him, "Yeah, I already got a look at your aircraft, Sloan—and I found the problem right away."

Kirk's eyebrow arched, "You did?" Only having been gone for a few minutes, he eyed her uncertainly. "What was wrong with it?"

Nodding to Ben, who handed Kirk the cell phone, Rae gave him her diagnosis. "There was a 'loose nut' behind the yoke." Rae smirked, pointing to the freeze-frame of Kirk at his aircraft on Ben's cell phone. "...And there he is right there." She touched the play button and as soon as the video began to play, Kirk's eyes widened. Rae glared at him, "You're about as subtle as a hurricane. I don't know what your game is, Sloan—but this is coming out of your pay—and from now on, so are any more of these annoying little things that keep happening to your aircraft!" Caught in the act, Kirk's face colored. Rae continued, "And you're in luck!—since you want it fixed right away, Ben has just agreed to take care of your aircraft *personally* from now on." With that, she turned and strolled off in the direction of her office, tossing her nitrile gloves into a trashcan along the way. Speechless, Kirk shifted his gaze to Ben, who smiled broadly, waving with his fingertips. Deflated, Kirk frowned and pushed the cell phone back into Ben's hands, then stalked away.

The next day was Rae's day off and she came by in the afternoon carrying her nephew, J.J. on her hip and a diaper bag on her shoulder. She stepped into the hangar through the front roll-up door, encountering Kirk almost immediately. Seeing her, Kirk pasted on his most charming smile. "Hi Rae." His eyebrows arched at her cargo. *Rae has a kid?* At the same time, seeing an opportunity to curry endearment, his smiled brightened. "Cute kid."

Rae smiled easily, and combed J.J.'s hair with her fingers. "Yeah, his name is J.J.—he's Sam's." Rae glanced around the hangar as she spoke, "Have you seen him lately?"

Stunned at her disclosure, Kirk squinted at J.J. "He's Sam's? He looks a little like you."

"Yeah, I think he has my nose, but mostly he looks like Sam." Rae's answer was matter-of-fact as she scanned the hangar for Sam.

Kirk stared incredulously, taken aback by her candor. *Rae and Sam had a baby together? I can't believe she just says it outright like that!* "So, you're playing 'Mom' today?"

"Yup, I get him on the weekend sometimes, too." She cooed into the child's face.

Kirk arched an eyebrow. *Wow, she sure is cool about it!* "So Sam has him the rest of the time?"

"That's right," Rae sing-songed the final word on two notes as she rubbed her nose against J.J.'s and tickled his tummy. Kirk just stared, trying to get his brain around what he was seeing and hearing. *His wife is okay with that?* Rae raised her chin to Kirk. "So, have you seen Sam?"

Kirk forced himself to focus on her question. "Um, yeah—I saw him go into the office a minute ago."

"Okay, thanks." Rae stepped away and Kirk stared after her. *Wow, she's sure in a good mood today!* He shrugged, *I guess motherhood agrees with her.*

Just then, Luke came around the corner—when he saw Rae he called out to her. "Rae, where are you headed when you leave here?" Standing between them to one side, Kirk watched and listened for Luke's reaction to the child on her hip.

Rae turned at Luke's voice. "Into town. Why?"

Luke drew closer, his eyebrows arched hopefully. "Would you stop by the post office and mail a package for me? I need to get into the air, and they'll be closed before I get back."

Rae nodded, hoisting the child up higher onto her hip. "Sure, just put it in my car."

To Kirk's utter amazement, Luke smiled and waved the tips of his fingers to the toddler and made kissing noises, then spoke in falsetto. "Hello Mr. J.J!" The toddler beamed and giggled at Luke, waving his arms. Kirk could only stare. *Wow! Everyone seems pretty cool with the whole baby thing!* Luke returned his attention to Rae. "Okay, thanks. I have class after work, I'll be home later tonight."

"Okay, I'll save some dinner for you." With that, Rae turned and headed into the office.

Wide-eyed, Kirk stared at Luke. "You two live together?"

Luke nodded matter-of-factly. "Yeah. Well, I gotta go. . . See you, Kirk."

Luke headed toward the apron door and disappeared through it while Kirk stood staring after him. *Well, that explains why she won't go out with me.* He hesitated. *No, wait a sec—Jesse said she dates whoever she wants. Wow, she really gets around!—and everyone is so okay with it. . .!* He just shook his head, amazed.

** *** **

The next morning, Joe squinted over the schedules Sam had left with him. *Business is booming; that's good—too bad we don't have enough pilots.* He sighed, thinking. After a moment, he picked up the handset from his desk phone.

"Patty, would you ask Rae to come in here?"

"Sure Boss. . ."

A moment later, he heard the overhead page for Rae echoing in the hangar next door, and a few minutes after that, Rae was at his door. "You need me, Boss?"

"Yeah, hon—come in a second and have a seat."

"Is something wrong?"

"Oh, no sweetheart, nothing like that."

Rae nodded and took the seat in front of her dad's desk. "What's up?"

Joe shrugged with his thumbs, "Well, the good news is, we're getting a lot of new business this summer."

Rae smiled, "That's great!—what's the bad news?"

"Well, we don't have enough pilots to support it right now." Rae sagged, knowing what was coming next.

Joe caught the sagging out the corner of his eye. "I'm sorry, hon—I know flying is not your favorite thing."

"It's not the flying, Dad—it's being hassled by the passengers because of my age and being female."

"I know hon, but look at the bright side: One day you'll be old and graying like me, and people won't judge you for being too young anymore," he teased.

"Sure, but by then, they'll decide I'm *too old,*" she teased back.

"Ouch!" Joe chuckled at his daughter, his eyes smiling. *She looks so much like her mother—got her sense of humor, too.* Joe sighed wistfully, then re-focused. "It's just until we hire some more pilots for the season; no more than a few weeks, I hope. Will you do that for me, hon?"

Rae smiled across the desk to him, "Sure Dad, but only for you."

"That's my girl." Joe smiled at her affectionately, his gaze lingering for a moment.

Rae tilted her head, noticing. "What?"

"Oh, nothing. . .I was just thinking."

"Thinking about what?"

Joe waxed melancholy for a moment. "That one of these days, you'll be swept off your feet by some nice young man, and before I know it. you'll go off and get married," He grinned mischievously, "—and then I'll be out a mechanic."

"Out a mechanic?" Rae grinned at him. "How sentimental of you." Joe chuckled as Rae shook her head. "No, you don't have to worry about that, Dad—you've spoiled me for ever getting married."

Joe squinted at this revelation. "Spoiled you? How?"

"Because I don't want to get married unless I can marry someone like you—and guys like you just don't exist anymore." She shrugged, "So it looks like you're stuck with me, and won't have to worry about losing a mechanic." They both smiled, even though they both knew she wasn't kidding. Rae returned to their discussion, "So, since I'm going to be in the air, do you think maybe the pilots could help out with some of my scut-work during their downtime? Then maybe I won't get buried while I'm on the flight schedule."

"Sure, hon—that's a good idea." He tapped the edges of the pages in his hands against his desktop, rotating them from edge to edge until they were uniform and aligned, then holding them in one hand, he flicked his fingers against them with his other hand. "Okay, well, that'll help a lot with the log jam, for now. I appreciate it, Rae. I'll let Sam know so he can rework these schedules. Tomorrow morning I'll be having a staff meeting to let everyone else know, I just wanted to ask you first."

"Okay, Dad. We through?"

"Yes, 'we through'—you can get back to work." They smiled at each other again, then Rae rose and and disappeared through the doorway.

First thing the next morning, Joe emerged from his office and trudged up the short hall and Patty looked up as he approached her desk. His eyes on the paper in his hand, he addressed her, "Patty, would you call everyone together for a meeting?"

"Sure Boss. For when?"

"Five minutes. I want to catch them before anyone gets airborne."

Patty nodded and picked up her handset as Joe let himself out the door into the hangar. Her page rang out over his head as he stepped into the enormous room and he stood watching and waiting as the young men who flew for him flowed in from the four corners of the hangar and assembled before him, eventually joined by Rae and Ben.

"Men, it looks like we're going to have a busy summer this year. We've already got several new students and a number of new charter clients lined up, with more coming in every other day, and Luke has done such a good job with the crop-dusting that we've even got a few new regulars lined up for that, too—good job, Luke." Joe smiled at his middle child, then continued, "Now, a few of you are back from last year, and we've added Kirk to our roster, but we're also losing Sam in the rotation, since his load has increased at the flight school. I'm going to be taking some of the long charters along with you guys, and Rae is going to be flying a few, too. So, until we get a couple more pilots in for the season, we're going to be spread a little thin. With Rae flying, that's going to put more work on Ben, so you guys do what you can to pitch in, doing some of their scut-work when you have some down time. Any questions?"

Joe paused, but no one chimed in, so he continued, "Now, I'm sure you've heard about the unrest they're having in Georgia. It's been on the news and in the papers about the demonstrations at the smaller airports up there, where groups of protesters are going out and sitting on runways and tying up the air traffic." Some of the pilots nodded, and Joe continued, "Well, lately, some of those have turned violent—even with shooting at aircraft. Mostly it's up around Atlanta, but they've had a few further south. We only have a couple of flights up to Atlanta per month—and you boys who fly those already know to be careful, but for those of you who fly into the rest of Georgia, all of you need to keep your eyes open and watch yourselves up there. Rae, you'll just be flying locally. I don't want you in Georgia at all."

Rae colored, embarrassed, and protested on two syllables and tones, "Boss. . .!"

Joe waved her off. "No, it's not up for debate, Rae—I don't want you anywhere near those demonstrations. Plus, I need you close by in case we get a complicated repair job or a re-cert—or if Ben gets backed up. I don't want you gone more than half a day at a time, you got that?" Rae nodded, frowning and Joe turned to the rest of the group. "Everyone got that?" Nine heads bobbed in response, and Joe continued, "The last item is your license—everyone keep track of your own medical certs. You let them lapse, and you don't fly—end of story. They are your responsibility, so stay on top of them. Any questions?" Joe arched an eyebrow waiting, but no one had any. "Okay boys, fly safe." Joe nodded and returned to his office.

Immediately, Kirk started in on Rae, smirking, "Gotta keep the little girl safe, don't we? Wouldn't want her to break a nail in Georgia, now, do we?" he chuckled.

Still embarrassed for being singled out, Rae was not amused. "Shut up, Kirk. You're an idiot."

"Maybe so, but I'm getting the long flights and racking up the hours!"

Rae sneered. "That's what makes you an idiot, Kirk; I don't need the hours, remember? I'm not bucking for the airlines—so there goes your reason to gloat."

Kirk continued to smirk, pretending to have something that she wanted. Rae just rolled her eyes and headed back to her office—something she had that he envied, where she could close the door on him.

Chapter 9

After twisting open the valves to the hot and cold water lines, Heath withdrew from under the kitchen sink and straightened up. Reaching for the handle, he lifted the tap lever. Turning on and off the faucet, he watched for leaks, just as Ruth pushed through the louver door. Seeing no further drips, he nodded, satisfied. "There you go, Mom, the sink's fixed."

Pleased, Ruth smiled appreciatively, "That was fast!—Thank you, Heath." He nodded, then leaned back against the counter, arms folded in front of him, his face pensive. Knowing the posture, Ruth eyed her son. "Got something on your mind, Heath?"

Heath smiled slightly at his mom's intuition, "Yeah Mom, I do. . ." He shrugged. "I've just been thinking about how Nate sure seems to love being here with you and the Gang everyday. . ."

Ruth smiled, ". . .And me and the Gang sure love having him here, too!" An illustration jumped to mind. "You should have seen Mr. Balcomb and Mr. Peterman today—arguing over whose turn it was to read Nate his naptime story!" She chuckled at the memory.

Again, Heath's smile was slight; such was the best he could muster these days. "Who won?"

She chuckled again, "They all did! Both of them read to him and Nate got two stories!"

Heath nodded. "I'm glad they like having him around. I like that he gets to be around older people, too—I think that's good for a little kid."

Ruth smiled. "I think so, too. She squinted, waiting for whatever it was Heath was leading up to. "So you're glad Nate likes it here—is that all that's on your mind?"

"Um, no. . ." Glancing at the floor, Heath shifted in place, then again met her gaze. "Um, I was just wondering, Mom—would it be okay with you if I moved back in here for a while?—Until the house sells and I figure out what to do next?"

Ruth smiled, "Of course, Heath. You might as well move in; you're practically living here with us anyways!" She chided, then arched an eyebrow, "I thought you didn't want to move twice. What changed your mind?"

Heath, shrugged. "Um. . .well. . ." He hesitated, hedging, "I was thinking about the drive up here every day to drop-off Nate. It just seems silly to get him up so early to drive all the way up here from Redlands, just so I can turn around and drive back there for work—and then do it again at quitting time. It just makes for an extra long day for him."

Hmm. . .For 'him'. . .? Ruth recognized a side step when she saw it. "It seems like it makes for a long day for you, too."

Heath nodded quickly. "Yeah, for me, too—especially with staying to supper and all. I just don't think it's good for Nate—shuttling him around like that."

Nate again. Certain there was more to this, she nudged him further. "You been doing it for over six months. What changed?"

Heath shifted where he stood and glanced away. "I just think there has to be a better way to spend those two hours ever day than driving back and forth," he hedged again, avoiding eye contact. Another thought occurred to him. "And with all that needs fixing around here, I just think I'd get a lot more done a lot sooner if I just moved back here."

Sensing something else was driving this, Ruth arched an expectant eyebrow. "And. . .?"

Exposed, Heath winced, shoulders sagging. *How does she do that?* Feeling eleven years old again, he shifted his gaze to the floor, grousing in his thoughts at his mom's knack for unmasking the truth—even to himself. After another moment, Heath signaled his acquiescence with a long sigh and a roll of his eyes. "—*And*," he exaggerated the word, "I'm just getting where I can't hardly stand to go back to that house every night."

"That why you've been sleeping over here more and more?"

Heath sighed, still looking at the floor. "Yeah, I guess. I know it took me a while to decide to list the house, but ever since I put it on the market back in March, it's like I just want to be rid of it. I wasn't planning to move out until it sold, but now I wish I had listed it a long time ago because. . ." Sagging dismally, he winced again, ". . .because I just want to be done with it. . .and with thinking about it all."

Ruth nodded, returning to his request. "I'm sure your furniture and things will fit in the barn—if not, there's always the garage. Are you thinking about your old room above it, or the one upstairs?"

"No, I want Nate to be where I am and the apartment is kind of small for both of us—plus, I don't think I want Nate going back and forth to the house on those stairs out there; he's too little. I thought I'd let him have my old room upstairs and I'd just move into Suzanne's across from the bathroom, if that's okay."

Ruth smiled, "I see you've given this some thought." She thought for a moment then nodded. "I think that is a real good idea, Heath. So, how soon are you thinking?"

Encouraged, Heath brightened a bit. "Well, right away for me and Nate and our every-day stuff. But I don't know for sure about the rest—I have a lot of sorting to do before I start bringing stuff over. If you were okay with it, I thought I would see if Nate could stay here tonight, then I could go home and start pulling together our clothes and his toys and things, and bring it over here tomorrow. Is that too soon?"

"Tomorrow...?" Ruth smiled, understanding his urgency. "No, that's fine, Heath." She tilted her head, "But just your clothes...? I don't know, Heath—waiting for a house to sell could mean a long time living out of boxes—you might want to go ahead and bring over yours and Nate's bedroom furniture."

Heath shrugged. "Yeah, I guess...." After a moment, he just sighed. "Thirty years old and I'm moving back in with my mom. . ." He shook his head, then shrugged it off and nodded to her. "I appreciate it, Mom—thanks."

"Are you staying to dinner tonight?" They both knew he was.

Heath straightened up from his lean against the counter, eyeing the collection of under-the-sink items on the floor around him, "Yeah, thanks. Let me just put this stuff back in the cupboard under here and I'll help set the table." Ten minutes later, the table set and dinner ready, Heath stepped outside the louver door and reached for the dinner bell and clanged it a few times, summoning the Gang to supper. Then he scooped up Nate and came to the table. It wasn't long before the Gang began shuffling in from the TV room and took their seats, and Ruth started the food around the table.

Mr. Peterman grinned wide at Nate. "Did you like that story I read you today, Mr. Nate?" Nate just grinned and waved a green bean at him, as everyone else looked on.

Mr. Balcomb was not to be out-done. "What about me, Nate? Did you like my story?" Again, Nate grinned. Mr. Balcomb tried again, "So which did you like the best, Nate?—It was mine, wasn't it?"

Mr. Peterman wrinkled up his nose; "Why would he like yours better? David and Goliath are lots more exciting than a kid floating down a river in a basket."

"Not the way I read it to him!"

Ruth interjected, "Do I have to separate you two?" The two men just chuckled.

Later that evening Heath eased his sleeping son into the crib that had once been his. He prayed over Nate, and then for his mom and sisters and the Gang, then returned to the den, where Ruth had tea waiting. Taking up his mug, he leaned back into the sofa. A thought coming back to mind, he turned to his mom. "You know, I've kind of been thinking I might go with you to your church on Saturday."

Ruth brightened, "The synagogue? Is that right?"

"Yeah—synagogue." He corrected himself. "I been thinking about it more and more lately." Heath shrugged. "You been taking Nate every week—I just think I should go, too. I mean, I'm his dad, and all. I've just been feeling like the Lord wants me to go."

"Well, I think that would be real nice, Heath. I'm sure Sid will be glad to see you again."

"Yeah, I guess." Memories of his only two encounters with the Rabbi revisited his thoughts and Heath winced. *Maybe this time I won't embarrass myself.*

It was close to ten when Heath kissed his mom goodnight and climbed into his truck and headed back to his home in Redlands. Pulling into his driveway a half hour later, he shut off his engine and stared through the windshield at the darkened house. Regrets and memories swirled together as he again felt that familiar stab in his chest. Shaking it off, he let himself out and made his way to the front porch, fiddling with his keys in the dark until he found the keyhole, and let himself in.

Getting right to work, Heath headed out to the garage and scrounged around until he pulled together a box of lawn bags and a few boxes. Starting in his bedroom, he emptied his dresser drawers into two yard bags. Securing those, he carried them out to the living room and deposited them near the door, then returned and cleared out his closet. Seeing his guitar case in its furthest corner, he reached for it, along with its stand, and took them out to the living room as well, then did the same with Nate's clothes and toys. Then, taking the empty boxes, he filled them with the contents of both bathrooms. Now out of boxes, he decided to get the jump on clearing out the attic. After several trips up the ladder and back, the camping equipment and boxes from up there were now stacked on the living room floor. Beginning to feel the fatigue, Heath glanced at his watch and decided to call it a day. By the time he had brushed his teeth and climbed into bed, it was after midnight.

Waking before his alarm, Heath rolled over to face his digital clock. *Six fifteen. . .* Anxious to get going again, he threw back the covers, heading for the bathroom. Quickly he showered, shaved, and dressed—then straightened up his bed and bathrooms, in case a realtor called—just a few of the joys of having one's house on the market. He hurried out the door, hoping to arrive at the movers supply store when it opened at 7a.m. By 7:30a.m, he was on his way back to the house with an assortment of collapsed small and medium-sized boxes, a tape gun, along with a few rolls of packing tape, and then pulled through a drive-thru for breakfast on the way home.

Upon arrival, he quickly loaded into his truck bed the boxes and yard bags he had filled the night before, along with the camping equipment, and set his guitar and stand in the cab.

Then, after taping up the bottom of several of the new small boxes, he took them into the kitchen and opened the pantry. *Mom can use this stuff.* He emptied the shelves into the boxes, then dragged the ice chest in from the garage and upended the ice bin into it, then everything from the refrigerator and freezer that wasn't foul smelling or fuzzy. Deciding to leave the rest of the kitchen for another time, he loaded those boxes and the ice chest into his truck bed. Then, since he was out on the driveway, he pulled together his hand and power tools in the garage and loaded those into his truck, as well.

So far, so good.

Carrying a couple of small boxes to the back bedroom, which he used as his office, Heath took a seat in his rolling chair and carefully emptied his desk drawers of files and office supplies. Then, after clearing the desktop into another box, he sat there in the chair and regarded the handsome piece of furniture for a moment, admiring it anew. Memories wafted through his mind as he stroked the cherry wood surface. *Amy gave me this desk on our first anniversary. . .*

Pressing himself back to the task, he rose and stepped to the closet and opened it. Startled, he stepped back, not expecting to see Amy's wedding dress hanging there. *Has it always been in here?* He didn't recall. The shelves were lined with mementos from their big day, each item making him wince a bit more than the previous one. Again, since he rarely had the need to open this closet, he was not certain how long those things had been there. His eyes fell on their Wedding Album. Heath squinted at it, disturbed—though not surprised—that she had left it behind. He attempted to soothe the sting, *She's married again—what would she want to keep it for. . .?* Deflating, Heath moved to close the closet doors, but hesitated. *Nate might want to look at that some day. . .* Heath winced again, then grabbed the album and set it in the box with the desk supplies.

Gathering the two boxes, he lugged them out to his truck and loaded them into his truck bed. Taking a box into the laundry room, he boxed up the cleaning supplies. *Mom can use these, too. . .* And loaded them into the truck, as well. With room for another couple of boxes, Heath headed back inside and back to his and Nate's bedrooms.

Scouting the shelves of his closet, he decided to leave those things for now, and turned, facing his bed, he nodded at the memory. *The first bed I had since I was a kid where my feet didn't hang off the end.* The sight of the bed provoking memories of a different kind, Heath pushed them aside and promptly moved on to Nate's room. He scanned the crib, the changing table, and the dresser, recalling the day he and Amy shopped for the Nate's nursery. His eyes panned the curtains and wall hangings. Everything had been chosen with such care and love in anticipation of their son's birth. Heath sighed; shaking is head. Finding nothing more in there that would fit in the space left in his truck, he moved on from that room, as well.

In the kitchen, he opened each cupboard and drawer, checking for anything he might need until the house sold. With each door that he opened, the task became increasingly difficult, each cupboard evoking memories—the red serving bowl, those mugs. . . that set of dishes. *That dinner party. . . that cake she made. . . her lasagna.* Finally, he could take it not longer and decided he would deal with the kitchen when he had a buyer for the house. Stepping out to the living room, Heath zeroed in on the stack of boxes he'd brought down from the attic. *Let's see what's in those. . .*

One and a time he opened them. *My school stuff—yeah, I'll take this box now.* A couple of boxes of seasonal clothes—*Those can wait. My football trophies—yeah, that can come now, too. . .* Finally, there was just one unmarked box remaining. *What's in here?* Heath leaned down and pulled open the flaps. *Pictures. . .Photos of him and Amy; photos of them when they were dating. . . Amy alone. . . Amy with friends. . .* Heath sunk to his knees, equally drawn and repelled by them. He leafed through them, all the while wondering why he would put himself through it—yet unable to stop. Trips they took together, events they attended. There were photos of them with friends, photos of them on their honeymoon, photos of Amy pregnant, and, finally—photos of Amy with Nate, after he was born

Breathing heavily, Heath struggled against the hurt, questions swirling in his thoughts. . . *Where did these come from? How long have they been in the attic? Why did she leave them behind?* And the hardest question of all. . .*Didn't she want them?* So careful had Heath been not to erase Amy from his life for Nate's sake— only to see that she had apparently erased him from hers—and not just him; Nate, too. *She erased us both!* Despite his distress, Heath hesitated. . .*Wait a sec. . .*He picked up a several photos. *These pictures used to be in albums. . .* Disheartened, he worked to fathom this. *She kept the albums, but not the pictures?* Wounded anew, he squinted at the photos again. *Who goes to the trouble of taking pictures out of an album and then leaves them behind and takes the albums?* Suddenly it hit him. . .*She had to know I would find this some day!* He shook his head at this final—and ultimate, slap in the face. Cut to the core, Heath trembled in his anger and heartache. Something else occurred to him. *That's probably why she left the Wedding Album, too. . .and her dress and all that stuff from our wedding day—she's just rubbing my nose in all of it.* He shook his head, appalled. . .*Wow. . .*

Furious and indignant, all at once, Heath pushed himself to his feet, then snatched up the box of memories and headed for the trash bin outside. Lifting the lid, he hoisted up the box, then suddenly hesitated; Nate flashing to mind—and just as he had with the wedding album, Heath reconsidered. *I can't just trash his mom's pictures like this. . .* So instead, jaw clenched, he turned and shoved the box down into his truck bed and slammed the tailgate.

Already crushed by this end—not just the end of the marriage, but of his dreams of their future together, Heath bolted back inside the house, wounded afresh over this final—and carefully orchestrated—rejection by her; the discarding of their son, the final blow. Jaw set, he snatched up the boxes that would remain and, one at a time, hustled them back up the access ladder and shoved them into the attic. His thoughts and emotions churning, he rushed back inside the house, striding down the hall to his bedroom. After shaking a pillow from its case, he gathered up his clothes from the hamper, and his pajamas and toiletries and stuffed them into it, then headed for the front door. Stopping short in the living room, he spied the two boxes he'd decided to take. Grabbing them up together with one great heave, Heath bounded out the front door with them in one arm, slamming it behind him with the other.

It was nearly 9am when Heath pulled around to the back of his mom's big old house, coming to a stop in front of the carriage house garage. Hanging sheets out on the line, Ruth approached when he pulled up, stepping up to the side of the truck bed, just as Heath shut down the engine. Jaw clenched, anguished and trembling, Heath gripped the steering wheel, trying to settle himself before getting out. Seeing that was not going to happen, and aware of his mom waiting, he pushed open his door. Turning, he stepped to the side of his truck and stared into the bed. Arms straight and spread wide, he leaned against it—his hands gripping the edge, and his face betraying his upheaval.

Ruth eyed her son uncertainly. "Everything okay, Heath?"

He worked to control his tone and his simmering temper. "No, Mom—not really."

Noting his unusual degree of agitation, Ruth arched an eyebrow. "It looks like I should be thankful you got home in one piece." She eyed her son, "I take it things didn't go well?" Heath's only response was to focus on keeping his breathing under control, so Ruth ventured, "You want to talk about it?" When Heath only glanced away, Ruth knew that time had not yet arrived. Surveying the loaded truck bed, she reached for a lighter subject. "I'm sure Orby wouldn't mind helping you bring over the bigger—"

"No—" Heath interrupted abruptly, surprising Ruth by his sharp tone. "I don't need Orby's help."

"You going to try to load that stuff by yourself? Even the washer and your desk?"

"No. The rest is staying." Again, his tone was sharp, his face resolute. After a moment, Heath glanced over at his mom—but only for a moment; just long enough to see her puzzled and concerned expression. He softened a bit, nodding toward the bed of his truck, "I got all I'm going to get right here. Me and Nate don't need nothing else."

"Not even Nate's furniture?"

"He can use my old stuff."

Ruth scrutinized her son. "Heath, tell me what happened over there."

It took Heath a minute, then he swallowed hard and began, "Remember those picture albums I was looking for a couple of months ago?—The one's with all the pictures of Nate when he was a baby?" Ruth nodded and Heath continued, "Well, I found them—well. . .I found *the pictures*; Amy left them in a box—but she took the albums!" He shook his head, still appalled.

Ruth squinted, puzzled. "I don't understand—you have the pictures, but the albums are gone?" Heath nodded resolutely. Ruth tried to clarify, "So, she took the pictures *out of the albums?*" Just hearing her say it dismayed Heath all the more. He could only nod slowly. Completely bewildered, Ruth shook her head, "But why would she do that?"

"I figured she knew I would find that box some day, and she just wanted to leave me one last slap in the face—not just my face, but Nate's, too. He didn't do nothing to her—why would she want to do that to him?" His voice breaking as spoke. Finally, Heath sighed, shaking his head in disbelief. " What makes a person be so mean, Mom?"

Saddened, Ruth again shook her head. "To some people, the best balm for guilt is lashing out."

Heath stared between his outstretched arms at the ground. "All I could think about was that all those years I was living under the same room with someone who hates me that much and I never knew it."

"It wasn't all those years, Heath—just those last few months."

Heath looked away, pressing his lips together; his jaw tight. "I guess." He shook his head, "I never could figure out what made her so mad; why she did like that. All I know is I couldn't fix it—no matter how hard I tried."

"Heath, I've found that, when something breaks, there are two kinds of people; those that want it fixed and those who just want 'new.'"

Heath winced, then nodded, "Yeah, and Amy just wanted 'new.' I just wish I knew what broke."

Ruth nodded, "What did you do with the pictures? Did you bring them over with you?"

"Yeah. I almost didn't, though; I almost threw them in the trash. But then, I realized it wasn't just a part of *my life* that I was throwing out—it was Nate's life, too; that part that he had with his mama. Those pictures are all he has of her. He's bound to ask about her someday, and he might want to look at those pictures and see what she looked like. I couldn't throw away part of his life like that just because I'm mad with Amy."

Admiring his fortitude, Ruth nodded, "That was very generous of you Heath."

His indignation easing, Heath shrugged. "I thought I'd just keep them up in the attic in case he ever does ask." Pressing his lips together again, he shook his head, then after a moment, shoulders sagging, Heath sighed, glancing around them, "Where is he?"

"He just went down for his morning nap."

"Heath nodded. "Well, I need to get all this unloaded, Mom. If it's okay, I'll just take this stuff upstairs and head to the shop."

Her forehead furrowed, Ruth only nodded. "Sure, Heath."

** *** **

His anger giving way to sadness, Heath was underway again by nine thirty. He made his way across the bridge over the interstate and on into Redlands, and noticed a furniture store ahead on the right. Though he passed this way every morning and evening, he'd never noticed the store until this moment. As he drew closer, he squinted, an idea forming, and he pulled into the parking lot and got out. Stepping to the front door, he tried it, but it was locked. He glanced at his watch: 9:53am. A man inside near the entrance glanced at this watch, then shrugged and unlocked the door. "Good morning. We still have a few minutes before we open, but I didn't see any reason to keep you waiting out there. Can I help you find something?"

"That depends—can you deliver it today?"

"...Locally?"

"To Tennyson."

The man glanced at his watch again. "Let me check on that for you." The salesman excused himself and hurried to a back office. A few minutes later, he was back. "Our trucks are loading up right now; if you know what you want, we might be able to get it on one of them." The man smiled, and stepped up closer to his new customer, tipping his head back slightly so that he could maintain eye contact. He extended his hand, "I'm Mark Wilson..."

Heath shook the hand. "Heath Dawson."

"Okay Heath, what can I help you find?"

"I need a dresser and a bed."

Noting Heath's height and frame, the salesman ventured, "Let me guess—a California King?" Heath only nodded. Guessing in his thoughts at the reason behind his customer's need for haste, the salesman glanced at Heath's left hand, taking note of the faded tan line where a ring used to be. His hunch confirmed, the salesman nodded to himself, then pasted a gracious smile on his face and directed Heath to their right.

"Over here we have the beds." He guided Heath over to the floor models as he spoke. "We carry those in three models: Firm, Plush, and Pillow Top;" He stopped at the foot of the nearest, gesturing to all three with a sweep of his hand, "and you're in luck!—this week, we are running a special: a free headboard and frame are included with each mattress set." The man opened a palm toward an assortment of headboards against the wall. "You can choose from any of those over there." Mark then glanced at his watch again. "If it's okay with you, why don't you try out the beds and decide which one is right, while I run to the back and see if I can hold a truck?" Heath nodded and the man hurried off. He stretched out on each of the three beds, then wandered over to check out the headboards. The salesman found him there. "Okay, great! We've got a truck standing by. Did you find a mattress that will do?"

"Yeah, that Pillow Top one was nice." Heath shrugged to himself, *Might as well be comfortable, right?*

"Did you find a headboard you liked?"

Heath shrugged, pointing to one near him. "This one seems okay." It was of dark wood and metal construction.

Mark jotted that down. "...And you said you need a dresser?" Heath nodded. "Anything in particular?" Heath only shrugged, so the salesman hurried him over to the bedroom furniture. Walking past several choices, he stopped in the middle of several displays of bedroom suites, and pointed to the closest one. "This one will go well with the headboard set you chose."

Heath glanced at it and sighed wearily. "Sure, that'll work."

The salesman quickly jotted down the skew number of the dresser. "Will there be anything else?"

Heath shrugged, shaking his head, "No, I'm good."

Delighted, the salesman hurried him over to a desk, and cleared off a stack of papers, replacing it with a folder from a drawer. Pulling out a printed form, he glanced briefly again at his watch as he handed the form to Heath. "If you'll fill this out, Heath..." He pushed the paper toward his customer and handed him a pen. "Let me total everything up while you do that." The man feverishly worked his calculator while Heath worked the pen, then he looked up again, "...And how will you be paying for this today?"

Heath answered without looking up or even batting an eye. "Cash."

"The salesman arched an eyebrow and smiled widely, "Yes, sir!"

Heath fished out his debit card and handed it to the salesman, who disappeared for several minutes as Heath completed the form. He straightened up just as Mark returned with his debit card and handed it back to him. "Okay, your bedroom furniture will be delivered between three and six this evening."

"Can you have the delivery guys call me when they head that way?"

"Sure, Mr. Dawson—I'll tell them."

Heath nodded, smirking privately: *So I pay with cash and suddenly I'm 'MISTER' Dawson?* The two men shook hands again, and Heath exited the store. Mark watch through the front windows as Heath pulled away from the store—just a little over twenty minutes after he had arrived. Another salesman stepped up to Mark, also watching Heath's truck pull away,

"That has to be a record."

Mark smiled. "It is for me!"

** *** **

In his shop, Heath sat on his stool at the back wall, the overhead projector several feet behind him casting a sketch, and also his shadow, onto his work surface. He forced himself to focus on transferring the design on the transparency to the prepared wood signboard in front of him. He squinted, his attention again taking a detour...*I don't want any of it—I wish I could just leave it all there!* He squinted at a new thought, *I wonder if it's too late to change the listing to 'furnished'?* A few moments later, he wrestled his attention back to the signboard. Just as he refocused, his cell phone chimed. With a sigh, Heath reached for it on the table behind him and squinted at the screen; it was an email from his mom's synagogue. Though Heath had not yet attended, he streamed it occasionally on-line, and had signed up for their

126

email list—which included eBlasts from the Prayer Force. He tapped the screen of his phone in a few places, bringing up the notice—after a moment he nodded, smiling slightly. It only took a moment to decide, before he tapped in the contact number, and touched 'send.'

He waited for the call to connect. "Yeah, hey. Is this Buddy Modden. . .? This is Heath Dawson—I'm Ruth Dawson's son. . .? Yeah, I just saw your prayer request. Yeah. . . Wow, a house fire; yeah, that is a real shame—but everyone's okay? That's good. Hey, listen, I got me a house full of stuff: furniture dishes, towels and sheets and all—and there's a real nice desk in there, too. You can have any of it that you want... Yeah, all of it. . .No, I'm totally serious—really. No, all of it needs to go; I was just sitting here wondering what to do with it when I got the eBlast. Yeah, the Lord sure does provide, don't he? . . .Any time—whenever it works for you." Heath's eyebrow arched, ". . .A half hour? Um, sure. . .okay, I can meet you there. . . No, that'll work. . ." Heath recited his street address. "Yeah, at the end of the street—a gray house with white trim and black shutters. Okay. . .sure, you're welcome. I'll see you soon—and bring a big truck!" The two ended the call and Heath lowered his phone, still staring at it, marveling his thoughts at his good fortune.

Chapter 10

After a couple of months of scouting trips up to Georgia, Joel finally hung out his shingle in Heartland, keeping his business in Jacksonville open, as well. A guest of Sid and his family a couple of days each week, he commuted back and forth between Georgia and Florida for another couple of months as he built his new venture. Finally, as things in Georgia began to fall into place, Joel turned his attention to finding a suitable apartment and relocating there. That accomplished, Joel awoke in early July, his final morning as a guest of the Edelberg's—and his first Shabbat as a resident of Heartland. He dressed excitedly, then joined Sid and his family for breakfast. After the meal, he glanced up at Sid, "So, what's the plan?"

"Well, you can ride with me, or wait and come later with Connie and the kids. Or, if you want to take your car, you can come whenever you want."

"I like getting there early; I think I'll just ride with you." Minutes later the two were on their way.

Unable to fully conceal his enthusiasm, Joel's mind drifted to the woman in—and of—his dreams. "So, how has Andrea been doing?"

Unaccustomed to seeing Joel so wound up, Sid smiled, shaking his head at his friend's eagerness. "I guess she's been doing pretty well. Connie says she's kind of opening up and meeting people and becoming more involved."

"Oh, that's a good sign. Do you think she will be there today?"

"I imagine she'll be there; she usually is—unless she has to work." He watched Joel for a moment, "You know, Joel, it's only been about four months since her husband passed away—if you're thinking of approaching her, you might want to cool your jets for a little while longer. If you do it too soon, it might put her off."

"I know, you're right." Joel made an effort to ratchet down his enthusiasm a couple of notches. "There's no harm in talking to her, though. Right?"

"It's up to you, Joel. I'm just saying. . ."

A minute later, they pulled into the near-empty parking lot of Beth Chesed V' Emet, and Sid took a space in the back row, preferring to leave the front row spaces open for visitors and the elderly. In the foyer, Sid turned to Joel. "Well, I need to meet with the elders, so I guess I'll see you after the service." He grinned at his friend, "Stay out of trouble, okay?"

Joel also grinned and nodded and the two parted ways. Sid turned down the hallway to his office as Joel lingered in the foyer. In the months since that Shabbat when he had first seen Andrea, he had only been back to Sid's synagogue once—so it still felt new. He introduced himself to the greeters and nodded to the Shammashim as they busied themselves preparing for the congregants to begin trickling in. Entering the sanctuary, Joel stood before the replica of the Western Wall in Jerusalem, draped his Tallit around him, and began to pray along with a few others. After several minutes, his prayers finished, he made his way down the left aisle, finding a seat on the end about six rows from the front. He set his Bible on it, draped his tallit over the chair back then returned to the foyer to mingle with those arriving, introducing himself and seeking to become acquainted with each new person he met. At the same time, he kept watch for Andrea.

"Well, hey!" A friendly voice came from behind him. Joel turned in its direction until he found himself facing a thirtyish young man with sandy brown hair and a crooked necktie. "I'm Orby Grumwall. I don't think I met you before, are y'all new?" The young man spoke slowly with a thick drawl.

Charmed and delighted at the man's manner of speaking, Joel smiled, extending his hand. "Hi, Orby. I'm Joel Greenbaum. I'm new in town." The two shook hands.

"Y'all are new in town? Well, that explains why I never met you, then." Orby nodded, grinning broadly. Getting better acquainted, the two stood and chatted near the large windows by the exit to the patio, opposite the entry doors. Orby had an endearing quality about him and Joel liked him immediately and Orby was delighted to learn that Joel has been his Rabbi's friend since their college days.

Ten minutes later, the two were still conversing as more congregants arrived. Across the foyer from Orby and Joel, they streamed in, greeting one another. Someone outside pulled open one of the big, wooden front doors and held it as a family walked through. At the end of the line of children there was a short gap, and then Andrea entered behind them—her entrance seizing Joel's attention on the other side of the foyer. When Joel's voice trailed off mid-sentence, Orby waited for him to finish his thought, but when that didn't happen, he followed Joel's gaze across the foyer; seeing that it fell on Andrea, Orby grinned at his new friend. It wasn't until Andrea disappeared through the sanctuary door that Joel realized what he'd done. "Oh, Orby, I'm sorry—I got distracted there for a moment. What were we talking about?"

"Oh, that's okay. I seen you noticing Ms. Andrea, over there, and I just waited for you."

Embarrassed that he'd been caught, Joel smiled and flushed a bit. "Was I that obvious?"

Orby grinned and nodded, "Yeah, but that's okay. Do you know Ms. Andrea?"

"No, we've never met."

"If you want, I could introduce you to her," Orby offered.

Joel's eyes widened, "You would do that?"

"Not normally, I wouldn't—since I just met you, but seeing as you're the Rabbi's friend and all, I don't see that it would do no harm."

Joel could scarcely believe his good fortune. "Orby, I sure would appreciate that!"

Orby smiled and nodded in his usual, easy manner and started for the sanctuary doors, beckoning Joel to follow. They found Andrea just inside, talking to someone who had stopped her as she came in.

Orby stepped up just as Andrea was stepping away. "Hey, Ms. Andrea—Shabbat Shalom!"

Andrea's head pivoted in the direction of her name. When she saw Orby, a smile spread across her face, dazzling Joel. "Well, hi, Orby! Shabbat Shalom to you, too!"

They exchanged pleasantries for a few moments before Orby turned to Joel, "Oh, Ms. Andrea—this here is Joel Greenbaum. He's new here."

Andrea's eyes shifted over to the man next to Orby, whom she had not even noticed before that moment. Now face to face with the woman who had captivated his thoughts and his heart for the past year and a half, Joel broke into a sweat and a nervous smile when their eyes met. "Hi, I'm Joel." He extended his hand, his heart pounding in his chest.

Smiling, Andrea shook his extended hand firmly. "Hi, Joel, it's nice to meet you." The greeting was as brief as the eye contact.

Still gripping her hand absently, Joel gazed at her. "It's so nice to finally meet you, Andrea." Puzzled, Andrea squinted at his odd eagerness, eyeing Joel uncertainly. *Why is he looking at me like that?* Her hand still bobbing in his handshake, she glanced down and tried to withdraw it, but Joel absently held on, still shaking her hand as he gazed at her. Andrea bristled, *Okay, this is getting creepy.* Suddenly, the tug at his hand registered with Joel and he glanced down and released her hand. "Oh... I'm so sorry... I wasn't thinking."

Puzzled, Andrea eyed him a moment longer. "It's okay." Hoping to talk more with her, Joel's mind raced for something else to say, but he came up blank. Feeling the awkwardness, Andrea, shifted uncomfortably. "Um. . .well, I need to go."

Disappointment showing on his face, Joel sighed. "Oh, okay. Well, maybe we can talk again sometime."

Already deciding against that, Andrea shifted her gaze back to Orby. "It was good to see you again, Orby." She nodded then glanced again at the strange man next to him, before moving away. Joel stared after her as Orby looked on, smiling curiously at him.

Suddenly, Joel came to himself and turned his attention back to Orby. "Wow, I was really nervous—do you think she noticed?"

"Well, now, Joel—I don't see how she coulda missed it."

Joel winced, "I forgot to let go of her hand."

Orby smiled, "Don't worry none, she got it back eventually." Joel sighed, feeling foolish and Orby eyed him curiously. "Do you know Ms. Andrea from somewhere's else?" When Joel shook his head, Orby squinted, "Well then, that's a mystery. . ."

"What's a mystery?"

"You said 'finally'—that's what threw me."

"When did I say 'finally'?"

"When I introduced you to Ms. Andrea—you told her it was nice to *finally* meet her."

Joel's eyebrows arched, "I said that?" Orby nodded and Joel's countenance fell. "Oh, I'll bet that sounded weird to her." Orby nodded again, grinning. Joel thought of trying to sidestep it, but something about Orby just made him want to come clean. "No, I just saw her here when I visited last spring. I've wanted to meet her, but I heard that her husband passed away recently and I just haven't felt it was the right time to go up to her and say hello."

Orby nodded easily, "Oh, that makes sense."

"She probably thinks I'm a stalker, or something."

Orby grinned and chuckled, "Oh, I wouldn't worry none about that just yet." A woman stepped up to Orby and spoke softly to him; he nodded and she scooted away. Turning to Joel, he smiled again. "Well, she says she's needing me in the toddler's room, so I guess I better go."

"You help out with the children?"

Orby shrugged, "Yeah, when they need me."

Joel nodded, impressed. "Good for you, Orby!"

He shrugged again, "I don't mind doing it—those little pedestrians sure keep you on your toes! Sometimes I go in and help feed and rock the babies, too." Orby smiled his big, toothy smile and extended his hand again to Joel. "Well, it was real nice meeting you, Joel. I hope I see you again real soon."

"Thanks, Orby—I hope so, too." They shook hands again, and Joel watched as Orby pushed open the sanctuary doors and made his way through the crowd in the foyer, until the doors swung closed and hid him from view.

A blast from the silver trumpets made Joel glance at his watch and then around the sanctuary; seeing it was filling up quickly, he decided to take his seat. Moving down the aisle toward the front, he found the chair with his tallit and Bible and sat down, then reached for a Siddur and began leafing through it, then a few minutes later, a blast from the shofar roused him from his perusing. Setting aside the Siddur, he raised his eyes just as Sid stepped to the Bimah, and the service began. For a fleeting moment, Joel thought about Andrea, wondering where she was, but she was quickly relegated to the back of his mind as he became absorbed in the service. After the time of praise and worship, and blessing the children, Sid gave a stirring message about boldness which Adonai had laid on his heart for that week. Throughout the message, Joel was a rapt listener, and when Sid was finished, he wished there was more.

Sid stepped down from the Bimah to give the blessing and everyone stood and reached out to join hands in preparation for it, reaching across the aisles to join with those in the adjacent sections as they stepped closer. As everyone was reaching to take one another's hands, Sid diverted to tell an anecdote, and Joel turned to greet the elderly woman to his right as he reached for her hand. The woman smiled and said something, and as Joel leaned down to listen, he reached out with his left, anticipating joining hands with whoever was across the aisle. Charmed at the elderly woman's words, he smiled and chuckled, feeling someone intercept his left hand from across the aisle. Still smiling, he turned to greet the person belonging to the hand that held his; to his utter surprise and delight, it was Andrea. His heart leapt and he nodded, speaking softly to her, "Hello again!"

Realizing that this man had been sitting across the aisle from her throughout the entire service, Andrea nodded uncertainly, noticing Joel looked just as surprised as she felt. She thought back on when she had sat down, wondering if his choice of seat had been deliberate. *When I sat down, there was a Bible and tallit on that chair.* She glanced at the tallit around his shoulders. *That tallit.* Which meant that the man who now held her hand had found his seat before she had arrived, and somehow that was of comfort to her. *At least that means he didn't follow me in and sit next to me on purpose—that would be weird.* Andrea chided herself for assuming otherwise, and dismissed the thought as silly. Meanwhile, Joel glanced down at their clasped hands, and marveled at Adonai's goodness.

Up front, Sid finished his thought and raised his arms for the Aaronic Benediction. "The Lord bless you and keep you; the Lord make his face to shine upon you and be gracious unto you. The Lord lift up His countenance upon you and grant you peace, in the name of the Prince of all Peace, Yeshua." He then chanted it again in Hebrew, and everyone joined him at the end chanting "Shalom." on a four-note scale.

With that, the service officially ended and everyone dropped hands and started talking at once. Across the aisle, Joel noticed Andrea immediately began gathering her belongings. Seeing his window of opportunity was quickly shrinking, and hoping to make amends for his awkwardness earlier, his mind raced for ideas. Sid's message on boldness jumped to mind. *He said Adonai orchestrates things for a purpose. . .and to be bold when God presents an opportunity. . .*

As Joel eyed Andrea across the aisle from him, mulling over what form this boldness might take, a friend of Andrea's stepped up to her. The two greeted each other and began chatting. *Maybe when that woman leaves I'll try to talk to her again.* Joel tried to linger inconspicuously, but instead of the woman leaving, another joined the two, and Joel just sighed. *Waited too long. Okay, as soon as those two leave. . .*He winced. *No, what if someone else comes? What if they all leave together*? He hesitated wrestling in his thoughts. *Maybe I should just wait, like Sid said* to—*there's always next week*. . .He shrugged. *Still, Sid did just say to be bold*. . . Joel smirked to himself. *Okay, so I'll be bold!*

Heart pounding, he summoned his courage and, inspired by Sid's message, he glanced across the aisle at Andrea, who chatted easily with her two friends. Drawing a deep breath, Joel offered up a quick prayer for favor—and in case that prayer was not granted, one for mercy, as well, and he stepped across the aisle to where the trio stood talking. As he did so, they stopped talking and eyed him curiously.

"Hi," Joel smiled and nodded to all of them. The other two ladies smiled and nodded back. Andrea, not so much. Joel turned his attention to her and smiled, "Hello again, Andrea!—we seem to have ended up across from each other." Then addressing the two ladies on either side of Andrea, Joel introduced himself to them. "I'm Joel Greenbaum." He put his hand out to the first lady, "And you are. . .?"

"Tammy."

Joel shook Tammy's hand then he turned to the other woman. "And you?"

"Donna." Joel shook her hand as well. Both ladies smiled warmly, though puzzled—especially after they noticed Andrea, who shifted uneasily, eyeing Joel.

He smiled at the two ladies warmly. "Um, I was wondering if I might borrow Andrea from you both for a moment." Eyebrows arched, the two ladies turned to Andrea, hesitated for a moment, and glanced around her as though there might be another Andrea nearby. Finding no other, she winced then shrugged, and stepped away from the other two, following Joel across the aisle out of their ear shot. After several moments of her expectant stare—and his awkward silence, Joel finally spoke, "Uh, I guess I just wanted to explain. . .um. . .*apologize*, for when I met you earlier—not letting go of your hand."

Andrea's expression relaxed a bit, relieved it wasn't something weightier. She shrugged simply, "Oh, okay, no problem."

When Andrea moved to return to her friends, Joel hastily added, ". . .I was just *really* nervous."

Puzzled at that, Andrea hesitated. "Nervous about what?"

Receiving a flash of inspiration, Joel grinned, "Um. . .you know, I would love to tell you all about that. Would you like to have lunch?" He was certain that was an innocuous enough invitation, but Andrea's relaxed expression suddenly changed to one of startled confusion.

She eyed him suspiciously. "Me. . .?" Joel nodded; hopeful. Andrea's head began to shake before the words came; her tone was gracious but the words, firm, "No. I don't know you."

"I promise I won't bite." It was lame, but was all Joel could think of.

"I'm sorry," Andrea re-asserted, "I don't know you well enough to go somewhere with you."

Joel began to feel the stare of her friends and wondered if they could somehow hear him. Reminding himself of Sid's message, he gathered his courage and, as jovially as he could muster, he made another attempt. "Now, how will you ever get to know me if you won't have lunch with me?" Surely his logic could not be refuted.

She paused, and seemed to actually be considering his words, or at least an answer to them. "Um, I don't know how." *I'll let you figure that out.*

"We could go as a group—then you won't be alone with me."

Andrea tilted her head slightly, folding her arms across her ribs. "Do you always hit on women at synagogue?" It wasn't hostile or accusing, but she did say it with increased firmness.

Way out of practice, Joel winced. "Is that what I'm doing?" Andrea only nodded, still eyeing him. Knowing this could really backfire—and hoping it wouldn't, he smiled playfully, working to keep his tone light. "Not all women—just you."

"Me. . .?" She rejected the notion immediately. "No, I don't think so—I don't know you." Andrea took a step back to return to her friends, signaling the end of the conversation.

"Are you sure you're not hungry? I'm starving."

"Yes, I'm very hungry—but I don't know you. I don't go places with men I don't know."

Joel tried again. "How about just coffee, then?"

Andrea arched an eyebrow. "You are *very* persistent! But unless you have a pot in your pocket, 'coffee' is still 'going some-place'—so *no!*"

Though her words were charged with emotion, the deadpan tone and expression with which she delivered them both amused and surprised Joel, and he chuckled without meaning to. "I'm sorry, I just want to get to know you and that's the only thing I can think of."

After years of indifference with Evan, this baffled Andrea. *Get to know me?—Why would he want to get to know me? I've never even seen him before today!* Doubting his interest in her person-ally, she groped for an alternative motive. *Does his think I'm some kind of rich widow, or something?—I've read about men who do that.* Her eyes narrowed as she addressed that possibility. "I don't have *money*—if that's what you're looking for."

Joel found it curious how she could be so gracious while obviously challenging him. He understood her implication, but chose to respond as though he didn't. Palms up, he answered as cheerfully as he possibly could. "My treat."

Shaking her head incredulously, Andrea sighed,. "I didn't mean *that.*"

Joel just shrugged and smiled. "But, *I* did."

She scrutinized the man for a moment. *Is he slow-minded or just can't take the hint? I guess I just have to spell it out for him.* Though she disliked doing it, especially right there in the synagogue on Shabbat, she could think of no other way. "Listen, the answer is *no*. I don't know you. I don't know who you are or what kind of person you are. I don't know anything about you, so *NO!*—okay?" Her voice trailed up with her final word.

That gave Joel an idea. "If I can get someone to vouch for me, will you have lunch with me?" He recognized the signs of an impending refusal, so he added quickly, "Someone you know and trust—who knows me and can vouch for me? Will you consider it then?" He held his breath, hoping. *I've known Sid for over twenty-five years. How can she refuse if her own Rabbi vouches for me?*

"Someone I know and trust?—Who knows and trusts you, and can vouch for you?" she clarified, certain that such a person did not exist.

Thrilled that she was even considering it, Joel confirmed, "That's right. If I can find someone to vouch for me—whom you approve of—will you have lunch with me?"

". . .And if you can't find someone that a fills the bill?"

"Then I won't ask you again," Joel assured her.

"In what time frame? I don't want to have to wait around here all day."

"Before you leave—say, in the next ten minutes?" Joel was sure that would be ample time to track down Sid and bring him back.

If it meant getting rid of this man, that sounded good to Andrea. In her mind, there were only a few people at the synagogue that met those qualifications, two of whom happened to be standing right next to her at that moment. Andrea held up an index finger to Joel, indicating she needed a moment. He nodded, smiling, and Andrea stepped over to her two friends. "Do either of you know this man, other than his name?" Frowning, they shook their heads, puzzled; eyeing Joel suspiciously. Andrea smiled to herself. *Neither of my friends know him, and he's new in town, so no one else knows him.* She turned to Joel, "Okay, you've got a deal."

Jubilant, Joel smiled widely. "Great! Wait right here!" He disappeared into the crowd of people filing out of the rows between them and the Bimah.

Tammy and Donna eyed their friend quizzically. Tammy ventured first, "What was that about?"

Andrea shrugged. "He asked me to go to lunch with him; he probably want to sell me some insurance, or something. I don't know him, so I told him 'no.'"

The two ladies nodded, agreeing with that decision, then Donna added, "It looked like you had to say it more than once!"

Andrea grinned slightly. "He kept asking, so I made a deal with him." She filled in the details for them.

Tammy and Donna were incredulous. "Why are you agreeing to that, Andrea?!"

She smiled confidently. "To get rid of him!" Her two friends only stared at her so Andrea tried to assure them. "Relax! Ruth is helping out in Shabbat school today and there's no one else out here besides you two that I would trust to vouch for someone—and neither of you knows him." She grinned smugly to herself and her friends. "He just made a no-win situation for himself. So, when he comes up empty, I'm off the hook and that's that."

"But Andrea, why would he agree to that if he didn't actually know someone?" Tammy had a point, there, and Donna had to agree.

As confident as she felt, Andrea still felt a twinge of fright at the possibility—however remote—of him being successful. That, plus Tammy's assertion that he seemed confident he *could* come up with someone, was a little disconcerting to her. But she quickly dismissed it, feeling certain there was no one on the planet that would fit that description. Even if he did come up with someone, she could simply say they didn't qualify, and she would still be off-the-hook. *He rigged himself for failure, so this is all but over!* She shook her head. "He doesn't. He told me earlier that he was new in town." Andrea smiled, assured, but Tammy and Donna didn't share her confidence.

Feeling like a salmon swimming upstream. Joel made his way through the flow of people coming toward him, as he scanned the crowd for Sid, finding him at the opposite end of the front row gathering up his jacket and tallit. Noting his friend's countenance, Sid grinned as Joel approached. "You look happy."

Joel smiled excitedly. "I am. I need a favor."

"What kind of favor?"

"I need you to vouch for me."

Sid squinted at him. "Vouch for you? To who?"

"To Andrea."

Sid eyed him, puzzled. "To *Andrea?* Why does Andrea need me to vouch for you?" Sid's eyes narrowed. "Joel, what did you do?"

"I'll fill you in later—I only have a few minutes. I just need for you to tell Andrea that I'm not the boogie man."

Sid chuckled, then he hesitated, his expression changing to suspicion. "Joel, please say you didn't ask her out or something."

Joel winced, a tad embarrassed. "Well, yeah—I did." Sid only rolled his eyes, Joel hurried to defend. "I didn't plan to, Sid—it just sort of *happened!* He shrugged. "Your message about boldness was inspiring, Sid!" Sid sighed, hanging his head. Joel took a quick look in Andrea's direction and noticed her glance at her watch, and he winced again. "She said 'no' because she doesn't know me—but she agreed to have lunch with me if someone she knows and trusts would vouch for me."

Sid shook his head. "Joel, I wish you hadn't done that—it really puts me in an awkward place. You know I have no qualms about vouching for you, but Andrea doesn't know me very well; she might interpret my endorsement as pressing her into a relationship with you." He shook his head again. "I don't want her thinking anything like that."

Shoulders sagging at that realization, Joel winced. "Oh, I didn't think of that." He sighed. "You're right—I'm sorry, Sid. Never mind, I don't want to get out ahead of Adonai on this. I'll just tell her I couldn't come up with anyone and we can just get to know each other gradually over time. I mean, I live here now, so what's the hurry, right?" He shrugged again.

Sid could see the disappointment on his friend's face and understood it well. After thinking a moment, he had an idea. "Okay Joel—how about this: I'll vouch for you, but I'm giving her a disclaimer, too."

Hope rekindled, Joel nodded readily. "Okay, that's fair—disclaim away!"

"Just promise me you won't tell her about your dream until you know each other better, okay?"

"Okay, sure—that's reasonable."

"And cool your jets, Joel! —Remember, you've got a year and a half headstart on her in this."

Joel nodded. "Good point."

Sid nodded, then glanced around him. "Okay, where is Andrea?" Joel pointed her out in the aisle, just as she took another glance at her watch. Sid zeroed in on her. "Okay, I have to catch Owen before he leaves—you go on and I'll catch up in a couple of minutes." Joel nodded again, smiling widely. Sid grinned at his friend, teasing, "You bag of bones!—I can't believe you asked her out!"

"Me either! Joel grinned back, then hurried back to catch Andrea before she left. Stepping up to the three ladies, he nodded to them and Andrea arched an expectant eyebrow. "He's coming," Joel assured.

He found someone? Eyes narrowing, Andrea shifted uncertainly, then shook it off, reassuring herself in her thoughts of the improbability that he might actually succeed. Joel and the three ladies exchanged nods and awkward smiles for a couple of minutes until Sid finally approached. The ladies expected him only to nod as he passed by, but when he stopped next to Andrea, she eyed him curiously. Sid nodded to her, "How ya doing, Andrea?" Surprised, Andrea nodded and said she was well, then Sid turned to acknowledge her friends. "And ladies. . .? Tammy? Donna? How ya doing?" The two puzzled women nodded and affirmed that they were also well, then Sid got to the point. "Listen, I don't want to keep you—I just have a question for Andrea." Andrea's eyebrows arched in surprise, as did those of her cohorts. Concerned Joel's 'voucher' might arrive while the Rabbi stood there, Andrea hoped this would be brief. Sid turned to her, "Andrea, do you trust me?"

Puzzled by the question, Andrea squinted at him. "With what. . .?"

"Just in general—do you trust me?"

Andrea thought for a moment—not so much about whether or not she trusted him, but wondering why it mattered to him at this particular moment. "Well, I'm not sure I would want you to work on my car. . ." Her matter-of-fact answer amused Sid, who never made any bones over the years about his complete lack of mechanical aptitude.

He grinned, nodding, "You are a very wise woman!"

"...And I don't think I would want to go fishing with you..." Andrea added, recalling a funny story about what happened to this 'city boy' when he tried his hand with a rod and reel.

Surprised to discover she had a sense of humor, Sid chuckled. "Again, very wise! I think I'd better make myself clearer—or your list could get very long!" The three ladies smiled and chuckled and Sid narrowed it down, "What I mean is, if I told you something was true, would you believe me or would you have your doubts?"

"Seriously...?" Familiar with Sid's antics, Andrea searched her Rabbi's eyes for any hint of teasing, wondering if she was being set-up for a punch line. Not finding any hint of anything, she shrugged. "Yes, I would believe you. Why? Do you have something 'unbelievable' to say?"

Sid again grinned, gesturing to Joel. "This is about my friend here—he asked me to vouch for him."

Three feminine mouths fell open. Incredulous, Andrea felt her face flush. "You know him?"

"Yes, for about twenty-five years." Sid quickly gave her Joel's mini-bio, "He was married for about twenty years or so, and lost his wife about four years ago. He has a daughter that is married, and he has two sons. You are the first woman he has asked out since his wife died, and there's a very interesting story about that, but I'll let him share it with you some day, if he chooses to. So, first, before I say anything more, I have a little disclaimer: I didn't know he was going to ask you to lunch until just now, when he asked me to vouch for him. What I'm saying is, I'm not trying to fix the two of you up."

The three women stood wide-eyed and mute. Her fingers over her lips, Andrea stood mortified. "This is embarrassing."

Sid quickly intervened, "It's not my intention to embarrass you or shame you in any way, Andrea, and I understand you not wanting to go to lunch with someone you have no idea about, and I respect that. In fact, I'm impressed with you for it," Sid laid a hand on Joel's shoulder, "...but I can say without reservation that Joel is a good, upright man, he has a pure heart. He's a wonderful husband and father, he loves God, and you have nothing to fear from him—and I say that with complete confidence. Now, I told him this and I'll tell you, too—I'm vouching for his character, but you are under no obligation to go out with him. That is totally up to you. I won't be disappointed or think less of you if you decide to say no. I'm just telling you that he's a good guy—he's not perfect, mind you, but I love him like a brother." Sid paused and briefly looked into each woman's eyes. "So, anyway, I'll let you get back to your day. Again, Andrea, I don't want you to feel any pressure to go with him, but I don't want you to feel any reservations about it, either." Sid excused himself, leaving Joel and the three women in the aisle, staring speechlessly at Joel

Not yet certain if bringing in Sid had helped or hurt his chances, Joel shifted uneasily from one foot to the other. "Well...? Was Sid someone whose word you can trust?" Joel arched his eyebrow hopefully.

The other two ladies now focused on Andrea, who couldn't decide whether to be angry or amused as she wrestled in her thoughts. Her pride rose up to resist, but she knew that she had agreed to it willingly—if not insistently, and like it or not, the man did come through; she couldn't just renege. She wanted to be mad, but she knew it could only be at herself. *This might be funny, if it weren't so annoying. That's what I get for being smug!*

She sighed heavily. "Well, we were going to Fabiani's—you can meet us there, if you want to."

Joel hesitated, wincing, "Well. . .um. . .I came with Sid this morning; I don't have a car here." Andrea rolled her eyes, and looked for help from her friends.

145

"I can't make it today, but you guys have a great time!" Tammy ran her words together as she bowed out, scooting off quickly before Andrea could object. Andrea turned to Donna, who made a similar excuse and left just as quickly.

Embarrassed and abandoned by her friends, Andrea squirmed within, realizing that, despite her many refusals, it was ending up that she would eat lunch with Joel, after all. Wincing at the irony, she wondered how in the world her plan could have deteriorated so quickly and completely. Seeing her looking so defeated and forlorn, it occurred to Joel to offer her a graceful way out, but he was too afraid she might take it. Resigned, Andrea sighed, "I'm parked in the back row." It was all she could think of to say, and started for her car as Joel fell in behind her.

Chapter 11

Climbing into her car, there was one thing Andrea wanted to make very clear to the man seating himself in her passenger seat: "This is not a date."

Reaching for his seatbelt, Joel smiled. "It must be, because I'm taking you out to lunch!"

Andrea shook her head. "No, I'm paying for my *own* lunch—it's only a date if you pay."

"Oh, c'mon," he cajoled, "let me pay—it's the least I can do after bamboozling you into coming—and driving."

Andrea was resolute, "No, this isn't a date! This is two people eating lunch together and paying for their own meals."

Choosing his battles, Joel decided not to push it. "Okay, okay. Dutch treat."

Arriving at Fabiani's, Andrea found a parking space. They went in together and waited in silence for a few minutes before being shown to a table. Andrea pulled her cell phone out of her pants pocket then took her seat at the table across from Joel, setting the phone down on the table next to the wall. Before Joel had even unfurled his silverware from his napkin, Andrea turned to the server. "Separate checks, please."

The server arched an eyebrow and nodded with an uncertain smile, then handed each of them a menu, then left them to decide. Silently, the two scanned the selections as their server soon returned to fill their water glasses. When she was finished with that, she set down the pitcher and scribbled on her tablet as Joel and Andrea each recited their choices. Retrieving her pitcher, the server left the table and Andrea and Joel sat through several moments of awkward silence. Finally, Joel spoke, "I guess this is when we talk about the weather," Joel grinned hopefully, but Andrea just sqinted at him, and he just sighed. "Wow, I didn't expect this to be so hard. I haven't been on a date in a long time."

"This isn't a date," Andrea reminded.

"Oh, I'm sorry, I forgot." Rephrasing it, he began again, "I haven't been on a *non-date* in a long time."

The server returned with a basket of soft breadsticks and a large bowl of salad. Grateful for the distraction, the two sat silently and watched as she set the bread and the cold plates on the table, then began tossing the salad, and finally grating parmesan cheese into its bowl. After she left, the awkward silence resumed as they served up their salads, then stared at them for a few moments before digging in. Andrea eyed Joel as she poked at her salad. "I have a question."

Reaching for a breadstick, Joel brightened. "Sure. What would you like to know?"

"Do, you always use the Rabbi to meet women?"

A little taken aback, Joel recovered quickly and smiled. "No, actually, this was my first time—but it worked well, don't you think?"

"I guess that depends on how you define success." Her bluntness reminding him of his home state, Joel grinned widely. Andrea took a bite of her breadstick. "So, what is this about?"

"Does it have to be about something? I thought we were just eating lunch together."

"Lunch is just the vehicle. You must want something."

"Why would you think I want something?"

"A total stranger asks me to lunch out of the blue? You have an agenda. Men always seem to have an agenda." she answered with certainty.

Joel wasn't sure if her statement was a commentary of the men in her life, or of her view of herself—or both. "I just wanted to meet you. . .talk to you—you know, get to know you."

"Why?"

"Why. . .?"

"Yeah, why? I mean, Sid vouched for you, so I guess I can rule-out 'predatory male who frequents places of worship looking for vulnerable, unattached women to take advantage of,'—so, what is it you want?"

Though a bit dismayed over her suspicions, Joel was delight-fully taken aback at her candor. "Wow, you are very direct!"

Andrea simply shrugged. "It saves time." She took another bite of salad.

He arched an eyebrow, "It saves time?"

"That's right."

The two munched their salads for a few moments and Joel mused. *Is she serious or is she just pulling my leg?* He squinted as he pondered her resistance, again reminded of his years growing up in Queens. *Nah—she's being too nice; I'd be wearing my salad if she were serious!* Feeling more certain, he smiled to himself. *Yeah, she's just messing with me. . .* He watched her for a minute, an idea forming. "You like directness."

"I do."

He chuckled at her response, "Remember that line."

Her fork on the way to her mouth, Andrea hesitated, "Huh?"

"Oh, nothing. . ." Joel just smiled, so Andrea shrugged and her fork finished it's arc to her mouth. He ventured again, "So, you'll be fine with it if I'm direct?"

"Sure."

"Okay, here goes—do you plan to ever get married again?"

Andrea flinched, but not much—her answer was immediate, and she didn't elaborate. "No."

Joel's eyebrows arched. "No? Just. . .*no?*"

"That's right."

"Why not?"

"Nunya."

"What's 'nunya'?"

"Nunya business."

He grinned at her spunk. "Oh, c'mon now," he coaxed, "we're being direct, right?"

Andrea shrugged. "Okay, how about, 'Because I don't want to.'"

Joel just arched an eyebrow but before he could comment, the server arrived with their meals, and cleared away their excess dishes. The two stared down at their plates.

"Looks good!" Joel picked up his fork and began probing his lasagna, resuming his thought, "But what if God's will is for you to be married?"

Andrea sighed and rolled her eyes. "Oh, not this again." She took a bite of her fettuccine.

"Again. . .? You've had this conversation before?"

"Yes, before I started dating my husband."

"Oh, really? So you didn't want to get married then, either?"

"No."

"But you did."

"I had a weak moment."

Skeptical, Joel grinned. "A weak moment, huh?—Somehow I doubt that. I think you prayed about it and felt it was God's will, and you walked in it. Is that how it went?"

"How would you know?"

"Just answer the question."

Andrea shrugged, "Well. . .Okay, yes. Where are you going with this?"

Joel smiled genially, "I'm just saying that because I intend to marry you—*that's* what 'this' is about."

Andrea's jaw dropped along with her fork. It clattered onto the table drawing glances from the diners around her. Fumbling to retrieve it, Andrea's face clouded then flushed. "Wow, that's quite an ice-breaker. You just jump right in, don't you?"

"It saves time." Joel grinned, amused with himself.

"So, I suppose the next thing you're going to say is that that it's Adonai's *will?*"

"I think so."

"Do I get a say in this?"

"Sure—just say your line."

"What line?"

"The line I told you to remember a minute ago."

Andrea thought a moment. "I do?"

"That's the one!" He chuckled, even more self-amused.

She glared at him. "Very funny. So, now what? Shall we set a date, or do you want to wait until dessert?" Her tone was decidedly sharper. Amused again with her sarcasm, Joel took a bite of his food, still grinning. Andrea didn't think it nearly as amusing as he did; feeling unsettled, she shook her head. "I have no intention of marrying you."

"Not now, but I'm hopeful. Besides, I haven't asked you yet." Suddenly, feigning seriousness, Joel pressed his palm against his chest. "Is it because I'm Jewish?" Immediately, he chuckled, grinning anew. Having met her at the synagogue, his joke seemed particularly amusing to him.

Andrea rolled her eyes. "No, that would actually work in your favor—*if* I were looking to get married again; I'm just not." Uncomfortable, she steered the conversation away from that.

"So, how did God give you this revelation? Did he write it on a wall? Send you a postcard? What?"

Amused, if not delighted, Joel smiled broadly, chewing his food. "Wow, you are very good at sarcasm—are you sure you weren't raised Jewish?"

Andrea sighed. "Pretty sure."

"Are you from New York?"

"No, California."

"Southern California?"

"That's right."

"Okay, that explains it!" Joel gestured with his fork, "—and it explains why you don't sound *'southern.'*" He grinned again.

In spite of herself and her objections, Andrea couldn't resist a tiny smile, and Joel noticed—pleased that he seemed to have finally broken through her resistance, if only a tiny bit. Suddenly, from somewhere deep within, a wave of anxiety pressed upward in Andrea. She tried to push it aside and get through her meal, but it gripped her inexplicably, turning into something akin to panic. Abruptly, she dropped her fork and pushed herself away from the table in one forceful movement, and gathered up her pocketbook. "I have to go." Her voice faltered.

"What. . .?" Joel stammered, his grin fading from his face, "But. . ." Before he could complete his thought or question she had hurried away, almost crashing into their server on her way, leaving Joel sitting there in front of his plate, stunned. He knew if he tried to go after her, he would likely be tackled at the door for not paying the tab. Feeling the weight of a roomful of eyes around him, Joel shrugged to them, "Um. . .she had to go." Then he offered lamely to the server, "Something came up."

The server nodded, feigning understanding. "Would you like me to box up the rest?" When Joel nodded and thanked her, she added, "I guess it will be one check, after all?" He grinned sheepishly and nodded again, then swallowed the bite of food that was still in his mouth.

Her mind reeling, Andrea rushed out to her car, jumped in and hurried from the parking lot, forcing herself to focus on the driving so that she didn't run over anyone. "Abba, is this some kind of joke?" She felt tears welling up, and wiped them away. "Please, not again. I can't do marriage again, Father! I want it to be just you—*only* you." She rambled, pleading, until she came to a stoplight. Trying to calm herself, she glanced down then over at the seat next to her, and her eyes froze on the Bible and tallit sitting on the seat—*Joel's* Bible and tallit. "Nooooo!" All she could do was grit her teeth and groan as the light turned green and she pulled forward from her stop. For a fleeting moment, she considered just throwing them out the window, rather than have to see him again next Shabbat to return them, but as quickly as it occurred to her, she rejected the notion. *No, that's God's Word—I can't just throw it out the window!* She groaned again, "Why did I even let him ride with me!?" As soon as she spoke the words, it hit her—and she hit the brakes. "Oh, no! He rode with me and I left him there! OOoooOh! I can't believe this!" She groaned again, "Oh, that's just great—now I have to go back for him!" She warred against herself, "No, I don't! I'm not going to!—He can just call someone!" But even as she spoke the words, she knew she couldn't just leave the man stranded at the restaurant. Another realization hit her, "Oh man! I just stranded the Rabbi's friend! What if that's who he calls!" Mortified anew, Andrea groaned as though in pain, "How will I ever face Rabbi again?" Embarrassed to death, she briefly considered a move out of state and changing her name. Sighing in resignation, she grudgingly circled back to the restaurant.

While Joel awaited the check, he stared at the table then noticed something on it near the wall and he reached for it. *She forgot her cell phone!* An idea occurring to him, he experimented with it until he found the way to her contacts, then entered his own name and cell number, grinning to himself as he did so—and relishing the opportunity to return it to her. As he chuckled to himself, his grin suddenly faded as a realization hit. *Andrea drove us here!* Now anxious, he waited impatiently for the server to return with the check and the take-out containers, hoping Sid would not have to find out about this. *Maybe she's just outside waiting for me. . .* He grimaced, hoping against the much less-desirable alternative. Once the server returned, Joel waited another excruciating few minutes while she slowly scraped the two meals from the plates into the boxes, then loaded them into the bag, seeming to be in no hurry whatsoever. Rather than use his debit card and have to wait again for her to return for a signature, Joel just paid with cash, left a nice tip, then grabbed the bag and the two cell phones and hurried for the door.

Outside at the curb, he scanned the section of the parking lot where Andrea had parked her car, but there was only an empty space where it had been. His shoulders slumping, he sighed. *Oh great, now there's no way to keep this from Sid!* He pressed his lips together, kicking himself in his thoughts, then grimaced and shook his head. *Sid told me to cool my jets! Why didn't I listen to him?* He shook his head, then switching the bag to his left hand, Joel put Andrea's phone with the bag, and addressed his own phone in his right, pressing a speed dial number, again shaking his head. *He will never let me hear the end of this!* After a couple of rings, he was talking to Sid. "Sid, it's me. . .um. . . I need a ride."

It took several minutes for Andrea to make her way back through traffic to the restaurant. As she pulled up in front, she saw Joel standing outside, looking in the direction of where she had originally parked the car, a bag in one hand, cell phone to his ear in the other hand, and a pained expression on his face.

Grumbling out loud to herself, she squeezed the steering wheel in frustration. "This is SOooOOooO embarrassing!"

Meanwhile, Sid wasn't making it easy for Joel, who worked at being vague. "Where's Andrea? Well. . .um. . .she kind of. . .left." Suddenly, a look of surprise crossed Joel's face, "What makes you say that?. . .Okay, yeah, I may have mentioned marriage—but I didn't say anything about the dream." Joel sighed and rolled his eyes. "Uh-huh. . .yes, Sid—I know you warned me not to. Okay, yes, you were right; I concede. Are you happy?. . .Great. . . .Yeah, well, when you are through laughing, will you come and get me? Even if I had my car, I don't know how to get to your house from here, and I don't have my map. . .Sid, I'm standing out on the sidewalk here—can we just talk about it later?. . .Where am I? That's a good question, I don't know exactly. . ." Joel craned his head around looking for a sign that would let him know the name of the restaurant, then found a small version of it next to the door. "I'm at a restaurant called Fabiani's. . .Okay, thanks. I'm right out front."

Andrea pulled up next to where Joel was standing and waited there for a moment. Still talking on his phone and focused on the former parking space, Joel didn't see her so she touched her car horn. Mildly startled, Joel turned toward the sound and glanced at her car then glanced away again. Realizing a split second later who that was, he turned again to her, surprise registering on his face, he smiled, relieved. "Never mind, Sid, I'm good. I gotta go." He ended the call abruptly and pocketed his phone, then stepped to Andrea's passenger-side door and stooped to look in, smiling widely as she let down the window. "You came back!"

Andrea couldn't look him in the eye, so she looked everywhere else, and muttered lamely, "Sorry. I forgot we rode together."

To her surprise, Joel accepted the explanation willingly as he opened the door and slid into the seat next to her, moving his

Bible and tallit so that he didn't sit on them, then set the bag of food on the floor between his feet. Anxious to return Joel to where this whole fiasco began, Andrea abruptly lurched her car away from the curb as soon as she heard the door latch, throwing Joel off-balance against his door. Surprised, but still grinning, Joel righted himself, bracing his arm against the dashboard as he fumbled to get his seat belt around him. That accomplished, they rode in silence for a few miles, Andrea because she preferred it, and Joel, because at the moment he could think of nothing to say. Andrea stared blankly out the windshield as she drove, ignoring the man in the seat beside her—not from rudeness, but embarrassment. She replayed their meal in her mind, trying to think of how to explain her behavior, unable to understand it herself. Joel quietly watched her face grimace and contort as she wrestled in her thoughts.

Finally, he could stand the silence no longer and groped for words. "Um...may I ask, what, uh...what happened back there?"

Andrea tensed. "I...I don't know." She waved him off, unable to look at him, waiting for him to explode in anger.

"I'm sorry, Andrea—I really didn't mean to upset you." He watched her closely and noticed her glance at him quizzically at his apology, then relaxed a bit. Joel continued, "I was just...you know, 'being direct.'" His voice caricatured the words as he smiled hopefully.

Andrea glanced at him again, still puzzled, but didn't respond right away. After a few moments, her shoulders slumped. "I'm sorry. I guess I just wasn't expecting that."

Trying to ease her tension, Joel teased at her apology, "Wow, our first fight! Glad we got that over with!" Andrea slowly turned her head toward him, staring wide-eyed. Joel couldn't tell if she was angry or appalled—or both, so he just smiled weakly and shrugged. "Just kidding."

They continued on in silence for a few minutes then Andrea turned onto the street to the synagogue. Approaching the entrance to the parking lot, she slowed and made the right turn onto the property, then pulled to a stop at the main entry. His elbow resting on the window ledge, Joel hesitated, fingering his hair, not wanting to leave the conversation where it had stalled. After a moment, something occurred to him, and he brightened at the thought. *As long as I sit here in her car, she is a captive audience!* He knew he might not get another chance like this. Turning to Andrea, he shrugged. "So, how about dinner?"

Amazed, Andrea just stared at him. "We just ate lunch!"

"Not so—all we did was *order* lunch. You agreed to a meal, and we haven't had it yet."

Almost whining, Andrea shook her head, "Why are you pressing this?"

"It saves time!" He grinned, relishing the phrase, "Why are you so opposed to it?"

"I just can't figure out what it is you are after."

Joel thought it interesting that she was so convinced of that. "I'm just after *you.*"

Mystified, Andrea shook her head. "But why me?"

Again, her disbelief struck him as odd. "Why not you? I just want to get to know you."

Andrea eyed him doubtfully. "Sure, you do."

Joel's eyebrows arched, his chin tilted slightly to one side. "Is it so hard for you to believe that a man is interested in you?"

Actually, yes. Andrea answered in her thoughts, but decided to skip it. "You don't even know me—how can you be interested?"

"Um...I can't tell you that yet. So, are you up for a steak dinner?"

"No, I don't think that would be a good idea."

Missing the point deliberately, Joel offered an alternative, "Then, how about Greek?"

"No! Neither—none! Not anywhere!"

"Why? Are you afraid you'll fall madly in love with me?"

"No."

"No. . .?" Joel feigned disappointment. "C'mon, you have to give me a chance to make up for upsetting you."

"No, I don't. Why don't you just tell me what are you after?"

"I already did—I'm after *you!* Why is that so hard for you to believe?

"Nunya."

"Hmm. . .there's that word again." Joel shrugged "So, I'm just not what you're looking for?"

"I'm not looking at all—*that's* the issue!" She softened a bit. "If it makes you feel better, there is nothing really off-putting about you. I'm just not in the market—or on the market."

His eyebrows arched. "Oh, so, maybe it's just too soon?"

Eternity would still be too soon! Andrea sighed, "You're asking me something I don't have the answer to. It's not you—I just don't want to get married again, okay?"

"Not ever?"

"Not in a thousand years."

Joel grinned, his eyebrows arching. "Well, you know the Bible says '. . .For with the Lord, a day is like a thousand years, and a thousand years are like one day.' (2Pet.3:8b)—so, how about tomorrow, then?"

Andrea grimaced, incredulous. *Is he serious?* "I don't get it—just tell me what you're after."

Joel smiled broadly. "I love how direct you are! Okay, if I had not mentioned marriage at lunch, would you have said yes to dinner with me tonight?"

Andrea lolled her head wearily and sighed. "Again, a question I don't know the answer to."

Joel shrugged. "Maybe we can discuss it over dinner."

Andrea rolled her eyes. *He's like a broken record!* "No!"

Joel pressed his lips together, his mouth askew, as he pondered for a moment. "Well, I guess I'll just have to reason this out myself. Let's see. . .your refusing to get to know me can't be because of my poor character because, as you know, Sid vouched for me." He directed a *touché* glance in Andrea's direction, then continued, "It can't be because I'm ugly, because my grandmother has always said I'm 'as cute as a bug's ear.' It can't be because I forgot your birthday, because we just met and I don't know it—yet." He grinned, his eyebrows arched hopefully. When she didn't offer the date, Joel sighed exaggeratedly and resumed his discourse. "And it can't be because I've neglected you, treated you rudely, lied to you, or let you down because, well, you haven't given me the opportunity to do any of that yet—not that I ever plan to. So, as far as I can tell, you have no reason to reject me." Joel folded his arms across his chest then gestured with a palm up, signaling to Andrea that the floor was now hers.

Andrea took a different tack. "Your premise is flawed."

Amused anew, Joel's eyebrow arched. "Do tell. . .!"

"You have made the assumption that I am rejecting you based on who you are or how you act."

"Which I have shown has no merit."

"Yes, but that primary assumption itself is flawed. I am not rejecting you because of who you are because I don't know you, and as you said, you haven't behaved badly, so I'm not rejecting you because of how you act—but, that can change at any time because you are really starting to get on my nerves!" Joel chuckled and Andrea continued, "Therefore, because I am not rejecting who you are, or how you act, you cannot say I'm rejecting you, per se. I am, however rejecting marriage—and since marriage is your desired end. . ."

"Oh, I see your point." Joel interrupted, drumming his fingers on his knees. "Can we pretend that I didn't mention marriage?"

"Sorry, you can't un-ring a bell."

Joel continued his negotiation, "Okay, how about we just ignore it, then?"

"That wouldn't be right—you know what the Bible says about knowing the truth, but ignoring it."

Joel nodded slowly. "Okay, how about we just take marriage off the table, then?"

Andrea squinted, tilting her head, "Oh? Are you saying you don't want to get married now?"

Joel grinned sheepishly. "Um, which answer to that will get me out of the corner I've just painted myself into?" Andrea tucked her chin and arched an eyebrow at him, so Joel just shrugged. "Okay, forget reasoning it out—it's over-rated anyway. How about bribery?" Andrea shook her head. "Extortion?" Again, Andrea declined and Joel shrugged. "All I have left is getting down on my knees and begging pitifully."

Andrea rolled her eyes, "Please don't do that."

Joel exaggeratedly feigned relief. "Okay, thanks—these are my good slacks."

Andrea grinned in spite of herself, then leaned her head against her side window wearily. "Are we done now?"

Joel sighed. "I guess—if I can't convince you to have to dinner with me."

"Thanks, but I don't think so."

"At least, you don't seem upset anymore," Joel offered. Andrea averted her eyes instead of responding, so Joel continued, "I'm glad for that anyway, because I don't want to leave on a bad note. So, are we good?"

Andrea shrugged. "I guess so. . ." then hurriedly added, "—and don't forget your Bible and tallit!"

Joel nodded, reaching for them, and realized her cell phone was still in his hand. "Oh, here, you left your phone on the table."

Andrea glanced at it, and then at Joel, surprised. "Oh, thanks." She received it from him and set it in her lap. There was an awkward silence as Andrea waited for him to get out of her car. When he made no move to that end, she squinted at him. "What...?"

Well, I guess I could *walk* to Sid's house from here." He shrugged, eyeing her hopefully.

Squinting, Andrea glanced around them, quickly realizing there were no other cars in the parking lot, then remembered the reason Joel rode with her in the first place. She hung her head, letting out another sigh. Easing her car forward, she circled the parking lot until she was back at the driveway and the street, then stopped and waited, arching her eyebrows expectantly. Joel just smiled back at her, but the car didn't move.

When she continued to stare at him, he got suspicious. "Is something wrong?"

"I don't know where Rabbi lives."

"Oh, yeah, I guess directions would be helpful." Joel chuckled, "I just assumed everyone knew where Sid lives." He told her which way to turn and she followed his directions until they pulled up to the curb in front of Sid's house minutes later. Joel removed her take-out container from the bag and handed it to her. "Your left-overs, Madam." Andrea accepted the box from him and held it in her lap until Joel opened the door and stepped out, then she set the box on the seat he vacated. Once out of the car Joel stopped for a moment and leaned down to face her, chiding, "Thank you, Andrea—that was a very interesting *first date.*"

Andrea bristled. "It wasn't a date!"

He grinned impishly, "Oh, but it was—by your own definition."

Andrea squinted. "What are you talking about?"

"You left."

"So? How does that make it a date?"

"I paid for lunch—and you know what you said: if I pay, that makes it a date." He smirked smugly, waving the receipt at her, just out of her reach. Before she could protest, he closed her car door and backed away, grinning, waving to her with his finger-tips as he retreated.

Andrea called after him, "It wasn't a date!—Come here! I'll pay you back!"

Joel turned and made his way up the front walk, calling over his shoulder to her, "No, I don't think so, Andrea. You can take me out next time if you want to, but this is now—and forever will be, *our first DATE!*" Grinning widely, he calmly stepped up the couple of steps onto Sid's front porch and rang the doorbell, then turned to Andrea and chuckled again.

"There isn't going to be a next time!" Andrea yelled to him, much too loudly.

"We can do Mexican!" Joel called back playfully, ignoring her protests.

Andrea started to argue, but stopped short when she saw that someone was answering the front door. Groaning in exaspera-tion, she gave up for the moment and quickly put her car into gear, lurching it away from the curb—making her get-away just as Connie's face appeared in the doorway. Hearing tires squeal, Connie followed the sound with her eyes just in time to see the back of Andrea's rapidly retreating vehicle. She turned to Joel, puzzled. As she stepped aside to let him in, Joel only grinned and shrugged. "That went well!"

Chapter 12

A ndrea readied herself for work distractedly, and finally gathered her tote bag and pocket book and headed out the door. After several turns, she was on Holmes Boulevard, heading toward the hospital and, lapsing into auto-pilot, her mind replayed her embarrassing lunch disaster from the previous Saturday. Stopping at a traffic light, she glanced ahead, the Coffee Corner Bistro sign catching her eye. *A Chai tea really sounds good about now.* She turned right off the busy boulevard, and right again into the alley that ran behind a row of drive-thru restaurants whose back driveways open to it. Doing a right-hand U-turn into the lane for the drive-up window, she absently pulled up to the speaker and recited her order. "I'd like a Large Chai Tea, non-fat, no whipped cream."

"Um, sorry—but this is Taco Tony's."

Hearing laughter in the background, Andrea stared blankly at the speaker for a second before it registered what the voice said. She glanced up at the logos on the menu and then the building, sure enough, it was Taco Tony's—Coffee Corner was the next driveway down off the alley. Blushing, she just muttered, "Oh great. That figures." She shrugged, addressing the the microphone, "I turned too soon. Sorry!" Hearing another burst of background laughter from the speaker, Andrea pulled around to the neighboring drive-up lane and tried again. By the time she arrived at work, the caffeine and sugar in the Chai tea, as well as the moment of chagrin at Taco Tony's, had combined to add 'flustered' to her distracted state.

"Morning, Andrea—how was your weekend?" Arlene asked in a sprightly mood.

"Um, fine."

Arlene chuckled, "You don't look like it was fine! What's the matter?"

"Nothing, really. I'm just having one of those Mondays." *Lord, don't let them find out about Joel—if they do, I'll never hear the end of it!* She stuffed her pocketbook into her locker and headed for the time clock.

That afternoon a delivery man arrived at the reception desk of Andrea's clinic with the biggest bouquet of long-stem roses anyone had seen in a quite a while.

"I have a delivery for Andrea Cullen."

Eyebrows arched from every direction as everyone within earshot turned at the name. At the nurse's station, Yvonne stepped up to the reception counter, smiling widely.

"Hi, I'm the charge nurse. Yes, Andrea's here. Just set them right there and I'll make sure she gets them." After he left, the nurses and the Unit Secretary gathered around.

"Is Andrea seeing someone?"

"I haven't heard her say anything."

"Maybe they're from a friend."

"That isn't a 'friend' bouquet."

"Read the card."

"No!—we can't read the card until Andrea has read it."

"If you're real careful when you open it. . ." One of them suggested and everyone chuckled.

"No, let's just wait until she notices them. When she asks her usual, 'Are those for me?' like she always does, we'll just tell her 'yes!' and watch while she opens the card."

And that became the plan as Andrea's co-workers lurked inconspicuously around the nurse's station awaiting her return. After several minutes she emerged from a patient room and stepped to the reception counter, her nose in a chart. Setting it down onto the counter, she continued to flip through the pages until the scent of the roses drew her attention upward to the flowers. Eyes wide, she marveled at them. "Wow, are these for me?" It was the long-standing first line of her playful ritual whenever flowers arrived on their unit—to which the answer was always a tired, 'No, Andrea—they're for so-and-so.' Then Andrea's next line would always be, 'Oh, lucky so-and-so.' Staring up at the exquisite flowers, Andrea awaited the expected response, anxious to learn who was the lucky recipient.

Arlene stepped up to the counter, grinning. "Yes!"

Andrea squinted at her. "'Yes,' what?"

"Yes, they're *for you!*"

Andrea squinted, puzzled. "They're for me?"

"Yeah, they actually are this time!" Arlene chuckled.

Puzzled, Andrea squinted curiously at her co-workers, then at the flowers. In all the years she'd worked there, this had never been the case. Squinting, it took Andrea a moment for it to sink in. The entire staff had come out to watch, and activity around the desk ground to a halt as everyone awaited the unveiling— even several patients in the hallway drew close. The weight of ten pairs of eyes finally convinced her.

"Is it your birthday, or something?"

"No, her birthday was in March," Arlene corrected.

"Oh yeah. So who are they from, Andrea?" another co-worker asked.

Finally reaching up for the attached envelope, Andrea opened it and slid out the tiny card and read it to herself,

Thanks for a great "first-date"—
Looking forward to actually eating with you!
LOL,
Blessings, Joel

Embarrassed and irritated at this invasion into her work environment, Andrea glared at the little card, which didn't escape the notice of a few of her co-workers. Suddenly conscious of her curious onlookers, she reined-in her reaction. Forcing a cheerful smile to her face, she cleared her throat. "Oh, they're from my sister! She shouldn't have gone to that expense!" Everyone around her sighed and smiled, thinking warm thoughts, but a tad disappointed it wasn't someone more interesting, and one by one, they returned to their work. With the eyes off of her, Andrea retreated to the bathroom, where she quietly gave expression to her frustration and indignation by slam-dunking the little card into the trash can.

** *** **

On Wednesday the following week, Andrea gathered up her pocketbook and keys and headed for the door, hoisting her tote bag onto her shoulder on the way out; it was Health Check Day at Ruth's again. Although she delighted in her visits to the elderly boarders every other Wednesday, with her distracted state over the past week and a half, she nearly forgot the day had arrived. If Ruth hadn't called that morning to ask her for a favor, she would have forgotten completely.

As was her routine, she checked the blood pressure of each of Ruth's boarders, discussed with them their medications, and listened to their concerns—and, if need be, made recommendations that they visit their physicians. When the health checks were finished, Ruth watched as Andrea packed up her paraphernalia. Setting something down, she forgot where she put it, searched for it, found it—then promptly lost the next item the same way—over and over, becoming more flustered with each lost item. As Andrea finally located and put away the final item, she glanced around to make certain she hadn't left anything behind.

Shaking her head slowly, Ruth sensed her friend was in need of a listening ear. "Are you ready for some tea, Andrea? I baked some muffins this morning, too."

"Oh, yes, please. That would be wonderful! Let me make sure I haven't forgotten something that I'm supposed to do after leaving here." Ruth watched as Andrea now searched for where she had left her cell phone—finding it in her pocket. Checking her 'to-do list' in her phone, Andrea nodded. "All clear, as far as I can tell. I haven't been able to rely on my memory lately."

"I can see you are pretty distracted today."

"Is it that obvious? Oh Ruth, I just can't think straight anymore. You know how they say you need to find a new normal? I'm beginning to wonder if this is it."

"I thought you already found a new normal."

"Well, I guess this is a 'new' new normal."

"Was there something wrong with the 'old' new normal?" Ruth grinned, but still flustered, Andrea just sagged pitifully. "C'mon into the Kitchen, Andrea, we'll talk in here."

Ruth disappeared through the swinging louver door into the kitchen, and Andrea gathered her things and followed, taking her usual seat at the cozy breakfast table. She watched as Ruth filled the kettle and put it on the stove. Absently, Andrea began twirling her ring around a finger of her right hand as she smiled at the toddler playing cheerfully at Ruth's feet. "Nate looks happy. How's Heath? He seems like he's doing better since he moved back with you."

Ruth reached for the mugs, and then the tea bags. "Yes, he's doing a lot better—and so am I. It's been good having his help around here."

"It's good seeing him at synagogue. . ."

Ruth nodded, "Yes, I think coming these last couple of months has been good for him." She smiled, "He seems to enjoy Sid, and I know he's been getting a lot out of his messages on Shabbat. He actually signed up for a Yachad group for the fall session—I was real glad to see that."

Andrea arched an eyebrow, "Really. . .? That's good—I'm sure it'll do him good to start mixing more with other people." She tilted her head, "I sensed a 'but' in there."

Ruth took a seat at the table. "But things take time."

"It's been almost two years."

Ruth sighed, "I know. Heath's feelings run deep—always have; just like his dad."

Andrea nodded then began twirling her ring again. "How about you, Ruth? You doing all right?"

"Oh, I'm doing just fine, hon. You, on the other hand. . ." She grinned at her friend. "I see you've started twirling your ring again—I haven't seen you do that in a while." She glanced again at Andrea, who just rolled her eyes. "What's got you so flustered today? This wouldn't have anything to do with a certain someone I've seen around you at services the last couple of Shabbats, would it?"

Andrea's blush confirmed her suspicions. "Ruth, I don't know what do to about him. He won't go away!"

"Go away? Why do you want him to? He seems like a nice fellow. Isn't he a friend of Rabbi's?"

"You knew that, too? It seems like everyone knew that but me."

"You had lunch with him a couple of weeks ago, didn't you?"

"Yes. . .well, no. Well. . .sort of. . ."

"What does that mean? I saw you leave with him—it didn't go well?"

"It was a disaster."

"I guess he didn't think so. He flits around you like a little hummingbird."

"I know. I wish he wouldn't."

"Why is that?"

"Ruth, he wants to marry me! Can you believe that? He doesn't even know me!"

The teapot squealed for attention, so Ruth left the table to tend to it. She called over her shoulder, "He told you that? Already?"

"Yes, that day at lunch! Who says that the first time they meet someone?"

Ruth reached for the mugs. "What's his hurry?"

Andrea shook her head. "I have no idea."

"What kind of tea do you want? How about something herbal—I don't think you need any caffeine."

"You've got that right!—Herbal is fine. Do you have any more of that fruity red tea?"

"Sure do." Ruth set the teas to steep then gathered the muffins, plates, and butter, assembling everything on the table in front of Andrea. That done, she brought over the cups of steaming tea and sat down across from her. "Now, tell me about your lunch date."

"It wasn't a date."

"What was it then?"

"An embarrassing, humiliating experience."

Ruth grinned. "I can't wait. Now, stop twirling your ring and tell me about it."

Andrea related to Ruth her ordeal with Joel, beginning with their 'deal' to find someone who would vouch for him, his declaration of intent to marry her, running out on him, and then having to return for him. Ruth couldn't help laughing.

"It's not funny, Ruth."

Still chuckling, Ruth begged to differ, "Oh, but it is, hon!"

When Ruth continued to chuckle, Andrea tilted her head, and eyed her impatiently, trying to sound indignant, "Ruth, this is serious!"

Though still smiling, Ruth checked her merriment. "I'm sorry, but it's a cute story! What happened after that?"

"Well, after I picked him up, I drove him back to the synagogue—but I forgot that he didn't have a car there, so then I had to take him to Rabbi's house. All I could think about was, what if he tells Rabbi I left him at the restaurant?"

"Maybe he didn't say anything," Ruth offered.

"Wouldn't you, if it were you?"

Ruth grinned again, "Well, I have to say, it would be hard not to! But at least you went back to get him!—Think of the story he would have to tell if you'd left him there, and Sid had to go get him!"

"Oh, that would have been terrible!" Andrea's eyes suddenly widened. "You know, he was talking on his cell phone when I pulled up to him. Maybe he had already told Rabbi! Oh, I'm so embarrassed! How can I face the Rabbi, now?"

Ruth chuckled again, "Andrea, you sound like a school girl!"

"I feel like one. I never did like the 'dating game'—even back when I was in school; it's too nerve-wracking!"

Ruth reached for a muffin. "So did Rabbi say anything when you dropped off Joel at his house?"

"I didn't talk to him; I never got out of my car. We just sat there for a few minutes having a debate over whether or not it was a real date. Joel kept insisting that it was, because I left and he had to pay for my meal, and I insisted it wasn't. Then I noticed someone opening the front door, so I just took off."

Ruth chuckled again, "That was subtle! Was it Rabbi?"

"I don't know, I just got out of there. I'm not ready for this, Ruth. I wasn't looking for it and I am not happy about it."

Ruth tucked her chin, eyeing her friend askance. "A nice man that wants to marry you? That's an answer to prayer for most widows."

"Well, maybe for some—but they are not *my* prayers. Ruth, being married was the most difficult and painful experience I've ever had. I'd rather be single forever than do it again."

"Forever is a long time, Andrea, and not all men are like Evan. I've talked to Joel, he seems like a very nice and sincere man."

"So did Evan."

"So, is Joel guilty because Evan was volatile and emotionally unavailable?"

"Pretty much," Andrea said, sipping her tea.

"I think you should give Joel a chance."

"I don't." Andrea reached for a muffin and cut it in half.

"What's the matter, are you afraid you'll fall in love with him?" Ruth chided.

Andrea's eyebrows arched. "Yes, Ruth—that's exactly what I'm afraid of! Love makes you stupid and blind. I'm too vulnerable right now. I just need to get through this adjustment period, and then I'll be fine. No, Ruth—one ride on the 'marriage roller coaster' is enough for me." She shook her head emphatically.

"It doesn't have to be a roller coaster again. Maybe next time it'll be a walk in the park."

"If it's up to me, there won't be a next time."

171

Ruth sighed, eyeing her friend sadly. "Andrea, just because yours was a difficult road, doesn't mean all marriages are like that. My marriage to Heath's dad was wonderful. I don't regret one minute of it."

"Then why don't *you* marry Joel?" Andrea offered.

Ruth chuckled, "Because he's almost young enough to be my son. Besides, it's you he has eyes for, hon. Have you heard from him since that lunch?"

"Yes. He actually sent flowers to my work! Can you believe that?"

Ruth chuckled, amused. "The monster!"

"Seriously, Ruth! I didn't want my coworkers to know about him; they're like Pit Bulls! I knew they would never let go of it if they heard about him, so I just wanted to keep it to myself. Then this huge vase of long stem roses shows up for me and right away, they all gathered around to find out who they were from."

"What did you tell them? They didn't just read the card?"

"Oh! I didn't think of that! I hope not! Well, if they did, they didn't let on. I just told them my sister sent them."

"Did they believe you?"

Andrea squinted. "I think so. . . I just threw the card in the trash—but they do keep mentioning it. . ." Andrea's forehead furrowed. "Every couple of days, either Arlene or Sandra will say something about 'your *sister's* flowers'—they keep emphasizing the word 'sister.'" Suddenly, Andrea's eyes widened, "You don't think they got it out of the trash do you?" Ruth only shrugged, then Andrea shook it off. "Well, whether they did or not, I'm sure they got the message that it isn't up for discussion."

"Don't be too sure, Andrea. If they did, they'll probably discuss it—they just won't discuss it with you!"

Andrea scowled. "I hope you're wrong about that."

Ruth shrugged. "Were they nice flowers?"

Andrea suddenly brightened, "Oh, they were beautiful! I've never seen such nice roses! It's been a week and a half, and they still look fresh."

Ruth grinned. "Oh, so you kept them?"

Andrea shrugged. "Well, yeah—I couldn't leave them at work! If I did, my co-workers would have wondered why I was leaving my sister's flowers there—so I took them home. They were so pretty, and smelled so good, I couldn't just throw them away." She leaned back in her chair. "I didn't know anyplace in Middle Georgia even sold flowers like that."

"Did you tell that to Joel?"

"No way! That would just encourage him." Suddenly, she eyed Ruth suspiciously. "—and don't you dare tell him, either!"

Ruth only smiled. "Your secret is safe with me. Did you say anything at all to him about them?"

"He asked me about them on Shabbat; I just asked him to not do that again. I think I hurt his feelings." When Ruth eyed her and she hurriedly added, "Ruth, please don't look at me like that. I hated to do it, but he just won't take the hint."

"What did he say when you told him not to do that again?"

"Oh, he wanted to know why, and then it just got awkward with me trying to explain, and him not getting it. It was embarrassing."

"Oh, that's too bad. Why don't you give him a chance?"

"No, Ruth. I don't want to even go there. I'm looking forward to it just being me and the Lord from now on, with no one to put the kibosh on me pursuing Him."

"Have you prayed about it?"

"Prayed about what?"

"About getting married again."

"Why would I pray about that? I don't want to get married again."

"Don't you want to know what God thinks about it? What if it's not his will for you to stay single?"

Andrea leaned back, her hands falling to her lap. She sighed heavily, almost glaring at her friend, her tone was impatient. "Ruth, I don't want to hear that!"

"Well, I don't want to derail your big 'single forever' plans, but we all need to ask God about the things we *don't* want, as well as the things we *do* want. After all, isn't it about what *He* wants?"

"Ruth, it's very Biblical to stay single. In First Corinthians 7:8, it says, 'Now to the single people and the widows I say that it is fine if they remain unmarried like me.'—and that's what I want."

Ruth tilted her head to one side, eyeing her friend. "Well, it sounds like you've been rehearsing *that* for a while." She grinned for a moment, then grew more serious. "Andrea, people are called to marriage just like they are called to singleness. Everyone needs to find out from Adonai what His will is for them."

Andrea sighed wearily, "But Ruth, why would it *not* be Adonai's will for it to be just him and me? Why bring in a 'third party' and muck everything up—again?"

"Well, what about the chord of three strands?" (Eccl. 4:9-12) Ruth ventured; Andrea only eyed her, exasperated. Ruth sipped her tea, and then set down her mug. "All I'm saying, Andrea, is that you should pray about it. We all need to seek Adonai's will for our lives—if you're not surrendered to that, you aren't surrendered at all."

"I *am* surrendered to His will!" Andrea frowned, trying to convince Ruth, as well as herself. "I just don't want to be married again."

Ruth smiled sympathetically. "How can you be, hon? If you won't even ask Him what His will is?"

"But, doesn't God give you the desires of your heart? My heart doesn't desire marriage!"

"Well, if it's Adonai's will, maybe you should pray about it and ask Him to change your heart."

"I don't want my heart changed. I like it the way it is." Andrea teased, but only partially.

"Then maybe you should ask him to change your heart about not wanting to change your heart!"

Andrea stared across the table. "Ruth. . .! She stretched out the name to three syllables, "My heart is fine the way it is!"

Ruth squinted at her friend. "Andrea, listen to you! I've never heard you say anything that even came close to not wanting what God wants—and here, you don't even want to find that out?"

"What if he says he wants me to get married, and Joel—or whoever—ends up just being another Evan?" Her voice was small and pleading, "I can't do that again, Ruth." She swallowed hard then took a sip of her tea, averting her tearful eyes.

Ruth watched her friend for a long moment. "Andrea, I've never seen you in such a state! Maybe this isn't about marriage at all. Maybe this is really just about trusting God."

Chapter 13

The summer had been busy but uneventful, and now that it was over Rae looked forward to being dropped from the flight schedule and catching up on her work in the hangar. When Labor Day came and went and she still found her name on the schedule, she was not happy. Halfway through September, she stopped at the bulletin board next to the break room, and zeroed in on the new schedule; once again, her name was all over it. Eyes narrowing, she snorted. Snatching the schedule off the bulletin board, the push pins flying in different directions, Rae went looking for Sam. Bursting into his office, she waved the paper in the air next to her head. "What is this?"

Surprised, and a little startled, Sam glanced up and answered in his calm, easy manner. "I can't tell for sure from here, but it looks like the schedule I just posted."

"Summer's over. What's my name still doing on it?" Rae glared at him.

Sam cocked his head to one side, surprised at her. "Your name is still on it because we still need you to take flights. I only had one student finish, the rest are still training." He watched as Rae's jaw clenched. "Is something wrong, Rae?"

"Yeah, something's wrong! First, I was only supposed to fly for a couple of weeks and that turned into a couple of months, and then it turned into all summer—and now it's turning into fall, too. I'm behind on everything because I'm flying your routes!"

Sam's eyebrows arched. "Rae, take it easy."

"No, I'm not going to take it easy. I've been 'taking it easy' since May. Now it's into September and nothing has changed. Dad said for the pilots to help me in their downtime, but no one has. I'm helping you guys out, but no one is helping me!"

Sam stared at her, stunned. Ignoring her diatribe, he squinted at his sister. "Is everything okay, Rae? It isn't like you to get so worked up over something like this."

"I'm fine. I just wish everyone would get off my back!"

"Off your back. . .? Look around you, Rae—no one's on your back. I'll talk to Dad, if you want, but you know he wouldn't put you in the air, unless he had to. Things just haven't eased up the way they usually do after summer. Business is good—what can I say?"

She flung the schedule onto his desk. "You can say, 'Rae, you don't need to fly anymore'—for starters. Then maybe you could say, 'What can I do to help you get caught up on your maintenance schedules and certs?'—*THAT* would be nice!" She gestured in the air animatedly, her speech heavy with sarcasm. "Or, how about, 'Can I type up your monthly reports for the last three months?—The ones you haven't *gotten to* yet?'—THAT would help a lot!"

Sam stared at her. "What. . .? Seriously, Rae, what is going on? I've never seen you like this—ever!"

"Well, get used to it, because maybe it's the 'new' Rae!"

"I was kind of hoping the old Rae would be back pretty soon." Immediately, Rae stiffened at her dad's voice behind her, then she grimaced and closed her eyes, blushing. Joe spoke again, "What's this I'm hearing, Rae? This isn't like you at all."

Sam hurried to intercede, "Um, she just saw that she's flying on the next schedule again. It's okay, Dad, we were just discussing it."

"That didn't sound like a discussion; it sounded more like a hissy-fit." Joe eyed Rae's back, waiting for her to turn around and face him, but she didn't.

Sam waved him off. "It's okay, Dad, really—I'm handling it."

"Okay, Sam, I'll just let you get on with things, then." His eyes shifted again to his daughter's back, "Rae, can I see you in my office when you're done here?"

Rae nodded wordlessly, still without turning around. After a moment, Joe moved on from the doorway.

Sam leaned back in his chair and leaned an elbow on one of its arms. Resting a cheek on the ends of his fingers, he sighed, waiting.

Rae deflated, "I'm sorry, Sam."

"Don't worry about it. Really." He watched her for a moment. "So, what's going on, Rae?"

Her eyes downcast, Rae just muttered, "Nothing." Her voice was barely audible.

Sam leaned forward, "Oh, I don't know about that. Anything I can do to help?"

"No, I'm handling it."

Seeing no evidence of that, Sam eyed her doubtfully for a moment, and then took a guess, "Is Kirk bugging you again? You want me to talk to him?"

Rae shrugged him off, shaking her head rapidly. "No, that's okay—thanks. He's not bugging me—well, no more than usual."

Sam sighed, "Okay, well, I wish I could take you off the schedule, Rae, but I'm really over a barrel right now, and I'm sorry to say I don't know when it will let up."

Rae shifted uncomfortably. "I'm sorry for going off like that." She gestured toward the mangled schedule on Sam's desk. "Just put me in where you need me. I'll deal with it."

"Okay, I'll do that. I appreciate it, Rae—and I'll lean on everyone to pitch in more and help you out with your scut-work."

Rae nodded, still hanging her head. "Thanks."

Shuffling across the hangar to her office, Rae suddenly remembered her dad's request and reversed her trajectory. Stepping through the door into the front office, she faced Patty. "Well, hi, Rae. Whatcha need?"

"Dad said he wanted to see me." Rae's voice was as deadpan as her face.

"Sure, Rae—just go on in."

Rae shuffled down the hall to Joe's office. She knocked softly when she came to his door and a moment later, Joe's voice beckoned her in. Head hanging, Rae slid into the chair across from her father's desk and began sliding her locket back and forth across its chain. Joe watched her for a long moment, waiting for her to raise her eyes to him. Letting go of the locket, she fussed in her seat, shifting uncomfortably, huffing and puffing as she wrestled within herself. She winced and snorted, glancing at the floor around her, then at the wall to one side, then the other, trying to figure out what to say, but no matter what spin she put on it, nothing she could come up with would justify her outburst in the hangar and snarling at Sam the way she had. Sighing heavily, her face reflecting her disappointment in herself, she finally raised her eyes to her father across the desk from her. Joe met her forlorn gaze and arched his eyebrows, but only for a moment before Rae again dropped her eyes to her lap.

An elbow on his desk, Joe rested his cheek in his palm waiting. After a few moments, Rae lifted her eyes to his, winced and looked away. Holding her mouth askew, she shook her head, sighed, then glanced up at her dad again. Joe tilted his head, one eyebrow arched, waiting expectantly. Rae sighed then nodded almost imperceptibly and Joe smiled and nodded as well. The tension visibly drained from Rae's face and shoulders, and she just sighed again. Joe smiled and chuckled, "I'm glad we could have this little talk, sweetheart." Rae smiled weakly in spite of herself, then stood and let herself out of his office.

** *** **

Two days later, Rusty came through the break room door, his chin skyward, his fingers probing his neck. "Am I bleeding?"

Luke glanced up, puzzled. Squinting, he scanned Rusty's neck. "No. Why?—Did you cut yourself shaving, or something?"

"No. Rae just bit my head off—again!"

Luke chuckled as he finished his chocolate milk. "What was it this time?"

"I don't know. Maybe I parted my hair on the wrong side." He examined himself and his clothes; "Oh, here's the reason—my socks are green," he chided, smiling, but only partially joking, "What in the world is eating her lately?"

"I don't know, but whatever you do, don't mention hormones."

Rusty grinned, "No, I would never go there! Who made that mistake?"

"Glen, and he barely lived to tell about it."

Rusty chuckled and nodded, "No, I'm a firm believer in never ticking-off your mechanic—if you can avoid it, that is." When Luke eyed him skeptically, Rusty quickly added, "I just haven't been able to avoid it lately."

Luke shook his head. "None of us can."

Jesse stepped to the doorway then hesitated, still staring back into the hangar for a moment before coming in. "Well, Rae seems to have developed a liking for pilots."

Luke squinted at him skeptically. "For pilots...?"

"Yeah, she's been eating them for lunch!" Jesse chuckled then nodded warily. "She just polished off Steve."

The other two chuckled, then Luke asked, "What did Steve do?"

"I think he's guilty of existing on the same planet as her," Jesse teased, but not completely, "Yeah, if she keeps this up, no one will be back to work for us next spring!"

A minute later, Steve bounded through the door, then side stepped, pressing himself against the wall next to it. "Hide me!" His antics elicited laughter from the others.

Jesse waved him in. "This is the man-cave—you're safe in here; Rae eats in her office."

For the next ten minutes, the four of them shared 'grumpy Rae stories' and poked fun at the trivial nature of her complaints. Somewhere during that time, Ben wandered in unnoticed. He stood at the door leaning against the jamb for several minutes before his presence finally caught Jesse's eye. Having an idea, he turned and squinted at Ben, signing and speaking, "Ben, you work with her. Has Rae been grumpy with you, too?" Ben only shrugged, nodding. Jesse shook his head, "Wow, it's been, what—two or three weeks now? How do you stand it, Ben? Day after day, like that?"

Ben shrugged and signed as he spoke, "I'm deaf, remember? I just close my eyes." Surprised and amused, the other four laughed out loud.

But Luke pressed it, "Seriously, Ben. What's her problem?"

Ben shrugged again and spoke in his distinctive tones. "She won't say, but I can take a guess, so I just let it go when she's grumpy."

"You just let it go? Wow!"

"So, what's your guess?" The four spoke together, leaning toward Ben.

Ben didn't expect Rusty or Steve to know or understand, but he squinted at his brothers, disappointed in them. "You don't have any idea?"

"No. What. . .?"

Ben shook his head, incredulous. "Do you ever pay attention to anyone besides yourself?" Still his brother stared at him blankly. Palms upward, Ben gave them a hint. "What time of the year is it?"

Shrugging, they answered in unison, "Fall."

Ben tried again, "What has Rae done every year at this time for as long as we can remember?" Jesse and Luke thought for a moment, coming up empty; still at a loss, they shrugged. Ben looked at them, disgusted, before finally spelling it out. "She goes holiday shopping with mom."

Steve and Rusty just stared, still puzzled, but the impact of Ben's words was immediate on his two brothers. They both grimaced, suddenly sorrowful, and their shoulders sagged, along with their countenances. "She's missing Mom and we're sitting here making fun of her?" Jesse closed his eyes and pressed his lips together, shaking his head slowly. "Man, we are absolute pigs."

He got no argument from Luke.

Chapter 14

Except for her disastrous lunch with Joel in July, the summer months passed quietly for Andrea who ventured out only occasionally with friends, going to the movies, a dinner, or to lunch after Shabbat services. Now, with the fall approaching, the congregants at Beth Chesed V' Emet, along with synagogues around the world, looked forward to celebrating the Fall Feasts—the annual prophetic 'rehearsals' for the second coming of Yeshua.

Sid led the services for Yom Teruah—the day of the 'Sounding,' symbolic of the 'Last Trump' and the return of Yeshua. Then, ten days later, Yom Kippur—the corporate Day of Atonement, symbolizing the *Kippora—the Covering*, who is Yeshua himself—who 'covers' the sin of those who have put their trust in Him. Finally, Sukkot arrived—the Feast of Tabernacles—or *booths*; the week-long celebration of when Messiah Yeshua again makes his abode with us. Each year, Beth Chesed V' Emet celebrated this event by reserving a lakeside picnic area and campsite, gathering together for fun and fellowship by day. And also by night, for those adventurous enough to pitch their 'sukkah'—or tent—and brave the outdoors under the stars for any or every night that week. The Fall Feasts culminated in the final afternoon and evening of Sukkot, and everyone who was able turned out for the celebration.

Parking her car in the grass alongside one of the roads near the campground, Andrea got out and made her way along the uneven ground as she circled to the rear of her vehicle. Opening the cargo door, she reached into her tote bag, pulling out her tube of sunscreen and quickly slathered her face, neck, and arms, then pitched the tube back into the striped bag. Her first Sukkot without Evan to carry the heavier things, she squinted, shaking her head at all she had brought; plotting out in her mind how to get it all to the picnic area on her own. Reaching for her folding chair and her small ice chest, she decided to come back for the tub of fruit once she'd located her friends and found a spot to set up. Closing her cargo door, Andrea hoisted the strap of the sheath that held her folding chair onto her shoulder then, taking hold of the tote bag and the small ice chest, she straightened up, glancing around to get her bearings.

The roads that intersected near where she parked her car were little more than paved paths. These paths meandered through the woodland campground and picnic area that nestled up to the surrounding lake in finger-like peninsulas—as though a giant hand reaching out into the water. Behind Andrea, one small peninsula held the campsites, where families had pitched their tents for the week. To her left, another smaller peninsula held the picnic area; the main gathering spot for the synagogue's festivities. Those at the campsites could easily walk up to the intersection and make a left to go down the gradual slope to the picnic area at the edge of the water.

Trudging up to the intersecting paths under her load, Andrea rounded the corner to her left, then weaved her way through the stream of people coming from the picnic area on their way to their cars, their campsites, or the bathrooms. Arriving at the clearing below, she scouted amoung the clusters of people relaxing and talking, enjoying their time with their families and friends from Beth Chesed V' Emet. At last, in the grassy area beyond the picnic tables, she found Donna and Tammy, with their husbands and children, and headed for them. The friends exchanged greetings and Andrea set up her chair and ice chest, then, leaving her tote bag, she set out again to retrieve the fruit she'd brought for the huge, synagogue-wide potluck that evening. Hiking back up the gradual slope to her vehicle, she retrieved the tub of fruit, and set out again to return to the picnic area. It was only a couple of minutes before she came upon a slight-framed, elderly woman, who frowned in deliberation as she pivoted her head in various directions. Andrea stopped next to her. "Are you lost?"

The small woman looked up hopefully at Andrea. "Oh, aren't you sweet to stop and ask!" Andrea immediately noticed a pronounced accent. The woman, gestured toward the path behind them as she spoke, "I just came up here to go to the restroom—and let me tell you, that was no small feat!—Do I look like someone who owns hiking boots? I guess I should have bought some before coming! Who knew? Anyway sweetheart, I think I made a wrong turn, or something 'cause now, I can't figure out which road I was on when I walked up here."

Andrea smiled as the woman spoke. *She sounds like she's from New York. . .or maybe Miami?* In her limited experience, Andrea could never tell the difference. She nodded to the woman. "Yeah, the roads sure do look alike from here. Are you looking for your campsite or the picnic area?"

Amused, the elderly woman scoffed. "Campsite? Oh, please!—Do I look like I could live in a tent?" The woman waved her off and the two chuckled, the woman continued, "The picnic area? Is that where all the people are?"

Andrea nodded, "That's right."

"Okay, then that's where I'm headed!"

"So am I—would you like me to walk with you?"

"Oh, bless you dear!"

Andrea extended her hand, "I'm Andrea."

Claire shook the hand. "Nice to meet you, Andrea—I'm Claire."

Andrea smiled, "Hi Claire. Just follow me." Andrea slowed her pace for the elderly woman and the two conversed easily as they walked along until the paved road gave way to gravel and dirt, and the way became uneven. Seeing Claire stepping unsteadily on the gravelly slope, Andrea moved her tub of fruit to her hip, holding it with one hand, and offered her other arm to the woman to help steady her.

"Oh, bless you, dear! Next year, I'll know to bring my mountain climbing gear!" Chuckling, Andrea returned the woman's smile, doubting Claire owned such a thing. The two picked their way around the ruts and dips until they arrived at the picnic area, where Andrea handed her tub of fruit to one of the ladies at the long food table. The woman who received it promptly removed the lid, added a serving tong, and deposited the tub into the proper section along the culinary runway. Andrea turned her attention back to the elderly lady at her side. "Can I help you find someone?"

"I'm here with my grandchildren; we're visiting from Florida. My son just moved here."

At that, Andrea decided her accent must be from Miami. "What do they look like?" Shielding her eyes against the sun, she turned to the crowd as she spoke, ". . .and how many of them are there?"

"There are four of them, three boys and a girl—all in their twenties, and then a baby."

Andrea scanned the clusters of people. "Is that them over there?" She pointed ahead to their left, "—by the barbecue?"

Claire followed Andrea's pointing finger. "Oh yes!—that's them! Bless you, dear!" She stretched the final word into two syllables. Pleased, Andrea escorted the woman the rest of the way to her family members.

As they approached, the twenty-something girl holding the baby raised her eyes, her relief was immediate. "Grandma, there you are! I was getting worried!" Though the elderly woman spoke with the accent, it was not so with her granddaughter.

"I'm sorry, dear. Believe me, the next time you offer to go with me, I'm going to take you up on it!"

"Did you get lost?"

"I sure did! But this nice lady found me and made sure I got back safely. That slope back down was a pill!" Two of the young men stepped forward and took her hands, the other pulled over a chair and helped her into it. Andrea felt as though she had seen two of the boys before, but couldn't place them, especially since they said they were from Florida.

The young woman with the baby regarded Andrea appreciatively. "Thank you so much! I was afraid she might fall and hurt herself, but she insisted on going by herself!"

Clair gestured animatedly with both palms out, "Yes, I know, dear, and I learned my lesson!"

That, with her accent, reminded Andrea of the little old Jewish ladies depicted in movies, which both charmed and amused Andrea. She smiled warmly, "Oh, it was no problem. We had a nice little chat on the way."

The five of them broke into a lively and congenial conversation that lasted several minutes before Joel stepped up to the small group, smiling brightly. "Well, hello Andrea!"

Andrea immediately bristled, then caught herself. Not wishing to be awkward in front of her new friends, she nodded to him. "Hi, Joel."

"You all look like you're having a nice conversation," he observed. Andrea tried to be gracious, but wished he would move on.

Looking up at Joel, Claire seemed amused by his remark. "Listen to you! *'You all'*—You've been here a few months and already you're speaking Southern!"

The others, including Joel, laughed out loud. Andrea squinted at them, and then at Joel, as the baby in the young woman's arms reached out for him and Joel received him from the girl's arms and cooed to him.

Suddenly uneasy, Andrea puzzled, "You know each other?"

"Oh, that's my son, dear," Claire bent her wrist toward Joel, "The one who just moved here recently." She reached up and patted Joel's elbow as she spoke.

Eyes wide, Andrea stared at Joel. "I've been talking to your family?" *No wonder those boys look familiar.*

Joel grinned that mischievous grin of his, obviously amused and delighted. "Yes, Andrea, this is my mom, Claire." He held the baby on one arm as he gestured to each person. "My daughter Madelyn—we call her Maddy—and my grandson, Shay." He gestured to the baby on his arm and then at the three young men, "My sons Jake and Micah, and my son-in-law, David." Andrea nodded at each one, trying to keep her breathing normal. Joel continued with the introduction, "Everyone, this is Andrea." He gestured to her with his palm up.

Claire brightened. "Yes—me and Andrea had a very nice chat on the way back from the restroom! She is an absolute delight, Joel—you should get to know her better!"

"I've been trying to, Mom." Joel blurted out without thinking—and immediately regretted it.

188

Suddenly Claire's eyebrows arched as she connected the dots. "Oh, is she the little lady you railroaded into having lunch with you?"

Joel blushed then mumbled, "Yes, Mom." Smiles broke across all faces of the Greenbaum family—except Joel's.

Blushing, Andrea spoke through a forced smile and clenched teeth. "He told you about that?" Although her question was directed at Claire, she stared incredulously at Joel.

Claire turned to Andrea, "Well, no wonder you wanted to leave, dear—that was *very* rude of him!" Everyone chuckled except Andrea and Joel.

Joel grimaced. "Um, Mom. . .?" He stretched her moniker into two syllables.

Waving him off, Claire continued, "Oh, don't pay no attention to him, dear—he's a good kid, but he can be a little pushy—and sometimes he says stuff before he has thought it through. But like I said, he's a good kid."

At forty-seven, Joel winced at being referred to as a 'kid,' especially in front of Andrea. As he hurried to shush his mother, Andrea smiled and chuckled in spite of herself, amused to see Joel in the hot seat this time. Anxious to make her escape, she leaned down to the elderly woman in the chair and took her hand, shaking it. "Well, Claire, my friends are waiting for me over there. It was very nice meeting you—maybe we'll get to talk again before you head back to Florida." She straightened up and smiled to each of Joel's children. "And it was very nice meeting all of you, too. I hope you all have a pleasant visit while you're here in Georgia." She nodded again to them and bowed out and away.

Claire turned to her son, "Such a nice lady, Joel! You need to hang onto her!"

Joel forced himself to smile as he rubbed his forehead, and then his chin, and sighed as he shook his head. "I'm trying to, Mom."

Chapter 15

Having read an e-Blast from the synagogue about an acquaintance who was an inpatient at Redlands Medical Center, Joel drove down there from Heartland to visit him. After spending nearly an hour with the man, Joel excused himself, and as he stood waiting at the elevator, he mulled over his thoughts. *Andrea works here somewhere. Where did Sid say it was? Wasn't it a clinic?* He glanced around him. Noticing the unit's reception desk, a grin crept across his face. *Well, it's at least worth a try. Nothing ventured, nothing gained, right?* Stepping up to the green-shirted woman at the desk, he leaned close. "Um, isn't there a clinic here in this hospital somewhere? For outpatients?"

"Yes, sir, it's on the second floor, in the back of the hospital."

He grinned widely, "How do I find it?" The directions she gave were sketchy and he tried his best to follow them, but since the hospital had been added onto a number of times, the further he ventured, the more maze-like the corridors became, and he had to stop a couple of times along the way for clarification. Rounding yet another corner, Joel stepped up to a reception desk, lost again. The two nurses at the desk conferred over something, and didn't immediately notice him until Joel leaned in. "Um, where can I find the outpatient clinic?"

Arlene and Yvonne stopped talking and glanced up. Arlene smiled, "Right here. You found it!"

Joel grinned, surprised. "Oh really? That's good!"

Yvonne turned her attention to the man at the desk. "I'm the charge nurse. May I help you?"

"Um. . ." Joel hesitated. Since his flowers seemed to have been received so tepidly, he began to wonder if this is such a good idea. Suddenly nervous, he had to clear his throat, "Um, is Andrea working today?"

The mention of her name by this unknown man arched the eyebrows of the two nurses at the desk and caught the attention of nearby nurses. Immediately, they stopped what they were doing and eyed the stranger at the desk. Yvonne was cautious, "Are you a friend of hers?"

Considering Andrea's aversion tactics since their lunch together, Joel was not sure how to answer that. So, he sought the easiest answer that would hopefully afford him his desired response. "We go to the same synagogue."

The two women in front of him—and those he could not see behind him—seemed suddenly delighted at that. Yvonne grinned, "Is that right?" She and Arlene exchanged glances furtively, then Yvonne winced. "I'm sorry, she's off today."

Joel's shoulders and countenance sagged. "Oh, okay. Thanks anyways."

Wishing for a way to find out more about him, Yvonne tried again, "Would you like to leave *your name* so we can let her know you were here?"

Joel considered that for a moment, deciding against it. "Um, no, that's okay—but thanks."

Always quick, Arlene connected a couple of dots and took a guess. "Are you the one who sent the flowers?"

Surprised by the question, Joel hesitated initially. In a nano-second, he thought back on Andrea's exasperation when she coolly thanked him for the flowers, then asked that he not do that again. Still, he found no reason to be coy with these ladies and shrugged. "Uh, yeah, that was me." Now he had everyone's *full* attention and a cluster of nurses closed in around him.

Thinking fast, Arlene jumped in, smiling widely, "They were beautiful. I'm Arlene." She extended her hand, hoping that would encourage the man to divulge his name—it worked.

"Um, thanks. I'm Joel." Though curious about Andrea's reaction to the flowers, Joel was afraid to ask.

Sandra leaned in, "So, are you two dating, or something?"

Waxing dramatic, Joel let his head droop, and exaggerated his sigh. "I wish. . ." The faces around him brightened as the nurses exchanged enthusiastic murmurs, and Joel ventured further. "I've tried, but she won't go out with me. I finagled her into going to lunch with me once, but I guess I got a little too eager and scared her off." He shrugged, sheepishly. "That's why I sent the flowers. I've been backpedaling ever since."

Blunt as ever, Arlene playfully asserted, "Andrea said her sister sent them."

Joel blushed, chagrined, and chuckled softly, "Yeah, that doesn't surprise me; she wasn't real happy with me for sending them. That's when I found out she hadn't mentioned me to her coworkers."

Amusement spread across the faces around him. Arlene grinned, "Oh?—Did she take you to the tool shed for that?"

Joel shrugged and nodded, "More or less." Soft laughter erupted around him.

Arlene's eyes narrowed, an idea forming. "Hey, Joel, can I get your phone number?"

A bit surprised, Joel squinted at her. "You want my phone number?" Then playfully suspicious, he added, "What for?—A mercy date?" The nurses laughed.

Arlene only shrugged. "I just have an idea, that's all."

Joel groaned, "Oh, please don't get me in hot water with Andrea!—I'm still in the doghouse for sending the flowers here!" Again, those around him laughed, amused at his candor.

"No, don't worry—I won't tell Andrea. Besides, she never stays mad for long." Arlene seemed certain, so Joel shrugged and gave her his cell number. After another round of bantering, he said his goodbyes and excused himself. The nurses watched his retreating back until he disappeared around the corner at the end of the hall. Grinning widely, Arlene averred, "I *knew* those weren't 'sister' flowers!"

Sandra stepped closer, "So, what are you thinking, Arlene?— Why did you get his phone number?"

She shrugged. "He seems like a nice guy. I'm thinking maybe Andrea needs a little help seeing that."

"Are you going to set them up on a date?"

Arlene's forehead furrowed. "I don't know yet. I think we should check him out first, for sure. Maybe all of us can meet him for dinner somewhere. If he seems nice, then we'll think of something." The others were all for that and put their heads together to figure out a day that would work. That very evening seemed to work the best for most, so Arlene called Joel right back. "Is this Joel...?—Yeah, hey—this is Arlene at the Outpatient Clinic...Yeah, that's right, Andrea's work." She chuckled, "Yeah, it *was* quick, wasn't it? Listen, we were wondering if you'd like to go to dinner with some of us." Arlene laughed again, "Yes, I'm totally serious!...You would? Is tonight good?...How about Fabiani's?...No, the one in Middleton—it's on the same street as the hospital, but it's closer to the Interstate—just Google it...

Six-thirty? Okay, great!—we'll see you then." Arlene ended the call as the ladies around her grinned excitedly.

When Joel arrived that evening, he was seated quickly with five of Andrea's co-workers and grinned, eyeing them uncertainly. "So, what's this about? Are you sure it's not a mercy date?"

Stacie arched an eyebrow at him. "Hey, if after six months you still can't get anywhere with Andrea—*then* we'll talk 'mercy date,' okay?"

Nodding, Joel chuckled, "Okay, I'll keep that in mind."

Arlene took the lead, "Well, we talked and we're thinking you need a little help with Andrea, but before we consider that, we need to check you out first."

This amused Joel and he couldn't help chuckling. "Check me out? You mean, like an audition?"

"No, more like *an inquisition.*" Arlene deliberately tried to sound intimidating. When Joel's eyes widened, everyone laughed. "But let's get our order in, and then we can talk."

Opening his menu, his semi-lunch with Andrea still uncomfortably fresh in his mind, Joel couldn't help groaning within himself over this reminder of it. The six of them dove into their menus then recited their choices to the server, an amused young man who playfully made reference to Joel and the harem of ladies around him. Minutes later, he returned with soft breadsticks and a tossed salad and offered to grate parmesan cheese over everything.

Once everyone had their salad and a breadstick, Arlene jumped right in. "So, where are you from, Joel?"

"Originally from New York, but I've been in Florida for the last twenty years, or so." He took a bite of his salad.

Arlene snatched her napkin off her lap and tossed it onto the table, feigning instant rejection. "Okay, forget it! We're not helping you out just so you can whisk her away to Florida!"

Joel protested, grinning, "No, no, no! I live here now. You asked where I'm from!"

Capitulating, Arlene retrieved her napkin from the table, and again took her seat. "Well, okay; but, if you end up marrying her, you're not allowed to move away, is that clear?" Arlene teased, but only partially.

Joel nodded, "I'll do my best." After that, the questions came in rapid-fire from everyone in turn.

"So, do you have any kids?" One of them asked.

"Yes, I have three. Two sons and a daughter. My daughter is married and has a baby."

Before he was able to take a breath, another piped up, "So, are you divorced, or what?"

"No," he explained, "my wife passed away about four years ago."

"Was that your first wife?"

"She was my *only* wife."

His answer was met with a chorus of "awwws."

"So why haven't you remarried before this?" Someone else asked.

Another chimed in before he could respond, ". . .Haven't found the right one?"

"No, I just haven't been looking," he answered, and then added, "...until Andrea."

His answer elicited another round of "awwws" until Arlene turned the questions back on, "So how long have you known Andrea?"

"I met her for the first time in July."

"So, it's been almost two months and you've never even been on a date with her?"

"Well, just that one lunch date—and it wasn't a whole date."

"Not a whole date? What does that mean?"

"Well, I kind of finagled her into a deal to go to lunch when I met her back in July. I forgot that I'd come to services with a friend and didn't have my car, so she ended up driving." This amused his audience and they chided him liberally.

"So you finagled a deal? What kind of deal?"

Joel winced. "Um, since she didn't tell you about me, I'm not so sure she'd want me telling you that."

"Okay, skip the deal for now. Tell us about the lunch. What happened that made it not a whole date?"

"Um, well, we went to the Fabiani's in Heartland and she. . .uh. . . left early."

"Left early? Why did she do that?" Joel squinted, amused with the ladies. *Wow, they weren't kidding about this being an inquisition.* Before he could answer, Arlene interrupted, "Wait! Didn't you say she drove?" Taking a bite off his breadstick, Joel nodded. Eyebrows arched again, and Arlene stared incredulously, "So she *stranded* you at the restaurant?" Joel winced at his unintended disclosure, and just shrugged as he chewed. The laughter that followed was even heartier, all in disbelief that mild-mannered Andrea would do such a thing. Through her laughter, Arlene had to know, "So, what happened then? Did you have to walk home?"

"No," Joel leaned back in his chair, still grinning, "When she realized that she had left me there, she came back and got me." Finally, as the laughter subsided, he shrugged again. "Oh well, like I said, I was too eager. I guess it's too early for her, she's probably not over her husband's death yet."

Arlene only rolled her eyes, blurting out in her familiar bluntness, "Oh, I don't think it's his death she needs to get over as much as their marriage!"

This revelation stunned Joel. He noticed the other nurses nodding in silent agreement. Surprised and curious, he tilted his head, staring intently, "Her marriage. . .?"

Not one to mince words, Arlene nodded, emphatic. "Oh, heck yeah—her husband was a jerk to her. Some of us tried to get her to divorce him, but she wouldn't because of her beliefs."

Dismayed, Joel uttered, "Really. . .?" Then he shook his head, his voice barely audible, "Wow, that explains *a lot.*" Moved in his heart with compassion, he winced, unable to respond to that. Yet, despite his sadness for Andrea, he tingled with excitement at the same time, so he folded his hands together, lest these ladies notice them trembling.

Redirecting the conversation, Sandra piped up, "So, you've been backpedaling ever since that lunch?"

Refocusing, Joel cleared his throat. "Yeah, pretty much." The ladies chuckled again and the inquisition continued on through the entire meal.

At last, while they awaited their coffee and dessert, Arlene got serious. "Okay, Joel, since Andrea doesn't have a father around here to ask this—I will. What are your intentions?"

"My intentions. . .?"

"Yeah, " she affirmed, ". . .your *intentions.*" Four other serious faces nodded along with Arlene's.

Joel hesitated, "I don't know, ladies. Telling Andrea my intentions is what abruptly shortened our lunch."

Five sets of eyebrows arched; Sandra's in particular. "Why?" Suddenly, she squinted, "You didn't tell her you wanted to marry her, did you?" When Joel winced, their eyes all widened further.

Arlene laughed out loud, "You told her you wanted to marry her on your *first date?*"

Joel sighed, "Yes. I think that was my first mistake." The ladies' response to that was immediate, hearty laughter.

Always facetious, Arlene chuckled, "Well, gee—I don't know why that would scare her off! We were thinking of helping you, Joel, but you're not making it easy by saying stuff like that!"

The banter continued, with Joel enjoying it as much as the nurses. Finally, after dessert, with mornings coming early, Joel bowed out graciously and headed for home. As soon as he left, the ladies huddled at the table to come up with a way to help Andrea see the light.

Chapter 16

In early November, Joe Gerrard leaned on the door jamb between the office and the hangar watching Rae as she worked on Luke's aircraft, noting her countenance. *She looks like she's carrying the weight of the world.* Rae stood on a stool, reached over the nose, and opened the oil hatch on top of the engine, then reached inside and pulled out the dipstick to check the oil level. When she pivoted to get the light to strike the dipstick markings, she noticed him; smiling, she nodded. Joe smiled and nodded back before stepping away from the doorway. He didn't leave, but stood there contemplating.

Patty glanced up at him over her computer. "Do you need something, Boss?"

Forehead furrowed, Joe thought a moment, "Patty, tell me what you think. Does it seem like Rae has changed lately?"

"Changed how?"

"She's always been so forgiving and has taken things in stride, right?"

". . .Or just made a joke of it and laughed it off—yes."

"Exactly. but lately—the last few months—she's. . .I don't know. She and Kirk just don't get along, but I've never seen her hold a grudge like this. I don't know when that changed—and I don't know how much of it is Kirk just being 'Kirk,' and how much of it is Rae being...so...whatever Rae is being...I don't know."

"Grouchy...?"

"Yeah, like she's got a chip on her shoulder. Have you noticed it, too?"

"Well, she's never been grouchy to me, but I've seen her be short with a few others, especially Kirk—and with people on the phone." Patty thought for a moment, "The rest of the time she actually seems kind of sullen—like she's stewing over something, but I don't know what."

"Yeah, stewing about something—that's what it is. I don't know if Kirk started it, or if he's just getting caught in the cross-fire."

"From what I hear, it may be some of both."

"I was just watching her and she just seems like she's got a lot on her mind. Has she said anything to you about anything being wrong?"

"No sir. I wish she would, because I'd sure like to help. I've tried a few times to get her to open up, but when I do, she just looks at me for a few seconds, and says she's fine."

Joe's eyebrows knitted. "Really? That's what she says? Just *'fine'?"* Patty nodded, and shrugged, and Joe sighed. "She used to be more open, didn't she? I've just been noticing it lately. I can't figure out if it's because she's growing up and getting more inside herself, or if something is wrong. I wish her mom was here." Joe winced at the memory of his loss. "Lynn always knew how to get to the bottom of things, and she always seemed to know what to say that would fix it."

"Yes, sir, Lynn was sure good at that."

With the mention of his wife, something occurred to Joe. "You know, I wonder if this really started with Kirk—maybe it was brewing before that. I mean, just talking about Lynn right then...maybe this has more to do with Rae losing her mom."

"What do you mean, Joe?"

"She was so upset when Lynn died but she would never talk about it. Then, didn't Kirk come to fly for us a month or two later?" As Patty nodded, Joe shrugged. "I was just thinking: maybe Kirk irritating her the way he does is just bringing all of that back to the surface."

"After so long?" Patty thought for a moment, then shrugged. "It could be, Boss. I don't remember Rae ever being like this before that."

"Either way, it isn't good—not for Rae and not for business." Turning again to the doorway, Joe watched his daughter for another moment. A hand on one hip, he leaned with his other hand against the door jamb, drumming it with his fingertips. "I need to get to the bottom of this one way or the other." Joe winced. "Still, I hate to rub salt in a wound and bring up her mom if that's not the problem." Coming to a conclusion, he nodded "I'll try talking to Rae about it tonight. Just pray that she'll talk about it *to me*, okay?"

"Okay, Boss. I'll do that."

That night after dinner, it was Rae's turn to do the dishes, and Luke and Ben shuffled out to the front room to watch TV. Hoping for a chance to talk to her alone, Joe stayed behind to help Rae clear the table. When they had piled the dishes into the sink, and Rae started the water running to rinse them, Joe stuck around to load the dishwasher, praying in his thoughts before he spoke. "Desirae, you seem kind of unhappy lately. Is everything okay? Anything you'd like to talk about?"

Rae squinted at her dad, and then glanced away. "I'm fine, Dad. Why?"

Joe frowned, *Hmm. . .Just like Patty said.* He tried again, "Things seem kind of strained between you and Kirk. What's going on between the two of you?"

Instantly, Rae grimaced, stretching his name into two syllables and two tones, her irritation evident. "Kirk. . .? Nothing is going on between us!" She rinsed the plate in her hand and passed it to her dad.

Joe accepted it and set it into the bottom rack of the dishwasher. "Sweetheart, I know it's pretty far from 'true love,' but it sure isn't 'nothing.'"

"What do you mean?"

"This feud you two seem to be having."

"Feud. . .?" She handed him a freshly rinsed serving bowl.

Joe set the bowl in next to the silverware caddy. "Don't be coy with me, Desirae. I'm not blind. Even your brothers are talking about it."

"My brothers. . .?" she snorted, making a mental note to threaten them in the morning. "I just don't like Kirk, that's all. He irritates me." She handed him another plate.

Joe smiled gently, "Sweetheart, to be honest, it seems like lots of things irritate you lately—and that's not like you. Are you sure there's nothing else wrong?" He hoped if it was about her mother that Rae would be the one to bring it up—so he wouldn't have to.

Rae watched her dad for a longer moment this time. Something inside longed to share her heart with him. *No, talking about Mom will just make him sad...I need to just handle it.* She glanced away and tried to smile again. "I'm fine, Dad. Really."

Joe frowned, *There it is again, the 'I'm fine' brush-off.* He sighed. "So it's just you not liking Kirk? Nothing else?" Rinsing another plate, Rae nodded without looking at him, then handed it to her dad. Eyeing his daughter, Joe accepted the plate, then set it into the bottom rack behind the other. With nothing else to go on, he addressed the 'Kirk' issue. "Rae, it just isn't like you to stay mad at someone for so long—and it seems like more than being mad; it comes pretty close to hostility. It's never been in your nature to be hostile."

"Well, maybe my nature is changing." She tried to make a joke of it, but the edge in her voice made it fall flat, even with her.

"Well, I hope not, sweetheart, because I always admired your good nature, so this wouldn't be a change for the better." Rae sighed and handed him a glass tumbler, then glanced away. Joe held the glass, eyeing his daughter for another moment, before setting it on the top rack "I'd like to help if I can, hon. What's the problem between the two of you?"

"Nothing. I just don't like him." She handed another tumbler to her dad.

Joe set it in the top rack, "Well, that much is obvious."

"He's annoying—full of himself."

"So is just about every other single pilot his age that has come through our hangar, and you've always found a way to get along with them. I have to say, sweetheart, personal differences aside, it's pretty unprofessional to be carrying on like that around the hangar where customers can hear you." Rae just stood at the sink, glowering. When she didn't answer, Joe pressed, "Rae. . .?"

"Dad, he's such a jerk!"

"I know he'll never win any popularity contests with you, but I've never seen you like this. Are you sure you're not taking something out on him?"

"Like what? I can't believe you're taking his side."

Joe kept his voice even. "What side? I'm just saying this isn't like you—and jerk or no jerk, he still works for me—and so do you, little girl, so this needs to stop. At least during business hours—and for your own good, too; it's not healthy to be so angry all the time."

"You act like it's just me. Like he's completely innocent or something."

Joe leaned a hand on the counter, speaking gently, "You know better than that, Desirae. Now, I know you two didn't exactly hit it off when he first came, but that was months ago. I've been staying out of it, hoping you two would settle it like adults, but that doesn't seem to be happening. Now your brothers have said Kirk has made some attempts at peace, but it seems like you're the one who's determined to keep the war going."

Crestfallen, Rae stared at her dad, handing him a handful of silverware. "They said that?"

Joe gathered the silverware from her hands. "Yeah, how's that for a shocker?" He leaned over and began distributing the knives and forks into the silverware caddy as he spoke. "Now, I know Kirk can be annoying; he even annoys me sometimes—but this has been going on for too long, sweetheart. Will you please just make an effort to get along with him? Someone has to make the first move, hon. Now, I don't know how he was raised, but I know how you were. Can't you forgive him for whatever he has done to get you so mad at him?" Joe straightened up and dried his hands.

Rae deflated. She stared dully at the spray of water in front of her, turning another plate over and over under it. After a moment, she softened and sighed, "I'm sorry, Dad. I'll try."

"I appreciate that, hon, I really do." He hugged Rae across her shoulders and leaned down and kissed her on the top of her head. "I love you, sweetheart."

Chapter 17

A blustery morning kept everyone on the ground the following day, as stiff gusts of wind buffeted the hangar. Rae and Ben were the only two not disrupted by it. The others found either busy-work to do, caught up on old paperwork, or helped Rae with hers; she always had plenty of busy work for anyone grounded due to the weather.

Rae threw her weight against the wrench handle trying to loosen a stubborn nut, and heard a faint ping and clink. Immediately, she stopped what she was doing and stepped back, looking around on the cement floor. Seeing her locket between her shoes, she groaned then reached down to pick it up and examined it closely. *Oh good, nothing is broken—the clasp just let go again.* Rae sighed, relieved. *I really need to get that fixed.* She slipped it into the breast pocket of her coveralls and resumed her battle with the nut.

"Hey, Rae!" Luke called out from the break room doorway.

"Over here!" Rae yelled back from behind Sam's Cessna.

"I sorted those files. Where do you want them?" He held a towering stack of manila folders stuffed with papers.

"My office. Just set them on the chair by the door."

"Yes, my queen," Luke teased, and started across the hangar toward Rae's office. Just as he passed in front of the outside door,

Sam opened it and came in—along with a stiff gust of wind that whisked the door, and the newly sorted files, out of the hands that held them. The door banged against the wall and the files gusted in twenty different directions as Sam forced the door closed again.

"You dog!" Luke yelled and laughed at Sam's startled expression, then dove after the scattering papers. Heads came up all around the hangar, and amused faces watched scrambling hands gather the wafting papers.

Rae peeked out from around the Cessna, seeing the files scattered across the floor in the middle of the hangar and the whirlwind of papers still floating to the floor around Luke. "That wasn't my stack of files, was it?"

"Sorry, Rae!" Sam would have had more credibility if he wasn't laughing when he said it.

Immediately, everyone scrambled after the drifting papers, chasing them across the hangar, scooping them off the floor, and snatching them out of the air like clumsy ballerinas as the pages drifted downward. Luke was the only one not completely amused by it. In a split second, two hours of tedious sorting was now everyone's source of entertainment. Joe waved Patty over to the door, not wanting her to miss this spectacle. She watched for a minute, amused, then returned to her desk, chuckling.

Rae found a box and put it on the floor in the center of the vast room; immediately everyone began dumping armfuls of papers into it—and joined those on the floor scrambling for them. In the commotion, Rae's locket slipped out of her pocket, clinking to the floor. It bounced and came to rest near Kirk. Instantly, Rae's smile faded and she lunged to retrieve it, but Kirk, always on the lookout for a new and better way with which to tease Rae, seized the opportunity.

"Oh, a locket!" He snatched it up with glee and examined it more closely. "With a pretty rose on it," he said mockingly, trying to lure her into a game of keep-away. Immediately, Sam, Jesse, and Luke stopped their cavorting, and looked on. Ben stopped when he saw the others staring, and followed their stares to Rae and Kirk.

"Let's look inside and see if there's a picture of the one you love," he teased playfully. Not amused, Rae rose to her knees and reached out to snatch it back, but Kirk was too quick. He pivoted away from Rae and pushed himself to his feet as he pried apart the clasped edges of the locket. Rae jumped to her feet as well and came after Kirk, who dodged her easily, mocking. "Why, yes, there's a picture in here!" He drew the locket close to his face to better see the tiny photograph. "Let's see who Rae loves. . ." He squinted for a moment then his face brightened, "Why. . .it's. . . *it's Rae!* The love of Rae's life. . .is Rae!" Kirk laughed out loud and held up the locket to the men standing around him, expecting them to be amused as well. Their stony faces took him aback. He tried again, "Are you your own best fan, Rae?" Surely, that would get a chuckle out of them. It didn't. He glanced at Rae who was furious and close to tears. Puzzled, he turned his attention back to the others just as Sam stepped forward.

His arm extended, palm skyward, Sam demanded frostily, "Give me the locket, Kirk!"

Baffled, Kirk couldn't imagine Sam's concern. "What's wrong, Sam? Did your picture used to be in here?" He snickered, his chuckle cut short by the unsmiling faces around him.

"Stop it, Kirk! Just give him the locket," Jesse pressed, trying to maintain his composure, "You've done enough damage."

Damage? Exasperated, Kirk huffed and threw up his hands. "Lighten-up, you guys! She has a picture of herself in her own locket!—what a hoot!"

"It's not a picture of Rae," Luke informed, unsmiling, "It's our mother—she died last spring."

Kirk's face fell instantly and flushed. "I. . . I'm sorry. I didn't know," Quietly, he placed the locket into Sam's outstretched hand without looking up, and Sam handed it to Rae. Kirk could see how wounded she felt. "I'm sorry, Rae. Really," his voice trailed off. A moment later, he took notice of Luke's pronoun. *Did he say 'our'?*

Rae accepted her locket back from Sam, then turned and walked away without answering. Disappearing into her office, she closed the door quietly and the men watched the blinds over the window close. The brothers standing around Kirk said nothing—no one knew what to say. They knew he didn't mean to hurt anyone, but they felt wounded, just as Rae did. All, including Kirk, silently wished they could somehow suck the words back from the ears that heard them.

No one condemned Kirk, but neither could any of them bring themselves up from their own tangle of feelings to exonerate him; his remarks had stung them all. After a very tense minute of weighty silence, Ben quietly backed away from the cluster of silent men and shuffled to the aircraft where he had been working before all of this started, and stood staring at the floor. Then, one by one, the remaining brothers, all feeling the need to be alone, sighed and did the same, each going off in their own direction until Kirk was left with Sam.

"I didn't know. . ." Kirk tried again, conscience-stricken and embarrassed.

"I know, man. It's okay."

"And I didn't know she was your sister. So, all of you are brothers?"

Sam nodded. "Uh-huh."

His shoulders slumped. "I didn't know that, either. I mean, the sign out front says 'Gerrard & Son'—not *'sons.'*"

"It's an old sign." Sam could only shrug, then he raised his left hand to Kirk's left shoulder and patted it lightly as he passed by, as he too walked away.

Joe had watched the whole thing from the front office hangar door. When Patty glanced up from her work, Joe's expression was not what she expected. "What's wrong, Boss?"

Joe shook his head. "Wow, sometimes things can turn on a dime."

Patty peered over the top of her glasses at him. "They're not frolicking after papers anymore? What happened?"

"Oh, who knows?—Kirk and Rae were going at it again. It looked like he was teasing her about something, and now Rae's upset. I don't know what he did, but this time it was big—even the boys were glaring at him." Shaking his head, he retreated from the hangar door back to his office, and closed the door.

Alone with his thoughts, Kirk struggled with the jumble of feelings churning up within him. *"OUR mom?"* He grimaced. In an instant, everything made sense—why the Boss thought Rae was so wonderful. Why Rae got along so well with the other guys. Why he couldn't rally even one of them against her—and why he couldn't seem to find his place in that circle. *They're all family!—I am the outsider! I can't believe I didn't figure this out before now!* Somehow, it just didn't seem fair.

Suddenly, Kirk's memory flooded with all the things he'd said to the others. All the times he tried to imply that Rae had relationships with just about everyone there. No wonder they seemed unconcerned—or worse—amused by him. He groaned with embarrassment and closed his eyes. *And Sam's baby really IS just Sam's baby! —No wonder it looked kind of like Rae—he's her brother! Ugh! I'm such an idiot!* He groaned audibly. *O man,*

I teased her about her dead mom. . .! He winced, then corrected. *THEIR dead mom. Why didn't I just stop when Sam said to?* Down to his socks, Kirk knew he was wrong—but he didn't want to be; he *hated* being wrong! He thought again of the wounded expression on Rae's face just before she walked away and closed herself in her office. He felt guilty and it irritated him—and he didn't want to think about how she felt, especially when it made him feel like this. *Wow, I've really blown it this time! How am I ever gonna get out of this one?*

A half hour later, Joe stepped out into the hangar and found no one there. "Sam. . .?" His voice echoed off the walls, "Rae. . .?" He noted the files still strewn across the floor. Exhaling loudly, he threw up his hands and turned and stepped back through the door to the office. "Patty, would you page someone?"

"Who?"

"Anyone! I don't see a single person out there, and no one came when I yelled. Ben could be out there with his head in an engine—put on his light, too."

Patty flipped the switch for Ben's paging light—a bright strobe light in his general work area. Then she reached for her phone and pushed the intercom button, speaking into the handset, "Boys, the Boss is looking for you. Please come to the office. Rae, that includes you, too."

It wasn't long before Jesse poked his head in. "We're all out here, Patty. Does dad want us to come in there?"

"Let me check." She pushed the intercom to Joe's office, "Boss, they're right outside in the hangar. Do you want them in your office or are you going out there?"

"I'll just go out there." Jesse heard his dad's voice over the speaker, and Patty glanced at him for confirmation. He nodded as he backed out, closing the door. A second later, Joe hurried past Patty and out the hangar door. Facing them, Joe glanced around, "Where's Rae? Is she in her office?" Everyone shrugged. Joe sighed and stepped back into the office, "Patty can you see if Rae is in her office?" When she nodded, he returned to the boys. "Okay. . .Is today a holiday I haven't heard about? Why are Patty and I the only one's working around here? I came out here a few minutes ago and there wasn't a soul around. Will someone please tell me what's going on?"

Just then Patty poked her head out the door, "Boss, she doesn't answer."

Joe spoke over his shoulder. "Thank you, Patty." When Patty again disappeared behind the door, Joe again addressed the group. "Okay, where's Rae?" The blank, somber faces offered him no information. "Kirk, these boys seem to have been struck speechless—do you have any insight?"

He only shook his head, "No, sir."

Joe threw up his arms. "Oh, just get back to work!—And somebody find Rae. . .and Ben, too." He turned to address his eldest son, "Sam, I'd like to see you in my office, please."

Sam's shoulders slumped and he nodded "Okay, Boss." As Joe stepped through the doorway back to the office, Sam glanced at his younger brothers, who eyed him symphathetically. At that moment they were glad they weren't him.

"The privilege of the oldest," Jesse offered, as he stepped away.

"Lucky me." Sam gestured with his chin, and headed toward the office door. Stepping inside, he nodded to Patty, then turned down the short hall to his dad's office and let himself in. "Yeah, Dad?"

Joe gestured to a chair in front of his desk and Sam sat down. "Okay, let's have it."

"Let's have what?"

"Sam, I saw what went on a little while ago. One minute you're all having a party chasing paper, and the next, everyone is mad and disappears. Now I want to know what it was about."

"You saw that?"

"Yes, I saw it—now tell me what 'it' was."

"Dad, it'll be okay. We're handling it."

"Sam, you know I normally stay out of your business and let you boys handle your own—but now it's affecting work and I want to know what's going on. What's wrong with everyone? Where are Rae and Ben?"

Sam sighed, thinking for a moment. Deciding against defensiveness, he opted for disclosure. Arms resting on the chair's arms, he shrugged with his hands, "Well, Dad, for the most part, everyone is sulking. Ben is around here somewhere, probably sulking, too. You know how he is when he doesn't want to be found. . .and, I don't know where Rae is. I wish I did, because I want to see if she's okay."

"Sulking? You're a bunch of grown men and you're all sitting around *sulking?*" Shrugging again, Sam just nodded and Joe was silent for a moment. "You know, I always thought we were a pretty close-knit group here, but lately it just seems like the whole family is coming apart at the seams." Sam took a deep breath and shrugged again, not knowing how to answer that. Joe continued, "And you don't know where Rae is?"

"No, sir."

"You wondered if she's okay? Why wouldn't she be okay?"

"Well, Kirk. . ."

Joe rolled his eyes, "Kirk, again?" Shaking his head, he leaned back in his chair and stared at Sam, pressing his lips together, thinking. Changing figuratively from his 'Boss' hat to his 'father' hat, he stood and came around his desk, and took the chair next to Sam. "Okay, son, I'm listening. What went on between Kirk and Rae today?"

Sam glanced down, shaking his head slowly. "Kirk didn't mean to, he was just teasing as he usually does. . .and I never realized it, but he didn't know all of us were brothers and that Rae is our sister."

Joe squinted at his son, "You never told him when you were introducing him around?"

"No, I guess not. There wasn't anyone around that day—and I didn't think of it after that. . .and probably since we all call you 'Boss' at work, he never caught on."

"Okay, well, that clears up a lot for me."

"Yeah, it did me, too."

"So, once again, what happened out there?"

"Dad, you know I don't like to talk about these kinds of things until after they are settled, but I don't know how to get this one settled." Joe arched his eyebrows expectantly, not wanting to ask the question again. Sam got the message. "Okay, well—Luke was carrying a stack of Rae's files that he'd just sorted and I came in the outside door at the wrong time. The wind took the door out of my hand and blew the files all over."

"Okay, that explains the fairy frolicking. . ." They both smiled briefly.

"While we were all scrounging for the papers, Rae's locket fell on the floor, and Kirk picked it up and wouldn't give back to her."

"Her locket? Oh, no—not good." Joe just shook his head slowly.

"No, not good at all. You know how he keeps teasing her. I think he just keeps trying to break the ice with her, but when it comes to him Rae's just permafrost." Joe nodded again, and Sam continued, "Well, anyway, all I heard was him saying stuff about looking in the locket to find out who Rae loves, and when he saw the picture inside, he thought it was Rae—you know how much she looks like Mom—and he kept teasing her about her being the love of her own life. That's when I stepped in. I should have stepped in sooner, but I didn't realize at first what he was saying, and when I did. . .well, it just happened so fast. I got Rae's locket back for her, but she just went into her office and closed the door and the blinds. Everyone just sort of walked away for a while after that. It just took us out, Dad—including me. I mean, we're all trying to not think about Mom's death, and without knowing about it or realizing it, Kirk just threw her into all our faces. He apologized to everyone, so we're not really mad at him—except maybe Rae—but it just threw everyone off their game."

Joe nodded, feeling thrown off his own game. After a moment he asked, "Has anyone tried Rae's cell phone?"

Sam winced, shaking his head, "I don't know, I didn't think of it. I don't know if anyone else did either. We didn't even know she was missing until you called the meeting. I guess we're all being pretty self-absorbed."

Joe stood and reached into his front pants pocket. "No, you just got the collective wind knocked out of you, that's all." He pulled out his cell phone, and pushed Rae's speed-dial button, then listened. After a moment, he ended the call.

"Voice mail," they said in unison.

Joe replaced his phone into his pocket. "Why don't you go on back out there and see if you can finish cleaning up Rae's files and maybe even get everyone together to sort them out again." Sam nodded and let himself out of the office. Joe sat back in his desk chair and stared out the window at nothing in particular. It was his turn to feel like the wind had been knocked out of him.

** *** **

That night at home, after sulking through a dinner of cold cereal and cookies, Kirk slouched in his over-stuffed chair still working his brain over Rae. Humiliation and guilt churned in his thoughts and his pride resisted and resented it. He desperately wanted to get rid of both, but they persisted. Desperate for relief, his mind did the only thing it knew to do; it searched for someone else to blame—and Rae was an easy target. *This is HER fault! She's always making me look bad—and she's done it again! Now, everyone is mad at me because of her!* Again his pride thundered in his mind. *If she wasn't always on my case making me look like a fool, I wouldn't have messed with her today—and this wouldn't have happened! She did that to herself, today.* He felt certain of it. *Yeah, it was her all right. She's just trying to make it look like it was me.* It was as balm to his flesh and Kirk felt better already. *She needs to be taught a lesson for what she did to me. . .A BIG lesson. . .*Kirk nodded. *Yeah, I'll fix her. . .And I'll fix her in a way that her brothers can't step in—and so none of them knows it was me!*

Staring through the images on his TV screen, Kirk worked his brain until a idea began to take shape. Formulating a plan, he mulled it over and over, trying on different scenarios to find one that would make it work. Finally, one clicked, and he sneered, entertained by his thoughts. *That'll work if I could just figure out how to get Rae to take my weekly charter to Georgia. I'll probably have to do some serious sucking-up—but it will be worth it.* Gratified with the outcome of his musings, Kirk's mood softened, his ego soothed. He reached for his cell phone and scanned his contacts for a number, then selected it, and smiled smugly to himself while listening to the soft rings. When he heard a click and a greeting, his face brightened. "Hey Hanson, it's Kirk in Florida—I need a favor. . . ."

Chapter 18

With his plan in place, Kirk waited for the right time to approach Rae. In the afternoon, on the day before the charter, he scouted the hangar and office area looking for her. He also had to make certain her brothers were nowhere around while he hatched his scheme. He knew Jesse and Sam were in the air, so he didn't have to worry about them for a couple of hours, and he saw Luke leave with the Boss a few minutes earlier; he just needed to make sure of Ben. A minute later, Kirk found him in the break room watching football highlights on his lunch break. *Perfect, that'll keep him busy for awhile. Now to find Rae.*

It didn't take a rocket scientist to know where Rae could be found; she lived in the hangar. This time of day the hanger was empty, but after a peek into the window, he found her in her office, slouched in her chair, feet on her desk, examining some paperwork in her lap while munching on a sandwich. Donning his groveling persona to set the scene, Kirk approached. By the time he darkened her doorway, he was looking as forlorn and pathetic as anyone could—without overdoing it. He hesitated at the open doorway for a few moments, until he was certain Rae felt his presence, then turned and moved to walk away, only to return to the door, and hesitate again. Rae noticed his hesitations through the window that faced the hangar.

Disgusted, she yelled to him without looking up from her work, "What do you want, Sloan?" Acting 'caught,' Kirk stiffened for her benefit, then sagged, stepping to her door. Sporting his finest 'hopeless and pathetic' expression in his arsenal, he sighed. "Um. . . nothing." He said it in his best 'everything' tone, then peered in at her, to make sure she noticed. She hadn't, so he retreated to give her another chance.

"Suit yourself," Rae muttered mostly to herself. Kirk lurked indecisively outside her office for a few minutes more, pacing, halting, retreating, and returning, until Rae became so distracted she had do something—which was just what Kirk was counting on. As he paced by her door again, Rae sighed. Exasperated and a tad curious, she called to him, "Sloan, spit it out, or go somewhere else to cry in your beer!"

Trying his best to look as though he'd been found out, Kirk stuffed his hands into the front pockets of his jacket and quietly plodded into Rae's office, stopping somewhere between the door and her desk, still not looking at her. Rae hated playing cat and mouse, so she just waited for him to speak, but he wouldn't. Impatient, she prodded him, "This isn't the principal's office." Kirk half-chuckled, but still made himself appear unable to bring himself to say what was on his mind. Rae drew her own conclusions. She gathered up the paperwork on her lap and set it on her desk, then sat forward in her chair, giving Kirk a direct stare. "Okay, what did you break?"

". . .Break?"

"You must have broken something on your aircraft, or you wouldn't be acting like this."

"No, it's nothing like that; my aircraft is fine." He kept his shoulders slumped, pleased that she was at least nibbling at the bait. Rae waited as he seemed to be summoning his courage. Just when he could tell she was about to become annoyed, his voice just above a whisper, he confessed, "I need to ask you a favor."

At first Rae couldn't believe her ears. *All this just to ask a favor?* "Is that so?" She sat back smugly, unable to conceal her delight.

Kirk rolled his eyes and sighed in mock-resignation. "I'd like to go to Panama City tomorrow."

"So what are you telling me for? Sam handles the schedules." Dispassionate, Rae reached again for her paperwork.

"I tried. Everyone's booked tomorrow. There's no one else to take my charter."

"Then find someone to trade with you. Is this really what you interrupted me for?"

"I already tried to find someone. No-go."

"Oh, I get it, so you need me then, huh?" She smirked at him, "Then you're in a bit of a fix, aren't you?"

Kirk nodded submissively, setting the hook. "Yeah. That's the favor. I need to go to Lynn Haven, and that's close to your route." He'd picked Lynn Haven for that very reason. "I was wondering if you'd trade with me." His voice was flat, without expectation, and he hoped she noticed.

"Isn't your charter to Heartland? My dad said he doesn't want me in Georgia with all that's going on at the airports up there." She shook her head matter-of-factly and leaned back in her chair.

"I was hoping maybe we could just keep the trade to ourselves," he ventured hopefully.

Rae leaned forward again, her eyebrows arched, and scoffed, "...And the reason I would want to lie to my dad for you is...?"

Kirk paused for a moment, not meeting her gaze. "Well. . .um. . ." he sighed for added effect then spoke softly, resigned, "I can't think of one."

Mildly surprised, Rae stared at him. "Can't think of one?" She eyed him for moment, *Wow, something must really be wrong. . .* Kirk felt encouraged by her silence. Finally, Rae shrugged. "Why don't you just go on your day off?"

"It has to be tomorrow." Kirk deliberately wouldn't make eye contact.

"Why tomorrow?" When Kirk didn't answer, Rae rolled her eyes again. *This is getting annoying.* "What's so important that it can't wait?"

Kirk appeared to wrestle with himself over the answer, then winced. "I can't say."

"Can't say or don't want to?" Rae didn't try to hide her sarcasm. She had always wanted to say that. She'd heard her dad say it to her and her brothers a thousand times, and relished how it felt to be the one saying it. Kirk turned his face from her and just shrugged, hoping Rae would pursue it. She made an assumption. "Forget it, Sloan, I'm not going to cross my dad just so you can chase girls in Lynn Haven." She set aside her paperwork and reached for a three-ring binder, then returning to her semi-reclined position with her feet on her desk, and resumed eating her sandwich.

Kirk didn't have to feign disappointment and had to think of something fast. "Now, there, you see?" He didn't have to fake the whine either, "I knew you'd think that. That's why I didn't even want to bother asking." He shook his head in mock-despair and turned to leave—slowly, so she'd have a chance to stop him.

"What's eating you, Kirk?" She sounded more annoyed than concerned.

Ha! She used my first name! I must be getting to her! Kirk smirked to himself then continued his act. He deliberately stiffened his back, took a deep breath as though summoning his courage, then turned to face Rae again. "I'm not going there to see a girl, I swear." He didn't have to lie about that because he didn't even know anyone in Lynn Haven; he had never even heard of it until he'd saw it on the map last night. "Can't you just say you'll do it without having to know what for?"

"No."

"If I tell the reason, I'll never hear the end of it."

"Bummer." Rae turned the page in her notebook, dispassionate.

"C'mon, Rae. Do this thing for me, and I'll owe you, big-time."

"You can't owe me, because you don't have anything I want. Plus, I won't even consider it unless I know the reason. Even then, I won't make any guarantees—and like I said, why should I cross my dad for you?" Suddenly her dad's request that she make an effort to get along with Kirk drifted to mind; she scowled at the notion. *No, this is not what he was talking about.*

Kirk sensed she was considering it, despite her protests. He coached himself in his thoughts, *Okay. I've got to be careful here.* Finally making eye contact, he appealed to her pride, "Aw, c'mon Rae—we both know you can handle that charter. Your dad is just being overprotective." Before she had a chance to decline, he added, "I'll only stay in Lynn Haven as long as I need to, so I'll be sure to be back when I would normally be if I'd gone to Heartland. If we time it right, no one will even know."

'No one will even know'. . .? Rae squinted at him, *Doesn't Dad always say that's what the Evil One says?* Rae scoffed in her thoughts. "There's the small matter of flight plans. . ."

"We can change them at the last minute before we leave. No one will check." True to form, Kirk had an answer for everything. Despite her protests, he knew she must be thinking about it, otherwise she would have told him to get lost long before this.

Setting the notebook aside, Rae shook her head, set her feet on the floor and leaned forward. As she did, her locket swung out on its chain and dangled freely. Arms folded on her desk, and shoulders hunched, she stared at him. "No. I'm not going to lie to my dad for you, especially when you won't even give me a reason why."

Again, Kirk didn't have to fake his disappointment. Just then, the locket caught his attention and an idea exploded into his mind. Reigning in his sudden delight, he humbly lowered his eyes. "I don't want it to get around. You know how the guys can be."

"I know how *you* can be."

"I know, Rae—I'm a pain in the neck and I act like a jerk most of the time, and now it's catching up to me." He glanced up to see how being humble was washing with Rae.

"No argument there." She smirked again, watching him—still waiting, but Kirk could tell she had softened a bit.

Stifling a grin, he eyed her locket. "Okay, okay—but you have to swear not to tell anyone," he insisted. Rae just rolled her eyes. Kirk sighed heavily for effect then spilled the beans, "There *is* a woman in Lynn Haven that I want to see."

"I knew it," Rae snorted in disgust, "We're done. Get out."

"No, it's not like that, really." He folded his arms over his chest, and lifted one hand to shield his eyes from her, again for effect. "It's. . . it's my mom. It's her birthday." He spoke softly, pretending to be embarrassed, and then he peeked briefly between his fingers in Rae's direction. To his delight, she looked positively stricken.

"Your. . .your mom?" Stunned, Rae had not imagined Kirk even had a mom—ever. "You're doing this because you want to visit your mom on her birthday?" Kirk nodded. Rae's emotions swirled through her heart and her mind, feeling both incredulous and touched at the same time—never imagining Kirk Sloan capable of being sentimental about anything.

Kirk could see her bewilderment, and went in for the kill. He stared at the floor, toeing the edges of the tile there, speaking softly, "I just didn't want anyone to know. I couldn't take the teasing—not where my mom is concerned." Stifling another grin, he felt positively triumphant. He knew he had her.

In the moments of silence that followed, Rae's heart warred with her mind. Suspicious of anything coming from Kirk that had to do with decency and caring, her mind didn't want to be persuaded. But her heart, pierced by her longings for her own mother, began to fill with compassion for this contrite soul before her. Again her dad's words from the other night drifted through her mind. Kirk held his breath—and wisely, his tongue—as he awaited her answer. Rae leaned back in her chair and stared at the frame on the corner of her desk that held a photo of her mother. After a long moment, her heart won the battle. Still gazing at the photo, Rae sighed audibly; speaking softly, without enmity. "Okay, I'll switch with you—now get lost."

Kirk didn't have to fake his delight. He thanked her profusely then disappeared out her office door. He had a phone call to make.

Chapter 19

"Heartland Tower, this is Cessna Two-seven-two-seven-Sierra." Rae waited for a response, checking her gauges. *Everything looks good. Fuel's good.* She glanced at her watch, smiling to herself...*and ten minutes to spare.*

"Two-seven Sierra, this is Heartland Tower."

"Heartland, Cessna-Two-seven-two-seven Sierra. Request clearance for landing, Heartland."

"Affirmative Two-seven Sierra; approach on Three-One."

"Affirmative Heartland. Cessna Two-seven-two-seven Sierra approaching on Three-One, Heartland." Rae circled around and maneuvered the aircraft for final approach. "Heartland, Cessna Two-seven-two-seven Sierra on final at three-one."

"Affirmative, Two-seven."

Rae throttled back and lowered her flaps.

In the tower, Rick raised his binoculars and scanned the skyway, then lowered them, scanning the ground and the runway with his own eyes. Movement below caught his attention. "What's going on down there?" He raised his binoculars and focused them, and swore. "Geez! What are they doing? Are they crazy?!"

Billy glanced up at him from his console. "What?"

"There's a bunch of people swarming the runway down there!"

"What? I have someone on final!"

"Tell them to pull up, NOW!

"There isn't time!

"Tell them anyway!"

"Cessna Two-seven-two-seven Sierra. Abort! Abort! I repeat Abort!" Billy's voice strained.

Rae's pulse quickened. *Did he just say 'Abort'?* She pushed her earphone against her ear and pushed the radio button on her yoke. "Repeat, Heartland? Abort? *Now?*"

"Affirmative, Two-seven, ABORT!"

"You've got to be kidding!" Rae's heart jumped into her throat immediately as she reversed her landing procedure from a near-stall, quickly raising her flaps and throttling up, then pulling back on the yoke as hard and fast as she could. As she did that, she strained to see down the runway ahead of her wondering what the problem was. Suddenly, she saw it. Something was on the runway. No, not something—someone! *It's a group of people! What are they doing on the runway?* Suddenly, she remembered her dad's warnings. She didn't want to think about plowing into that crowd with her propeller. *I'm too low! I'm not going to make it!* She breathed hard and fast, eyes wide, straining against the yoke, trying everything.

"Abort, Two-seven! Abort!" The Tower insisted.

Her finger on the yoke button, Rae shouted back, "I'm trying! I'm too close!—I'm at 'full' right now!"

"Pull up, pull up! Two-seven!"

"*I'M TRYING!*" Finally her aircraft responded and lifted just in time to buzz the crowd, not five feet above their heads. Rae saw faces—angry ones and scared ones. She heard something pelting her aircraft. *Are they throwing rocks at me?* Suddenly something stung her shoulder near her neck, and she almost let go of the yoke as she recoiled, but forced herself to hang on, banking hard to the left away from the terminal as she climbed.

"Nice job, Two-Seven!" The Tower crackled over her headset, startling her already jangled nerves. "What's your status?"

Rae thumbed the yoke button. "I think I just went gray."

Rick grinned briefly, "Two-seven, diverting you to Potterville Field." He paused then gave her a new heading. "ETA ten minutes—use channel two. Heartland tower will notify."

"Affirmative, Heartland Tower." Her pulse still racing, Rae released the button on her yoke, still breathing hard. Shoulder stinging, she shrugged and rotated it, guessing she had tweaked something in all the excitement. After a couple of minutes, an alert tone suddenly sounded and Rae's eyes jumped to the annunciator panel, zeroing in on the offending light. *What? Fuel? No way! I had a third of my load left!* She glanced at her fuel gauge, her eyes widening, *Empty?! That can't be!* Rae tapped the glass over the gauge, wondering if the needle was stuck, but it didn't budge. *How can I be out of fuel?*

Just then, the whine of her engine stopped—and very nearly, her heart. Rae glanced ahead out her windscreen at her windmilling propeller. *Oh no. Not now! I don't have enough altitude for this!* Her heart back in her throat, Rae again moved her thumb to the radio button. "Heartland Tower, this is Cessna Two-seven-two-seven Sierra." She tried to sound matter-of-fact, but was failing miserably. "Experiencing engine failure. Attempting re-start, Heartland."

The men in Heartland Tower exchanged glances, dismayed. "Affirmative, Two-seven. What's your position?" Rae read him the coordinates off of her GPS, "Affirmative, Two-seven. Notify after attempted restart."

I can't be out of fuel yet, I just checked it! The gauge has to be wrong. Rae went through her re-start procedure at light-speed and pushed the start button. The engine cranked but didn't turn over and her propeller continued windmilling. Forcing herself to concentrate, Rae glanced out her windscreen and side window at the land below her and swallowed hard, then glanced at her altimeter, shaking her head. "Heartland, this is Cessna Two-seven; restart attempt failed. I do not have enough altitude for retry. Looking for place to set it down." Her voice shaky, she added, "Switching on ELT." Her pulse pounding in her ears now, Rae flipped the switch for the Emergency Location Transmitter.

"Affirmative, Two-seven. Notify when on the ground."

"Affirmative, Heartland." Rae released the radio button and muttered to herself, "If I'm still alive—and conscious. Well, at least no fuel means no fire."

She scanned the landscape ahead of her, looking for a field or a road where she could set down. Gliding over the Interstate, she was able to make out details of the cars below her, and even read some of the green signs. She coached in her thoughts, *Don't want to land on the freeway. . .Just a little further, c'mon. . .c'mon!*

After clearing the Interstate, she glided over what seemed like an endless sea of trees, but could see patches of farmland opening up ahead. Feeling hopeful, she checked her altimeter again, just as a few treetops raked the underside of her aircraft. Her mouth suddenly going dry, Rae swallowed again, drawing a bead on the field nearest her.

Ahead, the field drew closer as her aircraft dropped down even lower. *Okay, this is it! Field, I need you!* The field ahead of her wasn't very large and was flanked on three sides by thick, dense wooded areas, but she was in no position to be picky. *Hopefully, I'll find a way to stop before I get to those trees over there.* Rae held her breath, willing the aircraft to stay up high enough, and long enough, to clear the trees under her. Once that was accomplished, she needed to touch down as close to the near end of the field as she could to allow as much room as possible to stop before she arrived at the trees on the far side. As she drew closer, she could see the field had been plowed recently and her angle of approach ran contrary to the furrows. *Oh, man, this is going to be bumpy.* Rae pushed visions of cart-wheeling out of her mind and again forced herself to focus. She heard more scraping underneath, unnerving her further. Suddenly, the trees ended and the field opened up, and Rae headed in, clenching her jaw so tight she thought her teeth might crack. "Down, down, DOWN!" she coached her aircraft, tears streaming down her face. Suddenly she touched down roughly and, as expected, she bounced and bumped over the furrows, her shoulder protesting as the trees skirting the far end rushed toward her. *I'm going to fast!* She watched tensely as the trees grew larger before her eyes. *Brakes. Brakes. BRAKES!* At the last second, holding her arms across her face, she closed her eyes, bracing for impact.

When she stopped moving, and the impact hadn't happened, Rae opened one eye, then the other, and peeked between her arms out the windscreen at the woods in front of her. The aircraft had come to rest with its nose between two trees, the wings just inches from them. Rae exhaled loudly, scanning the ground around her. *The furrows must have helped slow me down.* Sinking deeper into her seat, she dissolved in relief. Weak from fright and breathing heavily, she sat there limply for several seconds, unable to move. Finally, she reached up with a heavy arm and touched the button on her yoke,

"Heartland Tower, this is Two-Seven-Sierra," her voice trembled, "on the ground at. . ." She pulled herself forward using the yoke, and read off the GPS coordinates, then let go of the button and fell back against her seat again.

"This is Heartland Tower. Congratulations, Two-seven—you did it! Dispatching assistance now, any injuries?"

Rae wanted to say something cute and clever, but after all of that, she just couldn't come up with anything. "Not as far as I can tell." She breathed erratically, feeling as though she had just run a marathon. Her head rolled weakly to one side and she stared out the window next to her, trying to relax and get her breathing under control. Suddenly, she froze. *Oh, no.* Quickly unlatching her seatbelt and door lock, Rae flung open her door and rolled out. Landing on all-fours, she tossed what was left of her breakfast then collapsed onto her back in the soft dirt.

She lay there several minutes staring up at the underside of the wing, without really seeing it. Eventually, her eyes focused and she stared at it directly, and noticed a black spot. *What's that?* She puzzled a bit longer, until curiosity overruled her inertia. She rolled onto her side, and pushed herself up onto her knees, her shoulder stinging again, and stared at the black spot. Still not able to tell what it was, she dragged herself with the strut until she was standing. Examining it close-up, she touched the spot with her finger and squinted when her finger disappeared into it. *It's a hole.* Suddenly, she gasped aloud, "There's a hole in my wing!—*In my fuel tank?!*" Again feeling weak, Rae steadied herself on the strut and staggered over to the body of her aircraft, bracing herself against its side with one hand, holding her head with her other.

Puzzling over that, Rae's eyes dropped to the side of her aircraft, and she noticed another black spot in front of the door, and squinted at it for a few moments. Curious again, she finally reached for it. *Another hole!* She moved her eyes over the white fuselage, looking to see if there were more of the black spots. Not seeing any on that side, she walked around to the other side and resumed her search, finding three more over there. Two were in the cowling, and another in the underside. *What in the world?*

Suddenly, she remembered. *The mob of people—they weren't throwing rocks! They were shooting at me—just like Dad said!*

After another step forward, she saw another black spot where the other wing met the body, and shook her head again. *Both tanks! No wonder I was out of fuel!* Her eyes traced the length of the wing and back, not seeing any more holes, and continued her scan along the body of the aircraft on that side, stopping again at another black spot in the middle of the cockpit door on the passenger side. Crouching down, she drew her face close to it and peered through, adjusting her head until she got the correct angle and line of vision to see where the bullet went. Her seat came into view, and also another black spot near its top that was surrounded by a an elongated, reddish-brown stain.

Quickly, Rae straightened up and ran back to her open door on the other side. She leaned in and reached for the hole in the pilot's seat, probing it with her fingers, then rubbed them against her thumb as she withdrew from the cockpit. *Blood!* Immediately, she reached with her other hand for the stinging place on her shoulder, near her neck, and touched it, feeling a rut in her skin. Recoiling from the pain, Rae snatched her hand away immediately, and examined those fingers. *More blood.* Her eyes suddenly widened at the realization. *That was a bullet!* Reeling, and weak at the realization of her close call, Rae leaned on the strut, then she eased herself down until she could sit on the wheel. Trembling, she gathered her knees into her arms, and rocked herself, staring at the furrowed dirt. Her eyes brimmed with tears that trickled down her cheeks. Her first impulse was to fall to her knees and thank God for His mercy, but then she remembered that since her mother's death, she wasn't speaking to Him—and resisted the urge. Feeling very alone, Rae straightened a leg and reached into her front pocket, pulling out her cell phone.

** *** **

Patty knocked on Joe's door then opened it. "Boss, there's a call for you on two."

Joe muttered without looking up, "I can't right now, Patty, would you take a message?"

"I think you need to take this one, Joe—it's Mr. Patton. He says there is trouble at the airport in Heartland and his ride never showed up."

Joe's head came up. He squinted; puzzled. "Get Sam in here would you?" He reached for the phone, and punched the button for line two. "Yes, Mr. Patton. . . . What's that?. . . Your aircraft is a no-show?" He heard Patty's voice echoing in the hangar as she paged Sam. "What kind of trouble at the airport?. . .You don't say. . . No, sir, I haven't heard anything. The pilot probably got diverted if that's what is going on there. I'll look into it. Thank you for your patience. . . I'm sorry about that. . . No, I think you're right, if the airport is closed, sending someone else up there would not be helpful to you. . . Yes, sir, I'm sorry too, and thanks for letting us know. We'll contact our pilot and find out what happened. Thanks again." Joe hung up the phone then glared at it, thinking.

Just then, Sam appeared in the doorway, "Yeah, Boss—what's up?"

"Who flew to Heartland today?"

"Kirk. Why?"

"Have you heard from him?"

"No, is there a problem?"

"Yes, there is. Could you try calling him?"

Concerned, Sam pulled out his cell phone. "Sure, what's going on?"

"Maybe nothing. Just see if you can raise him." The office phone rang again and Joe heard Patty's voice up the hall answering it.

Sam scanned his cell phone contacts for Kirk's number, found it, and pushed 'send,' then waited. After several seconds, he ended the call. "It went to voice mail."

Patty stepped to the doorway behind Sam. "Boss that was Riley. He said to turn on the mid-day news on channel eight. There's a report on out of Georgia—he said there's a melee at the Heartland airport and he thinks he saw our 182 in trouble."

"Our 182?" Joe's heart rate quickened. He turned to Sam, "Did Kirk fly one of ours?"

"No, I saw him take off. He was in his."

Baffled, Joe rose to his feet and he and Sam scurried out to the hangar, heading for the TV in the break room, with Patty on their heels. His other three sons had already assembled there for lunch break. Their heads came up when their dad barged through the door. Joe grabbed the remote and pointed it at the blank screen, as the other three looked on.

"Channel eight," Sam urged. His heart pounding, Joe forced his fingers to obey. Seconds later, channel eight flashed onto the screen showing a mob scene on the runway of the airport in Heartland, Georgia. An off-screen reporter told the story. "This scene in Heartland, Georgia was filmed by a by-stander using his cell phone camera. For reasons yet unknown, a mob stormed the runway at Heartland Airport as a small airplane was coming in for a landing. As you can see in the video, the pilot had to abort his landing at the last second, narrowly missing the crowd, who then shot at the airplane. The pilot was barely able to pull up in time, and there is no word yet on the fate of that airplane."

"They shot at the aircraft? Are they crazy?" Sam was incredulous. "Was that Kirk's? Did anyone see the call-numbers?" Sam's eyes darted between the TV and his brothers.

Jesse wasn't sure he heard right, "Kirk? You think that was Kirk? That looked more like our 182."

"They tend to play these things over and over again. If they do, look for the call numbers," Joe suggested, trying to steady his pulse. Ben pounded on Sam's back, wanting to know what was going on. Sam began signing excitedly, as he pointed to the TV screen. Ben's eyes grew wide.

"There it is again." Luke alerted everyone. The talking ceased as all eyes focused on the screen. The scene replayed as the reporter said essentially the same thing, only phrased it differently.

"There!" Ben said in his hollow, nasal way and pointed to the screen, his eyes quick to pick up the tail numbers of the aircraft. "I saw November, Two-Seven-Two-Seven Sierra! That's ours!"

"It can't be ours. I saw Kirk take off in his own aircraft!" Sam insisted.

Jesse turned to Ben, "Are you sure you saw the tail numbers right?"

Before Ben could answer, a voice at the doorway startled them, "What's going on?" Everyone wheeled around in unison.

"Kirk!"

"Yeah. What's all the excitement about?"

Joe pushed through the cluster of his sons and took hold of Kirk's shoulders, delight and relief spreading across his face. "Kirk, it's good to see you!"

Baffled by this reception, Kirk squinted quizzically, "Really? Why?"

"We thought you crashed," Sam enlightened him.

"Crashed? Why would you think that?"

Letting go of one of Kirk's shoulders, Joe opened his palm, gesturing toward the TV. Kirk traced the gesture to the screen just in time for the video of the aborted landing to replay again and his mouth fell open. "Where is that?"

"Heartland, Georgia." Sam informed, with a hint of accusation, wondering why Kirk was not there.

Joe silenced Sam with just a glance, then turned to Kirk, "Can you tell us how one of our aircraft ended up in Heartland, and not you?"

Kirk froze and lost all color in his face. He muttered under his breath, "Oh no. . ."

"'Oh, no', *what?*" Sam pressed. All eyes were on Kirk, who was shaking his head nervously. Tension hung in the air as they awaited Kirks explanation.

But it was Ben's voice they heard next. "Where's Rae?" He uttered in his hollow manner of speech. Everyone stiffened, realizing a moment later what Ben had already figured out.

The brothers drew closer to Kirk expectantly and Kirk swallowed hard. "Um. . .we traded routes. Rae flew my charter today."

Alarmed, Patty's hands went to her face. "That was Rae?!"

"You sent my little girl into that mess?!" Joe was beside himself.

"I'm sorry—I had no idea!" Kirk not only feared for Rae, but also his job, and now, looking into the faces of her brothers, his own physical safely.

"Did you somehow forget that I told you I didn't want her up there!" Joe accused, eyeing Kirk, knowing the younger man had been fully aware of that.

"I'm so sorry." Kirk choked out the words—it was all he could think of to say. "She said she'd talk to you when she got back."

Joe's head came up, suddenly remembering his talk with Rae a few evenings ago. He cleared his throat, trying to rein in his emotions. "I'm glad you're safe, son," he muttered and stepped around the men, heading for the door.

All mouths fell open, and Kirk, expecting to have gotten an earful, was taken aback by Joe's words. Murmurs of protest erupted all at once; accusations flew. Just then, the ring of a cell phone split the clamor, and everyone glanced around searching for the source. Shaking his head at the poor timing, Joe paused at the door and reached into his pocket, pulling out the offending device. With all eyes now on him, he glanced at the display to determine if he would even answer it. Surprised, he did a double-take, then his lips parted. "It's Rae." Suddenly silent, everyone stared anxiously as Joe answered, hoping the voice at the other end would actually be Rae's, and not someone else calling on her phone with bad news. He raised the phone to his ear. "Rae, is that you?"

"Yeah. Hi, Dad. Listen I. . ."

"Rae!" Relief registered on every face. "Thank God you're okay! Where are you?"

"I'm in Georgia—please, don't be mad."

"Georgia? Hon, what are you doing in Georgia? I told you I didn't want to you up there with all the problems they are having up there." His voice sounded pleading.

"I'm sorry Dad. You said you wanted me to work on getting along with Kirk, then he came to me wanting to trade routes yesterday."

His suspicions confirmed, Joe's shoulders slumped in dismay. "Oh Rae, why didn't you say something to me?"

"Kirk didn't want anyone to know. Dad, I'm really sorry I didn't tell you." Rae's voice quavered.

Feeling responsible, Joe shook his head, "It's okay, hon—I'm just so glad to hear your voice. We were worried because the TV News showed a mess at the Heartland airport. There was an aircraft coming in that had to abort the landing—we thought for a minute it was you." The brothers watched as their dad's face lost color. "It *was* you?" Wide-eyed, he stared at his boys, who stared back and Kirk looked even more ill. "Oh, babe. . ." Joe's voice fell off. The brothers waited expectantly as their dad listened. ". . .You were able to pull up in time? That's good." Joe answered their unspoken questions as he answered Rae, enunciating so that Ben could read his lips. "Then your engine quit?" They all inhaled sharply, fear registering on their faces collectively. "You landed in a field?. . .No crash? That's a relief!" Everyone collectively exhaled. "What's that. . .? Bullet holes?" All six inhaled again in unison, slack-jawed. *"Both tanks?* Oh, Lord. . .And one hit your seat?" Suddenly weak, Joe had to lean against the lunch table. Everyone waited transfixed, reminding—and comforting—themselves that it was Rae herself giving the report, and not a coroner.

Joe's voice softened, "It's okay, sweetheart, calm down— you're on the ground now—just take your time." Joe listened for another moment then grimaced. Tears came to his eyes, and the fingers of his free hand combed through his hair. He continued relaying Rae's account, "One of the bullets grazed your shoulder by your neck?" Stricken, all six stared numbly, waiting. "There's some gauze in the first aid kit, hon. Put some of that on it to stop the bleeding." Joe's voice sounded weak as eyebrows on the faces around the room knitted together. At that moment Joe wanted nothing more than to hug his little girl. "It's okay, baby, you cry all you want; you've earned it—no need to apologize." Joe's voice broke as he spoke, then he glanced up at the boys. "Yeah, they're all here." He nodded, and nodded again. "Yes, sweetheart, I told them; we're all so glad you're safe. . .What's that?. . . Kirk? Yes, he just got back." Kirk paled again as all eyes focused on him. Just then, Joe's eyebrows suddenly arched, and he abruptly turned his back and lowered his voice, "No, hon, I'm not going to say that to him!—he feels bad enough already!"

Chapter 20

Huddled in the cockpit against the November chill, Rae pulled her jacket closer around her. It was nearly two hours before she spied the blue pick-up truck bouncing over the furrows toward her. Relieved, she let herself out of the cockpit and waited for it to pull up. When it did, the driver's side door opened and a man about thirty-five stepped out, clipboard in hand.

Surprised, he took off his sunglasses and drawled, "Are you the pilot?" Rae nodded and the man smiled. "No kidding, how about that!" He stepped over to her and extended his hand, "I'm Neal, from the NTSB. Sorry it took so long. I was on my way back from a job in Atlanta when I got the call."

Rae shook his hand, "That's okay. Rae Gerrard."

"What happened here, Rae?"

"I had to abort my landing at Heartland because a mob of people swarmed the runway when I was on final and they shot at my aircraft. I pulled up in time, and they diverted me to Potterville, but then my annunciator alarm went off saying I was out of fuel, so I had to land here—I almost didn't clear those trees down there."

"You ran out of fuel? Did you run it too close to the wire?"

"No, I still had about a third of my fuel load when I came in; they shot holes through my wings and cowling and before I knew it, I was out of fuel."

"Wow, that stinks." Neal scrunched up his face as he wrote and Rae chuckled at the good-natured man. Neal leaned over and glanced at the underside of her aircraft. "Yup, lost some paint under there." He did a cursory scan over the entire aircraft. "It looks like y'all landed good—don't see anything broken." He glanced at the nose of the aircraft between the trees, "—and you didn't stop a second too soon. So, your aircraft is all in one piece. Are you all in one piece, too?"

"Pretty much."

"No injuries?"

"Well, just this." She showed him the mark on her shoulder. It was still raw and oozing. Neal took a look at it as Rae explained, "A couple of the bullets came into the cockpit; one of them grazed me."

One glance at her wound, and its location, and Neal's pleasant expression changed to one of concern, "Whoa, that was close! Show me where it came through the cockpit." Rae took him around to the passenger side door and he peered through the hole, then walked around to the pilot side and leaned in, examining the seat. Resting his elbow near the head rest, Neal shook his head and peered over his shoulder at her. "Rae, you are one lucky lady." He shook his head again for emphasis, then pressed ahead. "Um, okay, let's see—is this your first event?" Rae nodded, hoping it was her last, too. Neal continued, "Okay, this is how this works. I'll inspect your aircraft, then we'll need to take you to a doctor to get checked out. Once that's done, I'll have a local mechanic come out and take a look, and he'll make his recommendations—unless you have someone you want to do that." Rae shook her head. "Okay, we'll go with my guy, then.

After that I'll need to file my report. All that usually takes me about a day, depending on how soon the mechanic can get here."

"A whole day? Can I just check it out myself? I'm certified."

Neal's eyebrows arched, "You're certified? No way! Really? How about that!" He smiled broadly, sounding delighted rather than skeptical. "But no, sorry, they frown on that if you were the one flying the aircraft." Rae figured as much, but wanted to try, anyway. Neal contiued, "I got a guy down this way who is real good. I'll just give him a call. Once all that is done, you can take the report and contact your insurance people, or whatever you need to do. How does that sound?" Rae shrugged and nodded, and so did Neal. "Okay, if you want to, you can sit and relax in my truck and keep warm while I do my inspection." Rae nodded and stepped over to his passenger side door and let herself in while Neal went about his business. It seemed like minutes later that Neal tapped on the window outside her door. Without realizing it, Rae had fallen asleep. She roused herself and she pushed open her door as she glanced at her watch; it had been nearly an hour.

Neal stepped closer as the door opened. "Well, I got all I need from here, at least for now. I just called our doctor out here, and my mechanic guy, and they are both available. So, let's get you checked out first, then we can swing by the Potterville airport and connect with the mechanic and bring him back here with us. Maybe get something to eat in there somewhere, too. You hungry?"

Rae nodded, "Yeah, I've been here since around ten this morning."

"Oh, yeah, you must be, then. Well the doc is waiting, so you think you can hold on until after we see him? We can eat after that, and then go to Potterville Airfield. Sound like a plan?"

"Yeah, sounds good. Let me get my wallet and lock up." Five minutes later they were on their way.

The doctor Neal had lined up was in Potterville, and they arrived in just over a half an hour. After his preliminary checks, the doctor simply cleaned and dressed Rae's wound, and signed her off, then Neal kept his word about getting something to eat. They passed a pleasant hour at a popular chain restaurant with rocking chairs and checkerboards, then Neal drove them over to the Potterville Airfield—a small un-towered airport not far from the restaurant. Neal pulled up to the red brick terminal building and parked his pick-up, and Rae followed him over to a large hangar just beyond a row of open hangars. Neal poked his head inside and called to a man who stood leaning over the engine compartment of a Piper. "Hey Edd, where's Orby at?"

Edd turned around at the sound of the voice. "Well, hey Neal, whatcha doing out here? Someone wreck their aircraft?"

"No, not this time. Just a forced landing in a field."

"Well, that's good, anyways. Orby's around here somewhere, let me call him." Edd lifted his hand-held radio to his face. "Orby, Neal's here. Where you at?"

"I'm in the office. Tell Neal I'll be there in about five minutes, will you, Edd?" Orby's voice crackled back over the radio, his slow, heavy drawl sounded like he was talking around a big wad of gum. Rae tried to picture the face that belonged to that voice, but couldn't imagine it.

Edd lowered his radio. "Did you hear that, Neal?"

"Sure did, thanks Edd." Neal turned to talk to Rae, but she had already found something interesting in an open hangar across the way, so he stepped into the big hangar to catch up on news with Edd. After several minutes, Neal turned to scan the area for Orby, spotting him on his way back, nearing the open hangar Rae had gone over to. Neal took a few steps toward it. Puzzling over what he saw, he waved Edd over. "What do you make of that, Edd?" Edd stared for a moment, curious. The girl who had come with Neal had wandered over to the open hangar and was now leaning into the engine of the Cessna with her forehead on the head of a long screwdriver, the other end somewhere in the engine. "What's she doing with her head on that screwdriver like that?" Neal asked the mechanic next to him.

Edd shook his head. "I have no idea. Look, there's Orby stopping to watch."

Orby stood nearby, his hands stuffed down in the pockets of his baggy overalls, grinning broadly. Neal couldn't make out what Rae and the three men around the Cessna were doing or saying, but they all seemed very animated. Two of the men had on blue baseball caps, and seemed to take exception to whatever it was that Rae was doing, but Rae seemed unfazed by them. Orby just seemed to be amused by the whole encounter.

Neal squinted at the two men. "Who are those guys with the blue caps?"

"Oh, they're some high priced mechanics Mr. H brought down from Atlanta. He's been having a problem with that aircraft—looks like that girl has an interesting trick up her sleeve, though. We'll have to ask Orby about it when he gets over here."

"Who's that older guy?"

"That's Mr. Hildenbocken. He's the owner of that Cessna. He owns GCT—that's Georgia Charter and Transport. He's got four or five aircraft out here and some more hangars around the state."

"Oh, yeah, I've heard of GCT—okay, so he's the owner. . ." Neal nodded, still watching them.

Just then, Rae tossed the screwdriver back into their tool cart and headed back over to Neal and Edd, but Mr. Hildenbocken called her back. She walked back over to him, said something, gestured to Orby, and walked away again. Neal and Edd watched as she approached.

"Who is she?" Edd asked Neal, "She looks kind of irritated."

"She's the reason I'm down here; her aircraft got shot at over at Heartland and she had to land in a field."

"That little girl is a pilot?"

"Yeah—she's a mechanic, too."

"No kidding?" Edd shook his head, surprised. "She start when she was two, or something?" The two chuckled over that just as Rae stepped up to them.

Neal introduced them, "Edd, this is Rae." Rae and Edd nodded to each other and shook hands. Neal gestured toward the open hangar and the three men. "What was all that about over there, Rae?"

"Oh, nothing I'm not used to. So, where's this Orby guy?"

"He's over there. You were just talking to him."

"What? One of those blue-capped clowns? Then I don't want him touching my aircraft!"

Edd piped up, pointing. "No, Orby's the one in the overalls." Rae turned around and zeroed in on the tall slim, thirtyish man with a big, toothy grin, and a mop of straight, sandy brown hair that almost covered his eyes.

"Oh, that guy? Okay, he's all right—but those other two are sorry."

"Yeah, we thought so, too." Edd confirmed, "But Mr. H brought them down from Atlanta to help figure out what's wrong with that Cessna." He shrugged. "None of us could figure it out." Rae squinted at Edd, then back at Orby and the men around the Cessna. Curious, Edd ventured, "If you don't mind me asking—what was you doing over there with that screwdriver?"

"My brother is deaf and he's training to be a mechanic—that's one of his tricks for troubleshooting an engine. He taught me how to do it."

Neal and Edd stared at her for a moment; Edd found his voice first. "No kidding! So, did you figure it out, then?" Rae nodded and shrugged, and Edd's eyebrows arched. "Just that fast? Well, I'll be... That's amazing."

Rae disagreed. "No, it's my brother that's amazing. That aircraft over there is making the same odd sound as a Cessna someone called us about back at home, and I couldn't figure it out either. Then Ben did that trick—*he's* the one who figured it out. I heard that same sound when I was walking by just now. I thought I could help them out a little. Ha!—my mistake!"

"They didn't go for it?"

"No. Silly me—I forgot and left my 'Y' chromosome at home."

The men chuckled, then Edd ventured again, "What did Mr. H say to you?"

"Is that the older guy?" Rae asked. Edd nodded. "He asked your friend Orby if what I said was possible, and Orby said it could be, and the older guy—Mr. H—said, 'How much will it take to get you to fix it for me? Just name your price.'"

Edd's mouth fell open. "No, he didn't!—really? Mr. Hildenbocken said that?" He was absolutely incredulous.

Rae squinted, "Yeah, so?"

"Ms. Rae, do you know who Mr. H is?".

"No. Why?"

"He's a big man around here. He has a charter and transport company with hangars all over the state and owns a lot of aircraft." Rae arched an eyebrow, but other than that, she didn't see how that changed anything. Edd leaned closer. "Did you give him a price?"

"No. I told him his guys could fix it."

Edd pretended to swoon. "Oh, no way!"

Rae shrugged again. "The repair is easy—it's figuring out what's wrong that's tricky. When my brother figured it out, I fixed it in about a half an hour. No, his guys can do it—I'm not getting into it with them."

"Ha! Oh, man!" Edd could scarcely contain himself. "If you'd've said a thousand dollars, he would have paid it, Rae!"

Rae watched Edd for a moment then just squinted at him and shrugged. "That repair isn't worth a thousand dollars." She turned to Neal. "So, when can we get this Orby guy to check out my aircraft?"

Neal glanced over at the open hangar. "Well, Rae, that 'Mr. H' just handed Orby the screwdriver, so I'm guessing it'll be about a half an hour—isn't that how long you said it took you?"

Rae sighed heavily, her shoulders sagging at the delay. "Oh, great."

The three turned their attention back to the open hangar. Orby stood holding the blade of the screwdriver in one hand, and tapping its head into his other hand as he talked to Mr. Hildenbocken, then glanced in their direction and excused himself. A few seconds later, he approached the three, his hand extended to Neal. "Hey, Neal, it's good to see you again! You doing all right? I'm sorry to keep y'all waiting like that."

The two shook hands enthusiastically, then Neal turned and extended an open palm toward Rae. "Orby, this is Rae Gerrard, the pilot I told you about. Rae, this Orby Grumwall."

The two shook hands as Orby nodded to her. "Oh, so you're a pilot, too. I'm glad to meet you, Ms. Rae. What you was doing over there just now was something else! You sure got Mr. H's attention! He wants *me* to fix it now—I guess he don't trust those other guys no more. But I told him I had to see to this first." He spoke so slowly that Rae found herself nodding her head to encourage him along.

Impressed that Orby kept them as his priority, Rae shrugged. "Oh, that's okay. Go ahead and take care of it—it won't take long."

Orby's eyebrows arched, "You sure, Ms. Rae?" Rae nodded, so Orby excused himself again.

Neal grinned at her, "I thought you were in a hurry."

"I am—but this is going to be good. I don't want to miss it."

Neal could see the glint in her eye. "What are you thinking?"

Rae gestured with her chin. "Did you see the way those blue caps were looking at Orby?—Sneering at him that way? They think he's stupid. My brother gets that a lot. I just want to see the look on their faces when he fixes it." Edd and Neal grinned, nodding.

Orby had it done in a half hour, just as Rae predicted, and she got her satisfaction with the look on the Blue Caps' faces. Another half hour later, Neal and Rae were once again bouncing over the furrows on the way to Rae's aircraft, with Orby following behind them. The two pickup trucks pulled to a stop near it and everyone got out. The two men circled her Cessna while Rae leaned against Neal's truck, unusually weary for so early in the afternoon. She yawned long and forced her eyes open again.

Neal pointed out to Orby the holes in the wings and the cabin, then Orby pulled out a a tool and opened up the cowling as Neal waved Rae over. She and Orby poured over the paths of the bullets in the engine compartment, going by the ricochet marks and the damage left behind. Neal watched and listened to them discuss it, Orby's eyebrows arching as he nodded, eyeing Rae. Feeling his way around the engine, Orby squinted then suddenly smiled broadly.

"Well, looky here." He worked at something with his fingers for a moment then withdrew his hand, holding up a spent bullet. "There you go, Ms. Rae—here's you a souvenir for your trouble!" He dropped it into Rae's open palm then leaned his elbow against the fuselage. "We can dig that other one out of your cockpit seat, and then you'll have a matched set—maybe make you some earrings out of them." Rae chuckled at Orby's idea then stared curiously at the bullet in her hand. Orby moved to examine more closely the other bullet holes in the wings and the doors, and probed them with his fingers, then found another hole in the tail assembly that neither Rae nor Neal had seen earlier. Neal showed Orby the hole in the pilot's seat and prodded Rae to show Orby the wound on her shoulder, but Rae just rolled her eyes and declined until Neal wore her down.

"Okay!" Rae feigned exasperation, and pulled her collar aside, exposing the gauze dressing. Orby again arched his eyebrows and shook his head.

"So, what do you make of that, Orby?" Neal questioned.

"Hmmm. . . What do I make of that?" Orby thought for a moment, rubbing his chin, "Well, it's a mystery to me why people would do something like that—mobbing the runway that way, and shooting at someone's aircraft just to protest something that ain't even related." He shook his head. "That just don't add up in my mind. But you kept your head about you, Ms. Rae, that's for sure!—And it's a mystery how you could be standing here telling me about it with your aircraft all shot full of holes like this." Orby rubbed his chin again, "Well, all I can say is, God had mercy on you, Ms. Rae—there's no doubt at all about that." He said it in all sincerity, with no hint of joking, his blue eyes piercing her soul, with Neal nodding heartily in agreement.

Rae could only stare at him. Eight months before, she would have received that readily and joyfully, and cherished it—and would have made it a point to tell it to everyone she met. But she had spent the last eight months convincing herself that God didn't give a rip about her, and Orby's take on her forced landing did not fit with her assertions—nor was she prepared to suddenly change them. She stared at him numbly, unable—or unwilling—to accede to that possibility. Still, there was something about

Orby that Rae couldn't dismiss so easily. As he leaned his elbow on the fuselage, Orby watched the battle briefly flash across the pilot's face. When Rae didn't answer, he watched her for another moment, then nodded. "Yeah, hearing your story, Ms. Rae—and seeing you and your aircraft," Orby tilted his head as he spoke, seeming to read something as though it was printed on her forehead, "I think you just came to the front of the line and God's getting ready to reveal something of His nature to you—and maybe getting ready to answer some big questions you been asking." Orby maintained his penetrating gaze. Unnerved by it, Rae took a step back nearly stumbling over a furrow. She stared back at the man in front of her, who seemed to be able to see into her soul. Something about him made her want to tell him everything—which is why she felt like fleeing.

Neal's voice broke the tension, "So, Orby, about the repairs—how long before you get Rae in the air again?"

Orby eyed Rae another moment before turning again to Neal. "Well, depending on if I need to order them parts, and how soon they come in—a few days, maybe a week. We can patch the holes while we're waiting on them—that ought to save some time. That's if I have enough patching materials on hand; there's a lot of holes." His slow, easy drawl made Rae want to finish his sentences for him. "I'll have to check and get back with you on that, too. You want me to go ahead and order them parts for you, Ms. Rae?"

"Yeah, sure. Can you write me up an estimate? I'll have to run it by my dad."

"Oh, sure. I was going to do that anyway. Since you're a mechanic, you'll be doing the repairs yourself, I expect."

Rae turned her palms upward, "I don't have any tools with me."

Orby brightened, "Well, I'll be glad to bring up some tools—and even help you, if you want."

Rae brightened. "Oh, that would be great! I've never done that kind of patching before—especially on fuel tanks. I could use the help."

Orby nodded, pleased. "Let me see what all kind of parts I got on hand, and I'll give you a call tomorrow, and maybe bring up what I have—then we can go from there." Orby nodded and smiled easily as he spoke.

Rae nodded again. "That sounds good." She and Orby exchanged contact information, entering each other's numbers into their cell phones as they were dictated.

Then Orby turned to Neal. "Well, that's about it for now, Neal. Is there something else I can do for you before I head back?"

Neal glanced at his watch. "No, I think that about covers it, Orby. I guess you can take it from here. I'll finish my report by morning and give Rae her copy. She can file her insurance when she gets your estimate. Do you have any questions, Rae?"

"No, I'm good for now."

Orby moved to wrap things up. "Well, okay then, Ms. Rae, I'll call you tomorrow. I should have your estimate ready for you by lunch time, and maybe come up here again, once you decide on a few things and call me back." Orby extended his hand to Neal, "Well, it's been real good seeing you again, Neal," and then to Rae, "I'll see you tomorrow, Ms. Rae. Y'all take care now." Orby smiled his big, toothy smile and waved as he climbed back into his pick-up and bounced his way out of the field back to the road.

Rae turned to Neal. "So, now what?"

"Now, I go find a place to spend the night and get to work on this report. Do you live here locally?"

Rae shook her head. "No, Florida—near Gainesville."

"Do you have someplace to stay?" Again Rae shook her head, so Neal continued, "Well, usually downed pilots don't have any other transportation, either, so what I normally do is bring them to where I'm staying and they get a room, too. That way I can just hand them their copy of the report as soon as I'm done. Then I usually take them back to their aircraft the next day, or to a car rental place if they want. You want to do that?"

Rae shrugged. "I guess."

"Out this way, I usually stay at a motel over by the interstate. There won't be much for you to do until I'm done so if you want to, you can get a room there, too. At least you can keep warm and watch TV or read or something—it's better than staying in your aircraft and freezing."

Rae nodded, "Okay, that sounds good. Do you think we can stop by a store somewhere so I can pick up a few things?" Neal was fine with that, so Rae gathered her tote bag and locked up her aircraft again, and climbed back into Neal's truck—and they bounced along the furrows back to the road for the third time that day. A half hour later, they were checking into their rooms at a motel on highway 49, next to the interstate. Locking her door, Rae turned on the TV, plopped onto her bed, and promptly fell asleep.

Two hours later a knock at her door dragged her back from dreamland; it was Neal.

"I was going to get some supper—you want to come?"

"Sure, why not." Rae grabbed her jacket, her wallet, and her key card, and followed him.

They ate at a nearby diner and Neal entertained her with stories of crashes and forced landings he'd investigated over the years, dazzling Rae with the stupidity of some of the pilots he'd encountered, some of whom didn't live to tell about their gaffs. An hour later, they were on their way back to the motel, stopping at a convenience store along the way so Rae could pick up some personal items, a few snacks, and a six-pack of bottled water. Back at the motel, Neal got back to work on his report while Rae turned in for the night. Before she climbed into bed, she called her dad with an update, then turned out her light, and was asleep quickly. The next morning, Neal knocked on her door again with an invitation to breakfast, and they spent another entertaining meal together. Back at the motel, Neal had another hour of work. "What do you want to do when I check-out, Rae? Do you want to stay here? If not, I could drop you someplace else—whichever you like."

"Well, Orby is supposed to come back to my aircraft this afternoon, so how about you just take me back there and I'll wait for him, so he doesn't have to come out here and pick me up."

"Are you sure about that, Rae? If you two get your wires crossed, you'll end up stranded out there, and there isn't much of anything around for miles."

Rae thought about that for a moment. "Yeah, I'm sure. By the time you drop me off, it should only be another hour or so before Orby calls and comes."

"Are you going to check out now, or stay here until you get your aircraft fixed?"

"Um. . .that depends on what Orby says. I think I'll just check out when we leave here, then, depending on what I find out from Orby, I can always check back in, if I need to. Or if it turns out it's going to take a week or more to get parts, my dad can just fly up this afternoon and take me home. If that's the case, then I'll just go back to Potterville with Orby and my dad can land there."

"Well okay, but I really don't like the idea of leaving you stranded at your aircraft, even for an hour."

"I think it will be okay—like I said, Orby's going to be calling around lunch time."

"Okay, if you insist. Give me another hour or so, then we can check out and get you back to your aircraft."

An hour later, the two checked out of their rooms and Neal drove Rae back to the field. He gave her a copy of his report and then wrote down his cell number, just in case. "Now, if something changes, give me a call—I don't want you stuck out here by yourself, okay? I'll be in Heartland all day, and that's only a half hour from here."

"Okay, Neal, thanks for your help." They parted ways and Rae climbed into her aircraft, and pulled out her book to read until Orby called or came.

Chapter 21

H ours later, her face against her window, Rae awoke with a start, chilled. She stared out absently for a couple of minutes before she noticed the sun was no longer over her left shoulder, but was now streaming between the trees in front of her. Suddenly, she was wide awake. "What time is it?" Her watch at her face, Rae stared at it in disbelief, "One-thirty?! Oh, no! Why didn't he call?" Distressed, she fished her cell phone out of her pocket, and touched the screen several times. "Oh nuts!—it's dead!" Frustrated, Rae groaned at the phone in her hand. "Now what am I going to do?" She flung it onto the seat next to her then forced herself to think. Staring through the prongs of the yoke, she drummed her fingers on its rim. *I should have listened to Neal and stayed at the motel!* She kicked herself in her thoughts. "I need to find a phone." Irritated, she slid back her seat, unlatched her door and jumped out, landing easily in the soft, furrowed dirt. *Well, at least having a nap made the time go by faster.*

Rae stepped out from the cockpit and surveyed the tree-bordered field around her. *This field is plowed, so there's got to be a farm house around here somewhere, right?* She wished now that she had paid more attention on the trips with Neal out of the field and back, but since they spent those trips talking about the landing, and what led up to it—and not paying attention to the scenery, she didn't have a clue in which direction to start looking. *Man, I sure hope Mr. Grumwall comes soon, and does what he needs to do, then maybe I can get him to drop me back to the motel—if he's coming, that is.* Irritated with herself, she crossed her forearms over her head and scanned the field again, then flung her fists down to her sides,

"I should have just had him pick me up at the motel, like Neal said!" She kicked the furrow in front of her, ruing her choice. Forcing her irritation aside, Rae focused on what to do next as she fiddled with her locket, sliding it back and forth along its chain. *Okay, let's see. Just in case he's planning to come out during his lunch break, I'll wait a little bit longer and give him until around two o'clock. If he doesn't show by then, I'll just scout around close to my aircraft for either the road or a house—if I don't find one, I'll come right back here and just radio for help again.* Nodding to herself, Rae climbed back into the cockpit and forced herself back into 'waiting mode'—and without realizing it, drifted off to sleep again.

Hours later, she awoke groggily, chilled to the bone. With a start, she gasped, realizing she was now shrouded in darkness. *Oh no, it's night! How could I have slept so long?* Immediately she brought her watch to her face, and pushed the illumination button—it was nearly one a.m. Sinking back into her seat wearily, she pulled her jacket up close around her then rubbed her throbbing temples, frustrated beyond words. Another thought struck her, adding to her dismay. *I never called Dad back! He must be worried sick!* Closing her eyes, she sighed, shaking her head, helpless to do anything about it.

The morning sun crept across the side of Rae's aircraft until it encroached into the shadows from the trees, and blazed into her sleeping face. Her forehead pressed against her window, mouth open and drooling, she breathed heavily and slept deeply.

In the sudden brightness, she squinted, and then rolled her head away from it. She closed her mouth to moisten the dryness, and coughed a few times, rousing herself from her sleep. *Man, I feel rotten. I must be coming down with something.* As the sun shone warm on the side of her face and neck, she forced open her eyes, then blinked a few times as the yoke and instrument panel came into focus. *What? What am I doing in my cockpit?* Glancing around sleepily, she recalled her plight with a grimace. Despite having slept, Rae didn't feel rested. Her head pounded, and she felt weak. *Probably because I haven't eaten since that breakfast with Neal yesterday morning.* As she stirred, her muscles ached. *Must be from those two white-knuckle landings.* Yet, more than the relentless headache, the overwhelming fatigue was getting to her. With the events of the last two days, Rae felt completely drained. She checked her watch. *Seven-thirty. Man, what I wouldn't give for a hot shower right now.* After a rumble from her belly just then, she added. . .*and something to eat.* She eyed the half-wheel in front of her. *I'm so hungry, I could eat that yoke right now.*

Forcing herself into motion, Rae unlatched her door and pushed it open, then climbed stiffly out of the cockpit. She stood in the furrowed dirt and scanned the surrounding field and woods, then glanced up at the sky; though it was overcast, the weather actually seemed warmer than the previous day, and much more humid with a stiff gusting wind at her face. That seemed like normal November weather to a Florida girl, but this was Georgia, and Rae wasn't thinking about what that kind of weather in November meant here. She traipsed around the Cessna, looking for some indication of which way would be the best way to go on her scouting mission. Even with the mild temperature, just that small amount of walking around her plane had left her winded and perspiring, so all she knew for certain was that she didn't want to set out across that multi-acre field. Rae fanned herself with the front flaps of her jacket then took it off. *It's warm and I'm only planning to scout for a short distance and come right back.* She tossed the jacket onto the cockpit seat, grabbed a bottle of water and her small I.D. wallet, then closed and locked her aircraft, pocketing her keys and the wallet.

Scanning the surrounding area, Rae thought back on the previous day. *Neal had to come from around those trees in front of my aircraft, and he turned off the road down there at the end of them—then drove along these trees until he got here.* She considered the distance, and the time the walk would take—along with her energy level, and nodded to herself. *It'll be quicker if I just cut through the trees to the road. Yeah, that seems easy enough. It didn't seem very far when we were driving the other day.* Satisfied, and anxious to get going, Rae formulated her plan. *If I can't see the road after a short way, I'll just come right back.* Eyeing the line of trees in front of her aircraft, and estimating the angle of Neal's approach in his truck, she calculated her path through the woods and started off into the trees to the left of her aircraft, feeling certain she would run into the road fairly quickly. After trudging through the woods for what seemed like an hour, her feet heavy, she stopped. Breathing hard, and perspiring, she leaned over, supporting her torso with her arms braced against her knees. After several breaths, she checked her watch and saw that it had only been 15 minutes.

"I've only been walking twenty minutes?—That's all?" Amazed at her level of fatigue after so short a time, Rae glanced wearily behind her and to each side, seeing nothing but trees, trees, trees—and ahead was no different. The stiff warm wind had stopped. *It seems cooler now. Is the temperature dropping?* The chill in the air nagged at her, helping her decide to head back to her aircraft and just use the radio. *I should have just done that in the first place!* She growled at herself. It was no different on her way back—the trees all looked the same to this suburbanite who had never been a girl scout, nor had even gone camping. After another half hour, when she should have been back at her Cessna, she was still in the woods wondering where it was—and despite all the work of walking, she was chilled to the bone. *Where is that rotten plane?* Worry crept up in the corners of her mind. *I guess I must have veered off somewhere along the way.* She decided to try backtracking.

After another hour of swishing through the fallen leaves and stumbling over protruding roots concealed by them, Rae still saw no road and worse yet, no Cessna. Weary, her feet became heavy and her gait unsteady as she trudged along, exhausted. Every step became a supreme effort and she plodded zombie-like for another ten minutes before deciding to rest a moment. She thought to pray, then caught herself, squashing the impulse, and instead plopped down wearily, sitting in the dead leaves and pine straw, gazing off alternately in each direction, searching for something familiar. Finding nothing but more trees, she checked her watch, 10:30a.m. *Wow, when did it get to be ten-thirty?* Rae let her head hang limply, unable to hold it up any longer. *I'll just rest a bit then start again.* She laid back into the leaves, gazing up through the branches at the gray, brooding sky high above her. As she rested there wondering why the sky might look so sad and gloomy, she fell dead-asleep where she lay.

** *** **

Back in Potterville, Orby stopped his work for a moment, champing on his gum, puzzling over the girl he was supposed to meet with the previous day. Edd watched him for a moment, "You ain't heard from that little girl yet, Orby?"

"No, I ain't, Edd, and that's a mystery. She seemed real anxious for me to get back out there. I been leaving her messages on her voicemail since yesterday, and I still ain't heard back from her." Orby thought hard for a moment, "Maybe she worked out something already or maybe she's just been tinkering with her aircraft and forgot to call." He shook his head. "No, no, that can't be—she said she don't have no tools with her. What do you think, Edd?"

Edd shrugged. "You think maybe Neal might know something?"

"Hmmm. . .There's a thought. Maybe I should just give him a call." Orby reached for his phone and brought up Neal's number. As he waited for it to connect, he glanced at his watch and pondered further, "It's already almost eleven, even if she calls right now, I won't be able to get up there until four or five. That won't give us much time to get anything done. This is a real mystery." Just then, Neal answered his phone. "Hey, Neal, it's Orby Grumwall. . .I'm finer than frogs hair split four ways—how about you?. . .Good, good. Say, Neal, where you at, right now? . . . Atlanta? Hmmm. . . Well, Neal, now I'm real curious. I'm just standing here wondering, I thought I woulda heard from Ms. Rae before now. I called her a bunch of times and left her a few messages and haven't heard nothing back." He glanced up at Edd suddenly, his eyebrows arched, "You say you dropped her off at her aircraft yesterday morning?" A look of concern crossed Orby's face. "Well, that's a mystery. . . No, let's not get worked up about it just yet—it could be she just made some other plans—still, I don't know why she don't pick up when I call. . . Maybe her phone died? Well now, that could be. She's been here a few days longer 'n she planned to be. Tell you what, Neal—since you're in Atlanta, how about I just run up there and see if her aircraft is still there, or if she got it towed somewhere. . .No, I don't mind a bit. I'll call you when I get there." Orby ended the call, but he didn't look convinced.

Edd squinted at him. "You think that's all it is, Orby?"

"I sure hope so, Edd. I hate thinking she's been stranded there all this time."

Orby retraced the route back to Rae's aircraft and pulled off the road at the edge of the woods. Pulling his truck around, he found Rae's Cessna right where he'd left it two days ago. He pulled up to it, thinking as he chomped on his gum, then got out, and called as he approached. "Ms. Rae?" He looked around, not seeing any signs of life. "Ms. Rae?—You here?" His only response was a stiff gust of cold wind. Wondering if she could be taking a nap inside her aircraft, Orby stepped closer and peeked in through the window; cupping his hands around his eyes, then sighed, "Well, no one in there." Through the window, he could see her jacket on the pilot seat and a tote bag on the floor on the passenger side, and something that looked as though it had been tossed into the corner of that seat. "Hmm. Well, there's your phone, Ms. Rae, but where are you?—And without your jacket, too!" Orby tried the door, finding it locked. Sighing, he turned around and stepped out from under the wing, then reached up and pulled off his cap. Holding it between his thumb and first two fingers, he scratched his head with the remaining fingers, eyeing the gathering storm clouds. Concern etched on his face, Orby snugged his cap back onto his head, reached into his pocket for his cell phone, and pulled up a number,

"Yeah, hey, Neal. It's Orby again. Yeah, I'm here at Ms. Rae's aircraft and she ain't here. . .Yeah, right where we left it. . .No, there's no sign of her here. Her aircraft is all locked up tight like she left it to go somewhere's. But her jacket and stuff are still inside, so maybe she's gonna be right back real soon. Her phone is in there on the seat, so you may be right about it dying on her." Orby suddenly brightened, "She said her dad might come up for her? Oh, well, maybe she's with him, then. Yeah, maybe they come up with a different plan and she just couldn't call me back. 'Probably couldn't get to my number, since she put it right straight in her phone when I give it to her and it looks like it's dead. I sure hope that's all it is—but then I wonder why she didn't take it with her when she left...Yeah, maybe they're coming back pretty soon. Okay, well y'all call me if you hear anything, will you? Thanks a lot, Neal."

Orby ended the call and looked around again in every direction, still uneasy. "I just wish I knew for sure..." He raised his eyes to the sky, "Father, I don't know what's become of Ms. Rae, but you know exactly where she is right now, and I know you're watching over her. I just pray for her that everything is okay, and if it ain't—that it will be real soon—and I sure would appreciate it Father, if you could tell her to give me a call so's I can be at peace about what's become of her." Orby glanced at the darkening sky, "...And, Abba, I sure pray she don't get caught out in this storm that's coming; it's gonna be a cold one. I ask all that in Yeshua's name, Amen."

Pulling out his little spiral bound tablet, Orby flipped it over to a blank page and scribbled down his cell phone number, and under it, 'Give me a call—Orby.' He tore off the page and, stepping over to the door, he took his gum out of his mouth and used it to stick the paper to the fuselage under the wing on the top of the door. "There you go, Ms. Rae, just in case your phone is dead and you can't get to my number." Orby now addressed the little piece of paper, "I hope under there, you'll make it through this storm, and won't get blowed away or nothing." Orby walked slowly back to his truck, taking one last look around before climbing in, and heading back to Potterville.

** *** **

Distracted, Joe Gerrard glanced at his watch again and frowned. Snatching up the sheet of paper at the corner of his desk, he pushed himself out of his chair and headed down the short hall to the front office, "Patty, has Rae called here today?"

"No, Boss, sorry." She glanced up sympathetically seeing the consternation in his face. "Have you asked the boys? I think they're all back right now." Joe nodded at that idea and headed for the hangar. He poked his head into the break room, seeing everyone but Ben. "Any of you talked to Rae?" They all answered in the negative and Joe was feeling increasingly uneasy.

Jesse frowned, "You still haven't heard from her?"

"No. When she called yesterday morning, she said she would call me back by lunch time, but I haven't heard from her. I was hoping maybe she had called one of you."

All of them shook their heads.

"Have you tried calling her?" Luke suggested, as if his dad hadn't thought of that.

"Over and over. It just goes straight to voicemail."

"Maybe her phone is dead. She was only supposed to be gone for half the day on Wednesday, she probably didn't take her charger with her." Sam volunteered.

"I thought of that, but it still seems like she would have found a phone somewhere and called. She's more than twenty-four hours overdue from when she said she would call!" His voice betrayed his edginess, "It's not like her to go this long without checking in, especially under these circumstances." Everyone had to agree, but no one had any ideas. "Even if she was busy working on her aircraft, she would have called by now. Something is wrong. Rae doesn't just forget to call!" It was rare for them to see their father so worked-up. He held up a sheet of paper in his hand. "I just looked at the weather service; there's a big storm bearing down on the area where she went down."

Jesse stepped forward, "You want me to go up there, Dad?" The other two echoed their willingness as well.

"Not with that storm coming. It's supposed to get there about the time you would. I don't need two of my own downed somewhere in Georgia." Joe shook the paper and disappeared from the doorway, leaving the three young men exchanging uneasy glances. Their concern for their sister ratcheted up a few notches. Face stern and jaw set, taking long strides, Joe made his way up the hall into his office, plopped into his chair, and started making calls.

Chapter 22

Late that afternoon, Heath sat in his tree stand, his six-foot-five inch tall frame squeezed down onto a twenty-two inch high stool. He hunched over pondering the ever-darkening sky, trying to decide how much longer he could hunt and still have time to get home before the storm finally let loose. He noticed the steam in front of his face. *Wow, the temperature sure has dropped since I got here; I can see my breath now. It's going to be a cold one tonight.* The weather forecast that morning said that a big storm would be rolling in later that evening, and as Heath surveyed the wall of black clouds headed his way, he concluded the storm had, in fact, arrived; it was early and Heath was not happy about that. He had hoped to hunt until nightfall, but he could tell he was not going to get his wish. The clouds were moving in quickly, and he knew if he didn't get down out of that tree stand and get moving, he would be trudging home in a very cold, soaking rain.

He glanced at his watch. *Four o'clock.* After a late lunch, he had hiked nearly a half an hour to this tree stand from his truck, so if he left right now, he might just make it back before the sky opened up on him. As if to confirm his decision, a gust of freezing wind blasted into his face, almost taking off his hat. Heath sighed heavily, resigned. Grudgingly, he unloaded his rifle and climbed down from his perch. On the ground, he rearranged his gear then consoled his disappointment by thinking about what was awaiting him back at his mom's. Right about now, she would be starting supper for the The Gang—at the thought of that, his mouth began to water. He smiled, shouldered his gear, and started back.

Trudging along his familiar path through the woods, Heath hopped over the creek in the usual narrow spot, using the larger rocks as stepping stones, and continued on his way. Occasionally he glanced up through the trees at that black wall of clouds looming ever-closer, and then at his watch. He was making fairly good time; twenty more minutes in these woods and he would be at his truck, and home not long after that. Heath could feel the air heavy with moisture, dampening his jacket as he walked, and pressed himself into a faster pace. Glancing at his watch again, and satisfied with the time he was making, he checked on the black wall he was heading for, which appeared even more menacing in the fading daylight. "That's fixin' to be some kinda storm!" he said aloud, shaking his head for emphasis with no one but the trees to hear him. As he returned his eyes to his path, something on the ground up ahead caught his eye. Curious, he squinted in the dimming light, trying to make out the unusual shape on the ground as he drew nearer. *What is that? An animal? It don't look like a deer.* Heath froze, his mouth falling open as he realized what he was seeing. *O man, it's a person!*

Quickly crossing the path, Heath approached the form lying under the trees in the dead leaves and pine straw, the leaves and twigs crunched and snapped under his boots with each step. As he drew closer, he saw it was a girl and his pulse quickened. She didn't stir with his approach, despite all the noise he was making. Heath wondered if she was dead or just unconscious— neither would be a good thing in his estimation. Stepping to her side, he knelt down, setting his rifle and gear on the ground beside him. He looked her over from head to toe. She lay on her left side, unmoving—nothing about her told him she belonged in the woods: pale green jeans and a coordinating pin-striped button down shirt. There was an odd-looking watch on her wrist that looked as though it had lots of gadgets, and he saw a dainty little ring on her right hand. Her long blonde hair, though now a bit tussled, had been combed and gathered into a ponytail on the crown of her head, and he noticed a gold locket on a chain, dangling from the collar of her shirt. Her shirt? Heath squinted, realizing what was missing. *She don't even have on a jacket! What in the world is she doing out here with no coat?* Heath squinted at her again. *She don't look like a vagrant—I've never seen a vagrant with their hair fixed or with a watch or jewelry like that. Probably lost. . .* Heath guessed. Then thinking on how far they were from town, he amended it. *Really lost—or maybe she's a runaway? She don't look even sixteen.* The girl lay so still, Heath wondered again if she was alive—afraid she wasn't. He pondered for a moment what he would do if that were the case.

He reached for her throat to find a pulse, but something on her shirt caught his attention. He leaned down closer to investigate. On her right shoulder near her neck, a dark blotch on the green pinstripes. *That looks like blood!* Heath's pulse quickened. A closer look revealed that the dried blood stain encircled an oval-shaped hole in her shirt close to her collar, and his eyes widened. *Oh, Lord, she's been shot!* He reached over to feel for a pulse, but as soon as he touched her skin, his heart sank. *Ice cold.* Dismayed, Heath shook his head slowly. *Now, that's a shame.* He sighed again, *Well, I guess I need to call the sheriff.* He reached into his breast pocket for his cell phone, and just as he did that, the dead body suddenly took a deep breath and stirred. Startled to the core, Heath gasped and reeled backward, clutching his chest.

He landed on his elbow then chuckled at his own fright, as much relieved as he had been startled. *Okay, that's good! She's alive.*

Rae slept hard and deep, oblivious to the world around her, or that she was chilled to the bone and sleeping on bare ground. Had she been in normal circumstances, the bugs crawling on her would have sent her into hysterics. Instead, she slept soundly and dreamed. Odd, disjointed scenes unfolded in her unconscious mind. She was back in Florida with her parents and brothers. Her mom was alive and vibrant. Even in her deep state of sleep, she yearned for her mom, to hug her again, but couldn't seem to get close enough to her. Every time she reached for her, her mom would be just beyond her grasp. Then Bosco, her black Lab from her childhood, came bounding up to her and jumped up, landing his front paws on her midsection, as he always did. She bent near his face to kiss his nose and Bosco spoke, "You doing all right?" he drawled. Rae's forehead furrowed as she puzzled in her dream. *Bosco is talkin?—With a drawl?* Before she could answer him, Bosco tugged her elbow and asked again, "Are y'all okay?"

The tug snatched her out of her dream and back to the woods. Rae opened her eyes to find a stranger looming over her. In a split-second, Heath glimpsed the alarm in her eyes, but didn't duck in time. In a flail of arms and legs, something—a foot or a fist, he wasn't sure—caught him across the mouth, and once again he was sprawling backwards, this time onto his back, as the girl scrambled away into the trees.

"Wait! I'm sorry!" Heath tried to assure, but the girl was quickly gone from view. Heath's hand cradled his face, his lip and cheek swelling, blood oozing onto his fingers. He heard her scurry away a short distance, then stop. Still clutching his jaw, he pushed himself to his feet and stared at the blood on his fingers, still stunned. He shook his head to clear away the stars he was seeing. Surveying the immediate area around him, he knew the girl was nearby, but couldn't see her. His heart went out to her. "I'm sorry, Miss. . ." Heath formed the words around his swelling lip. "I didn't mean to scare you. See? I'm not coming after you, or nothing. I'm just standing here seeing stars." He smiled, hoping to break the tension, but the smile made him wince. "I just saw you lying there and wanted to make sure you were okay. . .and since I can see you are—and that you sure can take care of yourself. . ." He rubbed his sore chin. "I'll just be on my way again." He wiped off his fingers and reached down to retrieve his rifle and gear, then turned and started back on his way, but was stopped by the Holy Spirit tugging at his heart strings. Thinking for a moment, he offered up a quick prayer, then turned back to face the place he had last seen the girl.

"I was just out hunting and thought I'd quit early because *it's gonna to rain soon.*" He emphasized the words, "That's how I stumbled onto you. I thought you were hurt or dead or something." Heath paused, hoping for some indication that the girl was listening. "I'm glad you're not—dead or hurt, I mean." He paused again, but still no response from the nearby trees. "So, like I said, I'll just be going *since it's about to rain, and all,*" he added, hoping she was not missing that fact. He didn't feel right leaving her out there, but wasn't sure what he could do about it, especially since the girl was not inclined to come out from the trees, then Heath had an idea. "I really don't like leaving you out here, 'specially if you don't have some place to go. If you want, I don't live too far from here. My truck is just outside these woods, then the house is just a mile or so away after that." He paused for a moment. It's a big old white house on the right side of the road. Actually, it's the only house on that road," he corrected, "I live there with my mom—her name is Ruth. Besides me and her, there's a handful of old folks, and the cutest little boy you'll ever want to meet; that's Nate—he's my son. He's almost two and, well, that's about it. He hoped the casual conversation might make him seem like less of a villain and ease the girl's fears.

Crouched behind a tree not ten yards away, her arms folded tightly across her ribs, Rae shivered against the cold. She breathed into cupped hands in front of her mouth, then alternately rubbed each arm to warm them, then tucked her hands back into her armpits, contemplating her next move. Peering through the trees in the direction the girl had run, Heath squinted as he scrounged in his thoughts for what else he might say to encourage her to come with him. *If she is tired enough to fall asleep on the bare ground in the woods, she's probably pretty hungry, too.* He felt another tug in his spirit and tried again. "You want to come have supper with us? My mom feeds us all, and she's a real good cook. Let's see, today's Friday, so we should be having either stew or a casserole. She alternates every other week. Now, let's see, is it stew this week or. . .?"

"Thursday." Rae's shivering voice came from somewhere in the trees, surprising both of them.

"What's that?" Relieved, Heath was pleased to know she was still near.

"Today's Thursday." Rae repeated, her teeth chattering.

"No, no, I don't think so," Heath gently corrected, furrowing his forehead, and shaking his head slightly. "Pay day is every other Friday and I just picked up my paycheck today from my accountant. In fact, I got the stub right here in my pocket." He patted his front shirt pocket through his jacket. "Anyway, I'm pretty sure it's Friday."

Rae puzzled over that as she rubbed her arms to keep herself warm, her head pounding. *How can it be Friday? Did I lose a day somewhere?* Heath continued, "Wait, that's right—stew night comes on payday. So, yup—it's stew night, all right." He nodded to himself in confirmation, then paused, pleased that the young woman was still at least within earshot and listening. After a moment, he tried adding a few details, hoping it might sway her to come with him. "My mom sure makes a good stew, too. Huge chunks of meat—sometimes it's beef, sometimes it's chicken. She throws in a bunch of carrots and onions, and celery and potatoes, and seasonings and all. I'm not sure just what all she does to it, but it's real good—I can't wait! Then she usually serves some kind of vegetable—she changes those around, so it's always a surprise, and the best bread you'll ever eat; she makes it herself. I love bread making day; when I come home, the whole house smells like *fresh baked bread.*" Heath emphasized again, hoping his words were enticing enough to coax the girl out.

Salivating, Rae wrestled with whether or not to believe him. *For all I know, it's just a trick to get me to come with him!* Her eyes narrowed—*a really GOOD trick.*

Heath glanced up again at the threatening clouds and then back in the direction of the girl's voice. "There's always plenty to eat, and you just have to give me a chance to make up for scaring you that way." Rae didn't answer. "Well, I'll give you a minute to think it over, but don't take too long because *it's fixin' to storm,*" he emphasized again, "And I, for one, don't want to be out in it." He paused and listened, but there was still no response from the trees. "Yeah, it's gonna be a cold one, too. You see all them black clouds?" He gestured toward the ominous black wall not very far off. "I didn't see no jacket on you. I hope you don't end up getting rained on. It's cold enough out here now, without being wet, too." He hoped that would add a little urgency in the girl's mind. Rae didn't doubt that it was going to rain, she could tell that by the clouds, but still wondered. . .*Is it really going to rain that soon. . .or that hard?—Or did he just make up that part to speed along his plan to ambush me?* As credible as he sounded, she didn't want to be a sucker.

When she still didn't answer, Heath sighed and tried to stall his departure a little longer. "You know, it only rains when I want to hunt. Like, just last week, the forecast all week was rain, so I didn't plan any hunting—and, wouldn't you know, it didn't rain once. Now, today, they said it wasn't going rain until later tonight, so I went in to work early so I could get out here and do some hunting and, you see? Rain! *And it's fixin' to start real soon,* that's why I was wanting to get home so quick." Out of ideas, Heath tried the direct approach. "So, y'all want to come have some of my mom's stew?" There was still no answer from the trees in front of him. "Oh, I'm sorry. I haven't even told you who I am. No wonder you're not beating a path over here. Can't expect you to want to join me for supper if you don't even know my name, right? I'm Heath—Heath Dawson. That's with a 'D.'" Just about out of things to say, Heath sighed. *Maybe it's because I'm standing here. Maybe she'll come out if I start walking.* "Tell you what—I'm starting to get cold standing here, so I'm just going to start walking again. He hoped his leaving might speed up her decision, but Rae only watched and shivered. Heath tried again, "You can follow along behind me, if you feel safer—or even come later, if you feel better doing that. But the nice thing about coming with me is that you won't have to walk that last mile or so, because my truck is parked out on the road, just outside the woods."

He turned long enough to point toward the road. "Like I said, it's straight ahead through these woods about a half mile. . ." He interrupted his directions, "I'd really like it if you could come along so you don't get lost. . .again." He hoped that might encourage her to join him, but he saw no movement among the trees. He sighed again, "Anyway, after you go out that way the half mile," he hiked his thumb over his shoulder, "then you'll come to a road, just go to the right and follow it for about a mile or so. Then, when it bends to the left, it's the first house—actually, it's the *only* house on that road. It has green shutters and a wrap-around porch. You can't miss it. Anyway, I'll just be on my way." Concern evident on his face, Heath sighed, then turned and started back on his path, forcing himself to not look back right away.

Seeing the stranger, and his offer for a hot meal, turn away, the power struggle heightened between Rae's stomach and her sense of caution. For a moment, she considered following him. Then, eyes narrowing, something occurred to her and she squinted past the stranger, recalling his hiked thumb. *So the road is that way. . .* She craned her head 180 degrees. *That means my Cessna is this way.* Considering that possibility, she glanced again at the man, and then back. *If I just go in this direction, I should find it and I can just radio for help.* That possibility took the risk out of following the stranger. *Yeah, it can't be that far and then I won't need his help.* She nodded to herself. *I can handle it from here.* Satisfied, Rae turned her attention back to the stranger and watched him another moment as he paused briefly to look up at the sky, then back in her direction. He hesitated for several moments, then turned, and pressed ahead through the woods, his retreating form growing smaller and dimmer as he made his way through the trees until he disappeared from view. At that moment, Rae's stomach growled loud and long, as if to protest her decision. She looked down and answered her belly, "It's too late, he's gone." Twisting again to the view behind her, Rae squinted through the trees, thinking. Certain her plane was not far away, she shook her head. *No, I got this.*

Heath continued through the woods to his truck, glancing back over his shoulder periodically, hoping to see the girl appear in the distance behind him, but she didn't. Once he got into his truck, he was home minutes later, and just as he stepped out of his truck the icy rain began to fall. Quickly, he jogged over to the back porch, climbed the steps then ducked under its shelter, already wet. He stood there on their wrap-around porch, gazing out through the rain, thinking back on the frightened look in the girl's eyes after he had startled her, and how cold she felt when he had touched her skin. *With this rain on her, she must be freezing by now.* Dismayed, he grimaced, not wanting to give up, but not knowing what else to do. Stepping to the railing, he leaned the heel of his hand on a post and watched the rain for a moment. Sighing heavily, then prayed softly, "Father, please help that girl find some food and shelter tonight. Help her to trust someone, Lord."

Finally, with the rain pounding on the porch roof above him, he pushed open the kitchen door and went inside the warm, inviting house that his mom had made into a home for all of them.

Having gotten her bearings from the stranger's gesture toward the road, Rae was now certain her aircraft was not far off. Unusually fatigued, despite her long nap on the ground, she set off in a straight line away from him, working her way back through the woods toward the field. What she didn't know was that her starting point from where she encountered the stranger was further west than she thought, so about the time she expected to break out of the woods and into the furrowed field, all she found was more woods. After continuing on for another ten minutes, she stopped. *I should be there by now.* She glanced around for a moment, and then up at the sky, pivoting in all directions. *Maybe it's just further than I thought.* She started off again. After another five minutes, she stopped again, certain she had missed it somehow.

Weak from fatigue and hunger, Rae's shoulders sagged wearily. "Where is it? I have to find it!" Exhausted, all she wanted to do was to curl up and go to sleep, but the black clouds looming so near excluded that as a possibility, so she trudged on. But without her realizing it, the straight line she thought she had been walking was in reality a wide arc, and each stride took her further away from her destination. As Rae trudged on, her thoughts drifted back to the man and his offer, wishing now—risky or not—that she had accepted. A stiff, cold gust of wind sent her into a spasm of shivering, as if to rub in her poor choice. She reproved herself in her thoughts—*Why didn't you just go with him? Why did you have to try to go back to the your aircraft?*

"Because I was sure it was close by!" She defended aloud in response. Winded, she stopped, standing with one hand on her hip, the other hanging limply at her side, she pivoted around her as she tried to catch her breath; nothing she saw gave her even the slightest clue. After a few moments, she shook her head. *Great Rae—now you're REALLY lost!* Irritated, she barked at the thoughts that accused her, "Yeah, I'm lost!—*okay?* I admit it!—I shouldn't have gone into these woods—I should've just stayed at the Cessna and radioed for help. There, I said it—are you happy?" She scowled to herself, then scoffed, "A lot of good that'll do me now." Rubbing her hands together, and then her arms, Rae grumbled, "Why did I have to leave my jacket? That was really dumb. . ." She shook her head. *Just another bad choice in a long list of them—starting with going against Dad to take Kirk's charter!* She berated herself in her thoughts, *What in the world is the matter with me?—I can't seem to make a good decision lately to save my life!* She shook her head, then stopped to swallow the last bit of water from her bottle, then she stared at the empty container as the fear she had kept at bay began to press in on her mind from all sides. *Man, this is serious. If I don't get inside somewhere before that storm hits, I could actually die out here!*

Just then, another icy gust of wind whipped at her hair and face. With the length of time she'd been searching, and the lack of results, Rae began to feel more and more hopeless and alarmed. Breathing hard, she leaned against a tree, attributing her weakness to her exertion and her chill to the falling temperature. With another chilling burst of wind, icy rain began to fall. First a few drops, but quickly, it poured down in icy sheets. "No!" Rae clenched her jaw in frustration, preferring the anger to the fear that had crept up within. Cold and heavy, the rain quickly soaked her clothing and she forced herself to press on, fearfully aware that she could not continue much further. She slogged through the mud and stumbled over branches and rocks, barely able see a path in front of her—let alone find her aircraft.

Twenty minutes later, it was now dark and still she had not found the Cessna. "I'll just go back to where I saw that man. Maybe I can find the house he talked about." The thought encouraged her, only now she was so turned around she had no idea which way that might be. Making her best guess Rae set out in that direction but, frustrated and completely exhausted, it wasn't long before she had to stop again. "It has to be here somewhere! But where? I don't even know which direction to try anymore!" She began to fret, "I have to find it! I can't stay out here all night—I'll freeze to death!" She set out again. Groping in complete darkness now, she pressed on aimlessly, not knowing what else to do, and after a short time, though she did not think it possible, the rain began coming down even harder and Rae shivered uncontrollably, feeling more hopeless with each passing minute. After another round of backtracking and detours, defeated in spirit, she had not found anything that even remotely resembled a house. Finally, she had to stop again to get her breath. Panting fearfully, a new realization crept into her conscious thought. *Man, if I die out here, no one will ever find me!* Her eyes widened. *My dad will never know what happened to me!* The thought was sobering, and spurred her on. She set out trudging through endless mud and trees. Slipping and staggering, twice she tripped over unseen obstacles and fell head-long into the mud with a splash. The freezing rain pounded down on her as she wondered where in the world the end of these woods could be.

** *** **

Still brooding over the girl at supper, Heath roused from his thoughts only long enough to occasionally nudge Nate along with his meal. Knowing these days that her son preferred to be left to his thoughts, Ruth tried to let him alone, but after another sigh, she had to ask. "You doing all right, Heath?" His mom's voice jarred him from his thoughts and he glanced up. Ruth stood across the big dining room table watching him as she ladled a spoonful of stew into Mr. Peterman's bowl. "What's got you so preoccupied tonight?" She'd seen his swollen lip when he came in from hunting, and he had been sulking ever since. He wasn't the brawling type, so Ruth was very curious, and had been waiting for him to feel ready to talk about it.

"Just thinking," Heath sighed, returning to his thoughts. He poked at the stew in his bowl with the spoon in his left hand, rubbing the back of his neck with his right, wrestling in his thoughts. He hated the thought that the girl was out there somewhere. Even more, he hated that he hadn't been able to convince her to come with him. *Maybe I'll just go out tomorrow and check on her. I wonder if she will still be there, or if she will have moved on by then? Isn't that what vagrants do?—Pick up and go?* He shook his head slowly and reminded himself. *She didn't look like a vagrant, though.* The more he thought about it, the more he became convinced she wasn't one. *No, she was lost. That has to be it—or maybe a runaway.* Whichever it was, he was sure she didn't have any business being in those woods. *I shouldn't have left her there!* The thought thundered into his mind like a freight train. Heath groaned within himself. *Man, I hope she makes it through the night in this weather!* He glanced up out the windows across from him, seeing and hearing the rain beat against them. He shook his head again, dismayed. Vexed in his spirit, his thoughts accused him. He shook his head trying to justify—*She wouldn't come! I tried everything I could think of to coax her out: food, warmth, shelter. . . But nothing worked! What was I supposed to do?—Drag her home with me kicking and screaming?* He sighed again, unsoothed, irritated with himself. *I hope her watch is water proof.*

"There you go sighing again. Now, what's eating you Heath Dawson?" Ruth had worked her way around the table filling everyone's bowls, and was now standing next to his chair.

"Huh?"

"You're sitting here lost in your thoughts, huffing and puffing like a love-sick school boy." She set the pot of stew down on the cart next to her, and reached for a large bowl of green beans.

"Not love sick, Mom, just a little heart sick," Heath replied, still staring out the window across the table from him.

Ruth could see he was truly troubled and ceased her teasing. She handed the bowl of green beans to Mrs. Balcomb who sat two chairs down from Heath, and gestured for her to take some and pass it on to her husband next to her, then across to Mr. Windom and Mr. Peterman. Ruth set the plate of her bread going in the opposite direction around the table, then she sat down in the empty chair next to Heath.

"Did something happen at work today?" she ventured softly, offering support now, instead of teasing.

Heath sighed again, "Not at work—after work." Heath leaned close to Ruth so that he could speak more privately without the Gang overhearing. "On my way back from hunting, I found this girl lying on the ground in the woods." Ruth's eyebrows arched. Heath continued, "I thought she was dead, or something, but I guess she was just sleeping. Then she woke up and saw me, it scared her and she ran off and hid. Anyway, she was really cold and I figured she hadn't eaten, so I invited her to come for supper."

Ruth's eyes widened, "You invited someone you found in the woods to come here? Do you think that was wise?"

Heath could hear the concern in her voice. "I know how it sounds, Mom, but I can't explain it. I just had this feeling that I should help her. I tried, but she wouldn't come. I guess I just scared her too much."

Ruth scoffed mildly. "Now Heath, you are about as scary as a bunny rabbit!"

Heath smiled weakly in spite of his anxiety, then sighed again and rubbed his forehead. He listened to the rain pounding on the roof of the front porch outside the window he stared through. "You know, Mom, when I found her, I thought she was dead. She was as cold as ice and she looked like she'd been shot."

Ruth kept her voice low. "What do you mean, 'shot'? Are you sure?"

"No, I didn't get a good look at it. She had blood on her shirt by her shoulder and I saw what looked like it could be a bullet hole."

"Do you think we should call the sheriff, or something?"

Heath thought for a moment, "I'm not sure. I mean, she didn't seem like she was hurt bad when she ran off. Maybe she just fell or snagged her shirt on something and it poked a hole. Who knows? That's just it, Mom, if I called the sheriff I'm not sure what I would tell them, or even what they would do—or could do." He thought for another moment and shook his head again. "No, I don't get the impression that I need to call the sheriff. I just got this. . .this thing, nagging at my spirit, that makes me feel like I need to help her—but she didn't seem to want any help."

"Is that what happened to your lip? She didn't want the help?"

Embarrassed, Heath touched his swollen lip, and smiled weakly. "Yeah, when she woke up and saw me leaning over her, it scared her. I don't know what I got hit with—it had to be her foot, from the force of it—but I was seeing stars for a few seconds." He fell silent again for a moment. "Maybe if I hadn't scared her, she would have been okay with coming here and we wouldn't be having this conversation."

"Now, Heath, you don't know that."

"No, you're right. I don't. I just wish it had gone better. I did everything I could think of to show her I wasn't some kind of 'backwoods boogie man,' but I just couldn't convince her to come with me. She wasn't even wearing a coat when I found her."

Ruth's eyebrows arched, "No coat? Oh, my—that isn't good, especially in a storm like this. Well, if she didn't want to come, you couldn't force her, Heath. We'll have to just pray for her and hope for the best." Ruth patted his arm, "She's in Adonai's hands, Heath. We just need to trust Him."

"I *do* trust Him, Mom—but I just feel like I got to do more than that. The fact is I shouldn't have left her out there! Maybe I should have trusted God more while I was out there, and waited longer for her to decide, instead of just leaving like I did."

"You did your best, son." Heath only sighed in response and Ruth could tell he wasn't comforted—and neither was she, for that matter. She laid her hand on her son's forearm again, and nudged him, and repeated, "Heath, you did your best."

"Did I, mom?" Heath leaned back into his chair, forgetting about the listening ears close by. "I was just in a big hurry to get home before it started raining, and that was so wrong of me—just thinking about myself like that! She could die of exposure out there, or run into a bear, or get tore-up by a pack of wild pigs or something." Heath stared at the table for a moment, shaking his head. "I'm sitting in here warm and dry, and she's out there freezing to death because I didn't stay and try hard enough."

"Heath..."

Heath would not be consoled. He sighed again then raised his chin, "You know, mom, I just can't sit here like this and 'hope' that she will be okay; it isn't right." He put down his spoon and pushed himself away from the table and left the dining room, through the doorway into the kitchen with Ruth following after him, then crossed the kitchen to the mudroom. Ruth watched as he pulled his jacket and rain slicker off their pegs, and his wide brimmed hat and the big floodlight torch from the shelf. Reaching down, he grabbed his boots and stepped back into the kitchen. Setting everything down on the table, he sat in the nearest chair, reaching for his shoe laces.

"You fixin' to go out in that rain and find her?"

"Yes, Ma'am." Heath's voice was gentle, but determined. Ruth knew her son's caring nature and studied his face for a moment. Seeing his tormented countenance, she decided not to press him. At thirty years old, he was long past being treated like a child.

"I just made some coffee, you want to take it with you?"

"Thanks Mom, I'd appreciate that." He put his foot into a boot.

Ruth stepped over to the stove and retrieved the thermos bottle from the cupboard above it. Pensively, she filled it with the steaming coffee. "You think you can find her again?"

"I don't know, but I'm praying I do—I have to try."

278

"What happens if you find her, and she still won't come with you?"

Heath finished putting on one boot, and reached for the other. "Maybe after being out in this cold rain this long, she won't be so hard to convince."

Ruth nodded twisting on the thermos cap and cup and brought it over to the table, just as Heath finished with his boots and stood to put on the jacket. "The wind has been picking up—I don't want a tree falling on you."

"I'll be careful." She handed him the thermos of coffee. "Thanks, Mom." Heath pulled the slicker over his jacket. "I'll be back as soon as I can."

He leaned down and kissed her on the forehead, then picked up his hat and the large flashlight from the table and stepped outside, closing the door behind him. Ruth listened to his footfalls along the porch until they faded away. After a few moments, watching out the window, saw his truck pull around from the back. She gazed after it until his red tail lights blurred and faded in the heavy rain.

"Father, watch over Heath. He has a good heart and just wants to make sure that girl he found is okay—and watch over her, too Father; please lead her to some shelter tonight."

Chapter 23

Andrea leaned close to her steering wheel, squinting through her windshield as she peered out into the night; her wipers swishing back and forth on their fastest setting, unable to keep up with the pouring rain. *I can't see a thing out there!* She didn't know her way around Heartland all that well to begin with, and now, between the darkness and the pouring rain, she wasn't even sure anymore where she was. Switching on her dome light, she glanced at the written directions in her hand as she crept along the road, reading each street sign as she searched for the intended cross street. Not finding it, she sped up to cross a wide, dark gap in the middle of a row of homes. Suddenly, a wave of water cascaded up on both sides of her car and surged up under her floorboards. Andrea winced, *Uh-oh, I guess there was some deep water across the road there.* Fortunately, it was brief, and she emerged out the other side and resumed her search. Instead of finding the street, she ended up back at a main road again, but not the one she was expecting. Glancing around her, nothing seemed familiar.

"Oh, great, this isn't where I'm supposed to come out!" She consulted her directions again, frowning, "Where in the world am I?"

She glanced at the road signs; neither street name familiar at all. The light changed to green, and she eased forward around the corner. Suddenly, except for the rain pounding on her roof and windshield, everything went ominously silent. Immediately, she reached for her key and tried to restart her engine. It cranked and whined, but didn't turn over. "Oh!" Andrea groaned, "Not now!" She turned off her headlights and tried the key again, with no success. Resigned, she switched on her hazard lights and steered toward the curb, hoping she could coast to the shoulder before her car stopped completely, praying all the while that she would not have to get out in that rain and push it. At the shoulder of the road, she tried again to crank it, but his time it only clicked when the key was turned. Exasperated, she exhaled forcefully, "Oh, that's just great." Reaching for her pocketbook, Andrea fished for her cell phone. Finding it, she pressed the speed-dial button for her son, then listened for the call to connect. When it went to voicemail, she ended the call and tried texting him. She glanced at her watch. "Rats, he's in class. He probably won't get that message for at least an hour."

Wondering who else she might call, she began scrolling through her contacts. Suddenly an unexpected name drifted upward on her screen. "What. . .? No way!" Quickly, she reversed her scroll, squinting to see if she had read wrong. Again the name drifted down her screen. "Joel Greenbaum? How did *he* get in here?" She puzzled for a moment, and then continued scrolling through her short list. Of the few names that were possibilities, she only got their voicemails, as well. Frowning, she thought about her options, "I can't call a tow truck—they'll want cash, and I don't have much with me." She sighed and tried her son again, with the same results. This time she left a message, "Matt, this is mom. My car broke down and I'm stranded somewhere in Heartland. Would you call me as soon as you get this?" She ended the call and sat there, thinking. Again, she began scanning her contacts, in case she missed someone. Joel's name scrolled past again. Shaking her head, she protested, "Noooo!" she stretched out the word, arguing with herself, "I don't want to call him!" After scrolling through her list twice more, and coming up empty, Andrea sighed in resignation, "Maybe he won't be available." She wondered why she would even hope that when it was obvious she needed help, then answered her own thoughts. "All I know for sure is that I don't want it to be *him* that helps me!" She stared at his name again, puzzling. *How did his number get into my phone, anyway?* She sighed again and hung her head, then pushed "send" to connect to Joel's number. "I wonder if he picks up on unidentified callers?"

After a couple of rings she heard Joel's voice answer, but she hesitated. When he repeated his greeting, she grimaced and sighed again. "Um, yeah, is this Joel?"

"Yeah, this is Joel. . ."

"Um, hi."

"Andrea? Is that you?"

"Yeah, it's me." Andrea's voice sounded weary.

Joel grinned with delight. "Well, this is a surprise!"

"Yeah. I know what you mean. I didn't even know your number was in my phone. Any idea how it got there?"

"Maybe it came with the phone."

"Right. . . somehow, I doubt that. Listen, I'm sorry to bother you. . ."

"Oh, I'm not bothered. What can I do for you?"

"Well, my car broke down and I'm stuck."

"Where are you?" Andrea gave him the names of the streets she'd seen on the signs. "What? What are you doing over there?"

"Well, you know. I'm looking to score some drugs to feed my habit," she tried to tease, but her heart wasn't in it.

"Well, from what I hear, you're in the right neighborhood for that."

Andrea's eyes widened. "Seriously?"

"Pretty close."

Suddenly frightened, Andrea defaulted again to sarcasm, "Oh, that's just great!"

"Did you call a tow truck?"

"No. They always want cash and I only have about seven dollars with me."

"Seven dollars?—And you don't have roadside assistance?"

"No."

"What is a single lady doing going around without roadside assistance, with only seven dollars in her wallet?" He reproved, but didn't wait for an answer, "Okay, I'm on my way. Stay in your car—and lock the doors!"

"I will. Thanks Joel, I appreciate it." Andrea ended the call, then tapped in another number, and waited for it to connect. "Marjorie? Hi, it's Andrea. . .No, it looks like I'm not going to make it; my car broke down. No, I'll be fine; help is on the way. . . Yeah, me too. I'll see you on Shabbat." When Andrea ended the call, she sat tensely for a moment, listening to the rain pound on her roof and windows. Suddenly remembering Joel's directive, she quickly locked all of her doors, and prayed as she anxiously waited for help to arrive.

Within ten minutes, to Andrea's relief, a police cruiser pulled up behind her car. *Oh, thank you, Father!* Andrea watched in her side mirror as the officer got out. He fastened his yellow rain slicker as he crossed between their cars, approaching her passenger side door, and tapped on her window. She tried to roll down the window, but with no power, she couldn't. Instead, she reached over and unlocked and unlatched the door and the police officer opened it a few inches. "Are you having some trouble, ma'am?"

"My car died."

"This isn't a real good place to be stuck in," he drawled. "You lost or something?"

"I think I made a wrong turn somewhere along the way."

"Yup. I'd say so! Have you called a tow truck?"

"No, sir."

"Well, let me do that. They probably wouldn't come out here if you called 'em, anyway." Andrea swallowed hard. Noting her strained expression, the officer offered, "Ma'am, would you like to come back here and wait in my car?"

Andrea nodded, her voice small, "Yes, sir, that would be really nice."

He closed the passenger side door and came around to her side of the car as Andrea gathered her things. Opening her door, the officer helped her out. "I'm sorry, I don't have an umbrella for you, ma'am."

"That's okay, I'm just glad you're here." He helped her into the back seat of his cruiser then took his seat in the front. The officer radioed for a wrecker, then the two sat in silence listening to the rain pounding on the roof.

** *** **

Exhausted and fighting panic, Rae coached herself, "I can do this. I just can't give up. Just a little further, and I'll be there—wherever 'there' is." The more she coached herself that she would make it, the more she doubted it—and the more she doubted it, the angrier she became. As she trudged along, breathing hard and shivering, she addressed her Maker for the first time in many months. "You have control over all this! —Why don't you do something? I'll tell you why!—because you don't care, *that's why!* Just like I thought!" She railed at God and raged at the storm, her trudging turning into stomping. "You didn't care about me when my mom died and you don't care now! You just sit there and let bad things happen, and don't do anything about it! You don't even—"

Suddenly, Rae tripped and fell head long again, landing hard with a splash, rolling against a tree trunk, the wind knocked out of both her—*and* her sails. Shakily, Rae pushed herself up from the mud. Unable to see from the rain and the darkness, she reeled and tottered on the slippery, uneven ground, just trying to bring herself to a stand. Finally upright, she cried and groaned in frustration, then glanced around her.

"Now which way do I go?" She squinted through the rain in another direction. "Which way did I come from?" She had no idea.

Where have you been, Rae?

The voice sounded as though right behind her. Alarmed, Rae whirled around wide-eyed, finding no one, "Okay, now I'm really nutting-up, here." She backed-up a few paces, tripping over an unseen tree root. This time Rae tumbled backward and slid several feet down an incline, sliding into a tree with a thud, yelping on impact. Upside-down with her shoulders in the mud and her legs halfway up a tree, she lay there stunned for a moment, collecting her wits and her bearings, then maneuvered herself around. Now sitting upright with her back against the tree that had stopped her slide, she drew her legs up close as the icy rain beat down on her. Increasingly fearful and thoroughly discouraged she clutched her knees and, shivering against the cold, she began to cry.

At that moment, a light flashed onto the trees ahead of her, and then away, then into the trees again. Glancing up anxiously, her crying abruptly stopped as she searched for its source, craning her head around the tree against which she leaned. Not far away from her place on the ground, she spied a light bobbing in the darkness; it seemed to float in the sky. She rolled onto her knees and pushed against the tree until she was standing, and faced the direction of the light—but as she did, the light disappeared, eclipsed by the branches above her. Kneeling again, the light flickered against the tree branches ahead of her—*There it is again! That's weird—I can only see it when I'm crouching down.* Suddenly hopeful, Rae straightened again, and quickened her pace toward the light, puzzling in her thoughts. *If I hadn't fallen, I would never have seen it!*

Her eyes fixed upward on the light, Rae hurried toward it. All at once, the ground fell away from under her feet as she broke out of the woods. Tumbling down an embankment into a cleared area, she landed with a splash in a wide puddle. Rolling herself over, she pushed up onto all fours, then sat on her calves. She stared skyward at the dancing, bobbing light, still ahead, though nearer. Immediately she was on her feet, trudging toward the swaying, flickering light until it was nearly straight above her. *Oh—it's a flood light attached to a tree!* The wind swayed the tree, making the light flicker through the swaying branches. *If there's a light, then someone must live close by around here—and since it's on, maybe that means they're home!*

Anticipation growing, Rae glanced around her, peering through the rain and darkness. Off to her left, in the flickering, shifting light, Rae could barely make out a building. Drawing near, she circled it. An old wooden structure with two large doors that stood side-by-side, hinged on the outside edges. *It's a garage!* Approaching the far side, Rae came upon a narrow stairway that rounded the corner and climbed upward, coming to a stop on a landing at the next floor. She peered up at it through the rain. It looks like a carriage house—*maybe that's an apartment up there!* Hopeful, she pulled herself up along the railing, until she stood at a door with a multi-paned window in the top half. Cupping her hands around her eyes, Rae peered in, but could see nothing. She knocked on the door and jiggled the knob, but it was securely locked. Further efforts with increased force, only proved useless. Deciding this was not an option, she hurried back down the stairway. *If there is a garage, there must be a house nearby, right?*

Rae stepped off the stairs next to the double garage doors and hesitated. *I guess, the house would be in front or next to it.* Rae pivoted. *If it's in front, it would be over there somewhere.* She peered through the pouring rain into the gloom. Seeing nothing, she just sighed and began walking in that direction. A swirling gust of wind sent her into another fit of shivering, and threw the flickering light against another building. Seeing it, Rae quickened her pace toward it. Drawing nearer, her eyes widened. *It's a house!*

Shivering in the rain, she took another step, then hesi-tated—suddenly concerned about approaching a strange house at night, and what manner of people might live there. Just then, another blast of cold wind convinced her to take the risk. In the flickering light of the floodlight, the house in front of her began to take shape. As Rae crept toward it, she could tell it was a very large and very old house, befitting of the carriage house behind it. As she circled around the near side, she noticed a dim glow coming from a side window near the middle of the wrap-around porch. She gasped excitedly, *Someone's home!* Hopeful again, she stepped toward the side of the house and climbed up the three steps to the porch.

Discouraging thoughts pounded in her mind. *There's no way they are going to open their door to someone who just shows up on their porch at night!* Desperate, Rae strained to think of something to say that would make them want to open their home to her, but nothing would come to mind. She stepped up to a side door, imagining how she might respond if the situation were reversed. *I wouldn't let a stranger into my house in the middle of the day—let alone at night! So, why should they?* Rae came to a hopeless conclusion. *Why should these people help me at all?—They don't even know me!* She moved to turn and leave, but the thought of going back out into the icy rain stopped her. *No, I won't make it if I go back out there. . .* Forlorn, Rae felt the tears well up again as hope waned . . .*but I need help and I don't know what else to do!* The thought tightened her chest, the very concept of needing help foreign and unwelcome.

Rae shivered as she stood there in the shelter of the porch. The soft light from the window shined down near her feet in amber squares on the boards beneath her feet. *Maybe I can just stay out here on the porch?* Then, as if to rebut the notion, an icy gust of wind blew a spray of freezing rain against her. Immediately rejecting that plan, Rae inched toward the side door. . .*but what if they say no? Where can I go then?*

But what if they say yes?

The thought popped into her mind, as though someone interrupting. Chilled to the bone and out of options, she turned, staring again at the amber squares. As she scoured her brain for some other way, a shrill sound came from inside. The squeal of the tea kettle summoned Ruth from the pages of her book. Setting it aside, she padded into the kitchen and shut off the stove, the squeal fading away as she lifted the boiling kettle from the hot burner. Pouring the steaming water into a waiting mug, Ruth bobbed the tea bag as the mildly spicy aroma wafted up. The floodlight at the back of the property by the garage swayed and bobbed in the wind, flashing into the kitchen window on that side of the house, illuminating the dim room with flickers and flashes. Ruth gazed out the window just as a gust of wind sprayed it with rain. *The storm is getting worse.* Her thoughts drifted again to Heath, hoping he had found that girl and was on his way back. She glanced up at the clock on the wall above the stove, and arched her eyebrows, surprised. *Almost eight—he's been gone over an hour. . .*

The light by the garage swayed toward the house again, splashing the windows with another flash of light. Hoping it was Heath's headlights, Ruth glanced out the window—but instead of seeing a truck pulling in, she caught a glimpse of someone standing on her side porch. Startled, her heart leapt to her throat, and her hand to her chest—and nearly spilled her mug of tea. Another flash of light revealed a girl, soaked to the skin, shivering in the cold, just standing there staring at her feet.

"Land's sakes!" Her fright now overcome by concern, Ruth set down her mug and hurried to the side door. Snatching it open, she surprised the girl. Remembering Heath's tale of how he'd frightened her off, she quickly softened her approach, speaking warmly, "There you are! I've been expecting you! Come on in here before you freeze to death!"

Rae only stood there, stunned. *Expecting me?*

Ruth waved her in. "C'mon now, hon, we're letting out all the warm air!" Ruth approached her gently, praying all the while for wisdom in bringing an unknown person into her home. "Let's get you inside. We've got to get you outta those wet clothes and into something warm and dry." With one hand to the girl's back, gently urging her toward the door, Ruth slipped her other hand around Rae's wrist. Feeling her cold, wet skin, her apprehension turned to deep concern. "Goodness girl, you're half frozen!" She drew Rae inside, and closed the door behind them.

All at once, the lights went on in Rae's mind. She turned to the woman at her side and gazed curiously into her face, marveling. Her voice was small, "You're Ruth."

"That's right, sweetheart, c'mon now. We've got to get you warmed up,"

Rae gazed numbly in amazement at the woman as she let herself be led through the kitchen, wondering how in the world she had ended up there. Ushering Rae through the louver door and across the front room, she stopped at the downstairs bathroom. Ruth grabbed a towel from the shelf and wrapped it around Rae's shoulders. "What's your name, hon?"

"Rae," she uttered, still mystified.

"Well, I'm glad to meet you, Rae." Ruth smiled warmly, with a genuineness that put to rest Rae's apprehensions. "I'm glad you finally made it. We were worried about you. Heath fretted all through supper over you being out there, and finally he just went out looking for you!"

"What. . .?" Rae could not comprehend a stranger doing such a thing.

"That's right, and he's still out there. He'll be so relieved when he gets back and sees you're here!" Ruth reached into the shower and turned it on, feeling the spray with her hand. "Oh, my, even the cold water is warmer than you are, girl! Now, there's soap and shampoo in there. You take as long as you need to, and I'll find you something dry to put on. Just leave the door unlocked and I'll bring them in while you're in the shower."

Rae nodded and Ruth left her in the bathroom, closing the door behind her, and began her search. Rae stared at the sink, bewildered. *I turned around so many times, all the times I back-tracked. . .* After a moment, her shivering reclaimed center stage, and she peeled off her icy, wet clothes. Testing the water temperature, she adjusted the faucet handles then climbed into the spray. Initially, it felt like needles, stinging her freezing skin, but after a few minutes, it soothed her. She stood there in the spray for a long time, holding her arms close, letting the water cascade down her head and face—unable to stop shivering. As Rae warmed, the spray began to feel tepid, so she turned up the hot water incrementally to keep it hot, until gradually, the the muddy water that ran off of her hair and skin began to run clear, and her shivering subsided—and for the first time in days, Rae finally allowed herself to relax.

Ruth knew for certain that neither she nor Heath had any-thing small enough to fit the slight framed girl. She thought a moment. *Maybe one of the Gang will have something that'll fit.* Most of them were slimmer than she, and much shorter than Heath; she hurried into the back room where her boarders were watching TV. Stepping through the doorway, four sets of eyes turned to her,

"Hey, y'all—do any of you have a set of fleece or a spare set of pajamas you can lend to an unexpected visitor caught in the rain?" Minutes later, Ruth was on her way back to Rae with a sweatshirt and pants—courtesy of Mr. Balcomb. At the bathroom door, she knocked lightly, and opened it a couple of inches. Seeing the fogged mirror, she knew Rae was behind the shower curtain, so she entered. Setting the dry clothes and two more towels on the bathroom counter, she gathered up Rae's wet, muddy clothes and shoes from the floor, and took them to the laundry room. As she lifted each piece into her washing machine, Ruth noticed the hole in the shoulder of Rae's shirt, and the blood stain around it—nearly washed out now from the rain, and shook her head slowly, wondering about the girl in their shower.

** *** **

After another ten minutes, headlights shone into the cruiser from behind. Since the new vehicle didn't pull around in front of her car, Andrea decided it must be Joel. The police officer glanced into his mirror, then opened his door and got out, standing at his door. Andrea turned and watched behind her as the driver's door swung opened and an umbrella emerged and unfurled, followed by a man in a light colored rain coat who turned and approached the police cruiser.

"Are you the guy that called?" The officer called to him, his voice reaching Andrea through the slightly open driver's side window.

"Yes, that's right. I'm Joel Greenbaum. She's a friend of mine. Is she doing okay?"

"She's fine—she was a little nervous, so I asked if she wanted to come back here and wait in my cruiser." The officer gestured to his left at Andrea, and Joel turned and leaned down and peered through her window, smiling,

"Hi, Andrea. How ya doing?" Andrea nodded and Joel returned his attention to the officer. "I called a tow truck."

"So did I. Between the two of us, we'll see if we can get one out here."

Joel leaned down to Andrea's window again, "Andrea, let's get you into my car while we wait for the tow truck."

Andrea nodded and re-gathered her things. Seeing no door handles, she waited for the door to be opened for her by the officer. Holding his umbrella over her head, Joel helped her out and thanked the officer as he escorted Andrea back to his car.

As they walked, Andrea eyed him curiously. "You called the police? I thought he just happened by."

"I didn't want you sitting out here by yourself waiting for me." Touched that he would think to do that for her, Andrea eyed him curiously for several steps as they walked to his car.

Stepping between the two cars, she noted the familiar emblem on the hood in front of her.

"You drive a BMW?"

"That depends," he teased, "are you impressed?"

Andrea grinned, "That you have a car? Yes."

Amused, Joel grinned and laughed out loud, "Well, at least you're impressed at that."

Still smiling, Andrea shook her head, rolling her eyes. "Wow, is it even possible to offend you?"

"Oh, is that your strategy?—To drive me away by offending me?" He grinned at her and Andrea only shrugged sheepishly. "Well, I'm from New York, so you're going to have to work a lot harder if you want to accomplish that." He reached for her door. "You're great at sarcasm, but I don't think you have it in you to be deliberately insulting. You have too good a heart for that." Andrea bristled a bit, but Joel didn't notice, and continued, "Well, whether you were impressed or not, I had an answer for you either way."

"Either way?"

"That's right. If you were impressed, I was just going to say my other car is a Bentley. if you weren't, I was going to say this is just a rental." Amused, Andrea grinned as Joel closed her door. As he did so, a flat bed tow truck passed by and pulled over in front of Andrea's car, then backed up to it. "I'll need your keys." Andrea reached for her pocketbook. "Where do you want it towed?"

"Don't they just take it to the nearest mechanic?" She handed him her spare key.

"That's if you have roadside assistance. If you don't, they'll take it to wherever you pay them to take it. Where's your mechanic?"

"I don't know anyone up here."

"Okaaay," his voice trailed up, "So, where's your mechanic?"

"What do you mean?"

"I mean, 'where is your mechanic?' It's pretty self-explanatory."

"You're not going to pay for them to tow it all the way to Redlands, are you?"

"Unless you think they'll take it there for free—do you have a better idea?"

"Well, no, but. . ." she just sat there frowning.

"Andrea, I can keep asking that question all night, if you want, but I'd really like to get in out of this rain." Andrea frowned, wanting to object, but couldn't. Sighing, she told Joel what he wanted to know. He closed her door and Andrea watched as he approached the tow truck driver, who was already talking with the police officer, and handed him her key.

As much as Andrea bristled that Joel was the one rescuing her, she was grateful for his help, "Thank you, Abba, for Joel coming to help me tonight—and thank you that his number was in my phone. I don't know how he managed that without me noticing it, but thank you. I don't know what I would have done if he hadn't been available."

As she listened to the rain pounding on the roof, Andrea watched the drops pummel and splatter on the windshield, blurring her view of the men outside and of her car being hauled up onto the bed of the tow truck. She watched as Joel shook hands with the police officer then made his way back to his car. Once inside, he started the engine and fastened his seatbelt, then turned to her. "Have you eaten?" Andrea only eyed him, not wanting to answer. Joel took it in stride. "I'll take that as a 'no'. We can either do drive-thru some place on the way, or dine-in somewhere after we drop off your car." He glanced over at her, noting how uncomfortable she seemed with that. "You have a really hard time receiving, don't you?" Her only response being a sigh, a mischievous grin spread across Joel's face. "Well, in the absence of any input from you, I guess I'll just have to choose—and I vote for dining-in—and since you said you only have about seven dollars on you, I believe that officially makes this our *second* date." He grinned at her again, and then suddenly brightened at a new thought. "—And since we're in *my car* this time—you can't run off can you? Looks like you're kind of at my mercy, doesn't it? But don't worry, unlike someone else I know, I won't leave you at the restaurant." Amused with himself, he chuckled.

Outmaneuvered, Andrea just eyed him. "You're enjoying this, aren't you?"

Joel grinned, "You bet! Who knows when I'll get another chance like this?" In her estimation, Joel could not be more delighted, even if he was being a bit smug. Rolling her eyes again, Andrea sighed. Staring out her side window, she could only shake her head as Joel pulled away from the curb behind the tow truck.

Chapter 24

As the girl showered, Ruth tried Heath's cell phone several times, only getting his voicemail. Hearing the water stop, she pocketed the phone and hurried to the laundry room to switch on the washing machine, then came again to the bathroom door, "I have some hot food out here for you, hon. I'll let you decide if you want to dry your hair first or just wrap it in a towel until after you eat."

Inside the bathroom, Rae's head came up at the offer of food. "I'll be right out."

Feeling clumsy and uncoordinated, Rae pulled on the sweatshirt and pants as fast as she could make herself move, then she wrapped a towel around her hair. A moment later, she opened the door and glanced around.

"Right over here, hon—this way," Ruth stood at the louver door, waving Rae back to the kitchen, then disappeared back through it. Rae pushed through the louver door and took the seat at the table where Ruth had set out a bowl of her stew, and the green beans and bread she had served the Gang earlier. Ruth took the chair across from her visitor and watched as Rae stared at the food, "Well, go on ahead, sweetheart—I know you must be hungry." Rae didn't need a second prompting and dug in. Ruth chatted as she ate. "It's so dark out there. I'm relieved you found the house!"

Rae raised her eyes to Ruth as she chewed her stew, thinking, then swallowed and shook her head, speaking softly, "I have no idea how that happened. I was so turned around, I didn't even know which way I was going. I didn't even know this was your house." She shook her head again, still perplexed. Biting into a piece of Ruth's bread, Rae did not remember anything that ever tasted so wonderful.

Ruth smiled warmly, "Well then, it was God who brought you here, hon. He's looking after you—that much is obvious." Ruth punctuated that with an emphatic nod, then smiled again. At her words, Rae hesitated mid-chew, feeling a twinge of guilt. She balked at the thought that God brought her there, but could come up with no other explanation. Only nodding uncertainly in response, she finished chewing her bite of potato. Despite her hunger, she could only manage half of serving of stew and a few bites of bread before her appetite failed. Almost as soon as the food hit her stomach, the extreme fatigue caught up with her and Ruth watched as Rae quickly lost momentum, and began to nod, "You are welcome to stay tonight, if you like, hon." Ruth framed it as an offer, still concerned about possibly scaring her off.

"No, I should probably go. You've already done so much," Rae muttered unrealistically, barely able to keep her eyes open.

Certain Rae would not be going anywhere that night, Ruth didn't argue. "Okay, hon. Let me know if you change your mind, but I just put your clothes in the wash, so it'll be an hour or so before they're ready." She hoped by then, Rae would be long asleep. "When you get done eating, we'll see if we can get your hair dried before you go."

Rae nodded as Ruth went in search of a hair dryer and brought it back downstairs to the bathroom Rae had showered in. Ruth pushed open the louver door, peeking around it to Rae. "I found you a hair dryer and a comb, hon. They're in the bathroom." Rae thanked her and pushed herself away from the table, reaching for her dishes. Seeing them, Ruth's eyes narrowed. "You didn't eat much, hon. You sure that's all you want?" Rae only nodded, her eyes glazing over. Ruth sighed, "Okay then, just leave the dishes for now. I'll get them in a minute."

Rae obliged and set down her dishes, then followed Ruth back to the bathroom. It took some doing to get Rae's tangled hair combed through, but once that was accomplished, and Ruth got her started drying it, she let Rae finish and left to clear the dishes. When the hair dryer shut off, Ruth returned to the bathroom. Standing at the doorway, she admired Rae's long blond hair and how it came almost to her elbows, curling at the ends, "You have very beautiful hair, sweetheart."

Rae glanced up into the mirror at Ruth's reflection. Almost startled, her eyebrows arched—then she smiled, lowering her eyes. "Thanks."

"You looked as though you don't hear that very often."

Rae glanced away from Ruth's reflection, suddenly melancholy—quiet for a moment before answering with a shrug. "My mom used to say that."

Ruth arched an eyebrow, "Used to?"

Rae glanced away. "Yeah, she died last spring."

Her heart pierced at Rae's disclosure, Ruth stepped close to Rae and hugged her across her shoulders. "Well, it's time you started hearing it again." She smiled warmly, watching Rae in the mirror. Rae raised her eyes again to Ruth's reflection, lingering on it for a moment. Ruth asked, "Would you like me to braid your hair or do you want to wear it down?"

Rae suddenly blinked, then swallowed, "Sure, you can braid it, if you want." Ruth smiled and gathered up Rae's hair, dividing it into three sections, then began weaving them into a single, long braid. She glanced at the girl's reflection in the mirror and noticed a single tear tracing down her face, "You doing all right, hon?"

Rae sniffed and quickly wiped away the tear, retreating from the emotions. After a few moments, she shrugged, and decided to venture out. "My mom used to like to braid my hair."

Ruth smiled again, as she worked Rae's hair with her fingers. "I used to braid my girls' hair when they were young."

"Where are they now?"

"Oh, they're grown and married. One of them lives in Indiana, the other married a military man and they live overseas." Ruth noticed the chain around Rae's neck and her eyes traced it to the pendant that dangled from it. Rae fingered it as Ruth braided. "That's a pretty locket."

Rae smiled, glancing down at it. "My dad gave it to me when I turned sixteen."

"From your dad? Well, that's real nice." Ruth smiled into the mirror at Rae's reflection, her heart warmed as it brought back memories of her own daughters' sixteenth birthday.

Rae reached up and opened the locket. "I keep my mom's picture in it." She held the open locket over her shoulder as Ruth stopped braiding to see it.

"Oh, my, you sure do look like her!" She glanced again at Rae in the mirror, "If she had blonde hair, I would think that was you!"

Rae smiled again, gazing at the tiny picture in her locket. "Yeah, that's what my dad says." She closed the locket and let it fall to the end of its chain, then drew her right hand up close to her and cradled it with her left hand, gazing at the backs of her fingers. "She gave me this ring—it was hers when she was young." Rae held up her hand near her shoulder, her palm toward the mirror, so that the ring faced Ruth.

Holding Rae's braid with one hand, Ruth took Rae's fingers into her other, gently drawing close to see the ring with the dainty rose and leaves crafted of Black Hills Gold,

"It's lovely, sweetheart. What a special keepsake." Ruth returned to her braiding and Rae returned to studying her ring for another moment then lowered her hand. In the mirror, she watched Ruth work. Deep inside, it was as though Rae could feel the wall around her heart begin to crack. The baggy sweatshirt hung loosely around Rae's neck, and as Ruth finished the braid, she noticed the rut where the flesh on Rae's shoulder seemed to have been scraped away. Remembering Heath's mention of it, Ruth had wondered how she might approach that subject—and now, seeing the wound there in front of her, she had a context in which to bring it up. She decided to just take it in stride for now, "Hon, this wound on your shoulder looks pretty fresh. I have a first aid kit, if you want me to help you put a dressing on it."

Rae's eyes shifted to meet Ruth's in the mirror. "Yeah, I guess I should. Thanks."

The braid complete, Ruth secured it with the elastic band Rae had taken out of her ponytail, then scurried off to retrieve the first aid kit. In a few moments, she was back with the kit and set it on the bathroom counter. "Let's see," Ruth opened the container and pulled out a large square of gauze wrapped in paper, and a roll of plastic tape, then reached into another section for a little brown bottle and a cotton ball. Unscrewing the bottle lid, she readied the cotton ball. "Now, this is going to sting some." Rae nodded, bracing herself. Taking hold of the loose sweatshirt collar, Ruth moved it around so that the entire wound was exposed. "Here Rae, hold this for me."

Rae's hand came up obediently, taking hold of the collar and stretching it a little further. Ruth began daubing the raw stripe of missing skin with the orange liquid from the bottle.

Rae tensed and grimaced tightly, her eyes watering immediately. *Man!—that stings worse than when it happened!* Ruth winced sympathetically; knowing that having iodine put on raw flesh was not a pleasant experience. Despite the intense stinging, Rae neither cried out, nor pulled away as Ruth fanned the wound with her fingertips. After a moment, she folded the gauze pad and laid it horizontally over the stripe, and taped it with three lengths of the tape—one across each end, and another across the middle.

She glanced up at Rae, who was still grimacing. "You can open your eyes now, hon," she teased. Rae smiled, feeling a little silly. "It'll still be a while before your clothes are dry, how about we go sit in the parlor and have us some tea or hot chocolate. How does that sound?"

Rae nodded into the mirror. "Sure, tea sounds good, thank you."

Ruth smiled at the girl's manners, her apprehensions diminishing a few more notches. She led Rae to the parlor and opened the door, flipping on the light switch,

"Y'all go right in and make yourself comfortable. I'll put the pot on the stove." Rae did as instructed and found a place at the end of the sofa and sat down stiffly, already feeling chilled again. Ruth scurried into the kitchen, re-filled the tea pot and set it on the stove, then rushed to the linen closet for a pillow and quilt for her guest, hoping to persuade her to give up her notion of going back out into the storm. Ruth returned with her arms full of the bedding and plopped them on the other end of the sofa from Rae, who eyed them uncertainly. Thinking fast, Ruth spoke as she unfolded the heavy quilt. "I know you said you had to go, sweetheart, but this room is a little chilly and I thought you can at least be warm and comfy while you're waiting for your clothes to dry, right?"

301

Rae shrugged and nodded, as Ruth draped the quilt around her shoulders, then slipped the pillow into its case and handed it to her. The teapot squealing summoned Ruth back to the kitchen, and she scurried off again. A few minutes later, she returned with a small tray holding two mugs of steaming tea—Chamomile, to encourage Rae's sleepiness. Rae still sat stiffly on the edge of the sofa, holding the quilt around her.

"Oh, sweetheart, go on ahead and sit on back and relax. Put your feet up and make yourself comfortable!" Ruth waited for Rae to do that, then handed her a mug of tea. "Do you like sugar in it?"

"If you have some; if not, I can drink it plain."

"No, I have some right here." Ruth lifted the lid of the sugar bowl on her tray, and dipped in a spoon, and Rae leaned forward and spooned some of the sugar into her tea and stirred. She leaned back with her mug, tucking her feet up next to her and Ruth switched on the table lamp next to Rae, then took a seat in the chair adjacent her, pulling her feet up into it, as well. She watched as Rae blew across her tea and sipped, having a million questions, but asking none of them, not wanting to make Rae uncomfortable and risk a decision to leave. Instead of pressing to satisfy her curiosity about her visitor, Ruth fell back on every mother's stand-by—she talked about her family. So entranced was she over the woman adjacent to her, it didn't occur to Rae to call her dad. Glad to not be the one talking and grateful to not be answering questions, Rae listened and smiled, and sipped her tea until her mind fogged and her eyes blurred. Not lasting even ten minutes into Ruth's story, her head lolled backward, and she was dead-asleep. Pleased at her success, Ruth eased the mug out of Rae's fingers and set it on the coffee table. After drawing the quilt around the sleeping girl, she quietly let herself out of the room, turning off the overhead light while leaving on the small table lamp, and closed the door behind her.

** *** **

After the half hour drive down to Redlands, Andrea's car safely touched down from the flatbed and was maneuvered into a parking space at her mechanic. Awkward and uncomfortable, Andrea watched as Joel paid the driver and shook his hand. Then, wrapping her spare key inside a note with her cell number, she dropped the bundle into the key slot of the mechanic's office, and they hurried back to Joel's car. After getting her door, Joel jogged around and returned to his seat next to her. "Now we eat!" He beamed at her. "So, where to? Any preferences?"

"Can't you just take me home?"

"Not on your life!"

"Joel, this isn't funny."

"Oh, on the contrary, I think it's a riot!" When Andrea's shoulders sagged, Joel eased up. "C'mon Andrea, we're talking dinner with me—not going to the gallows." He arched his eyebrows toward her, "Hey, after rescuing you like that and following your car all the way down here to Redlands, the least you can do is let me take you to dinner."

Andrea squinted at him. "Let you. . .?—Like it's your reward, or something?" Joel nodded readily. Amused with his reasoning, Andrea couldn't help chuckling. "Oh, all right."

"There!—was that so hard? Now, where to?"

"Anything is fine."

"Well, that's good, but I don't know what kind of restaurants you have out here—so where to?"

"For what kind of food? We have a few 'family dining' places, a couple of steak restaurants, um. . . Greek, Seafood, Italian, Asian. . ."

"How about Asian? Do you have one of those where your table is around a grill?"

"Yes, we actually do."

"Great! Lets go there!" Pleased, Joel followed her directions until they pulled into the parking lot. To her chagrin, they ran into someone from the synagogue and were seated with them at the grill. Andrea sighed. *What are the chances of this?* But, since Joel considered this his reward for rescuing her, Andrea purposed in her heart to have a pleasant evening with him. Between being entertained by the chef, who transformed slicing meat and vegetables into an art form—and the camaraderie of the other diners at their grill—the meal passed quickly and painlessly and was actually enjoyable.

** *** **

Heath stared numbly out the windshield, hypnotically watching the wipers as they tried to keep up with the rapidly re-gathering rain drops after each sweep across the glass. Disconcerted and discouraged, he pulled off the road onto their long drive a minute later, coming to a stop around back, at the carriage house garage. Ruth brought Rae's mug into the kitchen just in time to see his headlights shimmer past her kitchen window. Relieved, and smiling in anticipation of telling him her news, she glanced at the clock. It was nearly nine. Heath had been gone over two hours and the Gang had all retired to their rooms for the night. Ruth leaned against the counter near the stove sipping her tea awaiting his entrance.

His heart burdened, Heath let himself out of his truck and trudged heavily through the rain and puddles to the rear porch steps, then hesitated there, not wanting to give up and come inside. Finally, he sighed and plodded wearily, up the steps and along the porch. Stopping at the door, he wiped his feet as he pulled back the screen and pushed open the kitchen door and let himself in. When his eyes met his mother's, he shook his head sadly, then disappeared into the mud room.

Anxious to tell him her news, Ruth followed him in. "Heath, that girl you found. . ."

Distressed to the core, Heath didn't let her finish. "I looked all over for her, Mom." Setting his wet hat on the shelf, he pulled off his slicker as he spoke, hanging it on a peg . "I couldn't find her. I called and called for her, and nothing."

He shrugged off his jacket, Ruth tried again, "I know, Heath—she. . ."

He didn't seem to hear her as he kicked off his soggy boots and returned the flashlight to its shelf. "I don't know if she couldn't answer or just wouldn't." Resolute, he shook his head. "I never should have left her out there." The distress in his voice was obvious. He turned to leave the mudroom and Ruth backed out ahead of him.

She tried again to interject, "Heath. . ."

But Heath continued, his head still shaking in dismay as he emerged back into the kitchen and set the thermos bottle on the breakfast table. "The temperature is dropping fast out there—right now it's near freezing." He plopped into a chair and reached to peel off his wet socks, continuing his lament, "It'll probably be icing up some before morning." He sighed, grimacing. "I don't see how she is going to make it through the night, Mom. She's going to die of exposure."

Again, Ruth pressed, "Heath, she. . ."

Heath's voice broke as he interrupted her yet again. "I never should have left her out there, Mom. I really thought she would come. I told her how to find the house—she probably got lost again." He shook his head, distressed. How can I ever forgive myself for..." He shook his head, distressed. "How can I ever forgive myself for. . . ."

Ruth reached out, pressing her finger over her son's lips to silence him. Heath stopped and squinted at her curiously. Without a word, Ruth took hold of his hand and quietly led him to the parlor door and pushed it open, resting her hand on his arm to keep him from entering. Puzzled, Heath glanced around the room, lit only by the small lamp on the table next to the sofa, searching for whatever it was she wanted him to see. His eyes panned past the rumpled quilt on the sofa, and then stopped, as that seemed out of order. Backtracking, his eyes returned to the tousled quilt. Squinting through the dim light, Heath could make out a hand resting against the sofa back, and then the end of a braid dangling out from under the quilt near the arm of the sofa and his eyes widened. *There's someone's under it!* Suddenly excited, he turned to his mom, keeping his voice low. "Is. . . Is that her?" Ruth nodded, smiling and Heath dissolved in relief. "What. . .? How did. . .?"

Ruth put her index finger to her own lips and backed away from the door, and when Heath followed, she reached in and closed it again. She led him away from the door as she spoke softly, "I tried to call you. She just showed up at the kitchen door about an hour ago, soaking wet and half-frozen. She about scared the life out of me when I looked out and saw her standing there! When I opened the door, she looked as surprised as I was that she had found us. I set her up to take a shower and Mr. Balcomb lent her his sweatshirt and pants."

"Oh, thank God!" Heath shook his head again, this time in amazement. "Wow, what an answer to prayer!"

Ruth continued, "After her shower, I gave her some stew. She didn't eat much—I thought she'd be hungrier; I guess she was more tired than hungry. Then I helped her with her hair and put a dressing on that wound you told me about. She didn't want to stay."

"You're kidding!—after all that? How did you convince her?"

"Well, since she was so reluctant to come when you first invited her, I didn't even try. After she showered, I put her clothes in the wash. I figured that would keep her here at least an hour or so."

Smiling his approval, Heath was impressed. "Good move!"

"Then, I just brought her in here to relax after dinner—gave her the quilt and a pillow and told her to make herself comfortable. Then I made her some chamomile tea."

"Chamomile!" Heath beamed at his mother. "Mom, I never knew you could be so sneaky!"

Ruth shrugged. "I had to do something! There was no way I was going to let that girl go back out into that storm! Then I sat in there with her and just talked about you and Nate, and after a few minutes, she just fell asleep."

"Thanks, Mom." Heath grinned broadly and hugged his mom, so relieved he could barely express it.

"Heath—you're almost as cold and wet as she was! Why don't you go get a shower and some dry clothes, and I'll heat you up some more stew."

While Heath showered and changed clothes, Ruth put on the tea kettle again, and began re-heating the stew for the third time that night. By the time Heath came back downstairs, it was nearly 9:30. He pulled on some dry boots and brought in more firewood from the porch, then built a fire in the stone fireplace in the den. Ruth joined him there, bringing his stew and some bread with their tea on a tray—his appetite having returned, Heath ate hungrily. After gulping down his stew and bread, he leaned back with his steaming mug and the two sat together on the sofa in the soft glow of the fire, sipping their tea and listening to the rain as Heath recounted to her his search for the girl.

** *** **

Back in his car, Joel smiled at his passenger, nodding. "I had a great time, tonight, Andrea. You are really fun to be with."

"Yeah, when I have a bunch of fun people around me."

"Not just with them, Andrea, you're fun on your own." Immediately, she tensed and rolled her eyes. Joel puzzled. *Did I say something wrong?* Still smiling, he attempted to clarify, "Um, that was supposed to be a compliment." Andrea only nodded and turned to her side window, falling silent. Squinting at her, Joel hesitated, mystified. "Andrea, what just happened there?"

"Nothing." *He should have quit when he was ahead.*

He shook his head, speaking gently, "No, that wasn't 'nothing.' I'm pretty sure it was 'something'—you just tensed up all-of-a-sudden, and rolled your eyes—you did that earlier when you took off your coat and I told you that you look nice in that sweater."

As Joel squinted at her, Andrea shifted uncomfortably in her seat. "It's nothing, Joel. Can we just go?"

Joel's forehead furrowed. "Um, sure." In a quandary, he started his car, and then backed out of their parking spot, puzzling over the sudden change in the atmosphere between them. *What happened, Abba? Everything was going so well, then all of a sudden, just like that, she shut down.* He eyed her for a moment at a stop sign, then pulled forward and continued on. *All I did was pay her a compliment...* He glanced over at her again, thinking.

A compliment did that, Abba? After a moment he nodded to himself and turned to her. "I'm sorry, Andrea. I didn't mean to make you feel uncomfortable." He watched the road as he spoke, but in his periphery, he noticed her shoulders relax and the tension between them seemed to ease.

"It's okay." Her eyes still averted, she worked at quelling her initial response. "I'm sorry I reacted like that."

"I take it you don't like being complimented."

Andrea just sighed heavily. "I just really hate flattery. It's just another form of lying."

"Lying?" He tried to reassure, "Andrea, I only wanted to pay you a compliment—that's saying something nice about you that I believe is true—it's only 'flattery' if it's *not* true." Taking a guess, he arched an eyebrow. "Do you have a hard time hearing truths about yourself? Or is it just compliments you object to?"

Her face still toward her side window, Andrea side-stepped his question. "It just seems like people only say nice things when they want something."

"Um, so, are you saying when someone says something nice, they are just trying to manipulate?" Saddened, Joel winced, feeling as though he just caught a glimpse into her life. "Well, you've been known to say some pretty nice things, Andrea. Were you trying to manipulate when you said them?"

"No."

"Oh. Okay," Keeping his voice light, he gently turned the tables. "So then, you're the one person on the planet who is telling the truth when you say nice things?"

Andrea winced. "Noooo." Her voice trailed up uncertainly. After a moment, she turned toward him, attempting to explain "It's just that. . .well. . .people say nice things—and then later, they say the complete opposite, like when they're mad. So when people do that, were they lying when they were calm, or when they were mad?"

Joel thought back for a moment on his dinner with Andrea's co-workers, getting even more of the picture. "When you say 'people'—are you talking about everyone? Or are you talking about your husband?"

Her eyes suddenly widening, Andrea quickly turned away. "Um, you know. . . just. . . *people.*"

"Well then, what if the nice things people say are true, and it's the mean things that are the lies?" He glanced over at her just in time to see her forehead furrow as she seemed to be considering what he said. Joel sighed in his spirit. *Is this what she's had to deal with all these years? No wonder she's so. . .* He could only sigh. *Abba, what do you say when someone's trust has been trampled on like that?* He tried again. "All I can say, Andrea, is that I'm sorry that has been your experience. I can't speak to someone else's motives or behaviors when I don't know who they are, but I'd like to tell you that whoever said those things to you—were wrong. And it seems like, if a person were to experience that on a regular basis, I can see where it would really erode their trust. But does that make everyone who compliments you, 'one of *them*'?"

Andrea winced. "No, I guess it just makes every compliment suspect."

"What if most of the people who have complimented you were telling you the truth?"

Becoming flustered, Andrea just shrugged. "I don't know, Joel—I don't know how to tell. I guess I've just learned to dismiss compliments."

"Why?—Because it saves time?"

Andrea rolled her eyes, then shrugged again. "I don't know—I guess."

Joel squinted, saddened. "Wow, that's really a shame." He sighed. "If you dismiss compliments, how will I be able to tell you a 'nice truth' about yourself without you thinking I'm lying or trying to manipulate?"

"I don't know, Joel." She shifted in her seat, her voice developing an edge of frustration. "Can we talk about something else?"

His palms on his steering wheel, Joel waved her down with his fingertips. "Hang on." Joel groped in his thoughts for an answer. "How about if I promise to always tell you the truth?"

Andrea quietly scoffed to herself, discounting his offer immediately. "Joel, if someone is going to lie, then their promise to be truthful is a lie, too." She shrugged. "There's just no way to tell. You can't trust them either way."

Joel nodded patiently. "So, it's not my honesty that's in question here—it's your ability to trust."

Shifting uncomfortably in her seat, Andrea sighed. "Maybe. . .I guess."

"So, what's the solution, then? How do I gain your trust so that you can feel assured that I am sincere and authentic?"

"I don't know. I guess you'd have to have a reputation for honesty first."

Joel smiled. "But Andrea, that's just it—I *do* have a reputation of honesty; I just don't have that reputation yet with you. So, in your mind, how does one establish that with you? How does one go about winning your trust? Tell me how I can prove to you that you can trust me."

"I don't know, Joel—I don't know! I keep telling you it isn't you. Why do you persist in pursuing this?"

Joel arched an eyebrow, "Why do I persist? Because I believe you are worth the effort!" He nodded, affirming it. "I believe that you are worth knowing *and* pursuing. I believe what I said about you is true—and because of that, I *want* to persist."

Andrea squinted at him, baffled. "How can you say that? You don't know me!" She wanted to believe him, yet every 'belief' he'd uttered was as the stab of a knife. "What makes you believe those things? What have I done to make you think those things about me? Is it just some kind of wishful thinking on your part?"

"Andrea, I only want to cherish you—if you'll just let me."

Andrea groped in her thoughts to make sense of it. "But, why? Why do you want to cherish me? You don't even know me!"

Needing to give her his full attention, Joel pulled into a gas station and parked by the water and air hoses. Andrea eyed him uneasily, wondering if she had finally succeeded in making him angry, and perhaps he intended to oust her from his car and make her walk the rest of her way home in the rain. Thinking and praying, Joel stared at his steering wheel, his forehead furrowed, his hands still on the wheel. Raising his eyes to hers, he spoke softly, yet firmly, "Here we are again, Andrea—back at square one. Every conversation we've had comes back to this place." At a loss, he eyed her earnestly. "It's as though you are requiring me to prove I know you before you'll let me get to know you, and when I can't do that, you push me away."

"I'm not requiring that you know me."

"But you are, Andrea. You just implied that I can't possibly be interested in you because I don't know you. But interest *precedes* knowing; interest is what sparks the desire to know; but you're so suspicious of my interest, that we can't seem to move beyond this." He thought for a moment. "You know what I think? I think that, for whatever reason, you can't accept that there is a valid reason for me to be interested in you, as though the only reason a man would want to get to know you is to harm or exploit you in some way." Exposed, even to herself, Andrea just stared at him. Joel tilted his head, his tone gentle, "Am I close?"

Andrea shrugged, her gaze shifting to her hands in her lap. "What's wrong with wanting to know what the trip is about before you say you'll go?"

"Nothing at all Andrea. But we've already covered what this trip is about—*several times.*" Andrea eyed him doubtfully. Joel reminded, "Remember? Back when we went on that first. . ." hesitating, he caught himself before uttering the word 'date'. Wishing to avoid another ill-timed rabbit trail, he steered around it. ". . .Um, that first *get-together?* You said you liked 'direct-ness'—so I was direct with you. I told you my intentions right up front, but I guess that was a little *too much* directness so early on—and I apologize for that. I apologized then, and I have been backpedaling ever since, trying to make up for it. So I'm guessing 'directness' isn't what you're wanting—at least, not *just* that." He tilted his head again. "So, what is it that you need in addition to 'directness'? Is it a guarantee you're looking for, Andrea?"

Andrea shrugged uneasily, feeling a bit defensive. "Maybe. . ."

Thinking for a moment, Joel nodded, "Okay, I get that. You want to be sure the story ends well before you'll pick up the book." He nodded. "I guess I can understand where you're coming from, there." Sensing a nudge in his spirit, Joel drew a deep breath and ventured out gently, and in all sincerity. "You know what I think, Andrea? I think your wanting a guarantee is just looking for a way around trusting. Your ability to trust has taken a beating, so rather than having to heal and grow that again, you seem like you're looking for a way to *not have* to trust. But you know what? Adonai will never give you that Andrea, because He is always about growing our trust." Joel watched her for a moment, gauging her reaction, but she just stared at him. Thinking back on her earlier reaction to his compliment, he nodded slowly several times. "Yeah, that's what I think. I think you're hoping to somehow go through this whole process without having to trust—for Adonai to just hand you the package with it already stamped 'trustworthy' before you'll even set out on the journey.

"But where is the adventure in that, Andrea? Life isn't a package tour where you have a map and know every stop along the way, and how much time everything will take. People who live like that don't live—they just keep a schedule. True living is an adventure of trusting God, *without* a map. You want it all mapped-out and God wants you to use GPS. You want to know all the turns ahead of time, and He wants you to just go straight until He tells you to turn—and He isn't going to tell you to turn until it's time to do it. What you're asking for, Andrea, is to *not* have to trust God to follow Him. What you want is not *faith.*"

Andrea stared at him starkly for a moment, then shrugged uncertainly. "I don't know, maybe." She considered his words, then reached back to an earlier place in the conversation. "You said before that 'interest sparks the desire to know'—but I just want to know what sparked the interest? And I'm not asking to know every stop along the way, I just want to know why I should even sign up for this trip in the first place. I mean, right now it's just me and God and I prefer it this way. So, other than it isn't what *you* want—what is so wrong with that?"

His elbow on the window ledge, Joel sighed and rubbed his forehead for a moment. *Okay, so she's used to selfish motives along with being lied to.* Turning to her, and with more compassion than Andrea ever imagined a man capable of, he tried to answer her concern as well as express his own. He shook his head gently. "Nothing is wrong with that Andrea, nothing at all—if it's what God wants for you. It shouldn't be about what I want or what you want; it should only be about what *He* wants. If I didn't believe with all my heart that He wants us to be together, I wouldn't be pursuing this." Before she could take exception to that, he quickly added, "Not because you aren't worth pursuing, but because it would never work if it wasn't His will. It's all about His will, Andrea, and His will is good, and perfect, and is always for our best." He eyed her for a moment. "Answer me this, Andrea, have you stopped resisting the idea long enough to ask Him what he thinks about it?"

Andrea quickly turned her head away from him and toward her window. When she didn't answer, Joel felt that he should pursue it no further. *Okay, Abba, I don't know how to get past this wall and I think I've said enough for now. I hope I didn't mess things up saying what I did. If I did, I repent of myself and I pray You'll just work it together for good and straighten it out again.* He pulled out into traffic again and stopped at a red light. Not wishing to end their evening on a sour note, he tried to soothe. "Andrea, I had a very nice time with you this evening and I don't want our little impromptu date to end on a heavy note. I'm sorry that my compliments put you off—but I'm not sorry I complimented you because I meant it and I believe it was true. And I'm not sorry I said those other things just now, because I believe they are true, too, and needed to be said." He noticed that Andrea seemed to sag in her seat. "What I'm most sorry about is that we can't seem to get on the same page where this is concerned—or even the same chapter. . .or the same book, for that matter." The light changed and Joel eased forward across the intersection as he spoke, "But, I'm looking forward to when we can eventually get past this wall and move on to talking about other things—like getting to know each other." He leaned against the window ledge as he drove. *So, what do I say now, Abba? I don't want this evening to end like this.* Joel's eyes narrowed as something occurred to him. He checked in with the Holy Spirit, then turned to her. "Just out of curiosity, what was your relationship like with Adonai before you got married?"

Andrea shrugged. "It was okay, I guess. I didn't know Him like I do now, but it was okay."

Joel nodded, thinking. "Okay, Andrea, I know this is none of my business, but I've picked up that your marriage was not an easy road for you—am I close?" Andrea winced, then turned away, her shoulders sagging. Joel proceeded cautiously. "I'll take that as a 'yes.' So, think about this: with all that you went through, did that draw you *closer* to Adonai, or drive you *away* from him?"

Andrea squinted through the windshield as she considered her answer, "Closer. . .a *lot* closer." Her voice softened, "Instead of running away, or running into another man's arms—I ran to God." Her eyes shifting to the floorboard, she shook her head. "I don't know how I would have made it through it all if it weren't for Adonai carrying me."

Joel smiled, both at her answer, and *that* she answered. "Well then, it seems like God used the difficulties you experienced in that relationship to actually *strengthen and deepen* your relationship with Him."

Suddenly, Andrea's chin came up—her forehead furrowing, as she processed this. Surprised, she nodded ever so slightly. "Yes—it did."

Chapter 25

As Ruth and Heath talked quietly in the den, Rae awakened on the sofa in the parlor, perspiring and thirsty. Squinting, she glanced around at her unfamiliar surroundings then remembered where she was. Pushing the quilt off of her, she made her way to the kitchen for some water. When the louver door swung closed behind her, she stood in the semi-darkness glancing around, wondering where Ruth kept her drinking glasses—not wanting to snoop through her cupboards. To her relief, on the kitchen counter, she spied some drinking tumblers in the dish drainer and lifted out one of those, then filled it with water from the tap. The sound of running water caught Heath and Ruth's attention; they paused for a moment, listening. "One of the Gang?" For several moments, they heard nothing. Then, just as they were about to resume their conversation—suddenly, a crash. Their heads snapped around in the direction of the sound.

Heath was off the sofa instantly. "Did that come from the kitchen?"

"I think so." Ruth set down her mug.

In seconds, Heath was at the kitchen door and listened for a moment. Hearing nothing, he pushed open the louver door and peered in. There in the semi-darkness, between the door and the counter, stood a girl in baggy sweat clothes, staring down at her bare feet. Her head jerked up when the door opened, her eyes widening at the silhouette of a very large man that effectively took up the entire doorway.

"Are you okay?" the silhouette asked.

The girl nodded. "I'm so sorry!" she fretted, "I just wanted to get a drink of water. The glass slipped out of my hand. . ." she ran her words together, mortified at her remissness. "I'm so sorry. . ." She moved to take a step.

"Wait!" Heath's urgency startled her. "Don't move. There's glass all over." He stepped back and called to Ruth, "It's okay, Mom, a glass broke, that's all." Turning back to the girl in the kitchen, Heath glanced back and forth from her bare feet to the shattered glass on the floor between them, then at his heavy boots, considering his options. Taking hold of the door jamb, he planted one foot on the kitchen floor a couple of feet from the doorway, then reached in with his other foot, landing it near the feet of the barefoot girl, the glass crunching under his boot. He offered his free hand to the girl for balance. "Here, use my boots as stepping stones."

Initially hesitant, Rae gingerly took the man's hand and did as directed; as soon as her hand touched his, Heath's forehead furrowed with concern. Rae stepped one bare foot onto his boot as he gently pulled her toward him, then she reached forward with her other foot, landing it carefully onto his other boot. Heath let go of the doorjamb, taking her other hand to help her keep her balance. She glanced up as she passed in front of him and arched an eyebrow; her head didn't even *reach his shoulder. This guy is even taller than Sam...!* Ruth was there to meet her on the other side of the doorway as Rae stepped from Heath's boot to the threshold, and let go of his hand.

Seeing Ruth she winced regretfully. "I'm so sorry. I broke your glass. I was trying to get a drink of water and it slipped out of my hand."

"Oh, don't worry none about that, sweetheart," Ruth drawled, smiling her warm smile, "I'm just glad you're okay. Let me get you another." Heath stepped aside the doorway to let Ruth into the kitchen, and he and Rae stood facing each other.

"We meet again—I'm Heath," he offered his hand again, this time as a greeting.

"Rae." She squeezed his hand. Again, Heath's forehead furrowed at her touch. Rae noticed his swollen lip. Embarrassed, she winced and glanced away, then up at him again. "Sorry about your mouth."

Heath shrugged it off. "No, don't worry about that. I'm just sorry I scared you." Her face seemed a little flushed to him and her eyes had a glassy look. "You feeling okay?"

"I guess so, just really tired, that's all. I appreciate you both feeding me and letting me stay here tonight." Heath nodded, noting her plans to stay as he acknowledged her appreciation, though he was still unsure about her well-being. They heard water running briefly in the kitchen, then Ruth reappeared at the door holding a tumbler of water—plastic this time—which she offered to Rae, who received it carefully. Smiling sheepishly, Rae nodded, "Plastic. Good idea. Thank you." When her fingers touched Ruth's, the same look of concern as Heath's crossed Ruth's face. Not wanting to take a hand off the tumbler of water, Rae gestured with her head toward the parlor. "I guess I'll just head back to the sofa."

Ruth and Heath watched as she retreated to her designated room and closed the door. Heath spoke softly. "Did you feel her skin?

Ruth nodded, "I sure did."

"She was like ice when I found her in the woods—now she's burning up."

"She may end up being with us more than just tonight." Ruth's voice was full of concern, "If she will stay, that is."

Heath arched an eyebrow. "That's a big 'if.'"

Knowing so little of their new guest, who arrived with a bullet wound on her shoulder, Ruth wondered what, if anything, they may be facing. "Are we sure we know what we're doing, Heath?"

"No, but God does."

Ruth had to agree.

** *** **

Heath rolled over in bed and opened his eyes, not sure what woke him up. A light shone under his bedroom door. *Did I leave the hall light on?* He saw a shadow glide across the ribbon of light under his door as someone walked by, and he glanced at his clock, *3:27 a.m.? What's Mom doing up at this hour?* He pushed back his covers and got up. Pulling on his robe as he maneuvered his feet into his slippers, he opened the door and poked his head out, squinting at the light. Seeing Ruth at the cabinet in the bathroom across the hall, he stepped over to that doorway. "Mom?"

Startled, Ruth's head jerked toward him. "Oh, I'm sorry, Heath. I didn't mean to wake you."

"It's okay. Is something wrong? What are you looking for?"

"Do we have a thermometer? I couldn't find one in my bathroom."

"A thermometer? Why do you need a thermometer at 3:30 in the morning?"

"Oh, well, I just woke up worrying about our visitor downstairs, since she was so hot last night. So I went down to check on her. Heath, she is just burning up! Sweating and shaking, having chills and all, and completely out-of-it. I couldn't wake her up. I want to take her temperature, but I can't find a thermometer."

"So, she's really sick now—oh, man. . ." He shook his head, then focused on Ruth's quest. "No, I don't have one. I just use those strip-things for Nate. I think they are in one of the drawers."

Ruth shifted her search to the top drawer then moved to the second one, her long graying braid draped over one shoulder. Finding what she was searching for, she straightened up. "Here they are." She headed for the stairway with her prize, and Heath right behind. Entering the parlor on Ruth's heels, Heath was immediately alarmed at the girl sleeping fitfully on the sofa. Her eyes closed, shivering violently, beads of perspiration on her forehead. Ruth scanned the back of the box of temperature strips for directions, then took one out and pressed it to Rae's forehead. The girl didn't seem to notice.

Heath was anxious to help. "Can I do something?"

Ruth made a suggestion, "Maybe a pan of water and a cloth?" Acting on that, Heath was out the door in a second. By the time he was back, it was time to read the thermometer strip. Heath stood by with the cloth and pan of water at the ready, as Ruth examined the strip. "Oh my! It's 102.9!" She reached for her bottle of acetaminophen, and shook out two tablets. "Heath, would you refill her water cup?" Heath handed Ruth the pan and cloth, then reached for the plastic tumbler, and made another dash for the kitchen. Ruth set down the pan and dipped the cloth into the water, then wrung it out, and gently stroked Rae's face and neck with it. When Heath returned with the cup filled with water, Ruth tried to rouse the girl by shaking her shoulder. "Rae? Rae, honey—can you wake up and take some medicine?" Rae roused somewhat, but settled again quickly. "Rae?" Ruth shook her shoulder again. Rae grimaced, resisting the rousing. "Rae?"

Rae's forehead furrowed, then she arched her eyebrows, eyes still closed. "Mom?"

"No, sweetheart—it's Ruth." Rae's face showed her disappointment, then she settled back into her pillow, shivering violently. Her heart breaking for the sick girl who longed for her mother. Ruth pressed, "Rae? You have a pretty high fever, hon—I have some medicine for you." Slowly Rae's eyes opened and she stared blankly into Ruth's face, confused. Ruth tried again, "Rae?—It's Ruth. You need to take some medicine, hon."

Still shivering, Rae gazed around her, bleary-eyed. Not finding who she was expecting to see, she returned her gaze to Ruth—still mentally adrift. "Huh?" After a moment, a glint of recognition crossed her face.

"Here, Rae." Ruth held out the two tablets. "I need you to take these. Your fever is too high."

"It's really cold in here."

"That's from the fever, hon. Can you take these pills okay? Or do I need to squash them up?"

"Huh?"

"Are you able to swallow these pills? I don't want you choking on them, now."

Rae stared at the pills in Ruth's hand, her head wavering unsteadily. Finally, Ruth's words registered with her, and she raised herself up onto an elbow and groped for the tablets in Ruth's hand. Unable to get a hold of them, she gave up and sank back into her pillow.

"Here, Rae." Ruth jostled her again. With great effort, Rae again raised herself to her elbow, and Ruth transferred the tablets to Rae's mouth. That accomplished, Heath passed the cup of water to Ruth, who handed it to Rae, and helped support it in Rae's hand as she took a few sips. Rae waited for the tablets to go down then sank back into her pillow.

Ruth nodded, satisfied, "There you go, hon. Now, rest easy. I'll check on you later." Rae faded back to sleep quickly and Ruth rose and stood next to Heath.

Heath shook his head. "She looks terrible. How'd she get so sick so fast? Is that from the wound on her shoulder?"

"I don't think so. It didn't look infected when I saw it. She got so cold and tired, and she hadn't eaten—I'm sure her resistance is way down. And who knows how long she was out there before you found her?" Ruth thought a moment, then added, "Thank God you found her, Heath, or she would be sick like this out there." Ruth reflected on that for a moment, "And with that storm, and the temperature out there, she probably wouldn't have made it."

Heath's eyes widened at that realization. He nodded as he exhaled slowly. "Wow, do you think she'll be okay? I mean, she's not gonna die, or anything will she? Maybe we should call an ambulance or something?"

"No, I don't think she will die, and an ambulance may be a bit premature right now—let's wait a while and see. I'll stay with her and try to get her cooled down some, then check her again in a couple of hours." Ruth took the damp cloth and began to daub it on Rae's face. After a moment, she noticed Heath hadn't moved, and looked up at him. He just stood there next to the sofa, staring down at the shivering, perspiring girl—visibly disturbed. "Go on back to bed, Heath. There's not really much more we can do for now. Try to get some sleep—I'm sure we are going to need it."

** *** **

Heath came downstairs into the kitchen around 7:30 a.m, surprised and a little dismayed to find Ruth already up. "Mom, please tell me you haven't been up since I left you at 3:30!"

Ruth smiled, tempted to tease him then decided she didn't have the energy. "No, I went back to bed about an hour after you did. I just woke up a little while ago, and came down to check on her."

"How's she doing?"

"She is still running a fever, but not like she was last night."

"I guess that's good. What are we going to tell the Gang?"

"I hadn't thought about that." Ruth considered it for a moment. "They already know we have an unexpected visitor, but I don't think they need to know you found her in the woods with a bullet wound."

"Yeah, maybe we should keep that part to ourselves. We don't want to cause an uproar over her." Heath grinned and Ruth smiled, understanding. "We should let them know she is sick, though, so they can stay clear of the parlor. Plus, I want to keep Nate out of there, too. You know how curious he is, as soon as he sees us going in and out of there, he's going to want to see what's up. I don't want him catching anything."

"Me either. I'm keeping the door closed."

"Are you going to Shabbat service?" Heath knew how she hated to miss it.

"I thought I'd stay home and look after Rae. Are you going?"

"You looked after her last night. Why don't I stay home with her and you can go. You can take my truck, since your van is tore up. Maybe while you're there you can ask your nurse friend to come look in on her."

"You stay with her while I go? Are you sure you want to do that, Heath?"

"Am I sure?—No!" He grinned and shrugged, "But I'm willing to take my turn. Besides, I feel kind of responsible for her being here. No, you go on ahead if you feel up to it. No reason for both of us to miss it."

"Well, that's true. I think I'll talk to Andrea, like you suggested. I'll take Nate with me, that way you won't have to worry about him while you are tending to her." Heath nodded and Ruth sighed. "Well, the Gang will be out here pretty soon, let me get breakfast going." Ruth set about making breakfast as Heath headed back upstairs to get showered and dressed, then wake up Nate. As the Gang assembled for breakfast, Ruth scurried around in the kitchen, trying to pull together their morning meal. As she came to the table with a large bowl of scrambled eggs, and a plate of toast and turkey sausage links, she called out cheerfully, "Good morning, everyone!" The Gang nodded and greeted her in return. "Y'all, I just want to remind you about our guest—"

Mr. Peterman interrupted, "The one Heath found in the woods last night?"

Ruth's mouth fell open. "Mr. Peterman! Now, how did you know about that?"

"I was eavesdropping—how do you think?" Everyone laughed.

So much for Ruth's plan to keep it quiet. "Well anyway, she's in the parlor and she's running a fever, so you might want to steer clear so you don't get sick, too." Everyone nodded their assent, glad for the warning. Breakfast was over fairly quickly and Ruth hurried upstairs to get ready for Shabbat service, and Heath took Nate up to get him ready. When both emerged, Ruth gave Heath some last-minute instructions, "Just check her temperature every few hours, and give her more medicine if it goes up over 101. She can have the medicine every four hours."

"What if she wakes up and freaks out that I'm here?"

Ruth grinned, teasing, "Well, I don't think she has the energy to kick you in the face again, if that's what you're worried about."

Heath smiled tolerantly at his mom. "No, Mom I was thinking more along the line of not wanting to scare her again, but I'll be sure to approach with caution."

"You'll do fine, Heath. I'll stop by the drugstore on the way home and get a thermometer." Heath nodded and she and Nate kissed Heath good-bye, and they went on their way.

Chapter 26

About fifteen minutes before the service was to begin that morning, Orby noticed Joel leaning against the wall by the door on the far side of the foyer, gazing across the way at Andrea. Orby watched him for a few moments. *He looks awful frustrated, Abba.* Feeling a tug in his spirit, he stepped over to Joel and leaned his back against the door jamb next to him. Joel nodded a greeting and Orby smiled in return, then nodded toward Andrea. "I seen you noticing Ms. Andrea standing over there with her friend." Surprised at Orby's observation, Joel was ready to deny it, but changed his mind and instead just nodded dully. After a moment, Orby spoke again, "Yeah, women are a mystery, ain't they? I can't say as I know much about them, but you know—people are people."

"How do you mean?" Joel asked it without taking his eyes from Andrea.

Orby nodded. "I mean, human nature, and all."

Joel glanced at him. "Human nature..."

"Yeah. You know how we humans are: the harder someone tries to talk us into something, the more we don't want to be talked into it."

Suddenly interested, Joel turned to him. "What are you getting at, Orby?"

"Oh, me? Nothing. I was just thinking. . . It just seems to me that Ms. Andrea over there might could use a little more 'show' and a lot less 'tell.'"

Joel eyed him. "What makes you say that?"

Orby tilted his head to one side, and shrugged. "Well, forgive me for saying so, but I just been noticing—it seems to me like you been working real hard these last couple of months to get Ms. Andrea to like you, and all. But you gotta remember that you're way ahead of her in this relationship you're wanting with her."

That's what Sid said the day I met her! Embarrassed, Joel tried not to look it. "Now, how do you know that?"

"Oh, I don't—it's just a guess, seeing as how you told her you wanted to marry her on your first date, and all."

Abashed and stunned, Joel stared at him. "How do you know about *that?*" Orby only shrugged. Shoulders sagging, Joel sighed, "So what are you saying? That I should back-off or something?"

Orby shrugged again. "I don't know, maybe." When Joel sighed again, Orby added, "Or, you might could just take a different path to her door."

He had Joel's attention again. "What path is that?"

His eyes on his hands, Orby fiddled with a fingernail. "Has telling her over and over what you want helped things along at all?"

How does he know that? Joel sighed, shaking his head, "No."

Not surprised, Orby nodded, "I'm just wondering if maybe it looks to her like you're kinda focused on what *you* want—and not paying a whole lot of attention to what *she* wants."

Suddenly, Andrea's words from their rainy evening the previous night leapt to mind, '*Other than it's not what* you *want, what's wrong with that?*' Joel's mouth fell open as the light dawned. "Andrea said something to that effect—I didn't think about it like that. I made what she said into 'our will versus God's will'—but now that you say that. . ." He shook his head. "You're right, Orby, that's what I've been doing. I've been making it my will versus her will. I guess I just thought she would somehow feel as enthusiastic about it as I do."

"Like I said, you're way ahead of her in this. Have you tried to find out what she wants? I was just wondering—maybe if you spent some time on what *she's* wanting, she might be more accepting of what *you* want."

"I don't know what she wants—all I know is what she *doesn't* want."

"And what's that?"

"Me."

Orby pressed his lips together again, shaking his head, "Oh, I don't know about that—has she said she don't want you? Or has she just said she don't want what you want?"

Joel swiveled his head around and stared hard at Orby, suddenly hopeful. "What are you thinking, Orby?"

Orby shrugged again. "Oh, I don't know. It just seems to me like all she knows about you right now is that you want to marry her. And, like I said, I don't know much about the ladies, but it seems like a woman would want to know a bit more than that about a man before she would consider something like that."

"I'd like to tell her more about me, but I haven't gotten the opportunity."

Orby grinned. "Now, there you go again with the 'telling'! What I'm saying is you just maybe want to start *showing* her who you are."

"I'd like to, but she won't go out with me again."

"Then you just have to show her who you are before you start expecting her to want to go out with you again."

"Show her. . ." Joel considered that for a moment. "How do I do that when she won't go out with me?"

Orby shook his head, chuckling, "Wow, and they say us country boys are slow!"

"Help me out, Orby. It's been two and a half decades since I've had to do this, and women are so different now."

Orby nodded in sympathy. "That they are, that's for sure." Orby thought a moment, and prayed a little before answering. "I guess I just can't imagine Ms. Andrea's gonna go no where's with you until she knows what kind of person you are—and not from hearing you tell her, but from her seeing it for herself."

"But Sid vouched for me. Why wouldn't she trust me enough with that?"

"Well, it seems to me that was her trust for the Rabbi that bought you that ticket. You kind of spent that dime on your lunch with her. I'd say you're on your own now."

"How do you *know* about that? Did Andrea tell everyone, or something?"

"No, I don't think Andrea's told no one. I think she's kind of embarrassed about leaving you behind and all." Joel groaned, feeling his face flush. Orby smiled sympathetically. "You know, it's funny how restaurants are—sometimes you just never know who's there eating at the same time as you."

Joel wilted. "Oh great. Someone from here was there that day? So everyone knows about this now?"

Orby shrugged. "It's been a few months, and it's a good size group here, so you never know—there might be one or two who haven't heard about it yet." Orby teased, watching Joel for his reaction. When Joel groaned, Orby grinned. "Oh, I'm just messing with you!—no one else knows. I was there at the restaurant that day, waiting for Heath and Ms. Ruth. You just left before they got there."

Relieved, Joel grinned. "Oh, man, Orby, that was cruel!" Orby grinned as well, then Joel added, "But she came back, you know."

"Yeah, I saw that, too. I felt bad for you, so I came outside to see if you wanted to eat with us instead, and I saw her pull up again. When I saw she was gonna take you home, I went back inside. Don't worry, I never told no one about it, or nothing—not even Ms. Ruth and Heath."

"Well, I appreciate your mercy, Orby. Thank you. Now, would you help me understand what you mean by showing her who I am?"

"Oh yeah, that ain't no big mystery or nothing. I just mean you go about your business being who you are, and maybe when she sees that, she might be more inclined to want to get to know you better. It's that human nature thing—most people don't like having their mind made up for them; they want to decide on their own so you gotta give them something to think on."

"So you're saying I should stop pressing her and just be myself around her?"

"I don't know. It just seems to me that it might be a little more promising than what you been doing. It just seems like trying to talk her into something she don't want to do might give her the wrong impression—might come across to her as kind of self-serving."

Again, he winced over Andrea's words. "I guess I just always thought women wanted to be married and would be glad someone was interested."

"Well, like you said, women are different now. Hearing them talk, I think they just want to know they matter and that what they think matters."

Joel's eyebrows knitted. "But she *does* matter to me! She matters *a lot!* I just wish I could tell her why this is so important to me!"

Orby grinned, shaking his head again. "There you go again, did you hear yourself? You said 'why it's important' *to you.*"

Joel groaned again, seeing Orby's point. "I just want to treasure her."

"Well, then, I'm guessing that's what you need to show her."

Joel sighed. "It's not that easy, Orby—I've never met someone who is so afraid of being treasured!"

Orby watched Andrea across the room as he spoke. "Well, I don't know for sure, and I'm just guessing, but maybe Ms. Andrea's not so much afraid of being treasured as *not* being treasured." Suddenly, Joel's chin came up and he stared intently at Orby, his mouth falling open. He nodded as he followed Orby's gaze across the room over to Andrea. *She's afraid of* not *being treasured!*

** *** **

Heath had settled in at the kitchen table with a cup of coffee and the morning newspaper, and after about an hour, he decided to check on his patient in the parlor. Pushing through the louver door, he crossed the front room to the parlor where she lay sleeping, and peeked in at the girl on the sofa. Once again, she was breathing rapidly and shivered uncontrollably, soaked in perspiration. Instantly alarmed, Heath rushed over to her. "Oh, man!—not again!" He reached for the temperature strips and pressed another one onto her forehead, then hurried to the kitchen for a cup of water. When he returned, he sat on the edge of the sofa next to his patient, awaiting the full allotment of time for the strip on her forehead to register her temperature. When the time was up, he checked it and grimaced. "Oh, man—it's 103.2!" Worried anew, he reached for the bottle of medicine Ruth had left there on the coffee table and spilled two tablets into his hand, then tried to rouse the girl. *What did she say her name was?* His mind raced before he settled on the name. "Rae?"

332

He jostled her shoulder, "Rae?" The girl only continued her disquieted breathing and shivering, unaware. Heath jostled her shoulder more insistently, becoming increasingly uneasy. "Rae! Wake up—you need to take some more medicine. Rae?" The girl grimaced and protested with a moan. He shook her shoulder again, "Rae, wake up for a minute—you need to take these pills." The girl shifted and stirred, and immediately, Heath leapt out of range of her feet. Having merely just moved her legs under her covers, the girl resettled without awakening. Sheepish over his reaction, Heath briefly grinned, touching his still-tender lip with his tongue. The tablets still in his hand, he re-seated himself on the edge of the coffee table across from Rae's head, out of range from her feet, and tried again. "Rae?" He jostled her shoulder, being careful of the wound.

Rae raised her head slightly and opened one eye, staring bleary-eyed at the figure across from her and mumbled, "Who are you?"

"I'm Heath. Your fever is up again; you need to take some more medicine."

Rae eyed him uncertainly, her head unsteady. "Heath, who?"

Heath sighed impatiently, anxious to get the pills into her and start bringing down her temperature. Even in her compromised state, he could tell she was not about to take the pills he was offering without something more to go on. He thought for a moment, and decided to capitalize on his mom's success. "Ruth's son; the lady who is taking care of you."

Rae continued her dull stare for a few more moments. "Ruth?" She vaguely remembered the nice lady whose voice sounded like her mom's.

Heath nodded eagerly. "Yeah. She said you need to take more of this medicine for your fever." He could see she was considering it, however slowly. Finally, and again with great effort, she raised herself up onto one elbow and stared at the tablets in Heath's hand for several seconds before she reached for them clumsily, dropping them into her bedding. Heath retrieved the tablets, then turned her hand over and set them into her palm. Shakily, Rae raised them to her mouth as Heath reached for the cup of water and brought it close to her. With some difficulty, Rae tried to coordinate grasping the cup and bringing it to her lips, nearly spilling it on the way. Heath had to help her hold the cup as she managed her few sips, then she sank back into the pillow, taxed for the effort, and quickly drifted back to sleep. Reaching into the pan of water for the cloth, Heath wrung it out, then began swabbing her face, and neck, and arms, trying to cool her, as his mom had done. He stared down at her, his concern growing. "Lord, please help this girl. She's so sick. . .help me to know what to do for her."

He finished swabbing her arms then plopped the cloth back into the pan, deciding to move his vigil to where he could watch her more closely. Returning to the kitchen, Heath gathered up his newspaper and coffee, and then parked himself in the chair in the corner of the parlor by the door, and there he kept watch over the girl. After nearly forty-five minutes, her breathing and shivering settled, and Heath rose and stepped over to her. Touching her face and forehead with the backs of his fingers, he sighed, relieved, and returned to his chair across the room.

It was close to 2pm when Ruth and Nate returned, and Andrea pulled in behind them a few minutes later. Ruth carried the sleeping boy with her as she showed Andrea to the parlor. Remaining at the doorway with Nate, she waved Andrea in and Heath stood when she entered, nodding to his mom at the door. Ruth glanced over at the sleeping Rae, and whispered, "How's she doing, Heath?"

Heath matched her low volume, "Pretty much the same. Her fever spiked up high again, like it did last night, so I gave her some more medicine, and it came down some. How was the service?"

"Meaningful as always—but I was a little distracted, as you can imagine." She gestured with an elbow to her friend. "I told Andrea about her." Nodding to the child in her arms, she added, "Let me run and put Nate down and I'll be right back"

Andrea nodded and stepped forward. "I'll just check her vital signs and listen to her lungs and go from there." Heath followed her over to the sofa and watched as Andrea opened her little bag that she usually brought with her on Health Check Day. She pulled out her stethoscope and blood pressure cuff, and perched herself on the edge of the sofa next to Rae.

"Watch out, she kicks," Heath whispered his warning.

Andrea smiled and nodded as she took Rae's wrist in her fingers, staring briefly at her watch, as Heath stood near the coffee table watching. Setting down Rae's wrist, Andrea then wrapped her arm with the blood pressure cuff and set the prongs of her stethoscope into her ears, then squeezed the rubber bulb of the cuff several times, inflating it. Listening with her stethoscope, she watched the manometer needle pulsate and decline around the dial. Then, she reached around behind her patient, setting the diaphragm of her stethoscope onto Rae's back, moving it to a new place after each breath, for several breaths, then listened with it to Rae's heart. Rae slept through the whole process. Andrea turned to Heath, just as Ruth returned. "She feels pretty hot. Have you taken her temperature lately?"

"I checked it again about an hour ago," Heath reported, "It was 101.4, down from 103.2 earlier."

"Hmmm...That's still pretty high. Well, her lungs sound okay, so she doesn't have pneumonia—at least not yet. Where's that wound you told me about?" Heath stepped back, deciding that would be Ruth's department. Ruth stepped to Rae's side, and stretched the collar of her sweatshirt down, revealing the gauze dressing. Andrea loosened the tape and peered under the gauze, then pressed it back into place. "That looks pretty good—nice job on the wound care, Ruth." Andrea grinned at her friend. Ruth only smiled demurely. The three of them rose and left the parlor, and Ruth closed the door behind them.

Standing together in the front room, Ruth spoke first. "What do you think, Andrea?"

Andrea set down her tote bag. "I don't think the wound is the source of the infection; I'm guessing it's a virus." Palms up, she shrugged. "It's up to you: you can call an ambulance if you're uncomfortable with her being here. But if you decide to wait it out, I'd say just keep doing what you're doing and watch her closely, and keep water close by so she doesn't get dehydrated with all the perspiring she's doing. If she gets worse later today or tonight, or if she isn't showing improvement by tomorrow, she should probably be seen. You'll most likely have to take her to the ER, since you really don't know her or anything about her."

Ruth arched an eyebrow to her son. "Well, Heath, what do you think?"

Heath frowned as he weighed the choices and touched base with his Spirit. "I don't know, Mom—I don't feel right about calling an ambulance just to get her off of our hands. I'm fine with her just staying here for now. What do you want to do?"

Ruth nodded. "I feel the same way. Let's pray over it this afternoon and see how it goes, and check back with each other later, okay?" Heath liked that idea. "Okay, then that's the plan." She turned to Andrea. "Can I make you some lunch, Andrea?"

"Sure Ruth, that sounds nice."

Ruth arched an eyebrow toward her son. "Heath?"

"No, I'm good. I ate with the Gang."

So, the two ladies started for the kitchen as Heath settled back into his chair in the parlor. As Andrea took a seat at the breakfast table, Ruth busied herself at the counter, setting the kettle on the burner and retrieving some tea mugs from the cupboard. As she assembled a couple of sandwiches, she filled in more details of Rae's story for Andrea. When teapot squealed, Ruth filled the waiting mugs and brought them to the table, then retrieved the sandwiches, taking the seat across from Andrea.

"Well, you don't look as addled as you did last time you were here, Andrea. Things smoothing out between you and Joel? What's happened since I saw you last—anything exciting?" She cut her sandwich in half and picked up one side, taking a bite.

"Yes, but this time it was pretty tame compared to that lunch I told you about, but it was still embarrassing, though! I was out in that storm last night, too."

"You were? Whatever for?"

"I had a gathering I wanted to go to in Heartland—but I never made it; my car broke down."

"Whose car are you driving today?"

"Matt's. He's gone off with a friend today and let me use it." Andrea took another bite of her sandwich.

"So you broke down in Heartland? At night? In the rain?"

"Yeah, but not before I got all turned around and ended up in a high-crime area."

Ruth's eyebrows arched, "Andrea! By yourself?"

Andrea nodded, "Yeah, then I drove through some deep water that I didn't see. My car did okay for a little bit, and then it died." She shook her head. "It's the first time I've had car trouble since Evan's been gone; it was kind of scary. I'm so used to just calling him whenever something like that happens that I never gave it much thought. But there I was—broken down at the side of the road at night in the rain, and no Evan to call. I tried calling Matt, but he was in class and had his phone off, so I went through all the contacts in my phone. Did you know, most of my contacts are businesses? I guess I don't socialize very much."

Ruth sipped her tea. "What does this have to do with Joel?"

"Well, when I was scrolling through my contacts, I saw his name."

"Why was that a surprise? You didn't put it in there?"

"No! I would never have asked him for his number! I had no idea how it got in my phone—I still don't." She paused for a moment, her forehead furrowed. "I wonder if he has *my* number..." Shaking it off, she returned to her story. "Anyway, his number was right there in my phone—but I wasn't about to call him. So I tried everyone I knew and no one picked up; all I got was everyone's voicemail."

"So you had to call Joel." Ruth concluded.

Andrea just rolled her eyes again, nodding. "I guess he does have my number now, since I called him." She sighed and shook her head.

Ruth brightened. "So, Joel rescued you?"

"Yeah—and he called the police to come wait with me until he got there."

"Well, wasn't that nice!"

"Yeah, it was. Then, I only had about seven or eight dollars with me, so he paid for my car to be towed to my mechanic—all the way back to Redlands. I wrote him a check to pay him back this morning, but he wouldn't accept it."

"He did?—that was very generous! So you don't have road-side assistance?"

"No, I always had Evan—he was my roadside assistance."

"You're going around in the rain without roadside assistance, and with no money?"

"Yes, I know, Ruth—that's what Joel said."

"Then what happened?"

"He wouldn't take me home; he insisted on letting him take me to dinner. He said it was the least I could do for him rescuing me."

Ruth smiled, delighted. "Well, that's creative! So, did you go?"

"I didn't have a choice; he was driving! And he was being so ornery!—he said it was an 'official date' because he would be paying. He just took advantage of me not having money with me."

"Took advantage of you by rescuing you and buying you dinner?" Leaning back in her chair, Ruth folded her arms across her ribs. "C'mon Andrea! That was very sweet of him!" When Andrea again rolled her eyes, Ruth arched an eyebrow. "Now, that's only fair!—after all, you made that rule, yourself!"

"I know. Don't remind me." She sipped her tea.

"And that's the second time it's come back to haunt you!"

"Don't remind me of that either."

"So, did you two have a nice meal together? I guess since he was driving, you couldn't exactly run out on him." Ruth chuckled to herself, as she sipped her tea.

Andrea sighed, "No, I couldn't—and he reminded me of *that* too!" Ruth chuckled again, and Andrea sighed. "It was actually a pretty fun evening—but then he complimented me." Her countenance fell at the memory.

"He complimented you?" Andrea nodded sadly, and Ruth added facetiously, "The beast."

"Ruuuth. . .!" Andrea stretched out her name in protest.

Ruth shook her head, "Taking you out to meals, buying you flowers, rescuing you from harm—and then complimenting you. I can certainly see why you think he's such a villain, Andrea." Ruth eyed her friend expectantly.

"Ruuuth!" she whined the name again, "You make me sound ungrateful!."

Ruth arched an eyebrow expectantly. *"I make you sound ungrateful? –You're the one telling the story!"* Andrea's shoulders sagged, then Ruth tucked her chin. "Okay, hon, how about you explain to me why paying you a compliment is such a crime."

"It's not a crime. . ." Andrea sighed, flustered. "Never mind, I can't explain it."

"Never mind? Is it that bad, Andrea?" Ruth thought for a moment. "Let me guess, this is another area that has been tainted by Evan?" Glancing away, Andrea only shrugged and nodded. "What happened? Another knee-jerk reaction?" Andrea only sighed, her shoulders sagging. Ruth leaned an elbow on the table, her chin in her hand. "Andrea, hon—maybe you should spend some time with Joel, if for no other reason than to train you out of all these 'knee-jerk' reactions you've learned."

Andrea just sighed and rested her chin in a palm, not wanting to consider that. After a moment, she brightened a bit. "But he did say something I hadn't thought of. . ." When Ruth leaned in, Andrea did, too. "He asked how my relationship with God was before I got married, and how it was now. He actually attributed going through all that with Evan to what made my relationship with God what it is today." She shook her head. "I never thought about that before."

Ruth smiled, surprised. "Well, how about that—all of Evan's interference taught you to fight your way to God and hang onto Him, then—didn't it?"

Andrea shrugged and nodded. "I guess so."

Ruth leaned back in her chair. "Hmmm—I think it's very interesting Joel is the first one to see that."

** *** **

Rae slept the entire day, unaware of those so concerned for her. By evening, her fever had come down some and leveled off for a while, so Ruth and Heath decided to wait it out. They took turns checking on her through the night, rousing her periodically to give her more medicine when her fever spiked too high. The next day was Sunday, and Rae's temperature and breathing dropped to normal, but she slept heavily the entire day. Ruth kept a bottle of water on the coffee table, and replaced it periodically throughout the day. The empty bottles she took away were the only indication that Rae had stirred at all. That night, after Nate and the Gang had gone to bed, Ruth and Heath spoke quietly in the den in front of the fireplace. "Once she's up and around, we probably need to find out who we have here and how we can help her." Heath thought a moment. "Did she say anything to you about her family or where she's from?"

"No, we've not had a chance to talk, except for that first night after she arrived. She's pretty much just slept for the past two days. Has she said anything to you?"

"Except for walking across my boots that night, I've only seen her awake long enough to give her some medicine. When she wakes up, I don't know if I should sit her down and find out what's what, or if we should just wait and see if she opens up about it on her own."

Ruth shrugged. "I would hate to just pounce on her and start asking her questions, that might scare her off before we even find out if she needs help."

Heath nodded, thinking. "I'm still wondering about that wound on her shoulder—if we should call the sheriff or not. I mean, if someone actually did shoot at her, it needs to be reported. And if she is in some kind of trouble, or if she's a runaway, maybe the sheriff should know about that, too."

Ruth sighed. "I hope that's not the case. I can't imagine anyone wanting to hurt her—at least not on purpose. It could have been an accident; out there in the woods in hunting season. . ."

Heath shrugged considering the possibility. "Why don't we just give her another day and see how she is tomorrow?" Ruth was in agreement, so they let the matter rest.

Chapter 27

Early Monday morning, Ruth awoke and went about her morning routine, taking her shower and dressing, then looking in on Nate while Heath showered; he was already awake and standing in his crib when she poked her head in. Lifting him out, Ruth changed his diaper, zipped him back into his blanket sleeper then carried him downstairs with her. At the foot of the stairs, she set him down and he scampered off as she headed for the kitchen to start breakfast for the three of them. On her way there, she stopped by the parlor and peeked in on their visitor. This time though, unlike the previous two mornings, the girl slept peacefully.

Pleased, Ruth closed the door, making sure it latched, as Nate watched her with great interest, from the front room. Lately, for reasons unknown to him, he was no longer allowed in the parlor. Every time he tried the door it was securely closed and latched. For the past few days he had watched Daddy and Grandma come and go from that room, speaking in hushed tones about a mysterious visitor, and Nate was determined to investigate. So, every time he saw someone come from that room, he hurried to the door and pushed against it then jiggled the knob to see if it would open, and just now, he tried again. When it didn't open he headed back to his toys.

Beyond the mysterious door, the sound of it latching and the subsequent jiggling of the knob, tickled the subconscious of the girl on the sofa. She stirred, taking a deep breath then forced open one eye, and then the other. After a moment, the cobwebs in her mind began to clear and the room around her came into focus. Raising her head, Rae squinted as she glanced around the unfamiliar room. *Where am I?* Puzzled, she thought for a moment as vague images drifted through her mind: a woman, and then a tall man, offering her something. Uncertain, Rae wondered if they were snatches of life events or merely fragments of dreams she'd had. She sat up and scanned the room in the dim light, not sure if it was night time, or early in the morning. All at once, the room seemed vaguely familiar. *Oh yeah, I had tea in here last night...with that nice lady.* Rae pushed herself up onto her elbow and scanned the coffee table in front of her for her phone. Not seeing it, she squinted in thought. *Oh yeah, it was dead. I left it in the Cessna.* With some effort, she pushed herself up the rest of the way into a sitting position, then paused, dizzy, waiting to regain her equilibrium. *Wow, I'm whipped.* She stood, teetering, and shuffled to the door.

To his utter delight, Nate watched as the parlor door swung open. Wide-eyed with anticipation, he awaited the appearance of its mysterious occupant. Rae's face appeared in the doorway as she peered sleepily in both directions, then made her way to the bathroom she remembered showering in. Nate marveled as he watched from his vantage point. *It's a lady!* This delighted him all the more, because she was new and different from anyone else in the house—a 'story event,' for sure! And he scooted off to find his most-favorite book ever. Minutes later, Rae shuffled back to the parlor and through the doorway, leaving the door ajar. The trip to the bathroom having worn her out, she fell back into the sofa limply, her back to the door, and was quickly dozing again.

Returning soon after with his favorite storybook, his blanket, and his giant, plush stuffed caterpillar, Nate tried the parlor door, and to his delight, it swung open! Hurrying in, he pushed the door closed behind him, latching it securely, and then parked himself on the floor next to the sofa. Not allowed to wake anyone but Daddy and Grandma, he waited for the new lady to open her eyes. Resting his hands on the edge of the sofa cushion, his chin on his fingers—inches from Rae's face, he stared at her closely so that he would know the instant she awoke. After several minutes, Rae inhaled deeply, and rolled over. Drifting upward to wakefulness, she sensed the weight of the little boy's gaze. Opening her eyes, she found herself gazing into a little cherub face. Pleased that this new lady was finally awake, Nate smiled widely, and so did Rae. Her hand under the quilt, she surreptitiously slid it toward the boy, unnoticed. Suddenly, out it shot from under the cover, surprising the boy with tickles on his chest and tummy. "Booga, booga, booga!"

Nate squealed with delight, and jumped away, giggling. He picked up his book from the floor and brought it to Rae. Pushing back her covers, she sat up obligingly and patted the sofa cushion next to her, inviting the little boy to join her, which Nate happily did. Rae slipped her arm around him as he snuggled close, and opened the book and began to read. "David was a shepherd boy. . ."

From the kitchen, Ruth heard Nate's squeal and wondered what he was up to. Poking her head out the louver door, she didn't find him; she squinted, puzzling. *Hmm, where did he go?* She set out to look for him; after several minutes of searching, Ruth still had not found Nate. *Where could he be? He sounded so close by.* She had checked all of the rooms downstairs whose doors were open—the only room left was the parlor. Ruth cocked her head to one side, wondering, and stepped over to the parlor door and tried it, but it was latched so she moved to step away—but then something caught her attention. *Is someone talking in there?* She knew Heath was upstairs, so this puzzled her. *Maybe one of the Gang?* She returned to the door and listened for a moment. Curious, she quietly cracked open the door and peeked in—to her surprise, she spied Rae and Nate snuggled together on the sofa, with Rae reading to him from his book. Her heart warmed, Ruth smiled and waved to Heath, who was making his way down the stairs for breakfast, beckoning him to join her. As he joined her, Ruth signaled him into stealth-mode with an index finger to her lips, then again pushed open the parlor door just far enough to insert their faces, into the gap—Heath's above Ruth's, and together they peeked in at the sight.

Changing her voice according to which character was speaking, Rae used exaggerated inflections which amused and delighted her audience of one. Ruth and Heath grinned and glanced at each, looking on quietly, not wanting to interrupt. After a few more pages, Rae finished the little book and closed it. She cooed and snuggled playfully with Nate until he glanced up and saw his daddy's face at the door. Smiling joyfully, Nate immediately let himself down off the sofa and scampered across the room. Surprised by his sudden departure, Rae followed him with her eyes until she saw the two faces peering in, and pulled her covers around her self-consciously. "I think we're busted," Heath whispered to his mom, teasing as he glanced downward.

"I think you're right," Ruth laughed.

The two straightened up, and pushed open the parlor door the rest of the way, stepping in. Nate met them excitedly, arms reaching upward and Heath scooped him up into his arms, smiling broadly. "Hey, buddy!" Now perched on his daddy's arm, Nate turned and pointed to Rae; Heath nodded. "Who's that, Nate? Is that a new friend?" Heath tickled Nate's chest as the child nodded eagerly and Heath stepped forward into the room with Ruth.

Ruth smiled her warm smile at Rae. "Good morning, hon! We didn't mean to spy on you—we were just looking for Nate and then found him in here. It was just so precious! We didn't want to interrupt." She smiled again, "You look like you're finally feeling better." Rae didn't answer, only stared blankly. Ruth tried again, "In case you don't remember, I'm Ruth." Finally, a glint of recognition flickered across the girl's face and she nodded. "You feel like some breakfast, hon?"

Unable to resist Ruth's inviting smile, Rae nodded, speaking softly, "Um, sure, that sounds good." She eyed the older woman curiously. *Except for the drawl, she sounds just like Mom. . .*

Ruth nodded. "It'll be ready in about ten or fifteen minutes. Do you want to eat with us out in the kitchen, or would you like me to bring it in here?"

Drawn to the woman, Rae answered quickly. "No, I'll come out there."

Ruth smiled. "Okay, hon, we'll be in the kitchen—just come on when you're ready." She nodded and turned for the door, pleased to be able to get some food into this girl.

Heath turned to follow her, then paused. "Say bye-bye, Nate."

Nate raised his little hand and waved. "Bah-bah!"

Rae returned the wave weakly. "Bye-bye, Nate—it was fun reading with you!"

Heath and Ruth exchanged glances as they left the parlor, their uncertainty about their visitor diminishing another notch. Closing the door behind them, they silently gave thanks for the girl's recovery and waited until they reached the kitchen before they spoke.

Still smiling, Ruth turned to her son, her hand over her heart. "Wasn't that precious?"

Heath beamed at his son, still surprised at what he had witnessed. "Did you see Nate's face?"

Ruth smiled, "I did! I've never seen him take to someone like that!"

Heath squinted. "That's really strange, him going in there like that. He's usually not that open to new people."

Ruth shrugged, taking a guess. "Well she is in his house; maybe that just makes her a curiosity instead of a stranger."

"Maybe so." Heath turned to Nate, who was still perched on his arm. "Did you like Ms. Rae, Nate?" Nate just patted his dad's face with his open hands.

Ruth thought a moment. "She looks so much better today, I'm glad we held off on calling for help." She reached into the refrigerator and pulled out the bin of eggs and set them by the stove as she spoke.

"Yeah, me too—but it sure made me nervous there for a while." Heath nodded his head for emphasis. "When did she finally wake up?"

Ruth crouched to retrieve her frying pan from a lower cupboard. "I don't know. I heard Nate giggle and went looking for him. I'm not sure how long he was in there before I heard him."

"So he just sneaked in there when you weren't looking?"

"He sure did! I don't know how he got the door open; I know I latched it." Ruth started some oatmeal cooking then, then broke the eggs into a large bowl and beat them with her whisk.

Heath set out plates and flatware with Nate following him around the kitchen, 'helping.' Heath spoke as he made his way around the small table. "You know, Mom—as cute as that was, we really don't know anything about her; I'm not sure I should leave you and Nate here alone with her. Do you want me to stay home today?"

Ruth poured the beaten eggs into her frying pan. "Oh, I don't think so, Heath. I'm not exactly alone."

"I know, but I don't mind, really."

"Do you sense that she is some kind of a threat?"

"No, I guess not." When Heath finished setting the table, he set Nate into his booster seat in the chair against the wall and took the seat next to him. Ruth brought over some muffins and a small bowl of oatmeal for Nate and set them in front of Heath.

"Thank you, son, but she still seems pretty weak—I doubt she can cause any problems. I think I'll be fine."

The oatmeal cooled, Heath slid the bowl over to Nate and watched as the toddler picked up a spoon with one hand, and plunge into the bowl with his other. Heath chuckled, nudging the hand holding the spoon. "Use the spoon, Nate!" Then he picked up a muffin for himself and buttered it. "Okay, let me know if you change your mind—I can always come home if you need me to." He took a bite of his muffin.

Ruth turned and headed back to the counter. "I appreciate that, Heath."

Rae emerged from the parlor and steadied herself against the door jamb before slowly making her way into the front room, surprised how wobbly she felt. Unsure which way to go for breakfast, she glanced around then spotted the louver door, and recalled an ill-fated glass of water. *That's right, the kitchen is through there.* She made her way over to it unsteadily, shuffling her bare feet across the wood floor. Pushing open the louver door a few inches, she peeked around it.

"There you are!" Ruth smiled from the counter in front of the toaster, then nodded over her shoulder toward the table. "Have a seat hon, breakfast is almost ready."

Rae poked her head into the room and peered around the edge of the door in the direction of Ruth's nod, until two more sets of eyes met her, and Heath beckoned her over. "Come on, have a seat." As she approached, Heath inspected the sweat shirt and pants that hung so loosely on her and teased her softly. "Nice outfit."

Rae half-smiled without looking at him, her voice dead-pan. "I made it myself."

Heath grinned at her quip, surprised—especially given that she didn't even appear to be fully awake. Rae smiled at the little boy as she took the chair next to him, across from Heath. Nate smiled back, offering the new lady a handful of oatmeal. Ruth followed Rae to the table with her pan of scrambled eggs and began spooning them onto each plate, then returned the pan to the stove. Captivated, Rae watched her the entire time. Gathering up the plate of toast and the pitcher of juice, Ruth returned to the table with them, and sat down in the chair between Heath and Rae.

"I sure appreciate your help and what you've done." Rae addressed it to Ruth as though Heath was not there.

Ruth smiled warmly. "Why, sure, hon. We're just glad to see you up and around finally." Rae nodded, then puzzled at the word. *Finally?—It was only one night.* Ruth continued, "I only gave you that little spoonful of eggs because I thought you might want to start out slow after not eating in so long." Rae nodded, again puzzling. *So long?* Ruth reached for the pitcher of juice. "But there's more eggs if you want them, hon. Don't be bashful."

Heath blessed the meal and everyone started eating. Rae listened while Heath and Ruth made small talk, and answered an occasional question they asked of her. She ate a couple bites of eggs and half of a piece of toast, and suddenly felt full. Putting down her fork, she watched as the others finished up, wondering how Ruth knew she wouldn't eat much. Nate held his scrambled eggs in his hands and mixed them with his oatmeal, feeding himself and offering bites to Rae.

When Ruth was finished eating, she stood and picked up her plate. "Well, I need to get breakfast on for the Gang."

Rae squinted at her, puzzled. "The Gang?"

"We have some elderly people boarding with us—that's what we call them." Rae nodded, vaguely recalling Heath mentioning that when she encounterd him in the woods. Ruth eyed Rae's plate. "Are you finished, hon?"

"Yes, thank you."

"Heath?"

"Yeah, thanks Mom." Ruth retrieved their plates as well, leaving Nate's behind until he had eaten more. Heath rose. "Well, I need to get to work."

He rose and stepped into the mud room beyond the little table and reached for his jacket. When he returned, Rae was eyeing him, puzzled. "You work on Saturdays?"

Heath slipped his arms into the sleeves and shrugged on the jacket. "Nope—today is Monday."

Doubtful, Rae eyed him shaking her head. "*Monday?* No way!"

Heath smiled "Yes way—you've been out of it for two days."

Rae froze. "*Two days?*" Getting a nod of confirmation from Ruth, Rae's eyes widened in alarm. "Are you serious?" Suddenly, Ruth's references to the passage of time made sense. Ruth and Heath both nodded, exchanging glances. Fretting, Rae suddenly gripped the hair on top of her head. "Oh, no. . .!"

"What's wrong, hon?"

"I need to call my dad! He must freaking-out by now!" Seeing their concerned expressions, she tried to explain. "I was supposed to call him on Thursday, but my phone died. . .and now it's *Monday?* Can I use your phone?"

"Sure, hon, it's right outside the door—to your left."

Rae pulled herself out of her chair and hurried through the louver door. Ruth glanced at Heath, who still stood there, hands in his jacket pockets.

He shrugged, speaking softly, "Well, I guess she's not a runaway, so that's good."

Ruth nodded, also whispering. "She doesn't seem to be any of the things we were worried about."

Heath thought for a moment. "She said her phone died. Did she have one with her when she got here?"

Ruth shook her head. "I didn't see one." She sighed. "I just wish we could know more about her."

They heard Rae's voice through the louver door. "Patty? Yeah, it's me. No, I'm okay. Is my dad there yet? Okay, thanks."

Hands still in his jacket pockets, Heath hesitated at the porch door. Hearing the girl's voice carry so well into the kitchen, he grinned at an opportunity. Shrugging, he spoke softly, "Maybe we're about to find out?"

Ruth's mouth fell open, her whisper, intense. "Heath! We shouldn't listen!"

Heath shrugged, grinning. "You're right, we shouldn't—but we can't help it if we can hear, right?"

Ruth shrugged uncertainly and Heath once again took his seat. With both hoping to learn more about their visitor, they waited and listened. After a long pause, Rae's voice came again. "Dad? Yeah, I know. I'm so sorry! I didn't mean to not call you...No, I'm okay, really...Yeah, my phone died and I was stuck at the Cessna overnight and half the next day."

Ruth glanced at Heath and whispered. "Stuck, where...?"

Heath shook his head and shrugged. "I didn't catch it."

They fell quiet again as Rae continued, "No, I got lost in the woods trying to get to a phone, and then there was a big storm—and then I got really sick. I guess I've been out of it for a couple of days. . .No, I'm doing better now. . . Yeah, I guess so. I just woke up and found out *it's Monday!* I know, right?—I had no idea! When they told me I about had a heart attack, Dad!. . . 'They'?—These people I'm staying with. . .No, I'm not in the hospital; I'm at someone's house. . .I don't know who they are. When I got lost in the woods, I just stumbled onto their house and they took me in. . .Dad, I didn't have much of a choice!—It was cold and pouring down rain and I just ended up here. It was either that or freeze to death. . . Yeah, they took care of me while I was sick. . .Yeah, it *is* pretty amazing. . .Uh-huh, this really nice lady and some man—he's her son. . .I wish you could meet her, Dad."

In the kitchen, Heath's mouth fell open in a wide smile. *"Some man?"* Feigning indignation, he grinned, speaking softly. "You're 'a really nice lady' that she wants him to meet—and I'm 'some man'?" He chuckled, amused. Ruth only smiled as they listened further.

". . .No, I don't want to leave it here, I think I can fix it. . .Yeah, I was referred to someone local who said he would help me with it." Rae winced at that memory. " Oh, man! He's probably wondering what happened to me, too! I'll have to call him." That thought brought another wince to her face. "Oh nuts, his number is in my dead phone. I'll have to get a new charger today, for sure—so I can call him back. . .No, you don't need to come up. I hate to have you do that. You already have too much to do there. . .I'll be fine, Dad, really; I'm doing much better now. If I need to, I'll find a room somewhere until I can get it fixed. . .I won't know until I see his estimate and find out if he has the parts. . .A car? Oh yeah. I didn't think about that. Hmm, I don't know how I'll get around. I guess I'll rent one, or something. . .I don't know. I'll handle it."

Ruth squinted, whispering. "Is she old enough to rent a car?" Before Heath could answer, another thought occurred to her. "Get a room? Why would she do that?" Ruth looked stricken.

"I don't know. Maybe she feels like she's been here too long and needs to leave."

"Oh, that's nonsense. Why can't she stay here?"

"It's up to her, but I don't see why not. Especially since she's already here." Heath grinned at his mom. "You were so worried about me inviting her here, and now look at you—wanting her to stay!"

"Well, I should think so! What else is she going to do?" Ruth thought a moment, "What do you think it is that she needs to fix?"

Heath only shrugged and shook his head. "I don't know. Maybe her car?"

"There were some keys in her pocket when I washed her clothes, but they didn't look like car keys."

"No, wait. She just said she didn't have any transportation, so it must be something else."

Outside the door, Rae's voice came again. "I'll be okay. . .Yes, I'm sure. . .Yes, I'll get another phone charger right away, I promise. . .I miss you too. I'll call you when I find a room. . . Daaaad!" She stretched out the word, "No, it will *not* be another three days, this time! I'll call you tonight—*I promise!*. . .Okay, 'love you, too."

As soon as Rae hung up the phone, Heath jumped up quickly, hoping to escape before she returned to the kitchen and saw he was still there, and their eaves dropping be discovered. He leaned over to kiss his mom, speaking softly. "Bye mom, have a good day." He moved over to Nate, kissed his son, holding Nate's oatmeal and scrambled egg fingers away from his clothes, and whispered. "Bye-bye, Nate. Daddy loves you."

But before he could make his getaway, Rae reappeared at the louver door, surprised to find Heath still there. "Oh, I'm sorry, I thought you left." She turned to Ruth, "Am I interrupting?"

Ruth tried to sound casual. "Not a bit, hon. Is everything okay?"

Rae already seemed drained. "Yeah, thanks. I'm sorry that was a long-distance call. I'll pay you for it."

"Oh, don't worry none about that, hon. I get a flat monthly rate for the phone; it don't cost us anything extra."

Rae nodded and sighed, charmed by Ruth's drawl. "You've already done so much, I hate asking for this—but if you are going into town today, would it be possible for me to ride with you? I need to take care of a few things."

"Oh, I'm sorry hon, my van is tore-up right now."

"Tore up...?" Rae squinted, imagining parts of the car sheared away. "Were you in a wreck?"

Ruth smiled, amused. "No, hon—that's Southern for 'isn't working right now.'" Rae nodded, enlightened. Ruth continued, "But maybe Heath can take you into town when he gets home this afternoon."

Heath nodded. "Sure, I can do that. Or, if you want, I can take you now—before I go to work."

This time Rae actually looked at him. "You can do that?"

"Sure, why not?"

"Your boss won't mind?"

"Naw. I'm in good with him—it'll be okay." Heath grinned, as did Ruth.

Rae shrugged. "Um, okay, sure. That would be great." Rae reached for the louver door, then hesitated—again addressing Ruth. "It'll just be a minute while I get dressed. If that's okay." Heath nodded, but she didn't notice.

Ruth called to her back. "Heath can wait while you take a shower, if you want, hon."

Rae stepped back into the room, eyeing Ruth. "Seriously? You don't mind?"

She glanced at Heath, who shrugged. "Sure, why not?—If you're up to it."

"Are you sure it's okay with your boss?"

Heath grinned again. "Yeah, he's good."

Rae's eyebrows arched. "Wow, you must have an amazing boss."

Heath grinned and shrugged. "Yeah, *I* think so."

Ruth reproved mildly. "Heath!" Heath just chuckled, but Rae didn't seem to notice. Ruth turned to Rae. "I put your clothes on the table next to the sofa, hon."

Again, Rae focused on Ruth, smiling appreciatively. "Thanks, Ruth." And she disappeared through the louver door. Though still smiling, Heath shook his head at her indifference, and chuckled. Slipping off his coat, he stepped back over to the mud room and hung it back on its peg. Returning to the table, he sat down again next to Nate, who had given his face an oatmeal scrub.

Scanning his arms and legs, Heath grinned and shook his head. "Am I invisible?"

Ruth squinted, puzzled, "Invisible. . .? What do you mean?"

"I mean, is it my imagination or is she pretty much ignoring me?"

"Ignoring you? What are you talking about Heath?—She talked to you!"

"Yeah, when she *had* to!" He chuckled, shaking his head, "Even when I say something directly to her, she hardly looks at me. I mean, I ask her a question, and she answers you. What's up with that?" He thought for a moment. "Do you think it's because I scared her that night?"

Ruth waved off the notion. "I'm sure she's not holding that against you. Maybe she's just shy?"

356

"Yeah, at first I thought that—but she sure seems to like *you* all right."

"Maybe she's just shy around men, then."

"I don't know about that, Mom—there's 'shy' and then there's *indifferent!*" He chuckled again. "I mean, it's no big deal, I just think it's kind of strange. She looks at you like you're a movie star, or something."

"Well, I think that's just because she misses her mama—I think I must remind her of her."

"She's only been away from home for a few days."

"No Heath, Her mama died last spring. She told me so that first night she was here."

Heath winced, "Oh, wow—she told you that?" When Ruth nodded, then so did Heath. "Well, I guess that explains that, then." Heath thought a moment more. "Then there's another good reason for her to stay with us instead of by herself at a motel."

Ruth nodded, then set about getting breakfast on for the Gang. As Ruth worked, Heath added, "Well, by the sound of her, she's not from Georgia."

Ruth shook her head, "No, she's not." She thought a moment. "It's like she just dropped out of the sky into our neck of the woods, isn't it?"

** *** **

Rae found her clothes in the spot where Ruth had put them. Gathering them into her arms, she made her way to the bathroom. She had intended to shower and dress promptly, but in her weakened state, every movement seemed to require enormous effort and more time than she had imagined. Turning on the shower spray, Rae waited a minute, and tested the water temperature, then stepped in. With her back to the hot spray, her shoulder protested immediately with stinging that brought tears to her eyes. Rae winced and reached for it, pulling off the now-soggy gauze dressing, as she turned to face the spray, keeping her shoulder away from it for the remainder of her shower. She soaped up and rinsed off, tiring quickly, then becoming winded half way through washing her hair, she had to stop and lean against the shower wall while she caught her breath.

Remembering that the man was in the kitchen waiting for her, Rae prodded herself along, until she was finished. Stepping out, she wrapped her towel around her and, once again, her stinging shoulder demanded attention. Turning, she peered at it in the mirror, shaking her head as she examined it in her reflection. *Man, that's deeper than I thought!* Glancing around her, she noticed the gauze and iodine still on the bathroom counter from the night she had arrived. *I probably better cover it again.* Rae repeated the procedure she'd watched Ruth do two days before, grimacing at the iodine and gritting her teeth all over again. Dressing proved to be more demanding than Rae could have imagined, and by the time she was ready to comb out her hair, she was already exhausted. *Man, that was just a shower—I hope I make it to the store!*

After twenty minutes, they heard the hair dryer in the bathroom, so Heath rose and retrieved his coat from its peg and slipped it on again. "Well, I'll start warming up the truck. Be right back." A couple minutes later, Heath let himself back in. "Wow, it's cold out there!—And it's just barely into November!"

"I know. It just scared me to think about what might have happened to Rae if you hadn't run across her last night."

Heath pressed his lips together and shook his head, amazed. "God sure had mercy on her."

Ruth couldn't agree more. A few minutes later, Rae reappeared at the louver door, semi-wet hair in a ponytail, already looking worn out. Ruth greeted her, "There she is! I see you found your clothes okay." She noticed how they hung on Rae's slim frame. "Looks like you lost some weight, hon!" Rae glanced down at her baggy jeans, only nodding. Ruth's forehead furrowed over Rae's worn expression. "You doing all right, sweetheart? You look beat already."

"Yeah, thanks. I'll be okay. I'm sorry if I kept anyone waiting." She stepped toward the porch door. Heath smirked to himself at her use of the word 'anyone.' He glanced at Ruth, his eyebrows arched to make the point as he joined Rae at the door. Ruth ignored him, turning to Rae,

"Um, Rae?"

"Yes, ma'am?"

"Forgive me for overhearing part of your conversation earlier, but I want you to know—you don't have to rush off and stay in a motel. *Heath* and I talked it over," deliberately mentioning his name in case Rae had forgotten it, ". . .and we'd like you to stay here as long as you need to so you can take care of things."

Surprised, Rae turned around to face Ruth, leaning closer. "Seriously? You don't mind?"

Ruth shook her head. "Of course not."

Rae hesitated. "I'm not sure how long it will take. I want to pay you."

"We'll work something out, hon. Just don't you worry about leaving 'til you get things squared away, okay?"

Rae's relief was evident. "Oh, man. That would be such a big help! I sure appreciate it. Thank you *so* much!" She even glanced at Heath, "Thank you."

Heath smiled and nodded at her, then opened the door. Rae stepped out, and waited as Heath stepped over to Ruth and kissed her good-bye again. She smiled at her son, speaking softly. "There, that's settled—and she thanked you too, Heath. See? You're not invisible."

Heath chuckled and smiled. "Well, that's good to know. We'll be back soon." Reminding himself of the oatmeal, he just waved to Nate. "Bye Nate—Daddy will see you later!"

As Heath stepped out the door, Rae turned and began making her way along the porch toward the frosted-over truck that sat belching steam in front of the old carriage house garage. As Heath walked along behind her, he noticed the small hole in her shirt at her shoulder, then realized something was missing. "You need a jacket?"

Rae turned slightly, but kept on walking. "No, I'll be fine."

"You sure? It's not even forty degrees out here."

She stopped and faced him. "Do you have a heater in your car?" Heath nodded, so Rae shook her head, and turned and started forward again. "That's okay, then—I'm good."

Heath wondered if she really was good with it—or if she was just being stubborn. "You just got done being sick and your hair is still damp. Let me get you a sweater or something." He disappeared back inside for a couple of minutes and returned with a small, bulky jacket. "Here, this is Mrs. Balcomb's; she won't mind if you borrow it. I'd lend you one of mine, but you'd probably get lost in it." He held up the coat by the ends of the collar, waiting for her to slip her arms into the sleeves. When she didn't, he jostled it, coaxing, "C'mon. . ."

Rolling her eyes, Rae shook her head at his hovering, and wanted to say something sarcastic, but out of respect for Ruth, she bit her tongue. Instead, she sighed and stepped back over to where Heath stood with the coat ready, and slipped her arms into the sleeves as he drew it up to her shoulders. It was big on her, but not noticeably so.

"Thanks." She offered it grudgingly, and they started walking again.

After a few steps, Heath ventured. "I take it you don't like being looked after?" Rae eyed the man walking next to her, but didn't answer. Heath nodded. "I get it—you can take care of *yourself,* right?"

Rae shrugged without looking at him. "Nothing wrong with that."

Heath shook his head. "Nope, there isn't—and you sure been doing *a fine* job of that these last couple of days." He grinned, amused with himself. Bristling, Rae shot him a look, but Heath just grinned again as he opened the door of his truck for her. She squinted at him uncertainly as she got in and Heath just chuckled and closed the door behind her. Climbing in behind the wheel, Heath reached for his seatbelt. "So, where are we headed?"

"Do you have a Super Mart?"

"Yup, we do." As he fastened the seatbelt, he glanced at Rae, and noticed her pale face and drawn expression, and his grin left his face. "Are you sure you're up for this?"

Fumbling with her seatbelt, Rae rolled her eyes again, then shrugged and nodded without looking at him. "I need to be."

"We can do it later if you want."

"No, that's okay," she gazed out her side window as she spoke, "I need to just go ahead and get it done now."

Heath watched a moment longer, then, shrugged. "Okay, let's go." He put it in gear and eased the truck forward.

Chapter 28

After several minutes of riding in silence, Heath finally spoke, "So, aren't you supposed to be in school or something?"

"No." Rae answered wearily, staring out her window watching the scenery pass by. Heath waited for her to elaborate, but she didn't. Rae disliked small talk, especially when it came around to being asked about herself and what she did for a living. Weary of the doubtful, if not accusatory, reactions that she usually receives when telling people she was an aircraft mechanic, and forever having to prove it to everyone she talked to, she had found over the years it was easier just to focus social conversations on the other person. So, before he could start peppering her with questions, Rae decided to get the jump on him. "You must have a really nice boss if he lets you come in whenever you want."

"Yeah, I have the best boss I could have—me." He grinned, amused with himself.

"Huh?"

"I'm my own boss. I have a small business in Redlands."

"Oh." Connecting that fact with his earlier answers, Rae just rolled her eyes. "What kind of business are you in?"

"I'm a sign painter."

"A sign painter?" Unimpressed, she squinted at him. "You can make a living at that?"

Heath smiled tolerantly, again amused. "I do okay."

"Then why do you need to live with your mom?"

Arching an eyebrow, Heath chuckled, still smiling—but just barely. "You sure don't beat around the bush, do you? Well, for your information, Miss Nosey-face," he smirked, chiding her, "I don't need to live with my mom. My dad died a few years ago and I just moved back in a few months ago to help her out."

"Your dad died?" Stricken, Rae immediately changed her tune. "I'm so sorry. I was just giving you a hard time. I'm really sorry."

"No, it's okay." Her contrition surprised him. "I help my mom with the house and she helps me by keeping Nate while I work." Heath wondered if she would volunteer to him that her own mom had died, but she didn't.

"Your son is a cute little guy." *That ought to keep him talking for a while.*

Not surprising, Heath spent the next ten minutes on Nate, his favorite subject. When he slowed down, Rae reached for another subject. "What's wrong with your mom's car?"

"Nothing serious. The mechanic said it sounds like it needs a fuel pump. I'm taking it in tomorrow."

"What kind of car is it?" Heath told her the make and model, but Rae needed more, "Is it new?"

"No, it's a 2009."

Rae nodded, making a mental note. To cover her tracks she added, "Are those good cars?" She couldn't care less if it was a good car; she just wanted to keep him talking so that he wouldn't start in on questioning her. Heath obliged her by expounding for a few minutes about the virtues of the make of van Ruth drove, and Rae tuned-out his answer until she noticed his flow of information again slowing down, and then simply asked him another question about himself. She had an arsenal of them at the ready, questions about himself, his work, his family. Anything she could think of to keep him going, and from being asked about herself. Not so inclined as most men to go on about himself, Heath's answers were brief, and after only ten minutes, Rae was running out of questions, so resorted to the standard passenger's lamaent, "Are we almost there?"

"Pretty soon."

Rae surveying the stands of woods and open fields outside her window. "Wow, things are really spread out around here."

"Yeah, it's pretty rural. It's grown a lot in the last ten or fifteen years, though."

After miles of farmland, fields, and woods, she was skeptical. "This is 'grown'?"

Heath smiled, amused again. "You must be from the city, or something."

"Suburbs, by Gainesville."

"Gainesville, Georgia or Gainesville, Florida?"

"Florida." Seeing the conversation was again turning toward her, Rae pressed herself to think of something else to ask about. *Sports is usually a good bet with men, let's see. . . this is Georgia. . .* "So are you a Bulldogs fan?"

Heath arched an eyebrow at her. "You're into football?"

"No, but my dad and brothers are, so I've learned to speak 'football' as a second language."

Heath chuckled. "How do you know about the Bulldogs? I would think you'd only be into the Gators."

"The Gators have to play *someone.*" She rolled her eyes again, then glanced down as they crossed a bridge over the interstate. "Which interstate was that?"

"That's I-75." Heath squinted, *Brothers, huh?* Suspecting that might have something to do with her nonchalance toward him, Heath half-grinned, then probed further. "How many brothers do you have?"

364

"Four."

"You have four brothers?" He chuckled to himself, "That explains a lot."

Rae squinted, "What does it 'explain'?"

He smirked, "Oh, nothing."

Before he could ask her something else Rae tried again, "I'll bet you played sports in High School." Heath only nodded, so Rae took a guess, "You're tall enough for basketball, but you're not built like a basketball player. I'm guessing football."

Heath shrugged and nodded again. "Yeah, I played football."

"You're too lean for a lineman, too tall for a quarterback. I'm guessing you were a running back or maybe a wide receiver?"

Heath grinned at her reasoning. "Yeah, wide receiver. You're right."

"So, did your team win any championships?" *That ought to get him going for a while.*

Heath shrugged. "Some."

Rae waited. When nothing else came, she arched her eyebrows. "That's it?—Just, 'some'? With most guys, that would keep them talking for an hour."

Heath half-grinned. "Oh, is that your goal?—To keep me talking?" Rae only shrugged, and then Heath did too. "I'm just not real proud of my football years."

"Why? Didn't your team win enough games?"

"Oh, we won plenty. I'm just not real proud of my behavior back then, or some of the choices I made." When Rae arched an eyebrow, Heath decided to steer away from that. "What about *your* high school team?"

"I'm not in high school." Rae shifted uncomfortably, then, to her relief, she noticed the scenery giving way to businesses.

Heath's eyes narrowed, "Really?—You've graduated? I thought you were only about fifteen or sixteen!"

"Yeah, I graduated." Her answer was dead-pan. *Here it comes. Where's that stupid store?*

"Did you skip some grades?"

"No. How much further?"

Heath noted the edge in her voice. "Oh, c'mon now—I answered all of your questions." Rae tucked her chin and eyed him sternly and Heath arched an eyebrow. "I take it you don't like to talk about yourself."

"Not really. Why do you think I kept you talking for so long?"

Heath winced. "I don't know, I guess I just thought you were being friendly." He glanced at her for a moment. "So keeping me talking *was* your goal." He sighed. "Is that some kind of 'city girl thing'?"

"Suburbs. No, I'm sorry. I don't mean to be unfriendly—but like you said, I just don't like to talk about myself."

"Oh. I didn't mean to make you feel uncomfortable. Sorry." Heath noticed she eyed him curiously after he apologized. "What. . .?"

"Nothing." Rae broke off her curious stare, and turned back to the window.

"Why does talking about yourself make you uncomfortable? I thought girls liked to do that." Rae eyed him wearily again, and Heath back-pedaled. "Oh, sorry. Never mind." He glanced down the road ahead of them. "Well, you're off the hook because here we are." Much to Rae's relief, he turned left into the parking lot of Super Mart. Scanning the shopping center, Rae perked up when she saw a car parts store next to a pet supply mart on the end of the row of shops adjacent to Super Mart—and glad it was so close.

Heath glanced at his dashboard instruments. "Tell you what—I need to get some gas. How about I let you off here and I'll come find you inside in a little while."

Rae nodded. "Sure that's fine." *Actually, that's perfect.* Heath dropped her off at the entrance to Super Mart and Rae waited for him to drive off before she headed for the car parts store. She made her purchase there quickly and headed back to Super Mart.

About twenty minutes later, Heath found her in the toothpaste aisle. He noticed several clothing and personal items in her buggy, including a sweatshirt and pants, which Heath was certain had to be closer to her size that Mr. Balcomb's. Then he noticed the box in the buggy seat. "What's that?"

She shrugged. "Just something I picked up at one of the other stores."

Beginning to detect a pattern in her answers, Heath smiled. "Okay, I won't ask. I *can* be taught." Rae smirked, then tossed a box of toothpaste and a toothbrush into the buggy; it landed next to a cell phone charger. *Hmm. . .Mom said she didn't have a cell phone with her.* Heath eyed the charger curiously, but after his last remark, and their conversation on the way into town, he decided not to ask.

Rae shrugged. "Well, I think that's all I need right now."

They made their way to the check-out, and Rae pulled out her debit card from her wallet. When she reached up to swipe it, Heath's mouth fell open. "You're using a debit card?"

"Unless *you'd* like to pay for it."

Heath raised his hands, palms out. "No, I'm good. I guess I'm just stuck on the age thing. I keep forgetting you said you're eighteen."

"No, I didn't say that; I only said I had graduated." She punched in her PIN.

"But you said you didn't skip any grades."

"Are you phishing?"

"No. . .well, sort of. . ."

"Okay, I give! I'm twenty, okay? Are you happy now?"

Heath grinned. "Yes, very—you don't look twenty." Rae just rolled her eyes and sighed. As she completed her transaction, Heath gathered up a few of her bags and waited for her. Rae picked up the remaining two and they headed for the exit. Outside, his hands full—Heath gestured with his head. "I'm parked about half way up that row."

Her attention pulled in another direction, Rae didn't respond. To their right, near the entrance, sat a police cruiser and a small crowd of people gathered around two officers, the store manager, and a very upset twenty-something girl. At first, Heath moved to steer around the spectacle, but when Rae heard the girl's voice, with the familiar hollow, nasal sound, she stopped short. "Here, hold these a minute." Rae didn't wait for an answer and set her bags into his already full arms.

Diverting from the puzzled Heath, Rae drew closer to the crowd, peering around the bystanders, and found the source of the voice—the upset girl. Gesturing wildly and grunting, as she spoke in her hollow tones, she was trying unsuccessfully to make herself understood. One of the police officers reached for her arm, but the girl yanked it away, frightened, and began to cry. The people standing around gawking stepped back from her apprehensively. The store manager turned to one of the police officers. "I don't know if she's having some kind of problem or if she's just crazy, or retarded, or something."

Inhaling sharply at his words, eyes blazing, Rae snorted and stepped forward past the two officers to the distressed girl's side, and spoke sharply to the three men. "She's not crazy or retarded!—she's deaf!"

"Deaf?" The three men were almost in unison.

With an index finger extended, Rae turned to the girl and touched her own chin, then her ear, then pointed to the girl with the same finger; asking her in sign if she was deaf. The girl lunged toward Rae in desperate relief. Taking hold of Rae's hand, she nodded eagerly, immediately beginning to calm. The police stood by in surprise as the girl began signing rapidly, with Rae nodding frequently—then both the two girls rapidly exchanged signs for a minute, before Rae nodded again. The officers and store manager waited expectantly, as did the small crowd looking on. Rae turned to the three men and explained, "She locked her keys and her purse in her car and her mother is somewhere waiting to be picked up. She's late and she's upset because she knows her mom is probably worried sick about her." The three men smiled broadly, relieved and thankful that the situation was so minor and could be dealt with easily. As Rae waited, the men just kept smiling and nodding, and she became impatient. "Well, don't just stand there! Go get your Slim Jim and *open her door for her!*" Immediately the three men stopped smiling and stared wide-eyed at Rae, then one of the police officers sprang into action and jogged over to his cruiser. Rae turned to the girl and signed something else, then turned and scanned the crowd. "Heath. . .?"

Heath had been standing in the periphery, marveling. "Yeah, Rae, right here." The crowd parted around him, and began to thin.

"Can I use your phone?"

"Sure." He set down the bags from one hand and pulled his cell phone out of his pocket, then extended it to her.

Rae accepted the phone and returned to the girl, then began tapping in numbers as the girl signed them, and brought the phone to her ear. Waiting for the call to connect, Rae signed something else, and the girl responded as Rae nodded. "Yes, hello—is this Daphne's mom?" She paused for the response, "Hi, my name is Rae—I'm here at Super Mart with Daphne and she asked me to call you. She wants you to know she's fine. She's just running a little late because she locked her keys and her purse in the car. . .Yes, we have someone here who is helping her out with that. . .Uh-huh. . .yeah, she should be on her way in just a couple of minutes." Rae listened for a moment. "Okay, sure, hang on." She held out the phone toward Daphne, and sighed something.

Immediately, Daphne smiled and spoke in her hollow, consonant-scarce tones, "Hey, mom, it's me. I'm fine!"

Rae returned the phone to her ear. "Yes ma'am. I'll tell her that." Rae glanced up as the officer returned with the Slim Jim. "Yes ma'am, he's here right now with a Slim Jim. . .No, I'll just wait here with her until she's on her way, in case there's anything else she needs. . .Okay, sure. . . .You're sure welcome. Bye."

Rae handed the phone back to the stunned Heath, then began signing to Daphne again. She wagged an upright index finger in the air, and the girl stepped toward the parking aisles, leading Rae to her car—the store manager, the other officer, and Heath trailing behind. The two officers stepped to Daphne's car and maneuvered the Slim Jim until her door unlocked. Overjoyed, Daphne began touching her fingertips to her chin repeatedly, expressing her thanks—then started hugging Rae, the officers, and even the store manager. Jumping into her car, Daphne reached for something then turned to them holding up her keys, smiling happily. Rae and the three men smiled back, nodding, then Daphne closed her door and started the engine, and turned and backed out and, after another wave, she pulled away. The three men watched after her for a moment, pleased at the outcome. When they turned to thank Rae, she was already walking away.

"Young lady—thank you for your help. I don't know what we would have done if you hadn't shown up when you did."

Rae just nodded, smiled slightly, and kept walking. Heath jogged a few steps to catch up with her, still holding onto her shopping bags, grinning widely. "Wow, Rae—that was amazing how you helped that girl! How do you know how to do that?"

Rae shrugged wearily, without looking at him. "My brother is deaf."

They stepped up to the truck. Now full of questions, Heath couldn't wait to talk about the event, but once they were under way, the weary Rae just fell asleep against the window and didn't wake up until they pulled onto the drive at the house. When she came through the porch door into the kitchen, Ruth could tell she was well spent, "Now girl, you look like you're about out on your feet! Go on ahead and get some rest. I washed your sweatshirt and pants while you were gone." Rae nodded wearily and thanked her, then pushed through the louver door, not even retrieving her bags from Heath. Ruth turned to Heath, shaking her head. "That short trip really took it out of her. She sure looks beat!" She glanced at Heath who was still grinning broadly. "What are you smiling so big about?"

"Mom, you'll never guess what happened. . ."

** *** **

At his desk in his office, Joel's cell phone summoned him from his work. Glancing at the display, he grinned and held it to his ear. "Arlene! How ya doing?"

"Good. We're good. Um, our unit is having a get-together Saturday night at Sandra's place, and we'd like you to come, too. Are you busy?"

"No, I'm not busy. Um, is this another inquisition?"

Arlene grinned into the phone. "No, this time just about everyone from the clinic will be there with their spouses. Instead of an inquisition, just think of it as a gauntlet." Arlene chuckled, again deliberately trying to intimidate.

Unruffled, Joel shrugged. "A gauntlet? Okay, sure—that sounds good."

"Around six?"

"Six, it is. Can I bring something?"

"Oh, I don't know. You're a single guy. . .just bring a bag of chips or pretzels, or something."

"Okay, I can do that." Joel hesitated. "Um, will Andrea be coming?"

"Well, it wouldn't be much of a gauntlet if I invite her, would it?" Arlene dodged, grinning at Sandra.

Joel nodded. "That's probably best. I think it would make her uncomfortable if she knew I was going to be there. . ."

"Well, don't worry—she doesn't usually come to our parties. I'm not even planning to tell her about it." Arlene assured then grinned to herself. *I'll let Sandra do that.*

"Okay, that's good." Joel chuckled. "Because if she came and I was there, I'm sure it wouldn't go well for me."

Deciding it was a good time to change the subject, Arlene moved on. "I'll have Sandra call you with directions to her house—if I try to tell you, I'll probably get you lost." Joel was good with that, and they ended their call.

Sandra was eyeing her suspiciously when Arlene turned around. "He asked about Andrea?"

Arlene shrugged "Yeah, he said it won't go well for him if I invite Andrea."

"So, what did you tell him? Isn't getting them together the whole point of inviting him?"

"Yeah, and that's what we're going to do."

"But you just told him you aren't planning to invite Andrea."

"I'm not—*you're* going to."

Sandra shook her head, grinning. "Arlene, you are evil!"

Later that day, Sandra set the trap. "Andrea, I'm having a get-together Saturday night for all of us from work and our spouses. I was thinking around six-thirty. What do you think—can you come?"

Andrea balked, "Oh, I don't know, Sandra."

"Oh, c'mon! You need to get out more. You spend too much time alone at home. It's just a few hours with people you already know."

Andrea hesitated, still uncertain. "A few hours? Well, maybe."

Arlene stepped up, wanting some insurance. "You can ride with me, Andrea. I'll pick you up."

Andrea squinted at her, "You want to pick me up? Isn't that's kind of out of your way."

"That's okay. I think it would be fun."

Andrea shrugged, "Okay, I guess." She turned back to Sandra. "What can I bring?"

"I thought we'd just do wings and finger-food—nothing fancy. I'm doing the wings, everyone else is bringing the finger food."

Andrea shrugged again. "Okay, I think I can do that."

After Andrea moved on from her, Sandra turned to Arlene. "Why are you picking her up?"

Arlene shrugged. "So she can't leave when she sees Joel."

Sandra eyed her doubtfully. "Are you sure about this? It could really backfire."

Arlene waved that off, too. "Hey, Andrea needs a really nice guy, and that's what Joel is—she just needs our help to realize it. Just think of it as 'an intervention'!"

Skeptical, Sandra eyed her, "An intervention? Ha!—I hope you know what you're doing, Arlene! Either this will be a huge success or she will be really mad at us."

"Then we'll have to make sure it succeeds! Besides, if she gets mad, she'll get over it; she doesn't hold grudges. If she did, she would have divorced Evan years ago."

"Okay, she may get over it as far as we're concerned, but what about Joel? He may end up being dog-meat for life!"

"I didn't tell him Andrea is coming—that way, he has 'plausible deniability.'"

Again skeptical, Sandra shook her head. "I'm not sure him showing up at our party will be all that 'plausible' to Andrea."

"Just have all the girls bring their husbands so Joel will have someone to talk to if Andrea clams up."

Sandra nodded. "Yeah, good thinking."

Chapter 29

Around 3 pm, Heath turned onto the long driveway from work and pulled up in front of the garage around back. At the same time, Rae stirred from her nap on the sofa, feeling exponentially better than she had in days. Pushing the quilt off of her, she sat up and her eyes fell on the coffee table in front of her and the cell phone charger she'd bought that morning. *Well, I have a charger—now I just need my phone. If I could just figure out where my aircraft is. . .* She squinted. *I wonder. . .* Pushing off the sofa she headed out of the parlor. Ruth was in the kitchen having some tea when Heath clattered through the porch door.

"Hi, Mom, how'd it go today?" He ducked into the mudroom to hang up his jacket. At the same time, Rae padded softly through the kitchen in her bare feet. She smiled shyly to Ruth, then let herself out the door Heath had just come in through, closing it just as he emerged from the mudroom behind it. Heath puzzled at the door. "Who was that?"

Ruth's eyebrows were still arched. "That was Rae."

"Why did she go outside?"

"I have no idea—and she was barefoot, too!" Ruth puzzled for a moment then resumed the start of their conversation. "Today went just fine. You want some tea?"

"Sure, that would be great. Where's Nate?"

Ruth set the tea kettle on the stove. "He's down for his nap. He should be waking-up anytime now." Heath nodded and sat down at the kitchen table in his usual spot. He leaned his elbows on the table and crossed his forearms. "So, how is our visitor?"

"She's been sleeping most of the day—only got up a couple of times that I know of to go to the bathroom, and she came out after lunch for a short time and got her bags from her trip to the store this morning. I made her something to eat, but just like with breakfast, she only took a few bites."

"Has she said anything about how she ended up in the woods, yet?"

"No, except for that phone call we overheard, she hasn't said much of anything at all—just mostly sleeps." Ruth pulled a couple of mugs out of the cupboard and set out the tea.

Outside, Rae slowly circled around the back of the house on the wrap-around porch. Sliding her locket across it's chain as she scanned the woods at the edge of the clearing around the Dawson's house and property. Perplexed, she padded back around to the kitchen door and poked her head in from the porch. "Do you have a phone book I can look at?"

"Sure, hon, let me get it for you." Ruth pushed through the louver door as Rae stepped in and turned toward the little kitchen table.

Seeing Heath there, she stopped short. "Oh, you're back." She seemed almost disappointed. Hesitating for a moment, she took the seat across from him.

Heath nodded. "I just walked in. Were you looking for something out there?"

Rae only shrugged her response. Outside the louver door, Ruth retrieved the phone book from the desk and returned to the kitchen, setting it on the table in front of Rae then returned to the stove and the tea pot. Opening the book, Rae immediately began flipping through the pages. Heath watched her for a moment. "You look like you're feeling a little better." Rae just nodded without looking up, sliding her locket in short strokes across its chain.

The tea kettle squealed and Ruth turned to tend to it. "Rae, I'm fixin' to make some tea—you want some, too?"

Rae raised her eyes and smiled at the sound of Ruth's voice. "Sure, that would be good, thanks." Ruth smiled back at Rae and reached for another mug, and Rae returned her attention to the telephone book in front of her. Heath noticed how Rae gave his mom her full attention whenever she spoke, and smiled again to himself. He watched her from across the table as she combed through the phone book in the G's, while fingering the locket that dangled from a chain around her neck.

"That's a nice locket," he ventured.

"Thanks." Rae mumbled dispassionately without looking up.

Heath just rolled his eyes, again marveling at her indifference. Not finding what she was looking for, Rae closed the telephone book and pushed it aside, frowning. She pivoted in her chair and rested her arms on the chair back, watching Ruth prepare the tea.

Heath reached for the fruit bowl in the center of the table, eyeing Rae as he picked out an orange. The gauze on her shoulder showed through the neck hole of her baggy sweatshirt and caught his attention. "So, Rae…" he began, his eyes on his orange. Rae's head turned toward his voice. Remembering his manners, Heath paused and offered the orange to Rae, who shrugged and accepted it with a nod, and pivoted the remainder of her torso toward the table to face Heath, who picked out another orange for himself. He began again, "So Rae, it's none of my business, but if I was to take a guess, I would say that mark on your shoulder looked a lot like you were grazed by a bullet." He looked directly into her eyes as he started peeling his orange, and waited for her to answer. Ruth set their steaming mugs down on the table, and retreated back to the stove to let Heath take charge.

Rae sighed wearily, knowing already where this conversation was going to end up—where *all* conversations about her inevitably end up. *As soon as I tell him that I was flying when this happened, things are going to change. They always do.* Rae glanced over at Ruth. *I don't want this to change.* She was not at all afraid of taking-on this man across from her, but he was Ruth's son—and not for the world did she want to offend Ruth. Rae studied Heath's face, finding it an odd mixture of concern and caution, with a hint of challenge. Not one to back down from a challenge, Rae's eyes narrowed, and she leaned her head to one side. *Maybe he won't pursue it like everyone else.* She weighed that for a moment then sighed and answered herself. *Yeah right!—He's a man, he'll pursue it all right!* She considered lying about it, but she was a lousy liar—and if he detected a lie, she might be asked to leave, which would mean that she wouldn't be able to spend any more time with Ruth. *Maybe if I just bite my tongue a lot, and don't go off on him, the inevitable won't happen this time.* Rae shifted in her seat, trying to detach herself from her anxieties for the moment. Nodding, she shrugged again, "Yeah, it's from a bullet." She decided to tackle the peeling of her orange so that she could focus on something besides the man across from her.

Heath watched her for a moment, nodding as well. *That's what I thought. At least she didn't lie about it.* He shifted his focus to his orange, working his thumb under the peel for another swath, waiting for her to elaborate—but, as usual, she didn't. Just then, Nate roused from his nap, his voice crackling over the baby monitor on the kitchen counter. *Yes!* Rae brightened hopefully at the interruption, expecting Heath to go and tend to his son. But not wanting the conversation to be thwarted, Heath glanced over at his mom. "I'll get him," Ruth volunteered, and set down her mug as Rae slumped in defeat.

Still working the orange, Heath raised his eyes to Rae again. "Can I ask what happened?" His tone had softened and Rae detected that she seemed to have passed some sort of test with her first answer.

Since he did not demand it of her, she decided she would answer. "Some people shot at my aircraft, and a couple of the bullets came through the cabin." She hoped he would be happy with that and just drop it, but wasn't holding her breath.

Heath wasn't sure what he had expected to hear, but this was not it. Her simple statement raised so many questions in his mind, he didn't know which one to begin with.

"Your *aircraft?*" Again he waited for more, and again, Rae only nodded and didn't provide it. "Was this in a private plane or something?" Rae nodded again, hoping again that that would be the end of it, but it only seemed to make Heath more curious. "You were a passenger in someone's plane and someone shot at you?"

Nuts, he didn't drop it. Rae sighed. "No, I was flying it." Rae braced herself. *Here it comes. . .* While awaiting the inevitable, she focused on trying to get her orange started, coaching herself to not react.

Heath squinted. "You're a pilot. . ." It wasn't a question, he just didn't believe her.

Seeing the usual look of doubt, Rae groaned to herself, then sighed. *Well, at least, he didn't scoff.* She held her orange up close to her face, peering at him over it as she answered. "That's right." She tried again to get her thumbnail into the orange rind, as she guessed at his possible response, wondering which it would be this time. *Will I be 'the liar' or 'the little girl with a vivid imagination'?*

Heath puzzled over the girl across from him. "Really? You're pretty young. You don't look old enough to be a pilot." Even though Heath seemed nice enough, Rae really didn't feel like bandying with him over whether or not she was in fact a pilot—or old enough to be one—she was too weary for that right now. So she only shrugged again. Heath decided to let it go for now and moved to another question. "Where was that?"

"At the Heartland airport."

"Heartland?" He squinted, thinking, "Was that on Wednesday?" Rae nodded. "I heard something like that on the news. How'd you end up out here in the woods in Tennyson?"

Rae's chin came up. "Tennyson?—Is that where I am?" When Heath nodded, wondering why she didn't know that. Rae made a mental note of it then answered him. "I got diverted to Potterville and I didn't make it—my engine quit, so I had to land in a field."

"So, your plane got shot at and then your engine quit and you had to land in a field?" Heath didn't know whether to laugh or be disgusted.

Rae smirked, knowing what he was thinking. *Looks like it's 'The little girl with a vivid imagination' scenario this time.* She nodded without looking at him, her orange holding her attention. "Yeah, it wasn't a good day."

Heath chuckled at her irony. "No, it doesn't sound like it!" He tried again, "Okay, but that doesn't explain how you ended up in the woods."

"Oh, my cell phone battery died and I needed to find a phone, and I tried to take a short cut through them—I guess I got turned around." Still unable to get her orange started, Rae squinted at it, then tried using her teeth.

Well, that explains the phone charger in her buggy. Heath nodded to himself as his fingers worked his own orange peel. "Yeah, it's easy to get turned around out there—the woods can be pretty tricky if you aren't familiar with them. So, where's your plane now?"

Rae shrugged again, this time she looked up at Heath. "Actually, I'm not sure."

He glanced at her briefly, then returned to his orange. "You're not sure?" *How convenient.*

"All I know is that it's in a field at the edge of the woods somewhere, but I don't know where because I lost it when I got turned around." She squinted at the piece of fruit in her hands. *What is with this orange? I'm from Florida—I should be able to peel a silly orange!* "I went outside a minute ago to see if I could even figure out where I came out of the woods the other night, but nothing looked familiar."

"So, how are you going to find your lost plane?" Heath removed the last of his peel, and pulled apart the two halves of his orange. Then seeing her struggling with her orange, he reached across the table and set down his two peeled halves in front of her, and held out his hand for her orange. She glanced at his orange, and at his extended hand, and laid hers into it then picked up one of the peeled halves.

"Thanks." She addressed his question. "I don't know. I thought I would try calling Mr. Grumwall again."

Taken aback, Heath's chin came up abruptly at the mention of the name. He lowered his new orange and stared at her. "Mr. Grumwall?–*Orby* Grumwall?"

Rae brightened. "That's right. Do you know him?"

He squinted, baffled. "Yeah, I know him. How do *you* know him?"

She pulled off an orange wedge and munched on it as she answered. "The man from the NTSB who came to investigate my forced landing referred me to him. He came out to my aircraft after the forced landing—that's why I want to call him. I was hoping he could help me find where I left it. I have his number in my phone, but it's in the cockpit. Plus, my battery is dead, so even if I had it, I can't look up his number. I just looked for him in your phone book, but I couldn't find his name."

Again her answer was nothing close to what he expected. *Where did she come up with all of that?* His head spinning, Heath eyed her curiously as he tried to process all of what he had just heard. Finally, he shook it off for the moment to address her last comment—the only thing she said that made sense to him. "He won't be in our phone book—he lives out in Potterville; that's Houston County."

Rae brightened, hopeful. "Do you have his number?"

Heath shrugged, setting aside his bewilderment, and his orange, for the moment. "Sure, it's around here somewhere." He got up and pushed through the louver door and stepped to the desk just outside it. A few moments later, he returned holding a scrap of paper. Again taking his seat, he picked up his orange.

Rae brightened again. "Oh, that's great! I'm saved! Is it okay if I use your phone again?"

"Sure." Heath smirked. *This will be interesting. . .*

The phone number in hand, Rae hurried back out the louver door to the phone. Moments later, Heath heard her speaking. "Hello, is this Orby Grumwall?. . .Oh, that's so great! Mr. Grumwall, this is Rae Gerrard—you came out to my aircraft with Neal on Wednesday?. . .Yes, that's right. I'm sorry I didn't get back to you. . .Oh, it's a long story. My phone died. . ." She nodded, even though no one could see her, "Yeah, I got caught in that storm, too. . .No, I'm doing pretty well, now. Anyway, Mr. Grumwall—huh?. . .Orby? Okay—'*Orby.*' I know this is going to sound crazy, but do you think you could find my Cessna again? I sort of. . . *lost it*. . .Yeah, I tried to go and find a phone and I got all turned around in the woods, and now I don't know where it

is. . .You will? Oh, that's great!. . .Tomorrow at lunch time? Okay!
. . .No, that's perfect! Thanks so much!. . .Yeah, if you wouldn't
mind picking me up, that would be great. . .Where am I?—I have
no idea—somewhere in Tennyson. Hold on a sec."

Heath grinned, as he peeled Rae's orange, waiting for her to
come get him to talk to Orby and relishing the idea of talking to
him about all of this. When she didn't return after several seconds, he began to wonder—then he heard his mom's voice. "Hey,
Orby, it's Ruth Dawson. . .Yes, this is a coincidence! I'm not sure
what this is about, but Rae here says you need to know where
she is. I didn't even know you knew Rae! . . . Yes, she's been here
with us for a few days." Puzzled, Heath listened from the kitchen,
wondering why Rae had not simply asked him. *Well, I guess mom
just showed up at the right time.* He shrugged, wondering if Rae
would even be coming back in to finish her orange—or their
conversation. Stepping to the louver door, he pushed it open just
as his mom hung up the phone, still holding Nate on her hip;
looking puzzled. Rae stood near her, smiling triumphantly. Ruth
turned around to Heath, and, seeing his daddy, Nate reached for
him. As Heath stepped close, he held out his arms to Nate and
Ruth transferred the child to his dad as she tried to make sense
of the call. "Now, how did Orby become part of this?"

"He's going to help me find my aircraft." Rae's voice came
from behind Ruth, and Ruth turned back to her.

"You have an airplane, hon?"

"Rae tells me she is a pilot." Heath smirked then smiled
and cooed at this son. At his skeptical voice, Ruth pivoted back
around again to him.

"Rae is a pilot? Really?" Ruth pivoted back to Rae. "You're a
pilot, Rae?"

Though used to men looking at her askance, Rae couldn't
stand the thought of Ruth doubting her. She hesitated, "Um, yeah."

"What did Orby say?" Heath interrupted, "Is he coming?" Turning her face back around to Heath, Ruth began to feel as though she were watching a tennis match.

"How about if you two stand together, and I'll stand over here." Ruth maneuvered Rae over next to Heath, and stepped back toward the desk, facing them. "There, that's better." She addressed Heath first. "Yes, he's coming." She shifted her eyes back to Rae. "So Rae, how did you lose an airplane?" Rae just stared at her, hesitating. "Rae. . .?"

For the first time in years, it bothered Rae how incredible her story sounded, and she suddenly couldn't bring herself to tell it to Ruth. Ruth waited, curious at her hesitation. Heath stared at her quizzically. *She had no trouble telling me about it a minute ago.* Seeing Rae just standing there wide-eyed, Heath interjected. "What she's trying not to say is that she landed in a field near some woods around here somewhere, and her cell battery died, so when she set out to find a phone, she got turned around in the woods, and now she isn't sure where her plane is. Did I get that right, Rae?"

Shoulders tense, Rae stared at him anxiously, as though he had given away a sacred secret. Suddenly seeming very child-like, she nodded uncertainly at him then slowly turned to Ruth. "You believe me, don't you?"

"Sure, hon. Orby sounded like he knew all about it, so what's not to believe?" Heath's eyes widened at this disclosure and Rae's shoulders relaxed—the relief showing on her face. "People don't believe me a lot of the time." She glanced at Heath, resisting the urge to stick out her tongue at him.

Heath winced, his mouth dropping open. "It wasn't that I didn't believe you. . ."

Rae begged to differ. "Oh yes, it was!"

Heath stared at her, then just grinned and sighed, letting his head fall forward again. With one arm supporting Nate, he gestured with the other, its palm up; acquiescing. "Okay, what can I say? I'm sorry." He shrugged, still smiling.

Surprised again by his apology, Rae let herself relax. "Well, at least you weren't mean about it—I'll give you credit for that."

"Why, thank you, ma'am." Heath nodded and mock-bowed, getting the impression that the ice between he and Rae had finally broken. "So, when is Orby coming?"

"He said he would be here at lunch time tomorrow." Rae answered, still grinning.

"Can I come with you when you go to find it?" Heath asked hopefully.

"Heath!" His mom scolded, indignant.

"What?—I believe her!" He defended, "I just want to see her airplane!"

Chapter 30

A couple hours later, Heath descended the stairs. Pushing through the louver door, he stepped into the kitchen, and glanced around. "Where's Nate?"

"He's in the parlor with Rae, listening to another story." Ruth answered him from the stove, stirring the pot in front of her. "You're just in time; supper's ready."

"Great! I'm starved. You need me to set the table?"

Ruth smiled, "No, thanks. Rae did it a little while ago."

Heath arched an eyebrow. "She did?" He shrugged, surprised, "Okay. I'll just ring the bell, then." Heath pushed back through the louver door, and turned to the bell that was mounted on the door jamb above his head. Reaching for the leather strap that hung from the clapper, he gave it a few tugs, summoning the Gang from the TV room. Next, he stepped across the front room to the parlor and knocked on the door. Pushing it open, he called from the doorway. "Nate, it's time for supper." Nate's head came up and he smiled happily as he climbed down from the sofa and scampered to his daddy. Heath scooped him up and addressed Rae, nodding his head in the direction of the dining room. "Y'all wanna have some supper with us?" Rae glanced down at her sweat clothes and fingered her hair, hesitating, and Heath took a guess. "Oh, don't worry, we don't have a dress code." He beckoned to her with his fingers as he and Nate waited for her at the door. Rae smiled slightly and pushed herself off the sofa.

Heath set Nate down and watched as he scooted off into the dining room and Rae followed where the little guy went. When she stepped to the doorway into the dining room, five sets of eyes fell on her, bringing her up short. She had not expected anyone but the three she had already met. Behind her, Heath spoke, "Everyone, this is Rae. Rae, this is everyone." The elderly foursome all nodded and jumbled their hellos together, inviting her in. Rae smiled shyly and stepped in, taking the first available chair, between Nate and Ruth—which happened to be Heath's. Heath simply shrugged and took the remaining seat at the end of the table. It was Mr. Windom's turn to pray over the meal, and when he finished, everyone dug in. For Rae's benefit, Ruth pointed out each new face, giving Rae their name as she nodded to each one individually.

Mr. Peterman eyed the young girl, who quietly ate her meal in the chair diagonally across the table from him and, as usual, was the first to jump in. "You need me to cut your meat for you, little girl?" He chuckled, playfully harassing their visitor. Rae smiled tolerantly, but just kept eating. He tried again. "Where are you from, Rae?"

This time, she answered. "Florida."

"Oh, that's nice, we've been there." Mrs. Balcomb, smiled and nodded, "What part?"

"By Gainesville."

"You got any brothers and sisters?"

"Four brothers."

"Four brothers? What a thing to do to a little girl!"

"I think it was my brothers who felt *done to.*" Rae smiled, correcting, and everyone chuckled.

"You got any family up here in Georgia?" Mr. Windom finally got a word in.

"No, just you." All the Gang liked that. Heath and Ruth exchanged glances and smiled.

Mr. Peterman eyed her again. "Y'all can come watch 'Spin to Win' with us after dinner, if you want—unless that's past your bedtime." He chuckled, again amused with himself. Rae smiled with her lips, but her eyes flashed at the elderly man.

"Oh, I'm sure Rae is well beyond bedtimes, Morris." Mrs. Balcomb defended her unnecessarily. Mr. Peterman just grinned at Rae, his eyes twinkling, and moved on for the moment.

"How long are you here for?" Mr. Balcomb jumped in.

"Not much longer. I need to be getting back soon."

"Oh, too bad you used up all your time here being sick. Have you got to see or do anything in Georgia yet?"

Rae shrugged, "So far, I've just seen the Heartland airport and taken a walk in the woods." Ruth and Heath again exchanged glances.

"Well, I sure hope you can come back again and have a look around Middle Georgia, and see something more than just the ceiling of our parlor." The Gang muttered their agreement to that. Rae nodded and smiled, charmed by their friendliness.

"Those are my sweat clothes y'all have on." Mr. Balcomb was proud of his contribution to Rae's comfort.

Always the feisty one, Mr. Peterman couldn't let that go unanswered. "Oh, keep 'em sweetheart, you look better in 'em, anyway." A chorus of laughter went up with that, including from Mr. Balcomb.

Heath watched, amused, as Rae fielded each question, shifting her head back and forth from inquisitor to inquisitor, as Ruth had earlier. He and Ruth glanced at each other, grinning and nodding; the Gang seemed to be getting all their questions answered for them.

"So, is your name Rae, or is that short for something?"

"Short for Desirae."

Mrs. Balcomb smiled warmly. "Oh, that's my niece's name—it means 'Desired one.' I'll bet after four boys, your mama named you that."

Rae's smile stayed in place, but her eyes suddenly seemed sad. "Yes, she did."

"What are your brother's names?"

Rae jumped on the new subject. "Well, the oldest is Sam, then Jesse and Luke. Then there's me, and Ben is the youngest."

"Bible names—that's nice."

"'Jesse' is a Bible name?" Mr. Windom was skeptical.

"Sure it is. You know, 'David, the son of Jesse.'" Mr. Balcomb assured him.

"Oh, yeah. It just makes me think of Jesse James."

"Me, too," Mr. Peterman chimed in. "So, you're the second to the youngest?"

Rae nodded, then began asking some questions of her own, until everyone knew each other. Ruth's and Heath's concerns about their mysterious visitor melted away with each new round of questions. Mr. Peterman eventually pulled the conversation back around to himself, setting them up for his thought of the day. "Anyone read the paper today? Did you see what those crazy politicians are coming up with now?" Either no one had read the paper, or no one was up to talking politics with Mr. Peterman. He waxed thoughtful for a moment. "You know, why do they call them 'politicians', anyways? They're not 'poli'd'—they're elected; they should be called 'electricians.'" Everyone except Rae grinned at Mr. Peterman's usual mealtime antics. Rae just squinted, puzzled.

"They call them 'politicians' because they are elected at the 'polls,'" Mrs. Balcomb explained.

"Well, why do they call them 'polls'?" Mr. Peterman pressed, "They don't look nothing like a pole—all they are is a little, bitty booth. So people running for office should just be called 'booth-iticians,' then." He considered that for a moment and came to a decision. "No, 'electricians' is better; I think they should change it to 'electricians.'"

"But, if we changed 'politicians' to 'electricians', what would we call electricians instead?" challenged Mr. Windom.

"You can call them voltiticians, or ampiticians, ohmiticians. Or how about, zapiticians?" Mr. Peterman laughed, amused with himself.

"Mr. Peterman, you are an original," chuckled Ruth.

Mr. Peterman feigned exception. "I'm not 'an original'—*I am a classic!*" He smiled smugly at his new epithet.

"Well, a classic is just an *old* original. . ." A chorus of laughter erupted from everyone present, as all eyes searched out the source of the zinger—finding Rae, who shrugged matter-of-factly, eyeing Morris Peterman as she took another bite of bread.

"Ha! She's got you there, Morris!" Mr. Balcomb laughed heartily.

Mr. Peterman, having just speared a cube of meat with his fork, grinned in amusement and shook it at Rae, menacing her playfully, his eyes sparkling. Not the least bit intimidated, Rae returned the grin and shook her fork back at Mr. Peterman, to everyone's delight. Enchanted, Mr. Peterman laughed out loud again, his hand over his heart. "I think I'm in love!" Another chorus of laughter erupted from Ruth and the Gang.

Unnoticed by the others, as he chewed his mouthful, Heath smiled and chuckled a bit, which was as much merriment as he had shown in a couple of years. He eyed the young lady in the middle chair to his left, admiring her pluck, amazed and amused that she took on—and bested—the feisty old man.

After Dinner, the Gang hurried so as not to miss the beginning of 'Spin to Win,' leaving the Dawson's and Rae at the table. Ruth got up to clear the dishes and Rae immediately joined her. Heath lifted Nate out of his booster chair and carried him upstairs, cooing to him as he walked. In the kitchen, Rae helped Ruth with the dishes, peppering her with questions,wanting to know all about her, and telling her about her dad and brothers.

When they were finished with the dishes, Ruth dished some pieces of pie onto plates for the Gang. "Rae, would you run upstairs and see if Heath would like some pie? He's probably giving Nate his bath. Top of the stairs, to the hall—first door on your right."

Rae nodded and set out on her errand. Topping the staircase of the big, old house, she followed Ruth's directions and stopped at the bathroom door. Pausing before she spoke, Rae watched Nate as he playfully splashed his daddy, and watched Heath as he spoke softly to his son while shampooing his hair. Warmed by the interaction, Rae smiled and thought about J.J., her young nephew. Remembering her mission, she tapped on the door and Heath and Nate raised their eyes to the sound. Nate's eyes sparkled at Rae and he clapped his hands at her, sending little foam flecks into the air, which and made Heath grin and chuckle.

"Hi, Nate!" Rae smiled cheerfully and waved. She turned her attention to Heath. "Ruth wants to know if you'd like. . ." She glanced at the little guy who was about to go to bed. Knowing what the word would do to her nephew, she amended her question before asking it, "If you would like some P-I-E?"

Amused, Heath glanced over his shoulder at her, and chuckled. "Sure, tell mom I'd love some P-I-E. I'll be down as soon as I get Nate into B-E-D."

Rae grinned for a moment, watching Heath bathe his son, it suddenly struck her that she had not yet met, or even heard anything about Nate's mom.

"Would you hand me that towel?" Heath's voice broke into her thoughts, and Rae retrieved the towel for him. He wrapped it around Nate as he hoisted him out of the tub, mopping his head and shoulders with one corner. "Okay, Nate-ster, let's find your pajamas." He glanced at Rae. "I'll be down in little while—go ahead and start without me."

Downstairs, Rae pushed through the louver door. "He said yes, but to start without him. He said he'll be down in a little while."

Ruth nodded, and dished up slices of pie for herself and for Heath. "What about you, Rae? Would you like some pie, too?"

"Um, sure, maybe a little one."

"How about putting on the teapot while I set these on the table."

Once Nate was tucked in, Heath found Ruth and Rae sharing hot tea and pie at one end of the long dining room table, and took the chair where his mug and plate sat waiting.

"So, Rae," Ruth began, "Heath told me earlier about how you saved the day at Super Mart this morning. Good for you!"

"Yeah, that was so cool!" Heath nodded, putting a forkful of pie into his mouth. "I'd like to learn to do that. Could you show me?"

Rae looked over at him, certain he didn't realize what he was asking. "Sure, I guess. When do you want your first lesson?"

"How about now?"

"Right now?"

"Sure, why not?"

Rae shrugged, wondering at the practicality of this plan when she would only be there a few more days. "Well, I guess we can start with fingerspelling and maybe some basic signs." The two nodded in anticipation. "Okay, well. . .the first thing you should know is that Sign Language isn't just what you do with your hands. Your face has to match what your hands are saying. You can't just stand there with a blank look on your face while you're signing something happy or sad or exciting." Ruth and Heath nodded, already enlightened and Rae continued. "The Deaf are really honest with the way they communicate and with how they feel. In our culture, we act all cool instead of showing our feelings and a lot of the Deaf think that hearing people are not being honest because of that."

This surprised them, too. "They think we're not being honest?" Heath confirmed.

Rae nodded matter-of-factly. "Yeah. Think about it, for us that hear, when we talk, what we mean depends so much on how we say it—like with being sarcastic. When someone does something really dumb, we say, 'Well that was real smart!'" Her voice was heavy with sarcasm, then she continued in her normal voice, "The Deaf can't hear that, so it looks to them like we're not telling the truth.They are really straight-forward; they don't try to hide their feelings like we do, and when they communicate, they say exactly what they are thinking and feeling—and their faces show it. If they're sad, they cry. If they're excited, they grin real big and their eyes get all wide. They just *show it*. So, when you're signing, make sure you say what you mean, and that your face matches it."

Heath marveled, "I never thought about any of that."

Rae just gave a little shrug. "So, do you want to start with some fingerspelling?" Heath nodded, genuinely interested, and watched Rae as she formed each letter of the alphabet with her hand. Between bites, he tried to imitate the shape with his own hand. Rae made a suggestion, "If you want something to help you study and remember all that, you can print off the fingerspelling alphabet from the internet."

Heath nodded. "Okay, I'll do that. Show me some signs. You went so fast this morning, I couldn't make any connections."

"Well, how about starting with choosing your name sign?"

"Okay, what's that?"

"Instead of you and everyone else spelling out your name every time, you can pick out a name sign to refer to yourself."

"Okay, how do I do that?"

"Well, a lot of times people start by picking the first letter of their name. Like this is my name sign." She formed the letter 'D' and touched the side of her thumb to her heart.

Heath squinted at her, "But 'Rae' starts with an 'R'—wasn't that a 'D'?"

Rae's eyebrows arched. "Wow, I can't believe you remembered that already!"

Heath beamed at his accomplishment, then, remembering the dinner conversation, something occurred to him. "Oh, I know—it's 'D' for Desirae, right?"

"Right again."

"So, why did you touch the 'D' to your heart like that?" Ruth asked.

"Touching your heart shows 'feeling' like affection or caring—or it can even show pain, depending on how you do it." She showed them how to sign a few emotions. "You can use different signs and touch them to your heart to make it express that sign with emotion. This is the sign for 'pain,'" She demonstrated, with her index fingers pointing to each other, then twisting them. "Like if you hurt physically, but if you do the same sign over your heart, it means emotional pain; like sadness. You can do that with name signs, too."

Ruth nodded, "Okay, I see. So, your name sign might mean something like, 'affectionately yours, Desirae'?"

"Sure. I guess you could say that. My mom gave me my name sign when I was little." She sighed for a moment, then pressed on. "You can touch the initial to your heart like that, or you can just denote male or female. Like, you show male gender by signing at the side of your forehead, and female by signing at the jaw. "So, if my name was 'David', I could put my 'D' up here." She shaped her hand into a 'D' and touched the end of her thumb to the side of her forehead. "Or I could put my 'D' at my jaw, and that would mean a 'girl' starting with a 'D', like 'Desirae'. Or, you can do something fancy with your initial, like associate it with the sign for something about you. I used to know a musician whose name started with a 'J', and her name sign was a 'J' incorporated into the sign for 'music'." Rae demonstrated that for them.

"Oh, wow, that's pretty cool!" Heath was getting caught up with it. "So, my name starts with an 'H', and I'm a guy, so my name sign might. . ." He held out straight his index and middle finger together, with his thumb sticking up, and held it to the side of his forehead then frowned. "That seems like I'm shooting myself in the head." The two ladies laughed.

Rae grinned. "Yeah, that's because you have your thumb sticking up. Keep your fingers out straight like that for your 'H', but fold down your thumb." Heath obliged, as Rae turned to Ruth, "And you could make an R and hold it by your jaw, but that looks too much like another regular sign—so you might do better holding it over your heart, like mine."

Ruth tried shaping her hand into an 'R' as Rae had suggested, and placed it over her heart. "Oh, I like that one."

"Oh great," Heath teased as he groused, "you get an affectionate 'R', and I get a gun to the head."

Rae shrugged. "Well, since your name starts with an 'H' and you paint signs, maybe you can just wave your 'H' into your other hand like a brush for your name sign." Rae suggested, as she demonstrated, "or since your name starts and ends with an 'H', you can just slide one 'H' into another." She demonstrated that by simply wagging her 'H' back and forth in the air a couple of times.

Heath brightened. "Okay, that's a good one—I like that better."

"And since we don't know what Nate will do when he grows up, his can be like this for now." Rae formed an 'N' and held it to the side of her forehead.

"'For now...?'" Heath squinted at her, puzzled, "You mean you can change your name sign as you go?"

"Sure, it's *your* sign—you just don't want to change it real often or it will confuse everyone. We 'hearing people' change our name as we go through life, too; it's like going by 'Billy' when you're little then changing to 'William' when you are grown."

"Yeah, okay, I get that."

"Okay, well, you guys practice that and we can have another little 'family signing class' tomorrow, if you want." That was agreeable to both Heath and Ruth, then a thought revisited Rae's mind, and she squinted, curious.

Ruth noticed. "You look like you have a question, Rae. Are you wondering about something?"

"I guess I'm just wondering about Nate's mom; I haven't met her yet—or even seen her." Suddenly the atmosphere in the room tensed and Ruth and Heath glanced at each other.

Heath cleared his throat, "Um, she's gone."

Rae gasped. "Oh no! She died?"

"No, she didn't die," Heath sighed.

Relieved, Rae exhaled. "Oh, so she's away?"

"Yeah, *far* away—she left." His voice was flat.

Rae's eyes widened, her mouth agape. "You're kidding!"

"I wouldn't kid about that," he said, shifting uncomfortably.

Diverting from Heath, Ruth interjected, "You know, Rae, usually when we tell someone she's gone, they just understand that she left. Just out of curiosity, why did you think she died?"

Rae shrugged. "I don't know. I guess I just couldn't imagine someone leaving your family on purpose." Ruth smiled, charmed by Rae's sincerity.

Heath put himself back into the conversation. "It was very 'on purpose.' She took off with some gym bum when Nate was a baby." There was an edge in his voice and sadness in his eyes that he tried to mask by being ironic. "And to think I paid for that gym membership!"

To their surprise, Rae was crestfallen. She shook her head slowly, dismayed. "Wow, that stinks."

"Sure does," Heath had to agree. Ruth eyed Heath, surprised. Usually, her son backed away from talking about this subject, but tonight, for some reason, he seemed to be full of commentary about it. She leaned back in her chair, hands in her lap, and became a spectator to the exchange.

"Why did she leave?" Rae pressed. She wasn't trying to be nosy; she just couldn't wrap her brain around it.

Heath shrugged. "I guess she didn't like me anymore."

Again, Rae gaped. "What? What's not to like? You're a decent guy. You work hard and take care of your family. What's not to like?" Her face and voice underscored her bewilderment.

Not expecting such an appraisal, especially given Rae's indifference to him earlier, Heath arched an eyebrow. Puzzled and amused by her indignation, he shrugged. "I guess she wanted more."

Rae snorted and folded her arms across her ribs. "Well, then she's the loser."

Surprised, Heath arched both eyebrows. "She's a loser?"

Clearly agitated, Rae gestured with her hands in the air. "I don't know, maybe she's that, too!" Shook her head, then frowned, clarifying, "No, I said she *is* the loser."

Heath half-smiled, not knowing what to make of this girl and her passionate indignation over a woman she had never met. "Are you sure about that? How do you know I'm not just a lousy husband? Maybe getting rid of me is the smartest thing she could have done?"

Rae didn't hesitate, "That's easy—*Nate!*" She gestured animatedly again. "She didn't take him with her. If she did, it would be just another man complaining about his ex—but if she left behind her own kid, that's pretty clear. I mean, what kind of mom would bail on a little guy like that?" Rae's tone softened a bit, "No, she's the loser, and she's gonna regret it someday. Maybe she'll be back when she does."

Stunned, Heath stopped chewing his pie and could only stare at Rae. After a moment, he shook off the amazement to answer her assertion. "No, she won't be back. As soon as the divorce was final she remarried and they moved out to California."

"She remarried?" Rae wilted. "And she still didn't come back for her son?" Rae looked as though she might burst into tears. Then, indignant anew, she shook her head. "Then she's a double-loser! Wow, what a selfish person! Poor little guy!—One of these days he's gonna ask why his mom left him behind and there's just no way to tell him the answer without it hurting his little heart. He's never going to understand why! He's always going to think it's because of him and that she didn't love him! How can—?" Suddenly self-conscious, Rae stopped herself, glancing at Ruth, then Heath, and blushed. "I'm sorry—I have no business talking like that. I'm so sorry." Rae pushed herself away from the table. "Please excuse me."

Quickly, she rose and left the dining room, leaving Ruth and Heath speechless; her passion both shocked and charmed them. For several moments, Ruth and Heath just stared at each other, stunned. Finally, Ruth folded her arms across her chest and cocked her head to one side, eyeing Heath knowingly. "See, Heath?—it's not just your *mother's* opinion."

Chapter 31

The next morning, after breakfast, Rae helped Ruth with the dishes as Nate played with his toys under the breakfast table, then Rae disappeared for a while. Assuming she had gone back to the parlor, Ruth never guessed that Rae was outside, under the hood of her van. Nearly an hour later, hearing an engine revving, Ruth scooped up Nate and stepped out onto the side porch, puzzled. Following the sound to the back porch steps, she peered around to the garage, finding Rae in the front seat of her van, grinning widely. Surprised, Ruth stepped around to the driver's side window. Shifting Nate to her hip, she puzzled at her van's occupant. "Rae, what on earth are you doing? How did you get my van running?"

"Who told you that this thing needed a new fuel pump?"

"Our mechanic. He just made a guess based on what I told him over the phone. Why?"

"Well, your fuel pump works fine; you just had a kinked fuel line."

Taken aback, Ruth just stared. "What? How do you know that?"

"I work on aircraft engines."

"You do? And you figured out what's wrong with my van?"

"Sure—a kinked fuel line is a kinked fuel line. The only difference is you don't fall three thousand feet out of the sky if it's the one on your car." She grinned again at Ruth. "I got you a new fuel pump yesterday; I was going to put it in as a way to say 'thank you,' but you won't be needing it so I'll just return it."

Ruth shook her head. "Well, if that don't beat all! Heath is going to be so glad—and surprised!"

** *** **

Later that morning, Heath's voice called from the kitchen, surprising Ruth. "Hello?—Anyone home? Nate!—Daddy's home!" The louver door swung open and he appeared in the doorway, just as Ruth emerged from the back hall. "Hey, Mom."

"Heath, what are you doing home this early? Orby won't be here 'til after lunch; that's at least hour or so."

Nate running to him from the parlor caught Heath's attention. "Hey Buddy!" He scooped up his son and kissed his cheek, then shifted his eyes to Rae, who came out of the room behind him. "Hey, Rae—you doing all right?" Still feeling sheepish over her outburst the previous evening, she only nodded. Heath turned again to his mom, answering her question, "I know. I got a new customer out on Henry Road that wants me to paint a sign on his barn; I was on my way to have a look and thought I'd stop by and see what's for lunch. I know you weren't expecting me until afterward—do you have enough for one more?"

"Yes, Heath, there's plenty to eat—but with you it's more like *two* more," she teased.

Heath chuckled, "Hey, you know I'm just a growing boy! So, what's for lunch?"

"Just some tuna sandwiches and fruit, and I have some Apple Betty ready for the oven."

Heath brightened, "Apple Betty?—Yours or store-bought?"

"Mine."

Heath grinned. "Okay, you talked me into it!

Ruth smirked at him, just as the buzzer on the washer sounded; she turned to Rae. "Rae, hon—would you mind moving that load to the dryer?—And I'll get lunch going." Rae nodded and headed for the laundry room.

When she was out of earshot, Heath ventured, "So, how's it going with Rae?"

"Just fine. She was reading to Nate just now when you came in."

"Reading to him? Well, that's nice. Yeah, he sure seems to like her." He turned to his son in his arms, "You like Ms. Rae, Nate?" Nate just smiled and clapped his hands.

Ruth continued, "She's been helping me with the laundry and a few chores, and I even saw her in the TV room with the Gang at one point. She and Mr. Peterman were talking and it looked like he was teaching her to play chess."

Heath arched an eyebrow. "Is that so. . .? Well, that's good! Sounds like you two have had a busy morning." He set Nate down. "Okay, I guess I'll set the table."

In the kitchen, Ruth busied herself getting lunch together as she chatted with Heath. "You know what Rae did this morning?"

Nate toddled after Heath as he circled the dining room table with a stack of plates, setting one out in front of each chair. No, what?"

"She got my van running."

Heath stopped suddenly, raising his eyes, "She did. . .?"

"She really did! She said the fuel pump is fine, it was just a kinked fuel line."

"How does she know that?"

"She said she's an airplane mechanic, and when I asked how she knew about cars, all she said was, 'a kinked fuel line is a kinked fuel line.'"

Skeptical, Heath hesitated, his eyes narrowed as he set down another plate. "Are you sure it's fixed?"

In the kitchen, Ruth nodded. "Yes, I'm sure. I saw it with my own eyes! When I heard the sound of an engine revving, I went outside and there was Rae in the driver's seat with a big grin on her face."

Heath shrugged. "Well, what do you know?" Not sure what to think, he resumed setting out the plates.

Just then, Rae returned from the laundry room and Ruth smiled, pointing out the glass tumblers on the kitchen counter. "Would you set those on the table, hon?"

Rae nodded, picking up a few of tumblers and headed into the dining room. Finding Heath already there with a stack of plates on his arm, she hesitated, glancing away, then back to him. "Um. . .sorry about going-off like that last night."

Heath smiled amicably and set down another plate. "Don't worry about it—all that is ancient history." His statement wasn't exactly true, but she didn't need to know that, and Heath didn't want her to feel bad. He shrugged easily, "Nothing wrong with caring about how a little kid feels." He beckoned her in with a nod of his head and Rae seemed to relax, then shrugged and reached to set down a tumbler. Heath eyed her for a moment before speaking, "Mom tells me you fixed the van." Rae only shrugged. "So, you work on cars, too?"

"No, not usually. I just thought I'd take a look."

From the kitchen, unaware of their side conversation, Ruth resumed her chat with Heath, "So, Heath, have you thought any more about what Daryl asked you to do?"

As Rae fell in behind Heath, setting a glass in front of each plate, she glanced up at him as he hesitated, a plate in hand. He winced. "Um, no, Mom. Not really."

"He needs to know pretty soon. Will you think about it?"

"Mom, I really don't want to do that—I don't know anything about talking in front of a crowd; I told him that when he asked me." He waited for her to protest, and she didn't disappoint.

"Now, Heath, it's not a big crowd and you know most everyone that will be there," Ruth encouraged from the kitchen, "You'll do fine, hon, just speak from your heart and don't over-think it."

"Speak about what, though?" He rolled his eyes, then grinned when Rae caught him. "That's the problem, Mom, I don't have a clue what to say to those guys."

Rae stepped around him and muttered with a smirk as she passed, "He got a donkey to talk, he should be able to do something with you."

Surprised and amused, Heath hesitated, eyeing her curiously as he set down another plate from the stack in his arm. "A donkey. . .?"

Rae glanced up, "Yeah, you know, Balaam's."

Heath chuckled, "Yeah, I know what you mean—I guess I'm just surprised *you* knew about it." Now realizing that she had some Bible in her background, he ventured further. "You know, you're welcome to come to services with us, if you want to."

Hesitating, Rae glanced up then away quickly, setting down another glass. "Um, no thanks. I'm not a church-goer."

Her abrupt retreat was as surprising as her Bible knowledge. "No?—You sure about that?"

"Very sure." She set down the last tumbler and headed again for the kitchen without looking up.

Heath eyed her curiously for a moment, and then Ruth spoke up, continuing their conversation, "Didn't Daryl say they were going to be studying that section that says something about 'being clothed but not getting warm, and working but losing your pay'? Maybe you could find that passage and just say something that ties into it."

Shaking his head, Heath balked again. "Oh, I don't know, Mom..." He shrugged as he called his answer to her, "I don't even remember where in the Bible he said that passage was."

"Haggai." Rae returned with another armful of tumblers and set down another glass where she left off.

Heath stopped in his tracks, surprised, and arched an eyebrow toward her. "Haggai?"

"Yeah, the first chapter." She stepped to the next chair and set down another tumbler.

Heath squinted at her, hesitating with a plate still in his hand. "You know Haggai?" Shaking his head, he eyed her with a grin. "No one knows Haggai."

Rae rolled her eyes. "You're right—forget I said it."

Heath set down the stack of remaining plates and stepped out to the front room. Retrieving his Bible from the bookshelf next to the desk, he returned, thumbing through the pages, then stopped to read for a moment. An eyebrow arching, he raised his eyes briefly, then read aloud to her as well as his mom, "'Think about your life! You sow much but bring in little; you eat, but aren't satisfied; you drink, but never have enough; you clothe yourselves, but no one is warm; and he who works for a living earns wages that are put in a bag full of holes.'" (CJB) Heath tilted his head, eyeing Rae, incredulous. "Verse six—you were right!" Rae hadn't expected him to look up the verse and just shrugged.

From the kitchen, Ruth affirmed, "Yes, that's the one, Heath."

Heath answered his mom, "I don't know Mom, I'll think about it." He turned his attention back to Rae. "How did you know that?"

Feeling exposed, she shrugged. "Lucky guess."

Doubtful, Heath scoffed, puzzled all the more at her back-pedaling. "A lucky guess?" Rae set down the last glass and returned to the kitchen for the flatware. Not willing to let it go so readily,

Heath waited for her to return, and challenged her playfully. "That was a 'lucky guess,' and you know Haggai, but you're not a church-goer?"

"That's right." Rae set a fork next to the closest plate.

". . .And you're a pilot and an airplane mechanic."

Becoming amused, Rae set down another fork. "Right again."

Heath ventured further, just wanting to make sure he had all her 'stories' straight. "And, there's an airplane out there some-where with your name on it."

Rae couldn't help grinning. "No, not on it—*in* it."

"Oh—my mistake," Heath corrected, rolling his eyes, ". . .with your name *in* it." He eyed her again. "C'mon, Rae, don't you think all that is just a little far-fetched?"

"Okay, you're right," Rae conceded, and Heath smirked, anticipating a confession, then Rae shrugged. "I lied about the lucky guess."

"That's it? Just the 'lucky guess'?—That's all?" He shook his head, smiling. Rae nodded as she finished setting out the forks. Heath leaned into the kitchen doorway. "Okay, Mom, the table is pretty much set. I'm going to run out there and meet that guy at his barn. It isn't far—I'll be back before lunch." He glanced back at Rae and added with a grin, his tone mocking, "And then we'll go and find the lady pilot her airplane." Heath smirked as he emphasized the words, and Rae just wrinkled her nose in return—both amused at their little game of verbal chicken.

** *** **

After lunch, Orby arrived at the Dawson's around one, just as he'd said. Ruth put the Apple Betty into the oven, and she and Rae came out to meet him at his truck. Orby greeted them with his usual big smile.

"Well, hey, Ms. Ruth—you doing all right?" He greeted Ruth warmly with a hug. "And Ms. Rae! It's real good to see you again. You ready to go find your aircraft?"

"Yeah, I hope it's still there."

"Oh, I don't know why it wouldn't be."

"I just left it in someone's field—you don't think they would have towed it away, do you?"

"Naw," Orby waved off the notion. "It seems to me they won't be using that field until next spring. They probably ain't even noticed it yet." Orby grinned his big, toothy grin. "Well, are you ready to go, Ms. Rae?"

"Well, I am—but Heath wanted to come with us, if that's okay. He upstairs changing Nate. He'll be down in a minute."

"Oh, sure, that ain't no problem." After a glance at Ruth, he grinned playfully at Rae. "He don't believe that you lost your aircraft out there?"

Rae shook her head. "He didn't believe I even *had* one until you talked to Ruth on the phone. I still don't think he's completely convinced."

Orby nodded and chuckled, "Yeah, I'll bet that was a hard one for him to swallow." The three stood in the clearing between the barn and the house and chatted for a few minutes until Heath came out with Nate. He stepped up to the three of them and handed Nate to Ruth, then extended his hand to Orby, "Orby, hey, thanks for helping us out with this." Rae squinted at him. *Us?*

"Oh sure Heath, that ain't no problem. Well, I guess we better get at it so's I can get back to work. We can take my truck; I got rope and stuff in the back already."

The three of them climbed into Orby's truck and he circled it around, then they waved to Ruth and Nate as they headed out the drive and made a left onto the road, and at the bend,

Orby went right. He drove parallel to a stand of woods on their left, and minutes later, pulled off to the left onto a dirt road that parted the trees. Doubling back along the dirt road in the direction they'd come, it angled away from the paved road for several minutes until it opened up into a field. The truck bounced along the furrows, skirting the edge of the woods for a quarter of a mile before Rae's Cessna came into view.

Heath dropped his jaw. "Wow, there it is! Just like you said!" Orby and Rae just turned and stared at him. Suddenly self-conscious, Heath could only shrug sheepishly.

The three got out and approached the aircraft and Rae stepped up to the cockpit door. Hesitating, she noticed a note affixed above it by a wad of gum; pulling it off, she read it then turned to Orby. "You came looking for me?"

Orby nodded. "I sure did, Ms. Rae—I called you a bunch of times, and when I didn't get no answer, I called Neal. We was both getting worried for you, so I come looking for you myself. Orby nodded. "I sure was glad when you called me yesterday; I called Neal and told him, too—he was real relieved to hear you was okay."

As she had over Heath's search, Rae marveled for a moment. "Wow, Orby—thank you!" Orby nodded and Rae smiled, then turned again to her aircraft. Unlocking its door, she reached in, retrieving her dead cell phone, her jacket, and her tote bag with her laptop. They circled the Cessna as Orby discussed with Rae about patching the bullet holes, and replacing the damaged parts.

Heath poked a finger into a hole in one of the wings. "Why didn't it blow up when the fuel tank got shot?"

Rae just scoffed softly, but Orby was gracious with his answer, "Oh, that's just Hollywood, Heath. It takes more than that to blow up a fuel tank."

Heath squinted. "Really?—No kidding." He circled around to the front of the aircraft, stopping at the nose. Seeing that it sat between two trees, he slid his fingers along the propeller as he glanced down the wings to each side. Noting the narrow gap between each wing and the trees in front of them, he shook his head. "Wow, Rae, you like to cut it close, don't you?" Rae only shrugged. Heath peered at her around the airplane. "You know, the place where I came across you is only about twenty or thirty yards into these woods from here."

Surprised, Rae looked over at him. "That's all?"

"That's all. You want me to show you where I found you?"

"Sure!" Her eyes shifted to Orby. "Do we have time?"

Orby nodded. "I believe so. Twenty or thirty yards shouldn't take too long."

Shouldn't take too long? Rae snorted to herself as she and Orby followed Heath into the woods. In just a few minutes, he pointed to the place where he had come upon her lying in the leaves, then gestured to their right. "My tree stand is over that way, less than a quarter of a mile."

Rae pivoted all around at the surrounding trees; sure enough, she couldn't see her Cessna from where they stood. "Wow, that's crazy! Less than ten minutes, and I can't even see my aircraft anymore. No wonder I got so turned around—every direction looks the same to me."

"Well, like I said, the woods can be tricky if you don't know your way through them," Heath reassured.

"Twenty or thirty yards. . ." Rae shook her head in disbelief, "I wandered around for a couple of hours that day—and that was before you happened by."

Heath stared down at the spot in the leaves, absently stroking his chin, then grinned and chuckled.

"What are you thinking about, Heath?" Orby's voice broke into his reverie.

Heath smiled, eyeing Rae. "I was thinking about a lesson I learned that day. Never sneak up on this girl!"

"What happens when you do that?"

"You get your teeth kicked in." Heath grinned broadly.

Rae rolled her eyes. "Am I ever going to live that down?"

Heath chuckled again, "Not if I can help it." He turned his attention back to the site of their first meeting. "I feel like I should erect a monument here or something; 'Here lies Heath's teeth.'" He chuckled again.

Rae exhaled forcefully, "Can we get back to work?" The two men chuckled at Rae's discomfort as they turned to head back to the Cessna. Once they arrived, Orby squatted down, again examining its underside,

"Like I said before, Ms. Rae—you did real good on the landing. I don't see no damage from that except for losing some paint under here from scraping the trees. Going against the furrows like you done probably helped you slow down some too, maybe kept you from hitting these here trees. Ain't nothing broke, so that's good." He nodded, then added, "Good thing you didn't cartwheel, though—that would've been a different story, for sure." Orby shook off that thought then turned, raising his eyes to Rae. "I figure when we get it out of this field, you're gonna want to take it somewhere to work on it. You got anywhere in mind?"

Rae shrugged. "I don't know, I hadn't thought that far. What do you think, Orby?"

"Well, we might could tow it on down to Potterville, where I work. That'll be a job getting it there, but we can sure do it, if that's what you want. We'll have to go slow and it'll probably take a few hours."

"It didn't seem that far when we drove there."

"No, it ain't far—just about thirty miles or so on the interstate. But we're gonna have to use surface streets to get your aircraft there, for sure—and that's gonna take a lot longer. Once you get on down the highway here, I think the most direct route will be to go across the interstate on White Road and take Highway 41 on down to Potterville, then back across the interstate on Thompson to the airport. What do you think, Heath?"

Heath rubbed his chin. "Yeah, that would be the best route, but that's kind of far, Orby."

Orby arched a hopeful eyebrow, "You got something else in mind, Heath?"

Heath shrugged. "Well, she's already staying here with us—why not just tow her plane to Mom's and work on it there? You can put it in the barn."

Orby grinned widely. "Well now, that's a real good idea, Heath! 'That be okay with you, Ms. Rae?"

Surprised, Rae groped for words, "Uh, yeah, sure! That would be perfect!" She eyed Orby uncertainly, and added, "If you don't mind driving back and forth from Potterville."

"Oh, I don't mind, that won't be no problem at all. I'll just bring up the tools with me when I come. Well, if everyone's agreeable to that, let's get to it!"

Heath glanced at Orby's truck and then the Cessna. "Is your truck strong enough to tow an airplane, Orby?"

"Oh sure, these aircraft are real light. If we was on pavement, little ole Rae here could pull it herself." Orby gestured to Rae and nodded as he spoke.

Heath nodded. "Okay, let's do it."

Orby backed his truck up to the tail assembly, and got out. Folding the blanket over several times, he wrapped it around the fuselage in front of the horizontal stabilizer for padding, then tied the rope around it securely and fastened the other end inside his truck bed. The three piled back into the cab and Orby eased the truck forward, gently pulling Rae's aircraft away from the trees. Rae turned around in the cab and faced the truck bed, keeping an eye on it as they made their way out of the field onto the road. They drove slowly back to Ruth's, getting curious stares from other drivers once they were out on the road.

Chapter 32

Fifteen minutes later, Orby turned into the long driveway of Ruth's property and pulled up in front of the barn, and Ruth came out to meet them, smiling widely. "Well here it is, just like you said, Rae! What a sight!" With a gathering motion, Ruth gestured for the three of them to draw close together and, using her cell phone camera, she snapped a photo of them in front of Rae's airplane tied behind Orby's truck. The three recounted their adventure to Ruth briefly before she needed to get back inside, waving to Orby as she turned to go. A moment later, Orby jumped into the truck bed and untied the rope around the tail assembly, then pushed the tail of the Cessna forward away from the bed. Straightening up, he addressed Rae. "You want it in the barn, Ms. Rae? Or do you just want to leave it out here?"

Heath chimed in, "Oh, I'll need to move some stuff around in there to make room for it, so out here is good for now, Orby. I know you need to get back; we can push it in later."

Orby nodded. "Well, then that about does it for now." He turned to Rae, "I expect you'll be needing your insurance people to come on out and have a look, now that you have your aircraft back. Y'all want me to order them parts and the patching materials now, or wait and see what they say?"

Rae waved-off the question with a flip of her wrist. "Oh, just go ahead and order them; I'll need them whether this is covered or not."

Orby nodded. "Yeah, I expect you do. I can't see them not covering those things, but you just never know." Orby offered a little shrug. "Well, okay then Ms. Rae, I guess I'll be heading back to work then. Y'all just give me a call once they get out here, and we can get started with the repair work after that."

"Sure, Orby, that'll be good. Thanks for all your help." Rae shook his hand, then so did Heath. Orby reached for the door of his truck as Rae and Heath turned toward the house.

Pulling open his door, Orby hesitated, "Oh, Ms. Rae, I almost forgot." Rae and Heath turned again to Orby. "You remember Mr. Hildenbocken?"

"No. Who's that?" She questioned as the two stepped back over to Orby's truck.

"You remember that day we first met when you and Neal come out to the airport?–You did that screwdriver-on-your-forehead thing and figured out what was wrong with that Cessna?" Rae nodded, remembering. Intrigued, Heath leaned his back against the truck bed, his arms folded across his chest as he listened. Orby continued, "Well, Mr. Hildenbocken was the older man who owns it—the one who offered to pay you to fix it."

Rae leaned her head to one side, "Oh, yeah. What about him?"

"Well, I was talking to him yesterday after you called, telling him about me coming up here today to tow your aircraft. He remembered you right away and how you figured out so quick what was wrong with his aircraft and all, after no one else could—and you know what he said?" Orby grinned again, "He said he's got a pilot out for a month and wondered if you wanted to fill in for him while you was waiting on getting your aircraft fixed. He told me to ask you when I come up here today."

Rae's eyebrows arched. "No kidding?—He said that?"

"That's right—no kidding!"

"Oh, wow! That would be great! I could really use the extra cash."

"I thought you might like that idea." Orby grinned even wider, "He said for you to give him a call if you want to do that. I can call him right now for you, if you want—he seemed real anxious to hear from you."

Rae nodded eagerly and Orby pulled out his cell phone, brought up Mr. Hildenbocken's number, then pressed send and handed it to Rae. After a moment, she spoke, "Hello, is this Mr. Hildenbocken? This is Rae Gerrard, I was down there. . ." She glanced up; surprised, "Yeah, that's right—the pilot from the other day. . .Uh-huh, the one with the 'screwdriver trick'—yeah, that was me. . .Um, yeah, Orby just told me about a job you have?" For the next several minutes, all Orby and Heath heard was a succession of "yeahs" and "uh-huhs" until Rae had all the details. Then suddenly, her eyes widened and her mouth fell open. "Seriously?—*Per route?*" She glanced at Orby, then refocused, ". . .On Tuesdays and Fridays—okay. Yes sir, that sounds really good. Sure, I'd like to, I'm not sure how long I'll be here in Georgia—but I can do that until my aircraft is fixed. . .*This* Friday? Sure, as far as I know, that will be fine. . .You'll file the flight plans? Even better!. . .The brick building—got it. Okay, great! I'll see you Friday morning at seven. Thanks!" Rae ended the call and handed back Orby's phone.

Orby grinned his big toothy grin. "What did he say?"

"He said it's just flying a route between his hangars two days a week until I go back to Florida or until his guy is back—whichever comes first—and he wants me to start this Friday! –and he's going to pay me this crazy amount of money per route!" She shook her head, "Wow! He doesn't even know me, and he just hired me over the phone like that! What did you say to him, Orby?"

Orby only shrugged. "Nothing that weren't true. I told him about what happened with your aborted landing at Heartland and your forced landing in the field and even getting shot at, and keeping your head through it, and all—and how there weren't no damage to your aircraft from the landing, except for where the trees scraped it. That was enough for him." Heath marveled at the list. *Everything she said is true!* He shook his head.

"Wow, this is so cool!" Rae glanced at Heath, "I can't wait to tell my dad!"

Heath grinned along with her. "So, this is at Potterville?" Rae nodded and Heath's eyebrows narrowed. "How are you going to get there?"

Rae froze, her shoulders sagging. "Oh, that's right, I don't have my car up here." Her forehead furrowed, as she contemplated having to call the man back.

"I can leave early and take you down there when I go to work," Heath offered.

"You'd do that?"

His arms still folded, Heath shrugged. "Sure, why not?"

"Wow, thanks, that would be great!" Then she quickly offered, "I'll pay you for your gas."

"Well, that settles that!" Orby grinned again with a nod of his head. "Okay then, Ms. Rae. I'll just head on back to work." Orby climbed into his truck and pulled the door closed as Heath straightened up from his lean against the truck bed. As Orby cranked the engine and then let his window down, he handed Rae a sheet of paper. "Here's that estimate you asked for—and I'll get them parts and things ordered." Accepting the paper, Rae glanced over it as she stepped back, then Orby added, "Y'all give me a call when we can start work on patching them holes, okay?" When Rae nodded, he waved and pulled away.

As Rae watched him pull out onto the road, Heath turned, hands on his hips, and stared again at the airplane now sitting in their clearing, shaking his head again; amazed.

Rae squinted at him, "What was that for?" Heath turned, embarrassed that he'd been caught. Recalling his earlier surprise when they came upon her Cessna, Rae wagged an index finger at him, challenging, "You didn't think there was an airplane out there, did you? Even when Orby showed up, you still didn't believe me!"

Heath hung his head then shook it slowly, grinning. Finally, he just sighed and raised his chin. "You are totally right," he grinned sheepishly, "I'm sorry, I didn't believe you—I tried to, but. . ." he could only shurg, "I just had my doubts."

Rae's mouth fell open at his words. "That's it? No argument? No justification?" *No ego?*

Heath chuckled to himself at her shock, amused at being able to render this girl speechless—if only for a moment. His hands on his hips, he grinned as he eyed Rae. "So, are you just going to stand there with your teeth in your mouth?—Or are we going to go in and have some Apple Betty so I can get back to work?"

Still marveling, Rae pulled her jaw closed then shrugged with a smile. "I guess we're going to go in and have some Apple Betty."

As soon as they entered the house, Rae scurried to the parlor with her tote bag and cell phone, digging out the phone charger she'd bought at Super Mart the day before, and plugged it in. Still in the kitchen, Heath scooped up a sleepy Nate as Ruth set out the dessert she had prepared, and stared out the kitchen window at the aircraft now in their yard. Swaying gently, he lulled his son as he shook his own head, chuckling softly as Ruth came back into the kitchen. "Mom, I never imagined I'd be looking out this window at an airplane."

"Not even when Orby confirmed it?"

"No, not even then, I'm sorry to say. I just can't get my brain around that that little girl is a pilot!"

"Well to begin with, Heath—Rae might be younger than you, but she's no 'little girl,'" Ruth chided. "That was your first mistake!—she is a young woman in a career field, not some 'little girl'" She disappeared into the dining room with a stack of dessert plates.

Heath shrugged and grinned again, calling after her, "Yup. I'm embarrassed to say you're right, Mom!" Heath shook his head again, glancing at Nate, who was now draped over his shoulder. "Well, I think Nate is down for the count. Let me go lay him down real quick."

Just as Heath returned from that, Rae came through the louver door. "Go ahead and start without me; I want to call my dad."

Ruth nodded, "Oh, you got time, hon. I'm still dishing it up."

Out at the desk by the louver door, Rae punched in the number. Once again, Ruth and Heath couldn't help but overhear Rae's telephone conversation.

"Hi, Dad, it's me. . .Yeah, I'm doing way better, thanks. I wanted to let you know we just finished towing the Cessna over here. . .Uh-huh, they said I could just stay here until I got it fixed. . . .Yeah, and that works out real well because it's so close by. You can tell the insurance guy to just come now. . .I don't know, hang on. . ." she pushed open the louver door, "Ruth, what's your address here?" Ruth recited it, and Rae relayed the information to her dad, thanked Ruth, and then backed out of the kitchen. Resuming her conversation, she brightened, "You know what, Dad? After traipsing around in the woods for a couple of hours that day, it turns out I was only a short walk from my aircraft!

Less than ten minutes!—go figure! And after another two hours out in that freezing rain, their house is only another half hour on foot and it's, like, five minutes by car!...I know, right? That's the last time I go into the woods without a GPS."

In the kitchen, Heath leaned closer to his mom and whispered playfully, "City girl." Ruth gave him a shove and Heath only chuckled more.

Rae continued, "Remember that man I told you about that was referred to me by the NTSB guy? Orby Grumwall?...Yes, '*Orby*'... No, I am *not* teasing you, Dad!—that's really his name. Honest!" She grinned at her dad's reluctance to believe that, then pressed on. "Orby looked the aircraft over again and is going to order parts today. We can start patching the holes after the insurance guy comes to look at it...Yeah, it's right outside. They have a barn that we can keep it in...I know, right? It's way better than towing it down to the airport and keeping it in a tie-down—and no fees!...Yeah, it's a huge relief, that's for sure...No, there was no damage from the landing, just from the bullets, and the underside got raked up by the trees...Really, that's it!"

Rae paused as she listened, then answered, "I don't know. It depends on how soon the parts get here. . . .No, Orby said he'd help me, so there's no problem there. . . I don't know how much he charges, I'll ask him. . .Thanksgiving?" The enthusiasm in Rae's voice suddenly vanished. "Oh man, is that next week?" Suddenly sad, Rae lamented, "I don't see how, Dad, I can't even start the work until the insurance guy gets here and I don't know when that will be. It could be any time between tomorrow and next week, and I still need to repair it—plus, we're waiting on those parts. . .No, not without leaving it here. . .Come and get me? But that's two round trips just for one day! No, that'll cost too much..." Now there was a tremor in her voice, "...I know, I'm sorry, too. Maybe we can celebrate it when I get back. . .I know, it's not the same—and it's our first Thanksgiving without Mom. I'm sorry Dad, I don't know what else to do. . . Are you going to be okay?" They heard Rae sniff, then her voice quavered, "Don't worry, I'll be okay. . .No, really, Dad. . .Yeah, I'll miss you guys, too. I'll call you when the insurance guy comes and let you know, okay?. . .I love you, too. Bye." Rae hung up the phone and slumped sullenly into the chair next to it.

Ruth and Heath eyed each other, wincing at Rae's plight. Ruth rose and pushed open the louver door, peeking around it. Seeing Rae still by the phone she asked, "Rae, would you take the dessert out to The Gang?" Rae just nodded dully and pushed herself up from the chair, then followed Ruth back into the kitchen. Ruth transferred the Apple Betty onto a tray, along with some dessert plates and forks, then set the tray into Rae's waiting arms. "I'll let you dish this up for them out there. You be sure and have some, too. Okay hon?"

"Sure." Rae nodded dutifully and backed through the louver door, turning toward the back hall and the TV room. With Rae now out of earshot, Ruth and Heath had a few moments and took the opportunity to speak freely as they ate. "What are we going to do?" Ruth spoke softly, just in case.

Heath shrugged, "Well, of course we're going to ask her to join us."

"I know that, Heath. I mean about it being her first Thanksgiving since her mom passed."

"I don't know what we can do about that. We'll just try to make it a special day for her, somehow. I feel bad for her family, though. They are going to be without their mom *and* Rae."

"And she's going to be without all of them." Ruth sighed and thought for a moment, coming up blank. "Well, I'll have to think on that for a while."

Heath shrugged, "Whatever we do, we can't let her sulk in the parlor by herself on Thanksgiving, even if means forcing her to watch football all day."

"You know Heath, since it looks like she's going to be here another week or so, we shouldn't just keep her there in the parlor; she's going to need a regular room."

"We're full-up. What did you have in mind?"

"How about, we clean out your old room above the garage?"

Heath brightened. "Mom, that's a great idea!"

"I'll see if I can get started on that—maybe get her to help me. Hopefully it'll take her mind off missing her family for a little while. It's too bad we can't just invite them all up here for Thanksgiving. . ." Suddenly, the two locked eyes for several seconds, smiles breaking across their faces. Without a word, Ruth pushed open the louver door and peeked around it again, looking both ways for Rae, then stepped over to the phone and picked up the handset, pushing the 'redial' button. After a moment the call connected, "Hey there," she drawled, "My name is Ruth Dawson Is this Rae's dad. . .?"

** *** **

Their plan in place, Ruth and Heath grinned mischievously at each other, then Heath kissed his mom good-bye and headed back to work. Pushing through the louver door, Ruth now headed for the back hall and the TV room, stopping in the doorway.

"Rae, hon—if you're done with dessert, I have a little cleaning project I could use your help with."

Glad for the distraction, Rae brightened some at the prospect of spending more time with Ruth. "Sure."

Ruth smiled. "Let me gather up a few things, then we can get to it." She scurried around gathering her cleaning products and supplies: rags, the vacuum cleaner, a broom and dustpan, and a box of trash bags, then retrieved a set of towels and linens from the closet upstairs. When she had everything together, she loaded what she could into Rae's arms, and gathered the remaining items into her own, and they headed down the back hall.

Seeing they were headed for the back porch door by the laundry room, Rae puzzled over it. "Where are we going with all of this?"

"Out back. Just follow me, hon." Ruth stopped again at the door to the TV room, setting the baby monitor on the table near it as she called out, "Mrs. Balcomb—we're going to be outside for a little while, can you listen for Nate?" Mrs. Balcomb smiled and nodded as usual, and Ruth and Rae continued on down the back hall, past the laundry room, and out the back door. Stepping out onto that leg of the wrap-around porch, the two headed down the steps next to the wood pile and passed the clothesline, on their way toward the garage.

"We're going to clean the garage?" Somehow, Rae couldn't imagine needing cleanser, all-purpose cleaner, and a vacuum cleaner for that.

"Not the garage, hon—above the garage," Ruth answered, and Rae lifted her chin, raising her eyes above the side-hinged double garage doors, to the apartment above, recalling when she'd come upon it, and then Ruth's house, in the rain that first night. Ruth took hold of the wooden rail and made her way carefully up the stairs, with Rae close behind her. "Be careful on these stairs, Rae. I haven't been up here in a few years and I don't know how sturdy they are." Rae nodded and they rounded the corner at the first landing, and started up the main flight. At the top landing, Ruth produced a key dangling from a plastic spiraled key fob, and unlocked the deadbolt alongside the multi-paned window in the door's upper half, then pushed open the door. "Here we are." Stepping in behind her, Rae craned her head around the dim room in all directions. Propped against a near wall was a mattress and box spring, and across from it on the opposite wall, sat a love seat and chair—all were encased in plastic, and every horizontal surface was covered with a thick layer of dust. Ruth set down the vacuum and the broom and dustpan. "Let me flip the breaker so we can turn on the lights." Ruth made her way to the tiny kitchenette and reached for the electrical panel on the wall. Opening it, she flipped the switch and a light came on over the sink, above a small window that faced the outside stairs. "We'll have to take down those curtains and wash them when we get done," Ruth noted, more to herself than to Rae. "Well, let's get started—how about we get rid of all this dust first, then we can start with the bathroom." It took the better part of the afternoon before they were finished, and the two glanced around the tiny apartment with satisfaction. "This cleaned up real nice, don't you think, Rae?"

Rae nodded, smiling as she surveyed the room. "Yeah, it's a cute little place. I love those window seats."

Ruth nodded. "Between the two of them, you can just about see the whole property; from the front one, you can see the backyard and the house and the whole clearing out by the barn, and the back window faces the woods." She noticed the dusty curtains again. "Oh yes, we need to get these curtains down." Rae climbed up and handed down the curtain rod from above the sink, and did the same in each of the window seats. That accomplished, Ruth turned to Rae, "So, what do you think, hon? Will it do?"

Rae's expression was vacant. "Will it do for what?"

"For you, Rae. Since it looks like you're going to be here a while longer, me and Heath thought you needed a regular room, instead of staying on the sofa like you've been doing. A girl needs her privacy."

Rae's eyes widened as she gaped, "This is for me?"

". . .If you like it, and don't mind being out here. Heath said he'd set up the bed when he got home from work today."

Rae panned the room with new eyes. "Oh, wow! Ruth, that's amazing! Thank you!"

Chapter 33

That evening, after the supper dishes were done, Ruth busied herself in the kitchen making cookies with Nate, and the Gang chose their usual form of entertainment; watching TV in the back room. Heath built a fire in the big, stone fireplace in the den and sat on the sofa gazing into the flames. After a few minutes, Rae hesitantly appeared in the doorway with a magazine. "Is it okay if I read in here? The Gang has the TV up loud in the other room."

Heath nodded, waving her in. "Sure. C'mon in." Rae circled around the sofa, then got down on her belly in front of the hearth. Leaning on her elbows, her chin in one hand, she thumbed through the magazine she had brought in with her. He watched her for a moment then, with nothing else to do, he thought he'd try talking to her. "So, how's your room? You like it okay?"

Rae nodded and smiled appreciatively, giving him her full attention. "It's great, thanks!—I love it!"

"You don't mind being out there by yourself?"

"No, it's pretty cool!—Ruth said it used to be your room?"

Heath nodded. "Yeah, back in high school."

"You didn't want to just stay in the house with your family?"

"No, I thought I was too cool for that, so I fooled myself into thinking I was living on my own out there." He chuckled for a moment at the memory, then wondered about her magazine. "Whatcha reading?"

"It's just a magazine I had in my totebag," Rae answered without looking up.

"What kind of magazine?"

Rae rolled onto her side, holding it up with the cover showing. "Avionics." She noticed Heath's eyebrows arch above a blank stare, so she shrugged and returned her magazine to the rug in front of her.

"Avionics?" Not exactly the answer he'd expected, Heath tried again, "What's avionics?—Something to do with airplanes, I'm guessing?"

Rae turned the page, keeping her nose to the pages. "That's right—electronics: radios, instruments and stuff."

"Right." He smirked to himself. *Of course—what else would she be looking at?* He could tell it would not be easy to find some common ground on which to have a conversation with this girl, and thought for a moment. "So, Rae, what's life like in Florida? What do you and your friends do?"

Rae shrugged, again without looking up from her magazine. "I don't know. I mostly spend my time at work or with my family."

"What? You don't, like, hang out at the mall with your girlfriends?"

"I don't really have any girlfriends." Suddenly she chuckled at an ad on the page before her. "Oh, that's funny—a pitot tube cover that looks like a shark!" She pushed herself up until she was sitting on her calves then held up the magazine, showing Heath the image; he squinted, not having a clue what he was looking at. Seeing that, Rae attempted to explain, "The pitot tube…you know—for air speed?" When his blank look persisted, she shrugged. "Never mind," and she resumed her belly-lying position and her browsing.

Heath tried again. "No girlfriends? Why not?"

"Because all they want to do is hang out at the mall, like you said. What a waste of time."

"You think hanging out at the mall is a waste of time? I thought that's what girls your age did! What planet are you from?" he teased.

Rae sighed. "Unlike other girls my age, I actually have a life and don't have time for that.

"Okay, so no 'malling' and you don't have any girlfriends?"

"Not really. Why are you asking so many questions?"

"No reason. I'm just trying to get to know you a little bit, that's all." He tried again. "So, if you don't have any girlfriends, who do you talk to when you need to talk?"

"No one, I guess. Patty sometimes—but I only see her at work, so I don't get much chance to talk to her."

"Who's Patty?"

"My dad's office manager."

"Why don't you get to talk at work?"

"Because we're working. Duh! Plus, I'm in the hangar or in my office, and she's out in the front office."

"You have your own office?" Heath didn't mean to sound incredulous.

Rae sighed tolerantly, "Yes, I have my own office—I'm the head mechanic."

"The *head* mechanic?" When Rae nodded, Heath could only shake his head, amazed anew at this kid in such a position of responsibility. "Wow, that's pretty amazing." *Maybe Mom's right—she's not such a kid after all. . .* He tried another subject, "Okay, so do you have a boyfriend, or something?"

Rae rolled her eyes and sighed at Heath's line of questioning, then hesitated, and then smiled to herself. "I used to have a boyfriend; we were going to get married."

"Really, what happened?"

Rae turned a page. "One day, I went over to see him and he was gone."

Suddenly serious, Heath's forehead furrowed. "He left?"

Stifling a grin, Rae nodded. "Yeah. I found out later he moved to Texas."

"Your fiancé moved to Texas without saying anything to you?" Regretting he had brought it up, Heath groaned within himself.

"Yeah. I cried for days."

Heath sighed. "Wow, that's awful." *If she's only twenty, this must be pretty recent.* "You must have been pretty young when you got engaged. How old were you?"

"Five."

"Five?"

"Yeah, he was six. It was a May-December relationship." When a mischievous smile broke across her face, Heath knew he'd been had. Scowling at her, he grabbed the throw pillow next to him and hurled it at her. It landed square in the middle of her magazine. Startled initially, Rae quickly recovered and had a good laugh over it. Eyes narrowed in determination, Heath reached for a second pillow and flung it at her. This one caromed off her head and Rae immediately snatched it up, ready for war. "Okay, now you're toast!"

To Heath's surprise, she jumped up from the rug, throw pillow in hand, and pounced on the couch, whacking Heath on the head with it over and over. Caught completely off guard, Heath recovered quickly and held her off easily with one forearm, as he scrambled for another pillow with his other hand. At last finding one, he immediately launched a counterattack, pummeling Rae with his new-found throw pillow, and Rae fought back determinedly. Their commotion carried into the kitchen next door, their shrieks and shouts reaching Ruth's ears. Curious and a little concerned, Ruth scooped up Nate and hurried to the doorway of the den, then stopped short, agape. She watched, amused for a moment, a hand on one hip and Nate on the other. Nate giggled and clapped his hands at seeing his daddy rough-housing. With the TV up so loud across the hall, the Gang missed all the excitement.

After watching a few moments, Ruth made her presence known. "What's going on in here?" she challenged, pretending to scold.

Caught in the act, the two combatants froze in mid-swings, their heads snapped around in her direction. Both grinned, and in feigned innocence, muttered in unison, "Nothing." Then, surprised at their unison, they turned to each other and laughed.

"Do I have to separate you two, or can you play nice?" Ruth teased in her most motherly tone.

Heath grinned at his mom, speaking as though a child, "Okay, Mom, we'll be good."

Ruth shook her head at the toddler on her hip. "Do we have to put Daddy and Ms. Rae in time-out, Nate?" He only giggled again and Ruth turned her attention again to the pair on the sofa, and smiled. "Well, Nate and I have some cookies to finish, so carry on." She moved to leave, then hesitated, adding, "Oh, Rae, he's very ticklish on his collar bones."

Rae eyed Heath menacingly; plotting. "Is that so. . .?"

Betrayed, Heath protested, "Mom!"

Ruth turned and disappeared from the doorway as Rae mounted a new attack, zeroing in on his clavicles—Heath's Achilles heel. Despite his best efforts to suppress it, Heath erupted into an embarrassing fit of giggles, further delighting his opponent who pressed her attack. Finally, in desperation, he lifted Rae up and pitched her off the sofa. Rae rolled harmlessly onto the plush rug, laughing triumphantly, as Heath caught his breath. Still chuckling, Rae pushed herself up and headed back to her magazine. Heath eyed her, smirking, "May-December relationship. Ha! More like January-February!" Then he got in one last shot with his throw pillow.

Rae wheeled around in mock-indignation, "Hey! That was a very serious relationship! He broke my heart!" She grinned again at Heath as she picked up the pillow he'd thrown and threw it back at him.

Heath caught the pillow in mid-air. "I can sure tell you were raised with brothers!" He chuckled again, and then pressed, "So, back to the question..."

Rae had to think back for a moment as to what the original question was, then shrugged as she resumed her position at her magazine. "*No*, I don't have a boyfriend. *Okay?*"

"You're kidding...! Working in a hangar and being around all those pilots? You must run into guys every day."

"I didn't say I didn't run into guys," she corrected mildly, "I just said I don't have a boyfriend." She turned a page.

"I can't believe no one has shown an interest in you."

"I didn't say that either; there's been plenty of interest—just not the kind I want. Most of the single pilots I've seen are just a bunch of cocky, ego-maniacs—not exactly boyfriend material." She shrugged. "And since my brothers say I'm a 'jerk-magnet,' I just steer clear of pilots."

"A 'jerk-magnet'?"

Rae nodded as she turned another page. "Yeah, you know, the only guys I attract are jerks."

Heath grinned. "Oh so, if I see a guy flirting with you, that should tip me off that he's a jerk?"

"You got it—it's a give-away."

Heath chuckled, "Are your brothers pilots, too?" He found another pillow and pitched it at her.

Rae dodged it easily. "Yeah, but my dad raised them right, so they aren't like that. If most of the single pilots were like my brothers, I wouldn't have a problem with them—but they're not." She reached for the pillow and hurled it back; it missed by a mile and flew over the sofa out of Heath's reach.

Surprised, Heath cocked his head to one side. "Wow, that's really great that you think that way about your brothers." He leaned forward, resting his elbows on his knees. "Do your brothers share your opinion of pilots?"

"Yeah—and they keep an eye out when there's someone new in the hangar."

"Protective—that's good." He thought a moment about Rae's plight. "I guess it didn't occur to me that you'd have to deal with that at work."

"Yeah, and it's not just pilots, sometimes it's the customers, too. As soon as they see a female working in the hangar, they start right in, like it's a singles bar and I'm just in there to meet guys. Some of them have even been dumb enough to say something trashy about me to my brothers!" Shaking her head at the memory, she grinned incredulously and chuckled. "My dad and brothers are real good about setting them straight—a couple have even gotten tossed out of the hangar.

"No kidding! Wow, that's lousy. At least you have them there looking after you."

"Yeah, they're great."

"I know how your brothers feel—even though my sisters were older, I chased off a few boys for them, too." He smiled briefly at the memory. "What about other guys?—I mean besides pilots and customers."

Rae shrugged again. "I don't really know any other guys."

"Not from school or church or anything?"

"No. I don't go to church—and I didn't have time when I was in school; I was busy getting a life."

"So, you didn't date at all in high school?" Heath found this hard to wrap his brain around.

"Oh, maybe once in a while. I usually got asked to the big dances, but not much besides that. As soon as they found out I'm a pilot and was studying A & P, I usually didn't get asked out again."

"What's A & P?"

"Airframe and Power plant—that's aircraft mechanic school. Even now, guys still get all weird about what I do, as if it makes them less of a man, or something. I don't get that—I mean, it's not like I throw it in their faces or put them down about *not* being a mechanic or a pilot. The only ones who came around again were the ones who were hoping to get something for free, whether it was a flight or lessons—or me. As soon as they found out they weren't getting any of those, they were gone." Surprised at herself for saying so much, Rae shrugged. *Oh well, It doesn't matter—I won't be here much longer. . .* At that, she decided that meant the man on the sofa was safe to talk to, and concluded, "The guys I know are just. . .I don't know. . .They're just on a whole different frequency than me."

Considering the magazine she was looking at, Heath grinned at her reference to radios. Then he thought for a moment about how far ahead Rae was from most girls her age. *She knew what she wanted to do early on, and did what she needed to do to make it happen—and now, she's twenty and is already into her career.* He watched her as she thumbed through her magazine, pondering that.

"So, what about you?" Rae's voice brought him back to the present.

"What about me?"

"Yeah. Do you ever go out?"

Though not sure why, Heath was a little caught off guard by the question. "Um, not really." Unaccustomed to talking to girls about his love life—or lack thereof—his initial response was to put her off, but then reconsidered. *Well, she'll only be here a week or so*. With that in mind, he decided, just as Rae had, that meant the girl on the floor was safe to talk to. Shrugging, he answered her, "No, I keep pretty busy with work and Nate, and helping mom keep up this old house—that pretty much takes up all my time." He knew it was vague, but didn't see any reason to go into more detail. "Besides, I don't think most ladies are interested in a man with a little kid."

"Not even ladies that are *your* age?"

Heath winced at the way Rae said it, as though 'your age' meant *ancient*. "No, mostly ladies my age are usually done having kids and don't want to start over with a baby."

Surprised, Rae squinted at him, "They're done already? How old *are* you?"

Again, Heath felt ancient. "Thirty—thirty-one in February."

Rae arched an eyebrow, "Oh, wow, you're even older than I thought. Yeah, I guess they would be." Heath grinned and rolled his eyes, shaking his head as Rae continued, oblivious, "Mine's in March." She moved on, "What about your ex-wife?"

Heath sighed, feeling that familiar stab in his chest. He leaned back against the sofa. "What about her?"

"Do you ever see her? Does she ever come back to Georgia to see Nate?"

Heath hesitated, reminding himself again of her brief stay, then shook his head, "No, and I'm pretty sure she won't—she's not interested."

Rae's head came up from her magazine. "Not interested? How can she not be interested in her own kid?"

Heath sighed wearily, "I have no idea—but when she left, she made it clear she didn't want the life of a mom."

"Really? She actually said that?" Rae's countenance fell and she pushed herself up onto her knees and sat on her calves.

"Yeah, she did, and it about killed me to hear her say it. I mean, I was all about being a dad—I just couldn't believe she didn't feel the same way about being a mom and about Nate. I don't know why she even married me now. . . I mean, she knew I wanted kids and all."

"Maybe she thought she did too," Rae offered, grasping at straws, "Maybe she just wanted to want them because you did."

Heath looked at Rae, not expecting something like that from someone so young. He tilted his head slightly, reappraising the girl on the floor, suddenly feeling more like he was talking to a peer, and amended his assessment of her. "Yeah, maybe. She sure didn't mind all the attention she got when she was pregnant and when Nate was born, though—but I guess the whole 'mom thing' just got old real fast. She didn't like how she looked, and that she couldn't go do what she wanted to because of having to take care of a baby." He sighed and winced, "That's when she started going to that gym. I was fine with it because I thought it would make her feel better. I never thought that. . ." Unable to finish the thought, Heath just shook his head.

Rae watched him for a moment, seeing his sadness. "I'm sorry—I shouldn't have brought that up."

"That's okay; it is what it is—but no, most likely she won't be back for Nate. And just in case she has second thoughts some day, I made sure that she can't just show up and take him away from me."

The thought of Heath losing his son like that suddenly alarmed Rae. "She might do that?"

"I don't know if she would, but you hear about stuff like that all the time in divorces and adoptions and stuff. The mom changes her mind and courts just hand the kid back over, even years later, just because she's the mom. It's like they don't care about dads and adoptive parents—or the kid, for that matter. I mean, I don't mind sharing him with her; he's her son too, after all—but I just don't want her taking him away from me, so I did what I could to prevent that."

"What did you do? I mean, how can you prevent that from happening?"

"Well, when we were in the custody phase of the divorce, she said all these ugly things about what a pain it was having a kid and how she didn't want to be tied down with him." Rae grimaced, horrified a mom could say that about her own child, especially one as sweet as Nate. "Yeah, that about broke my heart. So, as part of the divorce paperwork, instead of having her just sign something relinquishing her rights, I had her write out what she'd said in her own words and in her own handwriting, so that she couldn't claim later than she didn't know what she was signing."

Rae's eyes widened. "And she agreed to that?—And did it?"

Heath nodded, stone-faced, "Yeah, and she didn't even miss a beat—she just asked for a pen and paper, and did it right then and there. Now, it's part of the official divorce documents—so hopefully, if she ever comes back here and tries to take Nate away, the judge will think twice about just handing him over to her."

Rae shook her head slowly, pained over what she'd just heard, and stared at the floor. "I can see why you did that, but I sure hope Nate never sees that piece of paper."

Touched again at her concern for Nate's heart, Heath nodded. "Yeah, me too."

"I just don't get that. How can a mom act that way? I mean, I can hardly stand being away from J.J.—and he isn't even my son."

"J.J.—that's your nephew, right?"

"Yeah, he's two and a half."

"Which brother is married?"

"Two of them are; Sam and Jesse, but Sam's the only one that has a kid so far. Jesse and Julie just got married last February. I just love J.J. to death—I couldn't imagine walking out of his life. Nate reminds me of him."

"Yeah, when we found Nate in the parlor with you yesterday morning, you seemed like you knew your way around little kids. So, what does 'J.J.' stand for?"

"Joe Junior—he's named after my dad."

"That's cute. Nate's named after my dad, too—short for Nathaniel."

"Really? That's neat. What did he do?"

"He was a sign painter, too—acutally, he's the one who started my business."

"He did?"

"Yeah, when I wasn't playing football I used to work with him summers and after school, and he taught me what he knew— then, when I graduated, we worked together; I took it over when he got sick. He was an artist, too—he painted that picture over the fireplace." Heath gestured above the mantle to the painting of the three children on a tire swing. "That's me and my sisters when we were little."

Genuinely surprised, Rae marveled. "No way, really? He did that? I *love* that painting!"

"Yup, he did that. There's a few more of his paintings upstairs, too."

Rae stared at Heath, "No kidding! Wow, I never thought about a sign painter being an actual artist."

Heath chuckled. "I'll bet you thought we just stenciled letters all day."

Rae grinned, sheepish. "Well, yeah, that is kind of what I thought."

"No wonder you thought I couldn't make a living doing that." He teased her, grinning.

She shrugged, embarrassed, "Sorry. Wow, you didn't even get mad when I said that. You could have really bit my head off!"

Heath shrugged it off, "That's okay, I knew different." Rae arched an eyebrow as she scrutinized the man on the sofa for a moment, thinking about how many times she 'knew different' and didn't hesitate for a minute to let the other person know it. Heath continued, "Yeah, my dad's first love was art, but painting signs paid the bills."

"Did he ever sell any of his stuff? I mean, besides his signs?"

"Yeah, we have folk and craft festivals around here a few times a year. He used to take his stuff out to them to sell and make some extra money; he did pretty good with that."

"Wow, that is *SO* cool!" She thought for a moment. "Are you an artist, too? Can you paint like he does?"

Heath shrugged and glanced away. "Oh, I do okay."

Rae thought she saw a little smile on his lips, and got the impression that he was just being modest. She wondered if he did better than just 'okay'—especially if his skill came anything close to his dad's. She chuckled, "Wow, I never would have figured you for an artist."

"I didn't say I was an artist—but, just out of curiosity, why not?"

"I don't know—you just don't look like an artist."

"What exactly does an artist look like?"

"Not like you. You look like you should be out wrestling alligators, or something," she teased—but only partially.

"Well, you don't look like a pilot—or a mechanic, either."

Rae grinned, "Yeah, I guess." She shrugged, conceding the point.

He grinned at her, surprised she didn't have a come-back. "If you want, I'll take you over to the shop with me while you're here and show you some more of my dad's stuff."

"Sure, that would be cool! Maybe you can show me some of your work, too."

Heath shrugged. "I guess, if you want."

Just then, Ruth showed up at the doorway with Nate and a plateful of cookies. "Anyone ready for some fresh-baked cookies?" She didn't have to ask twice, and Heath and Rae filled their hands from the plate. "So, what are you two talking about?"

"Heath was telling me about his dad painting that picture over the fireplace."

Ruth raised her eyes to the painting of the children in the tire swing and nodded wistfully. "Oh, yes, that one has always been one of my favorites." Rae noticed a sadness in Ruth's eyes that reminded her of the look she sometimes saw in her dad's. Just then, the timer in the kitchen went off. "Oh, there's another batch!" She set the plate down, along with Nate, and hurried back to the kitchen.

Nate climbed onto the sofa into his dad's lap and Rae watched them watching the flames lapping at the logs in the fireplace. Rae thought for a moment about Heath and his dad, and something occurred to her. "How long has it been since your dad died?"

"It's been about four years now."

"Four years? So, he never knew Nate? That's too bad."

Heath nodded, taking another bite of cookie. "Yeah, it really is—they would have loved each other."

Pondering his loss, a question pressed in Rae's mind. After several moments, she asked tentatively, "How long did it take you to get over him dying?"

Surprised at her question, Heath scrutinized Rae briefly. Sensing a need to know in her countenance, he chose his words carefully. "I haven't yet."

Rae deflated. "You haven't?—After *four years?*"

Heath shook his head. "When someone you love dies, I don't think you ever really get over it—you just sort of learn to live with it. After a while, you get past the ache and sadness, but you never stop missing them—at least, I haven't. How can you when they took up such a big place in your life?" He held Nate's hands as he bounced him on one knee, watching for a moment as Rae processed that.

"Does it make you sad to think about him and talk about him like this?"

"It used to, but I actually like to talk about him now."

She brightened a tad, hopeful. "Really?"

"Yeah. At first, when I thought about him, it made me think of how he died and how hard that was—but then, after a while, I guess I just started to think more about his life than his death. Now, I cherish my memories of my dad; talking about him just helps keep them vivid."

Rae gazed at Heath for a moment, her expression softening. "That's really nice." Then, nodding almost imperceptibly, her gaze shifted to the floor and she pondered that for several moments more before she again raised her eyes to his, her voice soft, "Thanks for saying that."

"Sure." Heath nodded, watching her, waiting to see if she wanted to talk further or move on.

Rae thought about it a few more moments, then again stretched out onto her belly and turned the page to her magazine. "Do you like to fly?"

The change of page and subject was Heath's indication that she was through talking about it, so he leaned back into the sofa as he answered, "I've only done it once, when I went to visit my sister in Indiana."

"Really?" Rae's eyebrows registered her surprise at that. "Only *once?*" Heath nodded. Rae's eyes returned to her magazine then she glanced up again. "Have you ever flown in a small plane?"

He shook his head. "Nope. Never."

Rae arched an eyebrow. "Seriously? Never?"

He held Nate up in the air above him. "Nope."

"You want to go up when I get my aircraft repaired?"

Returning Nate to his lap, Heath smiled, appreciating the offer as one not just of an airplane ride, but of friendship, and smiled. "Sure—but how about I go with you the flight *after* the first flight that it's fixed."

Rae only smirked. "You don't want to go on the test flight?— You chicken!"

"Yup, that's me! Huh, Nate?—Daddy's a chicken, isn't he? Bok-bok-bok!" Heath did his best imitation of the barnyard bird, complete with flapping his bent elbows, which delighted his son. Rae grinned, surprised he didn't deny it. Heath grinned as well, then resumed their conversation. "So, you said all your brothers are pilots?

"Except for Ben."

"He's the one that's deaf?" Rae nodded. "And there are other pilots working for your dad besides your brothers?"

"Yeah, a couple of them are year-round, but most are seasonal."

"Is there enough work for all of them to fly?"

Rae grinned. "You mean, 'can they make a living at that?'" she teased.

Heath grinned, amused and a bit embarrassed. "Um. . . well, yeah, I guess."

"Yes, more than enough. They all fly, but they don't all do the same kind of work."

"There are different kinds of flying? I guess I've never thought about that."

"Sure there are. Sam and Dad are both flight instructors, and Sam heads up the flight school, and he also does the scheduling for the other pilots. Luke and Jesse, and most of the others, fly charters, and Luke does some crop-dusting."

"Crop dusting? No kidding!"

"Why is that so surprising? We do have crops in Florida, you know."

"I know. . . I don't know why that seems surprising. Do you offer sky diving?"

"No."

"Why not?"

Rae shrugged, "Because none of us sky dive."

"Well, I guess that makes sense. Why don't any of you sky dive?"

"I don't know about the others—but if you ask me, it seems kind of pointless to go up just to jump out."

"I don't know. . .people do it all the time—enough of them for there to be businesses that just do that."

"Good for them. I'd rather stay in my aircraft."

"I hope so, since you're the pilot," Heath chided.

Rae grinned, imagining a pilot jumping with the jumper. "Yeah, they both jump and after their chutes open, they look at each other. . ." Rae turned a page in her magazine, and without looking up, she voiced an improvised conversation between an imaginary pilot and a skydiver; a different voice for each. "'Who's flying the airplane?' 'I thought you were' 'Oh, nuts.'"

Heath threw his head back and laughed out loud—something he had not done for quite a long time.

Chapter 34

Close to lunchtime on Wednesday, the insurance adjuster finally arrived after spending a couple of hours taking an unscheduled tour of the back roads of Tennyson, Georgia. Once he completed his assessment of Rae's aircraft, he was on his way again —this time, with a set of detailed directions back to the Interstate, and Rae called Orby with the news. "The insurance guy was just here. How soon do you think we can get started with the repairs?"

"Well, Ms. Rae, I know how much you're needing to get back home, so how about tomorrow?"

"That would be great, Orby!"

"I'll just go in early tomorrow and knock off work here after lunch. Then we might could get a good start on it before it gets dark. But on account of Shabbat, I won't be able to make it up there again 'til Sunday and we can work on it that whole day, if you want to. Will that work for you?"

Rae didn't have a clue what 'Shabbat' was, but it seemed important to Orby. "Sure Orby, that'll work—if you don't mind missing church on Sunday." It wasn't a stretch for her to believe he attended.

"Oh, I won't miss out, Ms. Rae—I worship on Saturday, so you're good. Okay then, I'll see you tomorrow after lunch."

"Okay, Orby, thanks."

Unknown to Rae, as she was ending her call with Orby, her brother Jesse was touching down at Heartland Airfield. He followed the tower's directions until he found the tie-downs and pulled in. After he shut down his aircraft, he and his passenger shook hands and parted ways, then Jesse completed his checks, and headed over to the commercial terminal to find Ground Transportation. A half hour later, armed with his internet directions and local map, he was under way in a rental car, grinning in anticipation of surprising his sister. After a couple of left turns, he found Highway 49 and followed it through a small industrial area nestled into the rural landscape, and on into Peach County. Several minutes later, crossing into the outskirts of Tennyson, he approached the interstate, making a mental note of a Mega 8 motel and a few eateries near the on-ramp to I-75. The site of them prompted him to drive through one for something to drink before crossing the bridge into Tennyson proper.

Ten minutes later, fries in hand, and a soda in the drink holder, Jesse was underway again. He crossed the bridge over the interstate and not long after that he turned right onto Highway 42. He drove along the two-lane road until he passed a sign for Crawford County, doing just fine with his directions until he made his turn off the highway, and following the side streets proved to be challenging. The crossroads were few and far between, not to mention poorly marked, and he passed a number of intersections with no signage. After traveling several miles he got suspicious and stopped on the side of the road. *This shouldn't be taking this long.* He squinted at his directions and then his map, then pulled back onto the road. After yet another unnamed crossroad, Jesse sighed. *Don't they believe in road signs up here?* Finally finding one, he noted its name and pulled over again to consult his map, searching carefully for the street until he could determine his location. With a wince, he found he'd gone too far—*way* too far.

He sighed, and circling back, he retraced his route and drove up and down the two-lane country road three times before he gave up and decided to just try to find it on his own. "I guess this place is too remote even for the map makers!" He mused to himself, wishing he'd brought along his GPS, but then realized it too would likely not be helpful way out here. After another half hour of trying side streets and crossroads along the way, Jesse checked his watch. *Nearly 5 p.m. I've been wandering around here for almost two hours!* Clueless on these remote roads, he wasn't even sure anymore how to get back to the highway, and with it beginning to get dark, he was pretty sure he didn't want to be wandering around in these boondocks at night. Seeing he had no other choice, he had to resort to the bane of all male existence—asking for directions. *I'll just ask the locals around here.* He scanned the endless stands of woods and empty fields. *If I can find any.* It was another two miles before he spotted a house in a clearing in the distance to the left, surrounded by a stand of woods and turned up that road. As he drew closer, he eyed the big old, white house with green shutters and a wrap-around porch set back off the road, wondering about its occupants. *I hope I don't get shot coming on someone's private property out here. If this doesn't work, I'll just have to call Rae, after all.* He pulled onto the property and made his way up the long drive to the front of the house and got out

Rarely having unexpected visitors, the footfalls on the front porch caught Heath's attention before the doorbell rang. He opened the door to a tall young man with thick, wavy brown hair, and greeted the stranger with a smile. "Y'all must be lost to be knocking on doors out here!"

Jesse raised his eyes to the taller, thirtyish man with straight dark hair whose frame took up most of the doorway, and returned his smile. "Yes, I sure am—this must be an old map."

Heath chuckled. "What can I do for you?"

"I'm looking for Rae Gerrard. She's staying with some people around here somewhere—the Dawson's. Do you know them?"

Surprised and puzzled, and feeling a bit protective of their young houseguest, Heath's eyes narrowed at the twenty-some-thing man on his porch. "Yeah, that's us. Rae is here."

Surprise and relief registered on the visitor's face. "Really? Oh wow, that's great! Then, you must be Heath."

Heath hesitated. "Yeah, that's right. Who are you?"

"I'm Jesse—one of Rae's brothers." He extended his hand toward Heath.

Now it was Heath who was surprised. He hesitated for another moment then smiled and extended his own hand, not sure why he felt relieved. "Well, hey! Yeah, I'm Heath. This is a surprise! Rae didn't say nothing about you coming—did she know?"

"No, it was kind of spur-of-the-moment, and I wanted to surprise her."

"Well, c'mon in and I'll go find her." Heath stepped aside and waved Jesse in. "We were just fixin' to eat supper. Y'all want to join us?"

Surprised again, Jesse hesitated at the offer. "No, that's okay—I don't expect you to feed me when I barge in on you unexpectedly like this."

"Oh, it's okay, really. We always have room for one more and there's plenty to eat."

Jesse smiled again. "Well, sure, I guess. That would be amazing, thanks!"

"Just make yourself comfortable in here." Heath waved Jesse into the front room and the younger man took a seat in an overstuffed chair, then Heath added, "I'll let Mom know to set another place, then I'll go find Rae." Heath pushed open the louver door and poked his head into the kitchen. "Mom, we have a visitor for dinner—you'll never guess who's here!"

Ruth closed the oven door and glanced up at Heath. "Who?"

"Rae's brother! Where is she?"

"Rae's brother?—From Florida?"

"Yeah, he just showed up on the porch!"

"Land's sake! Have you tried her room or the den?" Ruth took off her oven mitts, set them on the counter and rushed to look past Heath. Seeing Jesse, a smile broke across her face and she hurried across the room. "Well, hey! Heath tells me you're Rae's brother?"

Jesse rose to his feet as Heath made the introductions, "This is my mom, Ruth Dawson...Mom, this is Jesse. Let me go find Rae."

"It's nice to meet you, Ms. Dawson. Thank you for taking care of my sister." He took Ruth's hand.

Ruth smiled brightly. "Oh, it's no problem. It's been a pleasure having her around." Something about Ruth warmed Jesse's heart. Retrieving her hand, Ruth smiled again, "Would you like something to drink?"

Heath found Rae in the den reading Nate a story and his son scampered to him when Heath stepped to the doorway. "Rae, there's someone here to see you."

Rae squinted. "Me?"

"If your name's Rae." Heath grinned at her playfully. "He's in the front room."

Rae eyed Heath curiously as she passed him in the doorway. When she stepped out to the front room, Jesse smile broadly. "There you are, little sister!"

Wide-eyed and slack-jawed, Rae gasped, "Jesse!" She ran to him and leapt into his arms. They hugged each other tightly. "What are you doing here? How did you find it?"

"I almost didn't—I can see how you got lost! I found it by accident, just like you said you did!"

"What are you doing up here?"

"I brought Mr. Patton back today."

"So he made it to Florida, then?"

Jesse grinned, chiding his sister, "Yeah—since you left him stranded last we*ek!*"

Arms instantly akimbo, Rae's mouth fell open and she eyed her brother with mock-indignation. "*Stranded him?* Well, my bad for getting shot-down!"

Jesse just chuckled, "So, I thought I'd come looking for you once we landed."

Rae eyed him, playfully suspicious. "Is Dad checking up on me?"

"No, *I'm* checking up on you—with Dad's full support!" He grinned at his sister. "Dad says you got your Cessna towed out of the field."

"Yeah, it's in the barn. The insurance guy came this morning, so we can start patching it tomorrow. Orby said the parts should be in soon, too. You want to see it?"

Jesse nodded. "Sure, I was hoping I could."

Rae glanced at Ruth, who seemed to read her mind. "Supper will be ready in about fifteen minutes."

Rae nodded and led Jesse out to the barn and he helped her swing open the big, double doors, then Rae flipped on the lights. A minute later Jesse was circling the Cessna, shaking his head at the bullet holes. He ran his hand along the underside of the wings and then the door of the cockpit and paused, reflecting.

"So, what do you think, Jess?"

Jesse glanced over at Rae, then stepped toward her, giving her a hug. "I think that we're blessed to still have you with us, little sister."

Heath watched from the porch as Jesse hugged his sister again. He couldn't hear what was being said, but he could tell that seeing the bullet holes in Rae's plane had an impact on her brother. He stepped back inside, scooping up Nate and he and Ruth chatted as she puttered around making her final preparations. On the way back from the barn, Rae showed Jesse her little apartment above the garage and he nodded his approval. As they descended the stairs afterward, and came in from the porch, they found Heath standing in the kitchen holding Nate and talking to Ruth.

Jesse brightened at the child. "And who's this little guy?"

Heath beamed. "This here is my son, Nate—he's almost two."

"Just a little younger than J.J." Jesse smiled at Nate and tickled his tummy. "Well, hi there!" Nate giggled and beamed at the new face in his world.

As Heath rang the bell, Ruth herded everyone into the dining room and she and Rae brought out the food. Supper around the table was lively as the Gang, especially Mr. Peterman, joked with their guest and peppered him with questions as they had Rae. Finally Mr. Peterman asked one that everyone wanted to hear the answer to. "So, Jesse, tell us what Rae was like growing up."

"No, they don't need to hear any lame stories about me," Rae protested.

"They're not *all* lame, Rae. Some of them are pretty funny," Jesse countered.

She shook her head. "They don't need to hear those, either."

"Sure we do!" the Gang assured her.

"No, you don't," she insisted.

Jesse shook his head as he chided, "I don't know, Rae—it sounds to me like they do!"

"Jesse!" Rae's eyes were pleading.

"Now Rae, your public awaits!"

"My public? Right." Rae scoffed.

"Has she always liked to fix things?" Mr. Windom asked.

Jesse grinned. "Oh, I wouldn't say 'fix,' but she sure liked taking things apart, though! She became a holy terror when she discovered hand tools."

"How old was she when she discovered those?"

Jesse squinted, thinking. "Three, maybe? When she found out how handy a screwdriver was, she went all over the house taking the plates off of all our wall sockets. Then one night at dinner, out of the blue, she announced that vacuum cleaners have different screws than the wall sockets do. My dad looked at her like this—" Jesse squinted; his expression, puzzled, "and he asked her how she knew that. Well, that's when my parents found out that Rae had taken apart the vacuum cleaner. They had to take it to the repair shop to get it put back together." A chorus of laughter erupted from those around the table—except for Rae, who glowered at him. "How many times did you do that, Rae? Wasn't it like four or five before you finally figured out how to put it back together?" Jesse chuckled. Rae only shrugged.

When the laughter died down, Ruth piped up, "In my experience, there are three kinds of brothers that sisters have: brothers that ignore their sisters, brothers that torment their sisters, and brothers that protect their sisters. Heath was very protective of his sisters. Which kind were you boys?"

Jesse chuckled, "All three at one time or another. But a few things happened that taught us to be more protective brothers—Dad insisted on it because of how Rae was."

"Is that so, Rae?" Mr. Peterman turned to Rae for verification.

Rae nodded. "Yeah, pretty much—sometimes *over*-protective."

"Well sometimes you needed some serious over-protecting!" Jesse qualified. Rae just grinned, knowing what he meant. Jesse shook his head, already recalling a few instances.

"You said 'because of how Rae was'—what does that mean?" Ruth asked.

Jesse eyed Rae, grinning. "Well, Rae was fearless—especially for such a little girl; *scary-fearless!* I think part of that was just because she didn't have the experience to be afraid; she would just do whatever she saw us doing. Only we were bigger and older than she was and she didn't realize how dangerous some of the things we were doing could be—especially for a little girl, and neither did we, for that matter! She just trusted us and copied us—and our parents had the Urgent Care bills to show for it! Yeah, she thought her brothers could do anything; we were her heroes—especially Sam. She was too little to realize we were just a bunch of crazy, stupid young boys. We got in trouble quite a few times until we learned to look after her like she needed. A couple of times we *really* got into trouble—it's amazing Rae made it to her teens!"

"Like when?"

Jesse thought for a moment then turned to Rae, looking for input. "Narrow it down to a couple for me," he teased.

Rae wrinkled her nose at him. "I'm not going to help you tell on me! You're on your own!"

Jesse grinned, then sighed, thinking back. "Let's see. The only ones I can think of that stand out are when Sam's propeller toy-thing landed on the roof and that time we jumped on the neighbor's trampoline." Jesse sighed, recalling that one. "Oh man, that was bad! Yeah, I think that trampoline thing is what really made us wise-up; it about finished us all off—especially Sam." Jesse shook his head and Rae nodded, agreeing.

"What happened?" Everyone wanted to know.

"You sure you want to hear that one? It's a real soap opera!" Jesse cautioned. They pressed him unanimously and finally Jesse relented. "Okay, don't say I didn't warn you!" He turned to Rae, "Sorry, little sister, what can I say? The people have spoken!" Rae didn't protest, but only shrugged, mostly because she loved to hear Jesse tell a story, even if it meant telling on her. Jesse thought for a moment before he began. "Well, let's see, how old were you when the trampoline thing happened?"

Rae shrugged. "I don't know. . .four or five?"

He nodded. "Yeah, that's sounds about right."

"It was when I had those pink overalls."

"Oh yeah, and you got those on your fourth birthday from Grandma. I remember that because you wore them for almost two weeks straight because you liked them so much you didn't want to take them off." Jesse grinned at his sister and Rae only shrugged, which elicited some chuckles from around the table. "That would make Sam about twelve?" Rae nodded. "So I must have been around ten, and Luke had to be. . .seven or eight? Yeah, he was pretty young when that happened."

"So you boys were quite a bit older than Rae back then," Mrs. Balcomb clarified.

Jesse nodded. "We still are," he teased, smiling; eliciting chuckles from those paying attention. Then he added, "Except Ben—he's a couple years younger than Rae; he was still a toddler when this happened." Jesse thought for a moment then began, "Well, let's see. . . A family that lived near us had gotten a new trampoline—they were behind us on the next street, and down a few doors. It was one of those really huge trampolines and it didn't have a net around it. We didn't know that neighbor, and the three of us—Sam, Luke, and me—had started climbing up on the fence and sneaking over to their yard and playing on their trampoline when no one was home." Jesse grinned sheepishly at their literal trespass. "Well, this one day, we three went over there and I guess Rae had watched us climb on the fence and she followed us without us realizing it. . ."

"She climbed on the fence?" Mr. Windom asked, puzzled, "How could a four year old reach a fence that high?"

Jesse grinned at his sister. "Well with Rae, it was ten percent ingenuity and ninety percent determination." He chuckled for a moment, then explained further, "In our neighborhood, the back yards on one side of the street backed up to the back yards of the houses on the street behind us. The fences were only about five feet high, and there was just this one long, continuous fence that ran across all the back yards, dividing the properties, and the rails and posts faced the houses on our side. So when we wanted to go to someone's house on the street behind us, instead of walking all the way around the block, we would just climb up on the fence and walk along the top rail, then let ourselves down into their yard—all the kids did that, so naturally, Rae wanted to do it too. We had this step stool chair we kept in the kitchen and Rae would drag that thing out to the corner of the fence and use it to reach the top rail. Then she'd just pull herself up and walk along it like the rest of us." He chuckled. "Like I said—fearless!"

Mr. Windom and the others nodded and Jesse continued, "So, we're in this yard. I remember Sam and I were watching Luke jump on the trampoline and he was holding his soccer ball while he jumped—I had thrown it at him while he was jumping just to tease him, and he caught it and kept it for some reason. Then, all of a sudden we hear Rae behind us, asking if she could jump, too. We about jumped out of our skin! Sam gets all irritated and says, 'Raaaae!'" Jesse stretched the name into two syllables imitating Sam, "'What are you doing here?' and we both looked around feeling like we were busted! But Rae didn't know the difference—it never occurred to her that we ever did anything wrong back then." Jesse smiled at his sister. "She eventually learned different," he qualified. Everyone chuckled and smiled as Jesse continued, "So she asks if she can jump on the trampoline, too. Sam says 'Oh, I guess, but you can't tell anyone—it's a secret.' And he tells her, 'keeping secrets is something big kids do. Are you a big kid?'—and of course, she bought it—'cause Sam was her hero, and would never lead her astray, right?" Jesse smiled and rolled his eyes.

"So Sam said she could have a turn after me and as soon as he said that, Luke lost his hold on his soccer ball while he was jumping, and somehow while he was trying to keep from landing on it, he accidentally kicked it—and before we knew what was happening, the ball bounced off a back window of that house, and shattered it. We all just froze in our tracks." Jesse demonstrated their stunned facial expressions. "We didn't think anyone was home there, but all of a sudden we hear this man inside yelling, 'Hey! What are you kids doing back there?' and all of us just freaked out and scrambled into three different directions and over three different fences."

"Did you get caught?"

"No—well, not yet anyways." Jesse resumed, "After we'd run in our different directions, we all finally met back in our own driveway on the next street. We were all huffing, puffing, and panting and bent over, trying to catch our breath, and all of a sudden, I looked around and noticed Rae wasn't with us, so I said, 'Where's Rae?' I figured she had taken off with Sam or Luke. Sam says, 'I thought she was with you.' And I said, 'She was standing next to you!' Then Sam started looking kind of worried when we realized neither of us had Rae with us!—And when I realized she couldn't have made it over the fence on her own without her step-stool chair, I started getting worried, too."

His audience stared at him, appalled. Mrs. Balcomb gasped, "You left a four-year-old in someone else's back yard?"

Jesse nodded, chagrined. "Yes, that's exactly what we did." Eyes around the table widened as he continued, "So when we realized it, we did what most brothers would do in a situation like that—we started blaming and shoving each other. Then all of a sudden, Luke figures out what's going on and says, 'You guys left Rae back there?' So we started in on him, and then we all shoved and yelled at each other until we were out of breath again. Finally, Sam points out that we better go back and find her and Luke says, 'That man probably already killed her!' He looked like he was about to cry—and of course, that scared us worse. So, being the concerned brother that I am, I said, 'We are *SO* going to get it!'" Jesse chuckled, shaking his head at his younger self. "Then Sam said, 'What are you guys worried about?—I'm the oldest! I'm the one who's going to get it!'" Jesse chuckled again, "Here we just left our little sister with a furious man, and all we can think about is how much trouble we are in for!

"Well, right then a police cruiser turned onto our street, and Luke says, 'Look! There's a cop. We can tell him that man killed Rae!' Luke's not even thinking about our involvement, he just heads for the curb to flag down the cop! So, I grabbed him back and yelled at him, something like, 'Are you brainless? If we tell him that, he'll know we were over there!' because all I could think about right then was not getting caught. Well, I'm sure the cop saw that whole thing, because he pulled up next to us and stopped. All three of us probably looked about as guilty as anyone could. Then Sam said, 'Don't anyone say *anything!*'" Jesse hissed it through his teeth, his neck veins distended, as Sam had done so many years before. "Well, the cop got out of his cruiser and called to us over the roof. He says, 'You boys know anything about some kids jumping on a trampoline on the next street?'

I'm sure he already knew it was us, but back then, we didn't know that.

"So Sam answers and says, 'No, sir.' Now, we were so freaked out about losing Rae that I'm sure the cop could tell by our faces that something was up. So, he says, 'What are the three of you doing out here?' and Sam tells him we lived there and pointed to our house behind us." Jesse hiked his thumb over his shoulder imitating his older brother. "Then he said, 'We're looking for our little sister—she wandered off.' Well, Luke and I were so impressed with Sam for coming up with that! To us, it sounded like the perfect alibi. We just knew the cop would help us find Rae then, and never suspect we had anything to do with where she was." Jesse chuckled at their naiveté along with the others around the table. "I'm sure the policeman knew he had the culprits, but back then, we thought we were in the clear at that point. Then the cop said, 'Is your sister about five, with blond braids, wearing pink overalls?' Of course, we were really relieved to hear his description, 'cause that meant he'd seen her. Then Luke steps up and says, 'She's alive?'" Jesse chuckled again, as did the others. "And Sam yanks him backward, and says, 'Shut up, you stupid-head!' Then, as if the cop hadn't seen all that, Sam just acts all natural and says, 'Um, yeah, did you find her? Is she okay?'

"I remember the cop smiled real big right then. I thought it was because he was happy to find where Rae belonged, but I'm sure it was because he knew he had us. Well, he says, 'Yeah, she's right here in my car. Can you come over here and tell me if she's your sister?' He was so slick—he just let us keep incriminating ourselves. He knew as soon as we said she was our sister that it would be admitting we were in that man's yard with her, but we were just kids and we didn't have a clue about things like that. So, like the suckers we were, we rushed up to the side of that police cruiser and looked in through the windows, and there was Rae sitting on the back seat, eyes as big as pie tins, scared half to death. I could tell she was scared because she was chewing on her knuckle." Jesse demonstrated on the middle knuckle of his index finger. "She only did that when something *really* scared her. When we saw her, we about fainted from relief, and when she saw us, she looked pretty relieved, too.

"So the cop says, 'Is that your sister?' Well, Sam got all excited and said, 'Yes, sir!' and the cop smiles real big, because Sam just incriminated all three of us. Then, he nods toward our house and says, 'And you live right there?' and we all nod. Then the cop says, 'Is your mom or dad home?' and Sam says, 'Yes, sir. My mom is home.' We think the cop is being so helpful, when he's actually just solving the crime with our help." Jesse grinned again. "So the officer just smiled again and opened the back seat door and got Rae out and walked her up to the front steps. She was still chewing on her knuckle—I don't know why that stands out in my mind—her chewing on that knuckle like that—I guess because it showed me just how much that whole thing scared her, and knowing that just scared me more, because she's usually so fearless." Jesse reflected for a moment, then glanced at Rae and smiled. Then he continued, "When the officer got to the porch, he just says, 'Would you go inside and get your mom?'—again letting us pave the way for him. When we went in, he says, 'Is it okay if I wait inside while you get her?' Ha! He was so smooth!—baiting us like that so he could stay within procedure!

"So, Sam just nods and shows him inside, and we left him there in the entryway with Rae while we went and found our mom—I remember she was in the laundry room when we found her. We told her, 'Mom, there's a policeman at the door with Rae.' She looked at us with her eyes like saucers, grabbed up Ben, and hurried to the door all worried. When she got there, she sees

Rae there looking all scared and chewing on her knuckle and it scared Mom even more. She leaned down and asked Rae if she was okay and Rae just lunged at her and grabbed her around the neck. She didn't cry or say anything, she just held onto Mom for dear life. I remember Mom saying later that she had never seen Rae look so rattled."

At the mention of their mother, Rae winced, letting her mind drift back to that moment that Jesse spoke of—that longing to hold her mother surfacing once again. She gazed over at Ruth as Jesse continued, "It wasn't until about a week later that we found out what happened to Rae in that yard after we left her. We thought she was just scared because she got left behind, but we found out from Dad that after we scrambled over the fences, that man came after Rae yelling, 'Hey, you! What are you doing in my yard?' So, Rae just ran for it. She climbed part way up on the fence, but she couldn't reach the top rail, and that man snatched her off by the back suspenders of her overalls and turned her around and shook her by her shoulders and yelled, 'What do you think you're doing, little girl? Who are those boys?'" Jesse acted out the scene. "A big man like that—and Rae was just this little, bitty girl!" Jesse shook his head, still incredulous over it. "My folks rarely raised their voices to us. Oh, they were plenty strict and doled out some tough punishments, but yelling just wasn't their style. So poor Rae had never had a grown-up yell at her or shake her like that, and it really freaked her out. It took her several days before she could even tell mom and dad that it happened." Several around the table shook their heads.

"So, what happened with the policeman?" Mr. Peterman was on the edge of his chair, both figuratively and literally.

"Oh, yeah," Jesse collected his thoughts and found his place. "Mom saw how freaked out Rae was and then the cop says, 'May I speak with you privately, ma'am?' and Mom's face just fell; she knew it was going to be bad. She told us to go outside and to take Ben with us, and we knew that meant it was really serious. I think that's when the three of us realized we were still in trouble, so now we were all worried again and we went outside and started to argue again. Ben was about two, and he couldn't hear, so he was oblivious and just played with Luke's soccer ball, but the rest of us started accusing each other again. Finally Sam had enough and said, 'Oh, just put a sock in it and let me think!' Then he said, 'I told Rae to keep quiet; if we stick together, they won't know anything. So, just be quiet about it!' He was still holding out hope that we wouldn't catch it for going in that man's yard. Then Luke says, 'Well, if Sam hadn't left Rae behind, nobody would know anything!' and Sam got mad again.

"Well, while we are sitting there blaming each other, our Dad pulls up into the driveway, and we all just froze. It turns out that the officer asked Mom to call her husband and have him come home, so that's what she did." Jesse glanced away, recalling, "Dad says when she called, all she said to him was, 'A policeman just showed up here with Rae and he wants to speak with you.' Dad said, 'I'm on my way!' I mean, we all knew Dad loved us boys like crazy—but Rae was, and will always be, his little girl." Jesse chuckled, "He must have broken every speed limit between the hangar and our house to get home that fast! So, Dad gets out of the car and he's looking pretty concerned, and he comes up to us sitting there on the porch steps and asks, 'You boys know anything about this?' and we all just stared at him, wide-eyed and shook our heads." Jesse demonstrated their dread. "Dad just gave us that 'Clint Eastwood' stare and went into the house—he knew we were lying; he *always* knew when we were lying."

"Probably because you hardly ever did it and you weren't good at it," Rae interjected.

Jesse nodded. "Yeah, neither were you!—None of us ever were. I guess that's a good thing to be bad at." Jesse shrugged and continued, "I just remember shaking in my boots and feeling terrible, and I remember watching Ben out there on the grass playing happily with that soccer ball, and wondering how he could do that when the rest of us were so miserable." Jesse smiled again.

"Well, I'm sure that policeman told Dad what he knew about how Rae had gotten left in that man's yard. Dad told us later he had called Rae over to him and asked her how she ended up there in that man's yard, and she wouldn't tell him! He said he was really surprised by that because Rae always answered when she was asked something. So, he changed tactics: he asked her if she broke the window, and she shook her head. Then he asked her if she jumped on the trampoline, and she shook her head. So Dad told her to tell him who did, and Rae wouldn't! She clammed up! Dad said she just hugged him instead of telling him, and that gave Dad a clue—so he asked her if someone told her not to tell and she nodded. Then he asked if they would hurt her if she told, and she shook her head. Dad said he could tell from her response that it was loyalty, and not a threat, that kept her quiet. He said we were the only ones Rae felt that kind of loyalty for, so he had his answer just by that one little thing. When he told us about that later, I remember thinking, 'Wow, my dad is so smart to figure that out!'"

"So what did he do?" Mrs. Balcomb pressed.

"Well, Dad had Mom take Rae out of the room so he could talk to the officer alone and tell him what he thought. That's when Dad called us back inside, and back we came—our hearts pounding and our knees knocking. Dad sent Ben off to find Mom, then lined us three up between him and the cop, and he says, 'Well boys, this policeman says some kids were jumping on a trampoline in someone's yard on the next street and broke a window. Do either of you know anything about that?' We all were about to faint, our hearts beating a million miles an hour, and sweating and hyperventilating—but none of us said anything. Actually, we were probably saying a lot—just not with our voices." Jesse grinned again. "So Dad called on Sam, and Sam just stared at the floor and could hardly talk. He finally said 'no' and Dad just stared at him. I thought Sam was going to faint. Then Dad turns to Luke and I and asks us, and we just copied Sam and shook our heads, too.

"So Dad says, 'Okay, boys, I appreciate your *honesty.*' Oh, man—when he said that, we just died inside. We knew that he knew we were lying, and it about killed us. Then Dad told us to go outside while he finished talking to the officer. Well, we didn't have to be told that twice and we about fell over each other trying to get out the door. So Dad tells the officer that he is sure we were the culprits and assured him that he would deal with us and that the window would be paid for. Dad said, when he showed the officer out, the three of us were just sitting there on the porch looking like we were about to be sick and that made him and the officer feel pretty confident we would be confessing soon. Dad just went back inside and talked with Mom for a little bit, then brought us three back inside. I'll never forget the way he handled this, he is so wise!" Jesse marveled anew at his Dad's actions so many years before. "He was carrying Rae with him when he called us back in, and Rae was holding onto her stuffed donkey. I just remember her holding it real tight with one hand and holding onto Dad's neck with the other. Dad sat us three down on the couch in the den and he took Rae into the living room and tried again to get her to say what had happened. I'm sure he put us in there so we could hear what was going on, because he spoke loud enough for his voice to carry into the room we were in. So we three are in the den listening to Dad and he says, 'Rae, the policeman is gone now, so I want you to tell me who you saw in that yard today,' And Rae *still* doesn't answer him! So he says, 'Rae, I know that you know, so if you don't tell me, that's disobeying and you'll need a spanking.'

"Well, that really scared us! Luke and I were looking at Sam, getting all freaked-out, and Sam was looking kind of worried, too—but he shook his head and said, 'Rae's never gotten spanked before.' I think Sam was trying to convince himself as much as me and Luke. Then we hear Dad say, 'Rae? Do you want a spanking?' I guess she shook her head, because Dad said, 'Then tell me.' Then Rae says real softly, 'I can't. It's a secret.' So, Dad says, 'That's good that you want to keep a secret, but there are 'good secrets' and 'bad secrets,' and this is a 'bad secret' because it is hiding something someone did wrong—so you shouldn't keep it.' Oh, man, we thought we were done for right then, but Rae still didn't tell on us! So Dad says, 'Rae, if you don't tell me right now, you'll get a spanking.' Dad was sure Rae would spill it after he said that."

"Yeah," Rae interjected into the story, "I remember thinking, 'Oh, no—would he do that?—Would he really spank me?'" She smiled at Jesse, not divulging anything of his story.

The suspense killing his audience, several spoke at once, "So, did she tell?"

Jesse smiled, relishing their captivated expressions. "No, she didn't!" Mouths fell open around the table, as Jesse pressed on, "Dad was floored that a four-year-old could be so resolute! Essentially, she called his bluff—but Rae didn't know that. Well, now, Dad felt bad, because now he had to follow through with his threat and he didn't think he would have to do that."

Mr. Windom arched an eyebrow. "So did he spank her?"

Jesse bobbed his head sadly. "Yeah, he leaned her over his knee, took a deep breath, and paddled her a few times. He said it broke his heart."

"And you boys just sat there and let her get spanked for that?" Ruth and Mrs. Balcomb were indignant.

Jesse nodded. "Yeah, we did. We were so sure he wouldn't go through with it, mostly because Sam was so sure. Wow, we were so surprised when he did!—And when we heard Rae cry, all three of us burst into tears. Sam was just freaked-out—he jumped off that sofa like a rocket and ran into the living room, sobbing worse than Rae was—and he was a twelve-year-old-boy! Well, he goes bursting in there and there was Dad sitting there holding Rae in his arms, crying too! Sam told me later how awful it was seeing Dad cry, knowing it was his fault. So he runs in and blurts out, 'I'm sorry dad, I lied! Rae didn't do anything wrong—it was my fault! I told her not to tell!' And he's crying and blubbering all over the place and says, 'I'm sorry, Rae—I didn't think you'd really get a spanking!' Well, that didn't set very well with Dad on a couple of different levels. First he didn't like that Sam was betting against him by not believing that he would follow through with what he said he would do. . . and second, that Sam had implied that Rae had gotten spanked for nothing—like Dad was being unfair, or something. Sam said Dad gave him this real stern look and said, 'Sam, Rae got a spanking for disobeying me—not for anything you did! Now, are you going to tell me what you were doing in someone else's yard without permission?' So then, Sam finally confessed the whole thing."

"Where were you and Luke while he was confessing?" Mr. Windom wanted to know.

"We were still in the den, listening."

"You let him take the full blame?"

462

"He told us not to tell!" Jesse shrugged sheepishly, "—It was a 'brother thing.'" Jesse grinned, assuring his audience, "Hang on—we're getting there!" And he resumed his story, "While Sam was still trying to keep his end of the pact by leaving us out of it, Luke and I were back in the den crying and feeling guilty, and we hear Sam say, 'I was the one jumping on the trampoline, Dad. I didn't know Rae followed us over there.' That meant he was taking the whole blame on himself, since he never did get a turn on the trampoline, but he slipped—he said 'us,' and Dad picked up on it right away. Dad says, '*Us?* Your brothers were there, too?' Well Sam just stood there, speechless, trying to think of a way to backpedal out of what he'd just said. Finally, Luke and I just couldn't take it anymore; we were sobbing our eyes out—and before Sam could answer, we just about fell over each other trying to get in there and confess, too. Dad looks at us and says, 'So it was all three of you?' We all just nodded. So Dad says, 'How did the window get broken?'

"That's when we all finally manned-up and quit hedging and lying and blaming each other, and Luke admitted everything and told him how he accidently kicked the soccer ball into the window. I was real impressed with him for that; he was only like eight-years-old back then, and he just stood up straight and owned up to it. I'm sure he would have done that sooner if Sam and I hadn't leaned on him to keep quiet—I mean, he was ready to tell the policeman everything when he first pulled up to our house. So Dad squints at Luke and says, 'Why were you holding your soccer ball while you were jumping on a trampoline?' That still seems funny to me that he asked that—I mean, here we are in the middle of all this drama, and that little detail bugs him." Jesse grinned, "Well, anyway, now it was my turn to confess; Luke just did, so I knew I needed to. I wiped my eyes and nose and stepped forward and said, 'I threw it at him while he was jumping; I was just teasing him, and he just caught it and held onto it.' Dad just sat there holding Rae and staring at the three of us, then he says, 'And when you were caught, the three of you beat it out of that yard and left your sister behind?' He glared at us all real hard." Jesse again demonstrated.

"Then he said—and this is what really made us realize what we'd done—he said, 'Boys, it's a good thing for Rae that all that man did was call the police!' Man that really nailed us. Here we were so focused on how we played on someone else's trampoline without permission that we completely missed the danger we'd left Rae in. Sam came forward and said, 'When the window broke, a man inside started yelling at us and we all ran in different directions, Dad—we didn't know we left her behind until we all got back home.' Then *he* owns it!—He says, 'I'm sorry dad, it's my fault; I should have made sure she was with me.' And then he really surprised me—I think this is where I really realized just how hard he was taking it. Sam is very quiet natured—like my dad; it's hard to tell sometimes what he's thinking—but, he went over to Rae right then and he asked her to forgive him! He was feeling so bad that his voice broke when he said it." Jesse shook his head. "We all felt terrible by then."

The Gang leaned closer. "Did she?"

Jesse nodded. "Yeah, she did. She climbed down out of Dad's lap and went over and hugged Sam. Then Luke and I started apologizing all over the place, and she forgave us and hugged us, too." Jesse smiled as he leaned back in his chair and tapped the table with a knuckle. "Four years old!" He nodded to Rae admiringly. "You would think she would just be mad at us for getting her into trouble, but she forgave us!" He smiled for another moment, then continued, "A week or so after this, when Dad found out how that man shook Rae and scared her so bad—wow, was he ever mad! He marched over to the man's house with his checkbook and asked him how much to make it square with his window, and wrote him a check right then. Once the guy accepted his check, Dad explained to the man that he needed to come and apologize to Rae for handling her so roughly and scaring her so bad, 'so that he wouldn't be arrested for it.'" Jesse chuckled again, "That's how he put it! And I guess the man understood just what Dad meant because he came right over to our house with Dad, and apologized to Rae! And you know what Rae did? She forgave him, too!" Jesse shook his head, incredulous anew.

Mr. Peterman piped up again, "So, what happened to you and your brothers? Did you get in trouble for all that?"

Jesse glanced downward and grinned again, nodding. "Ohhhh, yeah." Jesse stretched out the word and chuckled, "We got grounded big time! Once Rae was out of the room, Dad gave us a stern look and said, 'Boys, what you did today was careless and foolish toward your sister, and disrespectful of our neighbors. I'm going to pay for that window to be fixed, and the three of you are all grounded until you've worked off the cost. There'll be no more flying hours for Sam and nothing but school and chores for all three of you—that means nothing fun, nothing entertaining, and nothing even remotely amusing until that happens! You got that? And you get to take turns making Rae's bed, cleaning her room for two weeks each for being so irresponsible with her—and while you're at it, you might think about thanking God for his mercy that nothing worse happened to your sister after you left her stranded in a stranger's yard. Now go up to your rooms.' After that, we never let Rae out of our sight! Yeah, that punishment was really stiff.—especially for Sam, with his flying hours. We were grounded for over three months working off that broken window—but, considering what could have happened to Rae, I think all three of us felt like we got off pretty easy. As the years went by, the older we got, the more I think we realized that—even now, just thinking about what could have happened kind of freaks me out. Man, I just know I'm going to be the world's worst over-protective dad when Julie and I have kids!"

Jesse chuckled again then paused, marveling. "Dad was so amazing, here we were feeling so bad about how we'd disappointed him, then he told us later that once it was all said and done, he was actually, ultimately, proud of all four of us! He said he was proud of Rae for being so loyal in the face of getting punished, and of us boys for being bad at lying and for finally owning up to everything when we realized Rae had gotten in trouble over it. He said most kids would have never owned up to it, especially after it had snowballed as far as it had. His saying that really surprised us—how he could find something to be proud of in that. . .I just thought it was amazingly generous of him, considering all the trouble we'd caused."

Rae laughed, "You know what Dad always said to you guys. . ."

Jesse grinned and the two of them quoted in unison, imitating their dad, "I'm not raising you to be good kids, I'm raising you to be good men!"

They both chuckled, then Jesse stared off for a moment more. "You know, I just hope when I have kids, I can be even half the dad my dad has been."

They both chuckled and Jesse shrugged. "Well, end of story. I hope I didn't bore you to death."

"Heaven's no!—That was quite a story! Very entertaining!" Mrs. Balcomb assured, and the rest of the Gang, along with Heath and Ruth all nodded heartily in agreement.

After dinner, Ruth and Rae brought in pie and tea, and once the Gang finished theirs, they nodded their appreciation to Jesse, then filed out to get settled in front of the TV in time for their favorite game show. Jesse and Heath lingered at the table, talking, while Ruth and Rae cleared away the dishes and cleaned up, then joined the men.

When Heath excused himself to get Nate ready for bed, Ruth turned to their guest. "Jesse, where are you planning to spend the night?"

"Well, I saw a Mega 8 Motel on my way through town this afternoon. I was planning to just stay there tonight—if I can find my way back there without getting lost again!"

"Nonsense! You're welcome to stay here—no sense paying for a room! This way, you and Rae will have more time to visit, and you sure don't want to get lost out there at night!" That was enough to convince Jesse. Ruth and Heath decided to turn in around 10 p.m., but Rae and Jesse talked past midnight. She finally left for her room after Jesse was made comfortable on the sofa in the parlor.

The next morning after another lively meal with the Gang, Jesse gathered his things to go—and as he had with the insurance adjuster, Heath drew Jesse a map back to the main highway. Then, with Nate on his arm, Jesse bounced him a couple of times, gave him a kiss then handed him back to Heath, "Bye Nate!" He gave Ruth a hug then looked into her face for a moment, as warm thougths of his mother drifted through his mind. "It's been a pleasure meeting you Ruth. Thank you again for taking care of my sister." Next, he reached and shook Heath's hand appreciatively. "Thank you too, Heath—I'm glad Rae ended up here with both of you." Then he set out again for Heartland Airfield, surprised to discover it was only a twenty minute drive with good directions.

When he returned to Florida, his dad was anxiously awaiting news of his daughter. "How's Rae?"

"She's looks really good, Dad—she's looking more relaxed and happier than I've seen her in months. I think she's in good hands up there."

"Really? Well, I'm glad to hear that." Joe nodded, thinking for a moment. "And, how's her Cessna?"

"Shot up—just like Rae said. The insurance investigator was there yesterday morning and Rae said they'll start patching this afternoon, and the replacement parts should be in any day." Jesse nodded. "Those are good people Rae is staying with, Dad." The relief in Joe's face was evident, as Jesse continued, "That Ruth... there's just something about her." He shook his head. "I can sure see why Rae likes her so well—she reminds me of Mom in some ways... And if you close your eyes and listen, she sounds kind of like Mom—but with a drawl."

"Like your mom with a drawl?" Joe grinned, amused, "Well, that sounds *very* interesting!"

Chapter 35

Thursday, Rae followed Ruth around like a puppy all morning, helping her with the chores, chatting her up while scarcely letting her out of her sight. Amused and charmed, Ruth didn't mind the gab—or the help. She even let Rae follow her upstairs to the Dawson's personal living space, an area normally off-limits to their boarders. At the top of the stairs, Ruth stopped at the 'T' where the front and back hallways intersected. "Rae, hon, how about you collecting the sheets off all our beds." Rae nodded eagerly, as Ruth gave directions, "The bedrooms we use are down that back hall. Heath's is the first on the left across from the bathroom, and then Nate's is next to his at the end of the hall, and mine is across from Nate's, the last door on the right—don't worry about the other rooms. I'll get the towels from the bathrooms."

Rae nodded again and got right to work, starting in the back rooms and working forward. Entering Ruth's room, she was surprised at its large size. Getting to work, she turned back the quilt and blankets and pulled off the sheets, then shook the pillows out of their cases. As she gathered the pile of sheets into her arms and straightened up, she noticed on the wall a painting of a country scene that warmed her heart, making her smile. *I love that!* She stepped closer. *It must be one of Heath's dad's paintings—he said there were a few up here.* She gazed for a moment more, taking in the details, smiling to herself. Wondering about others, she glanced around the remaining walls, finding a second. This one, a portrait of an attractive red-headed woman on a porch swing. Captivated, Rae dropped the sheets and stepped over to it. *Is that Ruth?* Her hand to her heart, Rae gazed at it, awed and delighted. The woman's expression seemed to capture the warmth of that moment on her porch. *Wow! They must have been so in love!* Though she would never meet Nathaniel Dawson, Rae decided right then that she adored him. Gathering the linens she'd let fall, her gaze lingered on the painting as she headed for Nate's room, making a point to look for a painting in there, too.

Nate's walls displayed a series of smaller paintings depicting children, boys and girls—some playing, others cuddling and being cuddled. Rae drew close, examining each one. *The little boy in these paintings looks just like Nate.* She squinted, puzzling. But *Heath said his dad never knew Nate.* Suddenly, her eyebrows arched. *These must be of Heath!* Her mouth fell open at the resemblance to his son. *He looks just like Nate!* Returning to her task, she lowered the side of Nate's crib, she quickly gathered the sheet then stepped to the changing table by the window for a moist towelette to wipe down the mattress. Glancing out the window, she looked across and to her left at the carriage house garage, and to her right, she could see the woods beyond the clearing, again wondering how she'd ended up on Ruth's porch that rainy night...*and coming from the opposite direction I should have.* She shook her head, puzzled anew. *I must have gone around and way past it, then somehow circled back. Wow, I was really turned around!—It's a miracle I made it here at all!* Suddenly she caught herself, again pushing thoughts of God's help to the back of her mind.

Adding Nate's sheet and mattress pad to her bundle, Rae continued up the hall to Heath's room, repeating the process from Ruth's. When she came around the bed, she noticed a guitar on a stand in the corner, and arched a curious eyebrow. *He plays the guitar? Wow, who would have thought that?* Scanning the walls, she spied another painting, this one a close-up of a baby sucking on his fist as he peered over the broad shoulder of the man who held him. Again she drew close, moved by its warmth. *That must be Heath again.* She smiled as she lingered on the baby's sleepy eyes.

"It's like you can just reach into that painting and pick him up, isn't it?" Ruth's voice startled Rae, who turned suddenly, finding Ruth in the doorway with an armful of towels.

Recovering quickly, Rae nodded, her eyes and whole face smiling. "It sure does! Heath said there were more paintings up here. I saw the ones of him in Nate's room, too—and the one of you in your room. They're amazing, Ruth!"

Ruth nodded, smiling. "I think so, too and I never get tired of looking at them. Actually, this one in here isn't of Heath—it's Nate. Doesn't it look just like him?"

Rae squinted, confused. "I thought it was Heath when he was a baby; he said his dad never knew Nate."

"The pictures in Nate's room are of Heath and his sisters—Heath's dad painted those. This one is of Nate—Heath painted it from a photo I made." She smiled warmly at it, "But you're right, it does look like Heath. Their baby pictures look almost identical. The only way I can tell which is which is by what they are wearing in them."

Rae's eyes widened, "Heath painted this?" When Ruth nodded, Rae shook her head, marveling. "If he can paint like this, it's too bad he has to use all his time just doing signs."

Ruth chuckled, tilting her head. "Too bad. . .?" She smiled knowingly, "You just haven't seen Heath's signs!"

Tearing herself away from the painting of Nate, Rae glanced around for more, finding another on the opposite wall of an elderly man with a young girl in each of his arms, and a little boy riding piggy-back,

"These look like the same kids as the ones in Nate's room, only a little older. Are they Heath and his sisters, too?" Ruth nodded and Rae pointed to the man. "Is this Heath's dad?"

"No, hon, that's his granddad."

Rae studied it for a moment. "Really? He sure looks a lot like Heath—just old."

Ruth nodded. "Yes, he does. . . Odd how that is—the Dawson men all seem to look just like each other."

"I know what you mean—Sam, my oldest brother, looks like a younger version of my dad, and except for the hair styles, pictures of Dad at Sam's age look like the same person, too."

Ruth nodded. ". . .And you look just like your mama."

Rae also nodded and her eyes again fell on the guitar below the painting. "So, Heath plays the guitar?"

Ruth seemed suddenly sad. "Well, he used to. . . I haven't seen him pick up that guitar in a couple of years now. It's a shame, too—he was pretty good at it and he enjoyed it so much."

"If he likes it so much, why did he quit?"

Ruth sighed. "I don't know for sure—I think it had to do with Amy, but he never said. He still keeps it, though, so who knows? Maybe someday he'll pick it up again." She thought for a moment. "He used to watch his dad play when he was little, and wanted to learn, so his dad taught him. Maybe he'll teach Nate when he's up to it." She shrugged. "Well, let's get these sheets downstairs and start a load."

** *** **

That afternoon Orby arrived as expected. Rae had been watching for his truck and hurried outside as soon as he drove up. Patching materials in hand, Orby greeted her in his congenial manner, then they pulled open the barn doors and dragged Rae's aircraft out into the clearing. Orby began by going over the basics of the patching process. "It's just your standard patching—you already know how to do it, I just want to show you in case you don't use this brand. You know about all the sanding, so I'll just skip that—the thing with this is, when we get to the actual patching, you just got to be real careful with this fiberglass goo once it's mixed—and it smells real nasty, too, so we got to make sure we do that outside. The holes in the fuel tanks will be a little trickier—we got to reinforce the tanks before doing the fiberglass patching. I brung along the stuff for doing that, so I'll start on them today." He glanced over at Rae, who nodded, then he continued. "In the meanwhile, you can get started on sanding them other holes. I thought we could just get all that done first, before we think about mixing the goo. With all the holes we got, we may not even get to the patching for a couple of days."

Rae nodded, and they each found a bullet hole and began. Orby at the pilot-side wing, Rae at the cockpit door below him. As she began, Rae asked, "Oh, Orby—what about payment? Do you charge by the hour or by the job? I'll need an invoice for my dad when we're done—and don't forget to include when you came up to tow it out of the field."

Having sensed the Lord's hand that first day, Orby considered it a privilege to be included in Adonai's plans. He just grinned his big, toothy grin and shook his head. "Oh, Ms. Rae, I weren't expecting no payment from you! I'm glad to help you out. All you need to worry about is the cost of these patching materials and them parts I ordered."

Surprised, Rae stopped sanding, not knowing what to say. *He's a total stranger and he's going to do this for free?* She protested, "Orby, your time is worth something."

Orby shook his head. "No, no, Ms. Rae—I already made up my mind about that the day I come out to your aircraft with Neal and offered to help. Just don't you worry none about paying me, you hear?"

Orby returned to his work, but Rae stared at him a moment longer, eyeing him suspiciously—wondering about the catch. She tried again, "But this is going to take some time—and there are a lot of holes."

Orby glanced at her bafflement and just grinned again. "Yeah, I know. That's why we best go on and get started."

Rae still hesitated. "You sure?" When Orby only nodded, Rae stared at him another moment, then shrugged doubtfully. "Okay. Well, thanks. I appreciate it and I'm sure my dad will too."

** *** **

As Rae and Orby sanded, Andrea pulled off the road onto Ruth's long driveway. Squinting ahead to her left, she shook her head quizzically. *Is that an airplane?* As she drew closer, the aircraft in front of Ruth's Barn took shape. *What is Ruth doing with an airplane in her yard?* She stared to her left incredulously as she drove up the driveway, then looked again at a man in overalls next to it. *Is that Orby Grumwall?* Andrea puzzled, shaking her head again as she pulled up to the garage and got out of her car. She stood, pulling her coat close around her against the chill, her hand at her brow, shielding her eyes from the sun. The man in the overalls took notice. "Well, hey, Ms. Andrea!" Orby waved as he called to her.

Andrea waved back to him. "Hey, Orby!" Orby smiled his wide smile at her, then returned to his work. Andrea watched him a moment more, wondering about the girl with him, and why they decided to work on an airplane in Ruth's clearing. Full of questions, Andrea decided to ask them of Ruth—inside, where it was warm—and headed up the back steps onto the wrap-around porch to the kitchen door, and knocked. Laying Nate down for his nap, it was a moment before Ruth opened the door and beckoned her in. Andrea squinted at her. "Ruth, there's an airplane in front of your barn."

"An airplane?" She stepped past Andrea onto the porch, feigning surprise. "How did that get out there?" Ruth tried to look puzzled as Andrea stared at her, not buying her act, so Ruth just grinned, waving her in. "C'mon inside, Andrea—have I got a story for you!" She waved at Orby and Rae, then ushered Andrea inside. Reaching for the tea kettle, Ruth began filling it at the sink, speaking as Andrea set down her tote bag and pulled off her coat, "The muffins are in the oven, hon. Why don't you get your health checks done while I get tea on? Then we can talk without being interrupted." Andrea agreed and headed through the louver door into the front room. Ruth set the kettle down on the stove and turned the knob, then followed her. Stopping at the door, she rang the supper bell to summon the Gang. Andrea quickly went through her routine with each of the Gang as Ruth set the kitchen table for their afternoon tea.

** *** **

Outside, as Orby sanded, he glanced upward. *Okay, Father, I know you got something up your sleeve here with Ms. Rae—is there anything you want me to say to her?* Not sensing anything immediately, he decided after a few moments to just get to know her a little better. "So, Ms. Rae, what made you want to become a mechanic?"

"I don't know. . . I always liked taking things apart and putting them back together. I used to take apart my toys all the time when I was little, but most of the time I couldn't get them back together. My parents finally just started getting me toys that were *meant* to be taken apart."

Orby chuckled. "And what made you get interested in repairing aircraft and being a pilot?"

"My dad owns an aviation business—aircraft were always just part life for us. My brothers and I all started learning to fly when we turned twelve."

Orby grinned as he worked. "Well, now, how about that! You musta had all the kids wanting to come to your birthday parties!" Rae smiled, tickled and Orby glanced down at her. "So, Ms. Rae, didn't Neal say you was from Florida? How did you end up in Georgia?"

"I was flying a charter. I was just supposed to pick someone up and do a turn-around."

"A turn-around?" Orby chuckled, teasing, "—And you been here how long?"

Rae grinned. "A week."

"Well, it seems to me that's one long turn-around!" He laughed, "So what happened to your passenger? You figure he found another flight somewhere's else?"

Rae shrugged. "I don't know. . .maybe he rented a car—either that or he *walked* to Florida." She chuckled along with Orby. "I know he found a way down there though, because my brother just brought him back yesterday."

"So your brother was here?"

"Yeah, he left this morning."

"He come up to see you're okay?"

Rae smiled, nodding. "Yeah, Dad said that client is how he found out what happened; he called Dad wondering about his ride."

"That right?"

"Yeah, and while Dad was scratching his head about that, a friend called him saying he thought he saw our Cessna on the news—so Dad turned on the TV and there it was."

"Well now, that must have been kind of upsetting for him to know that was you in that mess."

"Well, he didn't know it was me right away—I had traded routes with another pilot and Dad thought it was him."

"How'd he find out it was you?"

"When the other pilot walked into the room and asked what's going on." Rae chuckled, imagining the scene anew. *"That's* when Dad got upset."

"I'll bet so!"

"Right then is when I called him after I landed in the field." Rae shrugged, "You already know the rest."

Orby nodded, reaching for another topic. "So you said you have brothers that fly?"

"Yeah, three of them and another one that's a mechanic like me."

"The other one don't fly?"

"No, he's deaf."

"Deaf? Yeah, well I guess that would make it hard with all the communication being by radio." Orby nodded. "You got any sisters?"

"No, I'm the only girl."

"The only girl in all those boys? I'll bet your mama was real glad when you come along."

Rae stiffened, her answer abrupt. "Yeah." She didn't elaborate.

Immediately picking up on her tension, Orby glanced over at her. *Just 'yeah'? That's it? Hmmm. . .* His thoughts turned heavenward again. *There a problem with her mama, Lord?* Orby ventured further, "Does your whole family work with you and your dad?"

Glad Orby had moved on from the subject of her mother, Rae nodded. "Yeah, all of us do. My uncle used to, but he retired."

"What about your mama? She work there, too? In the office or something?"

Rae winced, again abrupt. "No." She reached for another subject. "How about you, Orby? You got any brothers or sisters?"

Orby's eyes narrowed. *There's another one of them one-word answers about her mama—and she sure changed the subject fast this time! What do you make of that, Lord?* He put that on a back burner for a moment to answer her question, "I just have me a baby sister." He chuckled at himself, "Only she ain't no baby no more; she's married and lives in North Carolina—but I still call her my baby sister. I been calling her that ever since I was a little kid."

"I bet you were a good big brother."

"Well, I tried to be, but we had our moments."

"Yeah, I've had a few 'moments' with my brothers, too."

Orby paused a bit as though listening, then chuckled and continued. "You know, talking about 'being good'—it's real interesting how you think when you're a little kid."

Rae glanced over at him. "Like what?"

"You ever heard that saying about how 'the good die young'?" When Orby saw Rae's nod, he continued, "Well, I heard someone say that once when I was little, and it kinda scared me. I remember thinking, 'I'm gonna die soon if I'm good?'" He chuckled again, "So, I started being kinda naughty and mean, because I thought it would keep me from dying." Rae laughed as Orby smiled to himself at the memory, then a sadness crossed his face. "But it was hard to keep it up because I could see it was hurtful to my grandma, plus I knew it made God sad—and I just hated the thought of making God sad."

Rae glanced up from her sanding for a moment, unable to imagine such a concern in a child. "How old were you?"

Orby squinted to help him recall. "Oh, about four, I think—maybe five."

Rae stopped sanding. "Really? That young?" *Actually, that isn't so hard to believe that about him. . .* As she continued with her sanding, a thought struck her. "That's pretty young to be worrying about dying."

"Yeah, well, it was just a little boy trying to make sense of life—or at least, make sense of why young people die, especially little kids."

"Little kids?"

"Yeah, little kids dying is the hardest of all to understand. That's why I was doing all that wondering when I was a kid—I had me a little sister, but she died about then and I just couldn't figure it out. Then, I heard some grown-ups talking and one of them said that—about the good dying young, and it just got me to thinking."

"Your little sister died?" Rae was pierced through. "What happened to her?"

Orby shrugged. "I don't know, I never found out."

"Really?—Your parents never told you?"

"Nope. My folks was so sad about it they would just set to crying when I asked, so I didn't want to cause them no extra grief by keeping on asking. They was better, though, after my baby sister was born."

"So your sisters never knew each other?"

"Nope."

"And you never found out what happened to the other one? Not even when you got older?"

Orby shook his head. "Well, my folks passed a few years later, so I never found out."

Rae's eyes widened. "Your parents died when you were little, too? Both of them?"

"Yeah, when I was seven. They was in a car wreck—my grandma raised me and my baby sister after that."

Shaking her head, Rae exhaled audibly, "Wow, I'll bet you were mad at God for a long time over that."

Orby stopped sanding and turned to her, his elbow on the fuselage. "Mad? No, I don't remember feeling mad or nothing, Ms. Rae. I guess I just figured God was just as sad as we was." He eyed her for a moment, then resumed his sanding. "I think it's His pleasure to receive people who die, but I don't think He takes no pleasure in them dying."

Rae considered that then side stepped it, returning to Orby's childhood. "And your grandma never told you what happened to your sister, either?"

"Nope. Grown-ups didn't talk much about stuff like that—especially to kids."

"Where's your grandma now?"

"Oh, she's gone now, too—a few years back."

Rae's eyebrows knitted. *Wow, he's lost just about everyone.* "Orby, I'm so sorry."

Orby grinned. "Well now, that's real nice of you to say that, Ms. Rae—but it's okay; I still got my baby sister and my Heavenly Father."

How can he even say that? She eyed him for a moment. "How do you stay so cheerful like that after losing so many family members?"

"Oh, you just do your best. My grandma was real helpful, and I got the Lord to comfort me—no one can comfort a hurting heart like He can."

Rae scoffed under her breath. "But He's the one who took them—why would you even want to go to Him for comfort?"

Orby stopped sanding again, eyeing her for a moment. "Where else you going to go, Ms. Rae?"

Eyes narrowing, Rae thought about that for a moment, then just shrugged and resumed sanding. As he worked, Orby's thoughts turned heavenward. *Okay Abba, I can see there's something there, but I don't know exactly what. I pray you'll open a door.* He shrugged and nodded. *Okay then...* And again addressed Rae, "So, Ms. Rae—getting back to what you was saying about ending up in Georgia and swapping charters with that other pilot, you said your daddy didn't know you swapped?"

Rae winced. "No. I traded and didn't tell him—it's a long story." She shook her head. "I figured I'd just tell Dad when I got back." She shook her head. "Man, I never do stuff like that—I guess this was my punishment for going against my dad."

Orby stopped sanding again. "Oh, you think God is punishing you?"

Rae shrugged. "Yeah, maybe."

"Well, Ms. Rae, there's punishment and there's 'natural consequences.' It seems to me, punishment comes after breaking God's laws and not repenting once you know you done wrong—and stealing His Glory, too; that's something God just don't put up with—and sinning on purpose and stuff. But He's real merciful—He lets you know when you're straying and gives you lots of chances to come around. So, to have His punishment come down on you, you got to be real determined to keep on sinning." He paused a moment. "You know, it seems to me that sometimes when people think they're being punished, it's really just God giving them a test." Orby reached for the materials to begin patching the fuel tank in the wing he was working on.

Rae eyed him curiously. "So, how do you tell the difference?"

Orby shrugged, preparing the patch. "Well, a test is kind of like God checking in on something He already taught you, and sometimes stretching it some so's He can deepen your faith. Things like putting God first, sticking with Him when things get rough—or when they don't go the way you expect, or choosing His ways over your own—stuff like that. I had me a Sunday school teacher when I was a kid, and she told us about how God gives us tests and then gives us all kinds of chances to get it right. That made me think of my school teacher that same year, and how she seemed like she really wanted us to do good in school. She would have us take turns reading out loud and help us until we could get all the words right—or like when she would give us a spelling test on Thursdays. I usually missed a few the first time, but she always gave us another chance on Friday. I would practice my words that night and usually got 'em all right the next day.

"I imagined God to be like that—giving us a test and letting us keep on trying 'til we pass, instead of just letting us fail it and saying 'That's it!' God is like that teacher, only He usually gives us more than just two chances. He just keeps forgiving and forgiving, and helping you and encouraging you along the way. He's real *kind,* that way. I mean, how many times do we get the same type of thing come up over and over and over again? Oh, sometimes it don't seem like the same thing on the surface—but if you look real close, it's just the same old problem showing up again and again. That's just God giving us another chance to pass our test." Rae listened quietly, amazed at how true his example was to her own life. Orby continued, "Like Peter had him a test in Matthew 26. He said even if he had to die, he wouldn't deny

Yeshua, and when he said that, I imagine God saying, 'Well, now, I think I'll test him on that!' And that's what He done, and you know how that turned out."

Wondering why he called Jesus 'Yeshua,' Rae nodded. "He denied Him three times."

Orby nodded. "That's right—even before that chapter was over, he done that! But you know, God didn't just leave him there with that 'F' on his test. He encouraged him and let him at it again in John 21, when Yeshua asked him those three times if he loved Him—some folks think it was one for each time he denied Him. Then after that, Peter passed his test—and kept on passing it 'til he become what Yeshua said he would in Matthew 16:18—the rock He built His church on." Orby emphasized that with a nod of his head. "One day, I was reading the Word and in Isaiah 55, I come across this passage in verse eleven, where God said that 'His Word will not return to Him empty, but will accomplish what He desires and achieves the purpose that He sent it for.' And that set me to thinking about how that Word from God would just keep on and on until it gets done with what it was sent to do—and it kind of reminded me of that 'test taking 'til you get it right' business."

"So, which one is this?—A test or punishment?"

Orby stopped sanding for a moment as he considered that. "Well, Ms. Rae," he stepped over to the cowling and smoothed his hand over the bullet holes in it, marveling as he spoke, "the more I think about these holes, the more I praise God that He looked after you like He did. So I'm guessing it's some kind of test—because, it seems to me like He was too busy rescuing you to be punishing you." Pressing his lips together, Orby nodded again, then he returned to patching the wing.

Rae squinted; doubtful. "Rescuing me?" She chuckled, disagreeing. "I did someone a favor—and look what happened!"

She erected a finger for each event: "I had to abort my landing and almost crashed into a mob of people. My aircraft got shot up, *I* got shot, I lost my fuel load and nearly ended up in the trees, and when I landed in that field I almost didn't stop in time—and just about ran into those trees. Then, I got stranded out there for a couple of days and nearly froze to death—and about starved. Then, when I tried to get help, I got lost in the woods and nearly died of hypothermia in that storm—and then I almost broke my neck falling down an embankment. After that I got sick as a dog and just about died from that. Exactly how is that 'looking after' me?—It seems more like punishment to me."

Orby nodded slowly, more certain now than ever of God's hand on her. "Yeah, Ms. Rae, you sure been having a time of it since you been in Georgia, haven't you? But "Punishment? Hmm…Well, it seems to me, Ms. Rae, that them folks who feel like God's punishing them, usually have done something they think is deserving of it. You been having some issues with God, Ms. Rae? Something happen that's challenged your walk with Him?"

Rae bristled. "My walk with Him? What makes you think I had a walk with Him?"

Noticing the past-tense, Orby eyed her for a moment. "Why, I sense it in my spirit, Ms. Rae—I sensed it that first day we met when I come out to see your aircraft." He patted the fuselage as he spoke it, then he smiled, waving his sanding block at her. "You been away for a little while, but He's got His eye on you."

Rae's eyes narrowed at his remark. "Now, that right there— how would you know if I've been away a little while?"

"It was just an impression I got, that's all."

"An impression?"

Orby nodded then focused again on the fuel tank patch. "That's right."

"What?—Like from God, or something?"

Orby met her questioning gaze. "That's right, Ms. Rae." Satisfied with the patch on the fuel tank of the first wing, he moved over to the other. Also finished with the hole in the cockpit door, Rae moved around to the other side, as well. Squinting, she puzzled for another moment, wondering if he might have a few more of those 'impressions'—ones that could answer a few nagging questions. . .but she hesitated to ask.

Watching her, Orby noticed the squint, and asked, "You got something on your mind, Ms. Rae?"

Rae struggled within herself, not certain she wanted to hear—but very sure she wanted to know. Sighing, she fell suddenly serious. "Why are all those bad things happening, Orby? It just seems like God is trying to take me out or something."

"Well, Ms. Rae, first of all, it seems to me that God don't have to *try* to take you out: if He wants you dead, you'd be dead—end of story. So it ain't God that's trying to take you out."

"So, if He's not trying to kill me, then I guess He's just not trying to help me, either."

Orby shook his head. "Oh, I wouldn't say He ain't trying to help you—it seems to me that God's been helping you a whole lot! In that list you just gave me, I heard you say 'almost' and 'nearly' and 'just about,' about two or three times a piece—and I think I heard a 'thought I was going to,' in there, too." Orby nodded. "There was a whole lot of close calls in there, but you're still here—so it seems to me that God's been working over-time *rescuing* you from all of those things. In fact, it seems to me like you maybe have worn out a few of your guardian angels in all that—and the rest probably have taken up biting their fingernails."

Rae couldn't help but grin at the image in her mind of nervous angels. She watched him for a moment as he worked on the hole in the fuel tank he was reinforcing, then sighed again, her forehead furrowing. "So, God just lets you keep wearing out angels while He beats you down until you can't take it anymore?"

"Naw, it don't seem to me like it's God who's beating you down. It could be He's just using our troubles to steer us into his Will—and sometimes, it's the Evil One trying to get you to curse God—like with Job (Job 1:11 & 2:5). The devil likes to mess with us and get us to blame God for the bad stuff that happens—when God just wants to help us through it. But, if you don't want God, or His help in your life, He won't butt-in. He's real polite that way—He'll just wait until you ask Him."

"So, God just sits on His hands while everything goes to pieces, unless you ask? That just seems. . .well. . .*sick.*"

"Well, you're sick too, then—'cause you do that."

"Me? What do you mean? When?"

"When you and Neal came down to Potterville that day we first met. Those other mechanics couldn't find the problem with Mr. H's Cessna. You knew what it was, but they wasn't interested in your help. So, what did you do? You stepped away and didn't force your help on them—you waited until Mr. H asked you." He nodded. "You do it, so does God. I think sometimes He lets things happen just so's we'll see how much we need Him. It seems to me that people don't tend to think about God when things are going good—it ain't until things get rough that they call out to Him—and when they do, He promises to answer."

"Well, if you only call on someone when you're having a problem—aren't you just 'using' them?" Rae countered.

Orby shrugged, leaning on the wing. "No more than you're 'using' a plumber when you call one."

"Huh?"

"When your toilet overflows, don't you 'use' a plumber? It seems to me that when you have a problem, you can either call someone who knows how to fix it right, or just keep on in your troubles. So you can let that backed-up toilet keep on over-flowing, and keep on trying to clean up all that junk the rest of your life, or you can call someone who can fix it. Does that plumber feel 'used' when you call him? Naw, he wants you to call him—and last I checked, plumbers don't go door to door asking—it's pretty much up to you to make the call, even if it's only because you don't have nowhere's else to go."

Rae couldn't help but think of how a toilet overflowing seemed to be a good description of how things had been going the past eight months. She mulled it over in her mind, thinking about how she'd been trying to fix the toilet herself all that time, then Orby nodded to himself and continued. "Just like that plumber is waiting for your call, so is God. Now, what God wants is a relationship with us, so He makes Hisself available to us in our troubles, and in the process of calling on Him for help, He develops that relationship with us—kind of like that plumber. So, it ain't 'using' God to call on Him, it's just one of His ways to begin a relationship—or pick one up that someone walked away from." Her face toward the hole she was sanding, Orby didn't notice Rae winced at that, and he contnued, "Like take the two of us, for instance. You called because you needed some help with this here aircraft, and as a result, we're talking and becoming friends. So, was it 'using' me when you called for help?"

Rae shrugged. "I guess not." She smiled to herself, then drew a deep breath as her shoulders relaxed a bit. Just talking to Orby, she began to gain some clarity that she had not sensed in months. After a moment, she tilted her head and sighed, "If He can prevent all those things from happening, why didn't He just do that?"

Orby smiled. "Well now, how would you have knowed He was helping you if none of those things ever happened? You been looking at this all wrong, Ms. Rae, maybe that's why you feel like God is picking on you."

"So, what's the right way to look at it?"

Orby grinned that wide grin again. "That He's been helping you—*a lot!*—And you're just not seeing it. Like, where would you be right now if He didn't step in when you were coming into the Heartland airport?"

"What do you mean?"

"I mean, that bullet that grazed your neck—maybe, like you said, it would have gone clean through your neck if He didn't step in. What about the bullets that hit your engine? You're a mechanic—how good for your engine are bullets? It shoulda quit right then and there, and come down on the runway—maybe on top of all those people, or on the Interstate you flew over, and not waited 'til you ran out of fuel and come down in that field. And, speaking of that—you said all you saw was just trees everywhere you looked—and then a field just all-of-a-sudden opened up right in front of you—right when you was going down. So, if God didn't step in like He did all those times that day, where would you be right now?"

She shrugged. "Probably dead."

"And so would those people on the runway. What about a couple days later? Heath knew there was a storm coming—what woulda happened if he had changed his mind about going hunting that day? And what if he didn't go that way home from his tree stand? Would you have knowed there was any shelter nearby? And how did you find Ms. Ruth's house, at night, in the rain, when you was all turned around and lost in the woods?" He grinned. "Do you really think you just stumbled onto it? And when you were so sick for those few days? Do you know you 'just got over it'? Maybe you woulda died—'specially if the Lord didn't get you inside somewheres where there was someone to take care of you. You should be dead about seven times over, as I see it. Now don't it seem kinda silly to say He's trying to take you out, when He's doing so much to *help* you out?" Orby grinned at Rae's wide-eyed stare. "It seems to me, Ms. Rae, that it takes a lot more faith to believe you was that lucky than it would to just believe God was helping you in all that."

Rae shrugged at his observation. "Maybe...I don't know." Her eyebrows knitted. "So, when is all of this going to stop, Orby?"

Now it was Orby who shrugged. "I don't know."

"I thought you were the big expert on God."

Orby smiled shyly. "Oh, I ain't no expert—I'm learning right along with everyone else who follows Him." He grinned again, then added, "I do know that He ain't the one who just lets things get worse—we do that by not going to Him when we need help. So, I imagine the answer to 'when is it going to stop?' could be, 'when you stop running from Him and call on Him.'"

Bristling a bit, Rae stopped sanding and glared. "Running from Him? Who says I'm running?"

"You do."

"*I* do?"

Orby nodded. "Yup. You're lack of peace gives it away."

Rae tripped over that but proceeded as though she hadn't. "Besides, how can you run away from God when He's everywhere?"

"That never did stop no one from trying."

Rae eyed him uncertainly, then tried to seem amused. "What makes you think I'm running from him?"

Orby smiled as he worked. "Well Ms. Rae, it just seems to me that you used to walk with Him—I can tell by some of the things you say. But something big musta happened and you just turned around and took off running in the other direction—like maybe you run into something too hard for your faith." Each insight a jolt, Rae shifted uneasily. Yet, Orby spoke so gently and with such warmth, she could only stare. There was a part of her drawn to sit at his feet and listen to anything he had to say—the other part was fighting the urge to run for the hills. Divided within, Rae squinted, working to figure him out. Orby watched her, listening in his spirit. "And running's a real shame, too. You see now, God sent his Holy Spirit, not just to teach us and to lead us—but to comfort us, too—and no one can comfort us in our hurting the way He can. But it's real hard to comfort someone who's running away from you."

"What makes you so sure I need 'comforting'? Are you trying to get into my head, or something?"

"Oh, I don't need to get in your head, Miss Rae—what I'm seeing is plain as day."

"Oh, really?" She tried to side step with a chuckle, "And what exactly do you see, Mr. Prophet of God?"

Orby smiled patiently. "Oh, I ain't no prophet, that's for sure—but I do know that a man can run from places, and he can run from people, and he might could run from his problems—for a while anyways, but I ain't met no one yet who is fast enough to run from God." He watched Rae for a moment. "You mind me asking what it was that set you to running from Him?"

Rae winced, then swallowed. After a moment she tossed her sanding paper into the box near her, and pulled off her gloves. "I'm getting thirsty. You want something, Orby?"

Orby nodded, understanding. "Why sure, Ms. Rae. Whatever you're having is fine."

Chapter 36

A ndrea finished with the Gang a half hour after she'd arrived, and now joined Ruth in the kitchen. "I told Mr. Peterman I was going to start charging him if he didn't quit asking me out."

Bringing the tea mugs to the table, Ruth grinned. "Knowing Mr. Peterman, he probably thinks it would be worth it."

"That's just what *he* said!" Andrea chuckled as she took a seat at the table. "I can't wait to hear about that airplane. Where's the pilot? Why did he leave it in your yard?—How did he even get it here?"

Ruth set the plate of muffins on the table. "You're not going to believe this, Andrea!—Remember that girl that Heath found in the woods? The one you came over and checked on after Shabbat service on Saturday?" Andrea nodded as Ruth grinned "*She's* the pilot!"

Andrea's eyes widened. "What? She *is?*—That girl is a pilot?"

"That's right!" Ruth brought over the steeping tea and sat down across from her.

"How'd she go from flying an airplane to being lost in the woods?"

"This is quite a story—remember that riot mess that happened at the Heartland Airport last week?"

"Uh-huh." Andrea blew across her tea, then sipped it.

"Did you hear about a plane that was coming in right when the mob swarmed the runway?

"Yeah, I saw it on the news."

"Well, that was her! And she ended up landing in a field up the road from here."

"Really? No kidding! I wonder why she didn't just go land at a different airport."

"Well, that mob shot at her plane, and some of the bullets went through her fuel tanks. All of a sudden, she was out of gas and had to land."

"Wow. That sounds scary! How did Orby get involved?"

"He got called in by the man investigating her landing. He's out there helping her fix her plane."

Andrea's eyebrows arched. "I didn't know Orby fixed planes for a living!" She refocused on Ruth's news. "How long will she be here?"

"Until it is fixed, so however long that takes—that's why she's still here. She's staying in the apartment over the garage" "I'm sure going to miss her when she leaves." Ruth sighed at the thought of it. "She's sure been a delight to have around; Nate just loves her—and so does the Gang."

"You left out Heath."

"Oh, Heath enjoys her, too. She keeps them all on their toes—you should hear the conversations we've been having around the table. She's quite a character. She and Heath even got into a pillow fight in the den the other night." Ruth chuckled at the memory.

Andrea's eyes widened. "Heath in a pillow fight?" Heath always seemed so reserved, she couldn't imagine it.

"It was just throw-pillows, but it sure was a sight! And she's been a big help around here with the chores and cooking, and looking after Nate. It's been nice to get things caught up around here lately."

Andrea smiled. "Too bad she can't just stay, huh?"

Ruth nodded. "That's for sure!"

"Is she helping you out to earn her keep?"

"No, she actually pays rent, Andrea!—She just helps out to be helpful." Ruth smiled warmly for a moment, then another thought occurred to her. "She is a mechanic, too. Did I tell you she fixed our van?"

"The one the mechanic said would cost $500 to repair?"

"That's the one! That first day she was up and around, she went out and figured out what was wrong with it without telling me what she was doing. I just heard an engine revving and came out to investigate—and there she was, just sitting there in the front seat, grinning at me! It turns out it was just a kinked fuel line—she doesn't even work on cars, and she figured that out!"

"I thought you said she was a mechanic."

"An *airplane* mechanic. I guess she just applied what she knew about airplanes to the van, and winged it." Ruth laughed at her own pun.

"Wow, that's a handy renter to have!"

"She's been a blessing, that's for sure."

They heard footsteps on the side porch outside the kitchen, then the door swung open and in walked Rae. Upon seeing the two ladies at the table, she quickly demurred. "Oh, I'm sorry Ruth—I didn't mean to interrupt."

"Nonsense, Rae. C'mon in, hon." Rae wiped her feet carefully, then steeped inside, closing the door behind her, then stepped over to the sink and turned on the water, and reached for the soap. "Are you and Orby doing all right?"

"Yes, thanks—we're coming along. We were getting kind of thirsty though. Is it okay if I get us something to drink and maybe a little snack?"

Ruth nodded. "Sure thing, hon, don't mind us." Rae reached for a towel, and turned toward the table where Ruth sat with her visitor. "Rae, this is my friend Andrea. She comes every other week and does health checks for the Gang."

Rae finished drying her hands, then stepped to the table and extended one to Andrea, who shook it. "Health checks? Wow, that's really nice. Are you a nurse or something?"

"That's right. It's nice to meet you, Rae."

"Andrea came and checked on you when you were so sick, too," Ruth added.

"You did? Thanks, that was nice of you, too." Then added, "I'm sorry, I don't remember."

"Oh, I don't expect you would—you were pretty out of it that day. Ruth tells me you're a pilot."

Rae shrugged shyly. "Mainly I'm a mechanic—just with a pilot certificate."

Andrea's eyebrows arched. "Doubly impressive, especially for someone so young!"

"Yeah well, I got an early start." Rae hurried to shift the focus away from her. "It looks like you're having a tea party."

"A small one, yes."

"I used to have tea parties with my mom and grandma when I was little."

"Oh, that sounds nice." Andrea smiled warmly

"Would you like to join us?" Ruth offered.

"Oh, no thanks. I don't want to leave Orby out there in the cold."

Ruth nodded. "Yes, of course. Help yourself to whatever you can find, hon."

"Thanks. I'll be out of your way real soon."

"Oh, you're fine, hon. You don't have to rush."

Rae nodded and turned to the refrigerator and began rummaging through it as the two ladies resumed their tea and conversation. Ruth buttered half of her muffin. "So, let's hear about Joel. Any new developments?"

"Not really. Did I tell you I met his family at Sukkot? I think that happened after I was here last time."

"It must have, because I would have remembered if you'd mentioned that!" Ruth leaned closer. "So, tell me about Joel's family." Andrea chuckled at the memory, and Ruth smiled, glad to see her friend more relaxed this visit. Grinning, Andrea described for Ruth the scene at the campground, and soon had her chuckling as well.

"It was nice meeting you, Andrea." Rae's voice interrupted their reverie. The two ladies had forgotten she was still in the room. Having pulled together a snack for herself and Orby, Rae stood by holding a plate with some cookies and two bananas.

Pivoting in her chair, Andrea gave Rae her attention. "It was nice to meet you, too, Rae. Maybe you can join us next time."

"Sure that would be cool with me, if I'm still here." Rae smiled and stepped away from the two friends.

Seeing the two bottles of water in Rae's hand, Ruth added, "Did you see the sodas there in the fridge?"

"Um, yeah. That's okay. I'm good with just drinking water."

"Well, okay hon. You tell Orby 'hey' for us."

"I will, thanks." Rae let herself out, balancing the plate as she managed the door, and headed back to Orby and her aircraft.

Grinning, Andrea stared after Rae. "I didn't know kids her age knew water was to drink!" She turned her attention back to Ruth. "Wow, you're right, Ruth!—She *is* young! She didn't look that young when I saw her on Shabbat. How old is she?"

"I think Heath said she was twenty."

"Wow, she doesn't even look old enough to drive! And so polite, too!"

"Yes, she's the perfect house guest."

Outside, in the seats of the cockpit, Orby and Rae downed their cookies and bananas quickly, then got back to work. With both fuel tanks reinforced, Orby joined Rae in sanding the holes on the body of the aircraft. Keeping their conversation light, Orby moved to the holes in the cowling, and Rae returned to the passenger side of the cabin. An hour later, they stopped briefly to wave to Andrea when she pulled away, and soon after that, to Heath as he arrived home, resuming their work without missing a beat.

Looking up from his sanding, Orby smiled. "Well I hope me not coming up here on Shabbat don't set you back too much, Ms. Rae. I know it's gonna slow things down for you."

Rae squinted. *There's that word again. . .* "No, that's okay Orby. I don't mind working around your schedule—I just really appreciate your help." Curious, she ventured, "So, what is this "Shabbat thing" anyways?—It sounds like a pretty big deal."

"Well, it sure is, Ms. Rae—Shabbat is my day of rest and worship. "You probably head it called Sabbath; 'Shabbat' is the Hebrew wor*d for* it"

Rae wasn't sure what she was expecting to hear, but it wasn't that. "Your day of worship is Friday?"

"Friday at sundown to Saturday at Sundown."

Rae squinted at him. "Oh. So, are you like. . .Adventist, or something?"

"Nope. I go to a Messianic Congregation." He deliberately didn't elaborate but kept on sanding, letting her ask the questions.

Rae pressed, "Messianic? What's that?"

"That's a branch of Judaism where we believe that Yeshua was the Messiah. That's why they call it 'Messianic.' Yeshua is Jesus' Hebrew name—it means 'Salvation'. Don't that just fit that Jesus' Hebrew name means 'Salvation'?" Orby grinned widely. "I just imagine his mama calling him, 'Salvation, come on inside for supper, now!' or 'Salvation, your daddy needs you in the shop!' or something like that." Orby grinned again, then continued, "Anyways, 'Messianic' means we believe that Yeshua is the Messiah—the sent one from God; His Son—just like Christians do."

"So, you're Jewish, then?"

Orby nodded, matter-of-factly. "I weren't born Jewish—I'm grafted in, same as you."

Ignoring his assumption, Rae found that interesting. "So, you have a Rabbi, and everything?"

Orby nodded, smiling warmly. "Yup, we have us a Rabbi. He was raised Orthodox—then he got saved."

"He got saved?—So he's a believer. . .? *A Rabbi?*"

Orby nodded. "That's right, Ms. Rae; he's a *Messianic* Rabbi—and I ain't never met a man so fired-up for the Lord as he is."

"But, if he's saved, then he's a Christian, isn't he?"

"Nope, he's still Jewish." Orby grinned to himself at her puzzling.

Rae squinted. ". . .And he's a believer?"

"He's a *Messianic* believer—just like me."

Bewildered, Rae shook her head. "I've never heard of that."

Beginning to strain to see what he was doing, Orby glanced up and noticed the sun was close to setting. "Well now, what do you know about that, Ms. Rae? It's almost dark! No wonder I can't hardly see what I'm doing!" He grinned widely, "I was having me such a fine time talking with you that I didn't even notice the sun going down!"

Just as surprised by the encroaching darkness as Orby, Rae squinted at the sunset and sighed, not ready to let it go just yet. The two quickly gathered their materials, as Rae pressed to understand. "You said Messianic means he believes in Jesus, but he's Jewish, but you go to his church, and you're *not* Jewish."

"That's right. Like I said, I'm grafted-in, same as you."

Rae shook her head, bristling at his assumption. "I don't go to church."

Orby grinned widely, "Maybe not, Ms. Rae—but He's got His eye on you!" Rae bristled at that, as well. Taking a cue from the Holy Spirit that she already had much to think on, he sensed he needed to leave their conversation where it was. "Maybe we can talk some more about it when I come back next time, Ms. Rae—if you want to." Rae just shrugged, still puzzling and the two pushed the Cessna back into the barn and secured the doors. Orby chatted as they walked over to his truck. "So, Ms. Rae, you ready for your first day flying for Mr. H tomorrow?"

Rae brightened a bit, setting her puzzling aside for the moment. "Yeah, I guess. There's not much to get ready for—he said he was going to file the flight plans and take care of the details. I guess I'll just find out everything when I get there."

Orby nodded, climbing into the driver's seat and pulled his door closed, then let down his window. "I guess so. Maybe I'll see you tomorrow when you come out to Potterville, Ms. Rae—If I don't, I guess I'll just see you on Sunday, then?" He started his engine.

"Sure, Orby." Rae squinted, the questions returning, then shrugged. "Um, you have a good. . .um. . .'Shabbat thing.'"

His delight obvious, Orby grinned widely. "Well now, thank you, Ms. Rae! Shabbat Shalom, to you, too!" Then waved and pulled away.

Eyeing him curiously, Rae just waved. *Whatever. . .*

Chapter 37

Excited for her first day on her new job, Rae awoke early, showered and dressed quickly, and left her apartment and was at the breakfast table with her tote bag before Ruth even had the tea on. She sat tensely. "Is Heath up yet? I don't want to be late on my first day."

Ruth smiled. "Yes, he's up, hon—he's getting Nate up. Don't worry, you won't be late; he knows you need to be there early."

Rae nodded briskly, forcing herself to relax. "Can I do something to help?"

Ruth smiled. "How about setting the table?" Rae sprang into action, gathering the plates and flatware from the counter and Ruth grinned at her eagerness. Just then, Heath pushed open the louver door with Nate perched happily on his arm.

"'Morning, Mom, Rae." He set Nate in his booster seat, then stepped to the counter to pour a cup of coffee. Ruth nodded to him as she readied breakfast and Heath turned to Rae as she set the little table. "You ready for your first day, Rae?" She nodded excitedly, and Heath carried his mug over and took his chair. "So, how does this job work?"

Rae finished setting the plates and flatware in their places, then sat down in her place across from him. "Mr. H said he has a schedule and a list of contact people at each airport. I can call him if I have any questions."

Heath eyed her uncertainly. "So, you just have to figure it out as you go?" Rae nodded simply, and Heath arched an eyebrow. "—and you're good with that?"

Rae shrugged. "Sure."

Heath squinted; his protective instincts surfacing. "Have you ever flown to any of these airports before?"

"No."

His forehead furrowing, Heath pressed, "What happens if you get lost?"

Becoming amused at his line of questioning, Rae grinned. "Then I get on the radio and ask." The tea kettle squealed and Rae got up to tend to it, pouring the steaming water into two waiting mugs.

Heath sighed, eyeing her skeptically. "Well, that's good at least."

Glancing up from bobbing the tea bags, Rae chuckled, "You aren't worried, or anything are you?"

Heath arched an eyebrow. "I don't know—should I be? I mean, you're just going off by yourself to all these places you've never been. How do you find your way around?"

She set the two mugs onto the table, then again took her seat across from Heath. "That's what flight school is for."

"Heath just rolled his eyes at his own protectiveness; conceding. "Okay, okay I get it—you know what you're doing."

Ruth brought breakfast over and joined them. "So, you're going to fly to a lot of different airports. What will you be doing at each one?"

"Picking up and delivering stuff—I'm pretty much an errand girl."

Heath grinned, taking a bite of his pancakes. "A *well-paid* errand girl, from what I hear."

Sipping her tea, Rae chuckled. "That, too."

Twenty minutes later, they were hurrying out the door, and a half-hour after that, Heath was dropping her off at Potterville Airfield.

"So, what time do I pick you up?"

Uncertain, Rae shrugged. "Sometime after lunch; I'll call you when I know."

Heath just sighed, eyeing her uneasily. Rae grinned, amused with his concern.

** *** **

So far, her first day flying for Mr. Hildenbocken was going smoothly, and Rae landed at Heartland airport without being shot at or having to abort her landing. She followed the tower's instructions over to the building with the green awning and shut down her aircraft near the dock. After a quick call to Heath, she headed inside looking forward to finding something warm from the Canteen there.

Rae paid the cashier and turned with her tray toward the dining area—a room crowded with tables and chairs in varying stages of disarray. Most of the tables were empty and either piled with trays of dirty dishes or littered with trash—not unusual, in her experience, for a place frequented by young men; she imagined college frat houses looking similar. Rae wrinkled her nose at the mess around her and sighed. *Welcome to the feeding trough.* She found a semi-clean table near the back wall and seated herself there after pushing aside the clutter. The only other occupied table was an eight-seater near the windows where sat three men talking and laughing loudly. Two wore the uniform of the dock crew, and one looked—and acted—like a pilot. She stared blankly at her table as she absently spooned her soup into her mouth, when a burst of laughter erupted from the three men a the other table. She glanced up briefly, then away again, and resumed spooning her soup.

Before she was able to completely divert her thoughts away, one man's words wrestled her attention back to them. "No way, Hansen—you're full of it!" The speaker emphasized his conviction with a toss of his head then scoffed loudly. Rae's eyes narrowed. *Hansen. That's the name of the man I was supposed to meet when I flew Kirk's route.* She surveyed the three men, wondering which one he could be. *He isn't a pilot, so that leaves the other two...* One man spoke again and Rae recognized his voice as the one she had just heard mention Hanson. *So that other guy must be Hansen.* Thirty-ish and pudgy, Rae eyed him for a few moments, then turned her attention back to her soup—still half-listening. It wasn't difficult to follow their conversation—in fact, it was unavoidable since the room was essentially empty and they spoke so loudly.

"Yes, he did! And took the whole aircraft, too! You weren't there that day—it was the morning of that mob-thing, remember, Mick?" At her table, Rae nodded to herself. *So the pilot is "Mick."* Hansen continued, "It was the day that pilot out of Florida was supposed to be sending up that girl pilot." Hansen confirmed. Rae's chin came up suddenly.

"Oh, yeah—I remember that," the pilot nodded. "He wanted you to give her a hard time. That was the same day?"

"That's the one." Hansen confirmed again, nodding.

"So what's this about a pilot from Florida?" The scoffer diverted.

"Some cocky mama's boy from out near Gainesville—gave me a hundred bucks to help him put the drop on some female pilot he figured had it coming to her. I had it all arranged, too—I was supposed to make her think she was going to be an over night guest of Bibb County—compliments of the Sheriff's office." The three had another good laugh. Rae's mouth fell open.

"So, what happened?" The pilot ventured.

Hansen shrugged. "Don't know—she never showed up. I don't know if she got caught in all that commotion or if she just didn't take the bait that flyboy was trying to push on her."

"What was the bait?" The scoffer asked.

"Some baloney about visiting his mom on her birthday, or something—I don't remember, exactly."

"Visiting *his MOM?!*" The pilot laughed incredulously, "No fool would fall for *that!*"

"Well, *she* did—at least that's what he told me on the phone the night before. But she never showed up, so maybe not. Who knows?"

The three men continued to laugh and talk, but the sound of their words echoed to the back of Rae's mind as she stared off, recalling the day before she'd made the trip to Hartland. *So he WAS lying!* Rae clenched her jaw as her blood began to boil. *I almost got killed because of Kirk's warped sense of justice?! Some joke, Kirk—ha-ha. You're toast!*

A voice in the periphery of her mind floated forward, "She's a girl—ask her." But it didn't register completely because Rae was busy thinking up how she might perpetrate a slow, painful death on Kirk Sloan.

A loud voice snatched her thoughts back to the present, "Hey, you! Ain't you a pilot?" It was the dock crewman that wasn't Hansen.

"Yeah, so?" Rae didn't sound at all friendly and she didn't care.

"Would you do that?" The man pressed. All three were staring at her.

"Do what?"

"Would you fly someone else's charter so's he could visit his mama?"

Rae stared at them through narrow eyes. "No way. . ." she sneered, "Only a complete loser would believe a line like that!" In one motion, she abruptly stood and snatched her tray off the table, banged it over the trashcan, and tossed it onto the rack on top, then headed for the Canteen door. She could hear them laughing behind her, thoroughly entertained by her answer. As she tromped out the door, she heard the nameless man as he laughed, "You see, Hanson? No one in their right mind's gonna fall for that!"

Rae rolled her eyes and exhaled forcibly. *No one but me. . .*

** *** **

Disheartened and more than a little bit angry, Joe Gerrard pressed the 'end' button on his cell phone and lowered his arm. "Well, that explains a lot," he muttered as he rose and stepped to the door of his office, coming to Patty's desk. "Patty—would you get me Kirk's paperwork?"

Joe's voice drew Patty's attention to him and she raised her eyes. "His paperwork?—Sure, Boss. I'll bring it right in." She stared curiously at his retreating back. *Wow, he sure doesn't look happy!* A minute later, Patty laid Kirks file on Joe's desk. "Everything okay, Boss?"

Joe frowned; subdued. "No, Patty 'everything' is *not* 'okay' and it seems to keep getting less 'okay' by the day."

He didn't say it harshly, still Patty was concerned. "Anything I can do?"

Joe sighed, "No—but thank you." Elbows on his desk, he rubbed his face with both hands, and then his head. "I just got some disturbing news from Rae and I don't know what to do about it yet. I'm sure I need to pray before I can even begin to sort it out—but I want to look at this file first."

"Yes, sir. I'll make sure you aren't disturbed."

"Thank you, Patty—I appreciate that." Just as she was closing the door, Joe thought of something else. "Oh—Patty. . .?" She poked her head back into his office. "Is Kirk around, or is he in the air?"

"I don't know, Boss—I'll find out from Sam. Do you want to see him if he's here?"

"Uh, not right away. If he's here, I'll let you know when to send him in." She nodded and again retreated from the doorway, closing the door behind her. As Joe opened the file, he heard Patty's voice overhead paging Sam and a few minutes later she tapped on his door again. "Boss?" When Joe glanced up from the file she reported, "Kirk is in the air. He should be back in an hour or so."

Joe nodded, "That'll work. Would you tell him I'd like to see him when he gets in?" Patty nodded and retreated again.

Twenty minutes later Joe emerged from his office and stopped next to Patty's desk, arms akimbo—clearly agitated. He exhaled forcibly then pressed his lips together; glancing around, he drummed his fingers on his belt.

"Find what you're looking for, Boss?" Patty ventured.

"Unfortunately, *yes!*" He seethed, nodding his head stiffly. Patty stared up at him, wide-eyed. Joe Gerrard was not someone she saw angry often. Joe snorted again, "I need to go for a walk." Joe stomped to the front door and snatched it open, shutting it roughly behind him—the blinds covering the front window clattered in the concussion. Patty's eyebrows arched. *Wow!*

Jesse rummaged through the refrigerator in the break room, moving every item on every shelf, looking for two brownies missing from his lunch. *They're just gone! —Again!* He straightened up and snorted, exasp*erated* and took a look around him, wondering whom to accuse. *Oh, skip it; it's not worth it. . .*He told himself—but it irked him. *Who keeps taking them and then putting them back a few days later? No, I'm not going to 'skip it'—someone is messing with me and I'm going to find out who it is!* Just then, Luke came through the door, a soda in his hand, and headed for the refrigerator, pulling out his lunch sack. Jesse eyed him suspiciously then growled, "Luke!"

Luke turned toward his voice. "What?" He pressed open his can of soda.

"Have you been messing with my lunches?"

Luke took a gulp from the can he'd opened. "No—why?"

Jesse half-accused, "Because someone keeps taking my dessert out one day then putting it back the next. It's been going on for a few weeks, and I'm sick of it."

Luke's brow immediately furrowed. Hurriedly he opened his lunch sack, his shoulders hunched tensely. He peered in, then relaxed, relieved. "Oh good—mine's still in here." Luke reached in for his sandwich, unwrapped it, and took a bite. He glanced back at Jesse, speaking with his mouth full, "So, someone keeps taking stuff out of your lunch?"

Arms akimbo, Jesse's shoulders relaxed as well—only his, in defeat. He could tell by Luke's momentary panic that he was not the culprit. "Yeah, that's right."

"I don't know," Luke chewed between his words, "I haven't seen anyone."

Jesse sighed and left the room, crossing the hangar over to Ben, and began signing the same to him. Ben spoke as he signed his reply, "I saw Kirk in there before he left on his charter this morning," Ben punctuated his response with a shrug.

"It's, like, the fifth time in about three weeks!" Jesse seethed, "Is anyone else missing anything?"

Ben only shrugged again, signing, "Not me—I keep my lunch in Rae's fridge."

"Does it have a lock on it?"

"Not now—but it will before I leave today!" Ben assured in sign.

Jesse half-grinned at his youngest brother, then turned and stalked away. *I'm gonna nail that Kirk when he gets back!*

Joe returned nearly a half-hour later, walk-spent and prayed-out, but still clearly agitated when he came through the door.

Patty glanced up at him. "Are you okay, Boss?"

Joe paused at her desk. "I don't know, Patty. I just don't know."

"You want to talk about it?—Bounce it off me?" she offered.

Joe considered it for a moment. "Maybe it would be good to get someone else's perspective—maybe I'm just too close to the situation to be very objective."

"Tell 'Aunt Patty' all about it, Boss." She chided in her motherly tone, smiling up at him.

Joe smiled in spite of his agitation. "Well, I got a call from Rae a while ago. She was pretty mad. She said she found out from some men at Heartland Airfield that Kirk had set up that whole thing about trading charters last week—just to get back at her! She said he gave her some sob story about how he needed to switch charters so that he could go see his mom in Lynn Haven on her birthday, and said he didn't want anyone else to know because he couldn't take being teased about his mom. *That's* how he got her to cover it up! I just checked his file, Patty—his family lives in Orlando, *not* Lynn Haven." Patty's eyes narrowed as Joe continued. "Then he got someone he knows up there in Heartland to be in on the prank! This guy was supposed to hassle Rae when she got there and make her think she was getting arrested for something; she doesn't know how or what. But then that mob-thing happened and she almost got killed, and then she had to land in that field. She wouldn't have even been up there if it weren't for his stupid prank!" Joe shook his head. "I'm so mad—I just want to take him and throttle him! I can't decide if he's a monster or just a self-absorbed jerk—or maybe he's just both." Joe paused thinking. "Remember when I mentioned how he's been unusually cooperative lately and how he keeps looking away when I look at him?

"Yes—you said he looked guilty."

"Yeah, well, maybe this is why. What do you think, Patty?" He waited for her to shed her grandmotherly wisdom on the situation.

In her own words, Patty calmly reflected back what she'd heard, "So Kirk made up a lie that played on Rae missing her mother, and tricked her into going up to Georgia against your wishes, so his friends up there could take advantage of her when she's by herself, in another state—without her dad or brothers to interfere. And in the process she almost got killed—*twice.*" Patty arched an eyebrow for confirmation.

Joe squinted at her uncertainly. "Well, I didn't think about it all like that, especially the part about using the 'mother angle,' and getting her alone, away from us—but yeah, that's the gist of it." Patty's spin on it fueled his agitation all the more. "I've tried to pray about it, but I'm just too stirred up. What do you think, Patty?—All I want to do is go punch him in the nose."

Patty's eyes narrowed. "I think you should."

"How's that? You think I should *what. . .?*"

"Punch him in the nose, Boss—then fire the creep!" She snorted.

Joe squinted, shifting his weight to one leg. "Well, Patty, that wasn't *quite* the perspective I was hoping for."

Patty's eyes blazed as she opened-fire, "He's just so *full of himself!* The reason that boy was mad at Rae was because she didn't fall into his arms the minute he smiled at her—and that's the truth, Joe! Just pure ego! Kirk has antagonized Rae from the beginning—yes, she has antagonized him right back, but he was almost always the initiator! The things he keeps trying to get her back for were all harmless, Joe—and he mostly set *himself* up for them! They were nothing mean or destructive; nothing warranting a prank like that!—Talk about over-kill!" Joe could almost see the steam rising from her ears. "You don't have to do anything, Joe—all you have to do is tell her brothers!—*They'll* take care of him for you!" Patty ended her diatribe with an emphatic nod of her head.

Stunned, Joe stared at her, his eyebrows arched. In thirty-something years, he had never seen Patty so worked up. Embarrassed at her own outburst, Patty pivoted back to her work. Joe rubbed the back of his neck, half-grinning, eyebrows still arched. "Well Patty, I see your point—it wasn't the most *objective* view, but I do see your point," he understated facetiously. "And telling my boys may be an effective way of dealing with Kirk—but I'm *pretty* sure it would not be in anyone's best interest." He nodded as he spoke, although somewhat amused by her. "So, since I don't want to have to bail the boys out of jail, I would appreciate it if you didn't mention this to them."

Chagrined, Patty called over her shoulder. "Well, you asked."

"That, I did." Joe smiled after her.

Just then, Sam poked his head in from the hangar. "Boss, did you still want to see Kirk?—He just landed."

"Yes, I do, Sam—when he finishes shutting down and comes in, would you let him know?" Sam nodded and disappeared from the doorway. Joe glanced at his watch then turned to his office manager. "Patty, it'll take him a bit to make his way in here. I have to run next door and talk to Pete for a minute. Just tell Kirk to wait in my office—and please don't say anything to him about this, I'd like to see what he has to say before you have him for lunch." He was teasing, but only partly. Patty nodded, feigning indignation, and Joe dashed out the front door.

Twenty minutes later, Kirk pushed open the door from the hangar and stepped up next to Patty's desk. "Hi Beautiful." He smiled, pretending to flirt. When Patty eyed him frostily, Kirk's eyebrows arched. *Hmm. . .What's eating her?* He pressed on, "Sam said the Boss wants to see me?"

"Yes, he said to wait in his office—he'll be right back." Patty answered unable to look at him.

Kirk squinted at her, surprised. *Wow, what's her problem?— She's usually so nice. . .* He shrugged; puzzled. "Um. . .Okay— thanks." When she didn't respond, he shrugged again and made his way to the Boss' office. Kirk slouched into the chair across from Joe's desk, crossing one ankle over to the opposite knee, glancing around as he wondered what this was about. He scanned the room just for something to occupy his mind, coming around to Joe's desk—and a file in the middle of it caught his attention. *Is that my name on that?* He leaned forward craning his head to read the name on the tab for confirmation. *What's he doing with my file?*

Nearly fifteen minutes later, Joe bounded through the front door, pausing at Patty's desk. "Sorry, that took longer than I expected. Is Kirk here?"

"He's in your office, Boss."

Joe set his eyes on his office door, thanked Patty, and headed that way. As he entered his office, Kirk glanced up and away quickly, just as he had been doing for almost a week and a half. Joe squinted at him and slid into the chair behind his desk.

Seeing the file still there, he wondered if Kirk had noticed it—in a way, he hoped he had. "Kirk, how'd your flight go?"

"Fine, no problems."

"That's good." Joe glanced down at the file, wondering how to begin. *First, I need to find out where he's really from. He's either lying about Lynn Haven or Orlando.* "So, Kirk, I was looking at your file today—I noticed you're from Orlando." Kirk nodded. "Did you grow up there?" Again, Kirk nodded. "What part?" Kirk told him and Joe recognized the area, and nodded. "I know some folks out there—which high school did you go to?" Speaking easily, Kirk answered him, and Joe recognized the school, as well. *Okay, he's definitely from Orlando.* Then something occurred to him. *Maybe they moved to Lynn Haven later?* "So, are your parents still there?"

"Sure."

"In Orlando?"

"That's right. They're divorced, but they both still live there." Kirk nodded easily, glancing up, then away again, jiggling the ankle that rested on his knee.

His trap sprung, Joe smiled. "Well, that's confusing to me, Kirk because Rae is under the impression your mom lives in Lynn Haven." He stared hard at Kirk, waiting to see his reaction.

Immediately Kirk froze; his chest tightening, as well as his throat. Suddenly appearing ill, he had to clear his throat before he could speak. "Rae told you that?"

"Yes, she did." Joe continued his piercing stare. "She also told me about your friend, *Hanson.*" The foot resting on Kirk's knee dropped to the floor as he deflated. He closed his eyes, shaking his head in tiny movements. Joe leaned on one elbow, his other arm out straight beside him, palm on the desk, and glared at Kirk; his tone suddenly intense. "Do you want to tell me why I shouldn't fire you right now?"

Exposed, Kirk's chin dropped to his chest, his shoulders slumping—instantly overwhelmed by his guilt. He wanted to back-pedal and argue, or tell this man to shove-it, but he couldn't—even Kirk knew he was way out of line this time, so he didn't even try to fight it. Staring at the floor, Kirk shook his head, ashamed, barely able to find his voice. "There's no reason, Mr. Gerrard—none at all." He inhaled deeply a couple of times summoning his courage, then raised his eyes to his Boss. "Just, please, before I leave—let me say this. . ." A bit surprised, Joe arched an eyebrow waiting as Kirk gathered his thoughts. "I know it was a mean, stupid prank, but sir—I swear, I never meant to get her hurt. I was just going to mess with her a little."

Kirk grimaced. "I've been sick about it ever since it happened; I wish I could take it back. I wish it had been me instead of her that went up there." He thought for a moment, "But if it was me. . .and I came upon that mob. . ." He shook his head, unable to finish the thought. "She's got a lot more experience than me; she's a better pilot. . ." The only thing he hated more than admitting those two facts to himself was saying them out loud. "If it was me, I might not have. . ." Kirk's voice choked off and he hung his head. He swallowed hard and raised his eyes to Joe, "Mr. Gerrard, I've pulled a lot of junk on people over the years, but I have never regretted anything as much as this—and not because I'm losing my job—I mean, I almost got someone *killed*. If I had, I know I couldn't live with myself—I can hardly live with myself as it is. I'm just *so sorry*."

"I heard about your little act the day before, Kirk—is this just an encore?" Joe demanded, eyeing him suspiciously.

Though it didn't seem possible, Kirk deflated further. He sighed heavily, his eyes again dropping to the floor. "I deserved that." He looked Joe square in the eye. "No sir, it's not an act—this time I mean it. Maybe for the first time in my life, I mean it. I'm just so incredibly *sorry!* I was going to tell Rae that when she got back, but she's still up there. I guess I won't be able to now." He shrugged with his hands a couple of times as he tried to think of what to say. "I'm sorry. I know that doesn't say enough, but I'm *really so* sorry." He breathed shakily. Kirk desperately wanted to leave right then, but somehow felt unable, so he just sat there staring at the floor.

Joe watched the storm clouds come and go from Kirk's face in the space of a few seconds, until he appeared to surrender to something unseen, and then seemed lost. Compassion stirred in Joe's heart for the miserable and contrite young man before him. As Joe appraised Kirk, he shook his head slowly. *Guilt. It's a relentless taskmaster.* Finally Joe spoke. "Well son, I tell you what—I forgive you." Joe felt the peace as soon as he spoke the words.

Stunned, Kirk stared at him blankly, his voice almost a whisper, "*What. . .?*"

"I said *I forgive you.*" Joe added a nod.

Kirk's eyes narrowed and he shook his head, imperceptibly at first, then more so—still not comprehending. "Forgive—? How can you do that after what I did?" Kirk voice broke as he stared at Joe—half incredulous, half suspicious, waiting for the punch line.

Joe's eyes locked on Kirk's as he came around and sat on the front corner of his desk. "Son, if I've ever seen a man in need of forgiveness, it's you right now." Something else tugged at Joe. "And the job is still yours—if you still want it. The Lord was merciful to me in keeping my little girl alive and in one piece last week, and. . .well. . .I need to be merciful, too—so, just know that I forgive you." Kirk stared at him, not comprehending, then Joe added, "But, no more pranks—okay?"

Joe stood and extended his hand to Kirk, who only stared at it for a moment, before standing. Haltingly, he accepted it and Joe pumped his hand as Kirk stared, wide-eyed, dumbfounded. He shook his head rapidly. "No sir—no more pranks."

Joe watched him for another moment. "Now, get back to work—and don't forget to close your flight plan."

Still bewildered Kirk half-smiled. "Yes, sir, thank you—I'll remember. I'll do that," he stammered as he backed toward the door—then hesitated, staring at Joe for another moment, "Thank you, Boss." He walked past Patty's desk in a daze and let himself out through the door into the hangar. Joe followed him out to the front office and watched the door close behind him.

"I didn't hear any shouting—did you fire him, Boss?" Just seeing Kirk's face, Patty felt like she knew the answer.

"No, Patty—actually, I forgave him." When Patty's mouth fell open, Joe just smiled and returned to his office.

Jesse leaned against the wall outside the front office waiting for Kirk to come back into the hangar. Rehearsing his threats, he planned to give Kirk a good scare as a deterrent to any further cake, pie, or brownie snatching. As soon as he saw Kirk come through the door, Jesse advanced on him. Grabbing him by the shoulder, he yanked Kirk around to face him. "Is that your idea of a joke, Kirk?" Kirk's heart jumped into his throat, his eyes widening as Jesse drove an index finger into his chest. "You think that's funny?!—I've about had it with your *pranks!*" He snarled menacingly into Kirk's dazed, wide-eyed face.

Bracing himself for the impending impact, Kirk spoke hurriedly, panting; trying to explain, "Jesse, I'm sorry. It was just a stupid prank gone bad—I never thought anything like that would happen." Jesse hesitated, squinting. *Anything like what...?* Kirk continued rapid-fire, "But, for what it's worth—your dad knows and he actually *forgave* me." Anxious, Kirk hoped that might encourage Jesse to spare him the thrashing that seemed imminent.

Jesse squinted at Kirk for a moment; curious. *Forgave him for what. . .?—Dad doesn't even know about this. . .* He eyed Kirk. *I don't think he's talking about brownies.* Jesse arched an eyebrow. *Well, I guess I'm just going to have to find out.* Deciding to go with it, he backed off of Kirk for the moment. Legs astride, arms folded across his chest, Jesse assumed this threatening stance for dramatic purposes, and cocked his head to one side. "Is that so?—Just what did my dad say?"

Fearful, Kirk ran his words together, "He said God showed him mercy by keeping his little girl alive, so he forgave me for tricking her into going up there—even though he knew about the ambush. All he said was, 'No more pranks.'" Hoping for a second reprieve, Kirk braced himself, waiting.

As Kirk's words sunk in, Jesse's anger kindled. "That thing in Georgia?" Kirk nodded, still hopeful. Now simmering, Jesse stepped toward Kirk—again driving an index finger into his chest. "That was a *prank?*—You set Rae up for that?"

Now it was Kirk who was confused. Backing up, he squinted at Jesse. "But, you just said. . ."

"I was talking about stealing out of my lunch bag!" Jesse yelled, shoving Kirk backward, still coming toward him. Kirk staggered then regained his balance as it fearfully dawned on him that he'd just told on himself. Jesse took another step toward him, seething, eyes blazing; his face inches from Kirk's. "You sent my sister up there *on purpose?*—As a *joke*? She almost got killed!"

Kirk stepped backward again, eyes wide. Jesse snatched him up by the front of his jacket, wheeled him around, and backed him up against the wall between the hangar and the front office with a loud thud. Patty's head came up as a commotion erupted outside her office door; she called out down the short hallway as she stood. "Joe?"

Already on his feet, Joe had heard the 'thud' back in his own office and was in the hall as Patty was calling his name. A second later, he was out the door to the hangar, and a second after that he was pulling Jesse off of Kirk, as Patty anxiously stood in the doorway. Finally breaking Jesse loose, Joe shoved him away then stood between the two as Luke and Sam came running, summoned by the ruckus; the altercation catching his eye, Ben hurried over as well. Jesse strained against his dad's palm on his chest, grabbing around him for Kirk, snarling at him; threatening. Kirk dodged Jesse's groping hands, held at his collar by Joe's other hand. The other three jumped to their father's assistance, Luke and Ben laying hold of Jesse along with their dad, and Sam pressing Kirk back to the wall—Kirk didn't resist the much larger eldest brother. Jesse strained against the three holding him, snarling, threatening, and accusing the other.

"Jesse!" Joe yelled, pushing against him, with Ben and Luke each at an arm. "Jesse!" Jesse didn't seem to hear. He raged, straining and grabbing for Kirk. Finally, Joe took hold of his son's jacket front with both hands and shouted into his face, "*JESSE!*" All at once, Jesse stopped abruptly, staring wide-eyed into his father's face, panting. "What's this about?" Joe demanded.

"Rae almost got killed because of his stupid prank! He deliberately tricked her and sent her up there so his friends could ambush her!" Jesse raged, pointing animatedly at Kirk. The eyes of his three brothers narrowed and shifted to the wide-eyed pilot against the hangar wall—forgetting about Jesse, they stepped toward Kirk.

Joe stopped them all with a glare, then blazed at Jesse, "How do you know that?—Who told you?" He turned toward Patty, still in the doorway, who shook her head animatedly, eyes wide. Joe turned back to Jesse, insisting, "Who *told* you that?"

"I did." The subdued voice behind them arrested everyone's attention.

Joe stepped toward Kirk. "You?" He was incredulous, wondering if Kirk was harboring some sort of death wish. Joe sighed, shaking his head. "Kirk, go wait for me in my office."

Sam released him, but not before giving him an icy stare. Kirk shakily stepped around him and slinked past Patty into the office. Joe addressed his sons, "I'll see you boys in the break room in five minutes."

Jesse eyed his dad. "Dad, he said you *forgave* him!" The eyes of his brothers narrowed again. "That's it? That's all? You just *forgave him?*"

Gesturing toward the break room, Joe stared at them fiercely, and repeated, "*Five* minutes!" He stepped to the office door.

Patty retreated from the doorway to let him in, and sidled around behind her desk extension into her chair as he passed by her. As he stepped into his office, Joe closed the door behind him, and turned to address Kirk, "Son, telling that to Rae's brothers was not the smartest move."

Hapless, Kirk attempted to explain, "He came at me growling about some prank I pulled—I thought he already knew. It turns out he was talking about something else."

"Another prank?—You're just winning points all around, aren't you?" Joe scowled for a moment, thinking. "Maybe you'd better just take the rest of the day off."

Kirk nodded, not needing to be convinced. "And don't forget about that flight plan." Joe reminded again. Kirk had—and after a momentary blank look, he recalled that, then nodded. Joe added, "Just tell Patty I said to use her computer." Then as an afterthought, he advised, "Better use the front door when you leave." He waited while Kirk plodded past him, dejected—feeling unemployed for the second time in five minutes. "I'll see you tomorrow, son?" Joe added, seeming to have read Kirk's thoughts. Surprised relief spread across Kirk's face and he smiled weakly and nodded, then closed the door behind him.

Joe paused for a moment, thinking—offering up a quick prayer before he headed to the break room, passing Kirk at Patty's computer on his way into the hangar. Heated words from four voices sounded from the break room as Joe stepped into the hangar, and they stopped immediately when he appeared in the break room doorway. Joe stepped in and closed the door, then faced his sons, gesturing with his palms up. Inviting. "Okay, boys, let's have it." The room remained quiet initially, then as if on cue, the four erupted all at once, snarling, complaining, accusing—Joe just let them vent. After a few minutes, their grousing spent, they wound down and fell silent again. Then Joe spoke, "You boys are angry—I understand that. I was angry, too, when I found out."

"But you just *forgave* him, Dad—just like that. How can you do that? He deliberately sent Rae up there to be ambushed—and he almost got her killed!" The four wove their complaints together.

"Yes, boys, you're right. What he did was pretty low, but he didn't plan on that mob on the runway anymore than Rae did." The boys glowered at him, not wanting to acquiesce so easily. "I wanted to punch his lights out when I heard.—any of you feel like that?" He received a chorus of agreement, and then some. Recalling a passage in the Bible, he put his own spin on it. "Okay, if that's what you want to do, then go ahead. He's in the office closing his flight plan—if you hurry you can catch him before he leaves." He gestured with an upturned palm toward the door. His boys eyed him suspiciously, wondering. Joe encouraged them further, "Go on, I'm not going to stop you this time." The four glanced at each other and nodded, standing as one and moving toward the door. "Just one thing, boys. . ." They turned, waiting to hear the catch. "Whichever one of you who has never messed up big-time—he's the one who gets to throw that first punch."

Immediately, four faces grimaced and four sets of shoulders sagged. One by one, they plopped back down into their chairs, beginning with Sam. . .

...And the story continues...

"Hazak, hazak, v'nit'chazak!"
("Be strong, be strong and let us be strengthened!")

About The Author

J aclyn Zant was born and raised in rural and suburban California, where she graduated from nursing school, and then later met and married her husband; they have one son. The three of them moved to Middle Georgia in 1996, where they still reside. In 2005, Jaclyn received a Word spoken over her from the Lord who said, "You will pour into others as God has poured into you." At that time, and for years after that, Jaclyn had no idea what form this "pouring out" would take. Then, in 2011, through a series of unexpected, but very definite leadings, she sensed God laying on her heart to write Petrified Hearts, and 'pour out' of the lessons the Lord has impressed upon her through her life experiences. Petrified Hearts began as one book, but has now, so far, become three.

Glossary of Hebrew terms

Abba—"Daddy" Referring to a close, intimate relationship between child and father.

Adonai—"My Lord" or "God." The Jewish word for the God of Abraham, Isaac, and Jacob. The One and only true God, Holy and awesome; the Creator of the universe and the sustainer of life. The author of the Holy Bible.

B'midbar—the Wilderness. "The Place where God speaks."

Beth Chesed V' Emet—"House of Grace and Truth"

Bimah—"The Place of Truth." The platform at the front of the synagogue sanctuary where the Word of God is read.

Hanukkah/Chanukah—"Dedication." A Feast Day

Mishpocha—"Family"

Ner Tamid—"Eternal Light" A lamp that is set above and in front of the ark that contains the Torah scroll, and is kept lit continually.

Pesach—"Passover." A Feast Day: The Prophetic Rehearsal/ commemoration of the First coming of Jesus

Purim—"Lots" As in 'casting lots.' A Feast Day

Rabbi—"Teacher"

Ruach HaKodesh—"Holy Spirit"

Segula—"Precious Treasure"

Shabbat (Sabbath)—"Rest" A weekly Feast Day

Shalom—"Peace"

Shammash/Shammashim—"Servant/Servants" akin to Deacons

Shofar—"Ram's Horn;" a Trumpet

Siddur—"Prayer book." Scriptures used in synagogue liturgy

Sukkot—"Booths" (singular—"sukkah") also called Tabernacles. A Feast Day

Tallit—"Prayer shawl" (plural—"Tallitot")

Talmid—"Student" (Plural—"Talmidim")

Torah—"Teaching" or "Instruction" from God

Yachad—"Unity" The name of their fellowship groups.

Yeshua—"Salvation;" Jesus' Hebrew name.

Yom Kippur—"Day of Covering;" A Feast Day: The day of Corporate Atonement

Yom Teruah—"The Day of the (Shofar) Blast" A Feast Day: The Prophetic rehearsal for "The Last Trump"

Books by Jaclyn Zant in the Petrified Hearts series so far:

The Shaking
The Contending
The Beckoning